THE FIFTH EDITION
GAMEMASTER'S SURVIVAL GUIDE

by Dave Hamrick

Writing Dave Hamrick
Design Consultant TJ Phoenix
Proofing John Webb
Legal Noah Downs
Additional Assistance Bob Carnicom, Aubrey Moore
Iconography Noun Project

Printed in China
© Hamrick Brands, LLC
All Rights Reserved

First Printing
978-1-7333383-8-7

This book is dedicated to the 5,273 Kickstarter backers who made it possible.

TABLE OF CONTENTS

Introduction 13
How to Use This Book 14
Understanding the 5e Monster Stat Block 15
    Name 15
    Size 15
    Type (and Sub-Type) 15
    Monster Stat Block Diagram 16
    Alignment 17
    Armor Class 17
    Hit Points (and Hit Dice) 18
    Ability Scores 19
    Saving Throws 19
    Skills 20
    Vulnerabilities, Immunities, and Resistances 21
    Senses 22
    Languages 22
    Challenge 22
    Special Traits 23
    Actions 23
    Bonus Actions 23
    Reactions 23
    Legendary Actions 23
    Lair Actions and Regional Effects 24
Understanding the Overall 5e Game Design 25
    Campaign Design 25
    Session Design 25

>   Adventuring Day Design 26
>   Monster Design 26
>   Single Session Encounter Experience 30
>   Creating Encounters 31
> Tactical Basics 34
>   Monster Fighting Styles 34
>   Common Monster Combinations 45
>   "What is the Monster Type?" Flow Chart 46
>   Pre-Combat 47
>   During Combat 51
>   Ending Combat 58
>   After Combat 59
> Individual Monster Tactics 60
>   Aboleth 61
>   Acolyte 63
>   Angel, Deva 64
>   Angel, Planetar 65
>   Angel, Solar 66
>   Animated Object, Armor 67
>   Animated Object, Flying Sword 68
>   Animated Object, Rug of Smothering 69
>   Ankheg 70
>   Archmage 71
>   Assassin 73
>   Awakened Shrub 74
>   Awakened Tree 75
>   Azer 76
>   Bandit 77
>   Bandit Captain 78
>   Banshee 79

Basilisk	80
Behir	81
Berserker	82
Blink Dog	83
Bugbear	84
Bulette	85
Cambion	86
Centaur	87
Chimera	88
Chuul	89
Cloaker	90
Cockatrice	91
Commoner	92
Couatl	93
Crawling Hand	94
Cult Fanatic	95
Cultist	96
Cyclops	97
Darkmantle	98
Death Dog	99
Death Knight	100
Demilich	101
Demon, Balor	102
Demon, Dretch	103
Demon, Glabrezu	104
Demon, Hezrou	105
Demon, Marilith	106
Demon, Nalfeshnee	107
Demon, Quasit	108
Demon, Shadow	109

Demon, Vrock..........110
Devil, Barbed..........111
Devil, Bearded..........112
Devil, Bone..........113
Devil, Chain..........114
Devil, Erinyes..........115
Devil, Horned..........116
Devil, Ice..........117
Devil, Imp..........118
Devil, Lemure..........119
Devil, Pit Fiend..........120
Devil, Doppelganger..........121
Dragons, True..........122
Dragons, True (Wyrmlings)..........123
Dragons, True (Young)..........124
Dragons, True (Adult)..........125
Dragons, True (Ancient)..........126
Dragon Turtle..........127
Drider..........128
Druid..........129
Dryad..........130
Duergar..........131
Elemental, Air..........132
Elemental, Earth..........133
Elemental, Fire..........134
Elemental, Water..........135
Elf, Drow..........137
Ettercap..........138
Ettin..........139
Faerie Dragon..........140

Flumph 141

Fungus, Violet 142

Gargoyle 143

Genie, Djinni 144

Genie, Efreeti 145

Genie, Marid 146

Ghast 147

Ghost 148

Ghoul 149

Giant Eagle 150

Giant Elk 151

Giant Spider 152

Giant Vulture 153

Giant, Cloud 154

Giant, Fire 155

Giant, Frost 156

Giant, Hill 157

Giant, Stone 158

Giant, Storm 159

Gibbering Mouther 160

Gladiator 161

Gnoll 162

Gnome, Deep 163

Goblin 164

Golem, Clay 165

Golem, Flesh 166

Golem, Iron 167

Golem, Stone 168

Gorgon 169

Grick 170

Griffon	171
Grimlock	172
Guard	173
Hag, Green	174
Hag, Night	175
Hag, Sea	176
Half-Red Dragon Veteran	177
Harpy	178
Hell Hound	179
Hippogriff	180
Hobgoblin	181
Homunculus	183
Hydra	184
Intellect Devourer	185
Invisible Stalker	186
Jackalwere	187
Knight	188
Kobold	189
Kraken	190
Lamia	191
Lich	192
Lizardfolk	194
Lycanthrope, Werebear	195
Lycanthrope, Wereboar	196
Lycanthrope, Wererat	197
Lycanthrope, Weretiger	198
Lycanthrope, Werewolf	199
Mage	200
Magmin	201
Manticore	202

Medusa	203
Mephit, Dust	204
Mephit, Ice	205
Mephit, Magma	206
Mephit, Steam	207
Merfolk	208
Merrow	209
Mimic	210
Minotaur	211
Mummy	212
Mummy Lord	213
Naga, Guardian	215
Naga, Spirit	216
Nightmare	217
Noble	218
Ogre	219
Ogre, Half-	220
Oni	221
Ooze, Black Pudding	222
Ooze, Gelatinous Cube	223
Ooze, Gray	224
Ooze, Ochre Jelly	225
Orc	226
Otyugh	227
Owlbear	228
Pegasus	229
Peryton	230
Phase Spider	231
Pixie	232
Priest	233

Pseudodragon	234
Purple Worm	235
Rakshasa	236
Remorhaz	237
Revenant	238
Roc	239
Roper	240
Rust Monster	241
Sahuagin	242
Salamander	244
Satyr	245
Scarecrow	246
Scout	247
Shadow	248
Shambling Mound	249
Shield Guardian	250
Skeleton	251
Skeleton, Minotaur	252
Skeleton, Warhorse	253
Specter	258
Sprite	259
Spy	260
Stirge	261
Succubus/Incubus	262
Tarrasque	263
Thug	264
Treant	265
Tribal Warrior	266
Troglodyte	267
Troll	268

- Unicorn ... 269
- Vampire ... 270
- Vampire Spawn ... 272
- Veteran ... 273
- Wight ... 274
- Will-o'-Wisp ... 275
- Winter Wolf ... 276
- Worg ... 277
- Wraith ... 278
- Wyvern ... 279
- Xorn ... 280
- Yeti ... 281
- Zombie ... 282
- Zombie Ogre ... 283

Beasts ... 284
- 4 Things to Know About Beasts ... 284
- Beasts by Fighting Style ... 285

Appendix A: How to Create Fifth Edition Monsters ... 288
- Basic Design Concepts ... 288
- Using Simple Templates ... 290
- Tweaking Existing Stat Blocks ... 295
- Converting Monsters from Previous Editions ... 299

Appendix B: Alternative Spell Lists for Spellcasting NPCs ... 301
- Acolyte ... 301
- Archmage ... 302
- Cult Fanatic ... 305
- Druid ... 306
- Mage ... 307
- Priest ... 309

Appendix C: Tactics vs Specific Player Classes 311
    Barbarians 311
    Bards 312
    Clerics 314
    Druids 315
    Fighters 317
    Monks 318
    Paladins 319
    Ranger 320
    Rogue 322
    Sorcerer 323
    Warlock 325
    Wizard 326
Appendix D: Powerful Spells and How to Avoid Them 328
    Basic Tips 328
    Individual Spell Tactics 329
Appendix E: Monsters Organized by Fighting Style 334
Open Gaming License 342

INTRODUCTION

Welcome to the *Fifth Edition Gamemaster's Survival Guide!* This guide is designed to support and enhance your role as a gamemaster, providing you with the tools and information you need to create compelling and engaging adventures for your players.

Inside these pages, you'll find over 300 tactical guides for some of the most popular 5e monsters. These guides will provide you with a thorough understanding of each monster's abilities and weaknesses, allowing you to create challenging encounters that will keep your players on their toes.

In addition to the tactical guides, this guide also includes tips and tricks for creating believable running dynamic combat encounters, handling tactically-minded "mix-max" players, and much more. With this information at your disposal, you'll be able to adapt your encounters to suit the strengths and weaknesses of your players, ensuring that each encounter is a unique and memorable experience.

Whether your players are focused on combat, exploration, or role-playing, the *Fifth Edition Gamemaster's Survival Guide* is an invaluable resource for anyone looking to elevate their game. So, whether you're a seasoned gamemaster or just starting out, this guide is here to help you bring your adventures to life.

HOW TO USE THIS BOOK

The *Fifth Edition Gamemaster's Survival Guide* is designed to be a comprehensive resource for gamemasters of all experience levels. This book includes the following sections:

- **Understanding the Monster Stat Block:** This section provides a detailed explanation of the information contained in a monster stat block, including its abilities, strengths, and weaknesses.

- **Design Notes:** This section includes a variety of design-related topics, including campaign design, session design, adventuring day design, monster design, and encounter design. It provides tips and tricks for creating memorable and effective encounters that will keep your players engaged.

- **Tactical Basics:** This section covers the basics of encounter design, including how to set up encounters, what to do during combat, and what to do after combat. It provides a solid foundation for designing effective encounters that challenge your players and keep the action moving.

- **Complete List of Individual Monster Tactics:** This section provides tactics for all of the game's monsters, as provided by the Fifth Edition 5.1 SRD. These tactics will help you make the most of each monster's unique abilities and strengths, ensuring that each encounter is a memorable and challenging experience.

- **Appendices:** This section includes a variety of additional resources, including details on creating monsters, alternate spell lists for monsters, dealing with different players by their fighting styles, how to counter strong spells, and guest articles. These resources provide even more depth and detail to help you create the ultimate gaming experience for your players.

To use this book, simply refer to the sections that are most relevant to your needs.

UNDERSTANDING THE 5E MONSTER STAT BLOCK

The Fifth Edition monster stat block holds all of the information necessary to understand and manage all monsters and NPCs in Fifth Edition. This chapter breaks down each element of the stat block and explains its purpose and how it can help you understand the monster's tactics.

1 - NAME

A monster's name has no mechanical effect beyond giving you an immediate impression of what the monster is capable of. It may also trigger "meta" knowledge, helping players better prepare for a particular encounter. For example, if you identify a monster as a "troll," an experienced player might know to use fire against it. As a rule of thumb, don't refer to a creature by its name unless the creature is fairly prolific in your campaign world (everyone knows what a horse is) or there is a character with proficiency in a relevant skill. Using the troll example, a character with proficiency in Arcana or Nature might recognize a troll right away.

2 - SIZE

A monster can be Tiny, Small, Medium, Large, Huge, or Gargantuan. The Size Categories table shows how much space a creature of a particular size controls in combat.

A monster's size determines the size of the battlefield and any possible areas of escape. For example, a Tiny creature can easily slip away through small cracks and crevices in the wall, whereas a Gargantuan creature will have a lot of space to maneuver and large paths into which they may retreat.

3 - TYPE (AND SUB-TYPE)

A monster's type speaks to its fundamental nature. There are fourteen monster types in Fifth Edition: aberrations, beasts, celestials, constructs, dragons, elementals, fey, fiends, giants, humanoids, monstrosities, oozes, plants, and undead.

Certain spells, magic items, class features, and other effects in the game

DMDave

Medium humanoid (nerd), neutral

Armor Class 13 (natural armor)
Hit Points 44 (8d8 + 8)
Speed 30 ft.

STR	DEX	CON	INT	WIS	CHA
9 (-1)	10 (+0)	10 (+0)	12 (+1)	13 (+1)	11 (+0)

Saving Throws Int +3
Skills Insight +3
Damage Resistances force
Senses darkvision 60 ft., passive Perception 11
Languages Common
Challenge 1/2 (100 XP)

Sleepy. Dave has disadvantage on saving throws against effects that would make him fall unconscious.

Actions

Guitar Smash. *Melee Weapon Attack*: +1 to hit, reach 5 ft., one target. *Hit*: 2 (1d6 - 1) bludgeoning damage.

Bonus Actions

Nimble Escape. Dave takes the Disengage or Hide action.

Reaction

Pass Gas. When a creature moves into a space within 5 feet of Dave, Dave emits a cloud of noxious fumes. Each creature within 5 feet of Dave must succeed on a DC 10 Constitution saving throw or become poisoned for 1 minute. A creature can repeat its saving throw at the end of each of its turns, ending the effect on a success.

Legendary Actions

Dave can take 3 legendary actions, choosing from the options below. Only one legendary action option can be used at a time and only at the end of another creature's turn. Dave regains spent legendary actions at the start of his turn.

Attack. Dave makes one attack with his guitar.

The Fifth Edition Gamemaster's Survival Guide

interact in special ways with creatures of a particular type. For example, an arrow of dragon slaying deals extra damage not only to "true" dragons but also to other creatures of the dragon type, such as dragon turtles and wyverns.

As a gamemaster, type is most important when considering the types of spells to use against characters. All characters are humanoids; therefore, spells, effects, and magic items that specifically target types other than humanoids will not work against characters.

4 - ALIGNMENT

A monster's alignment provides a clue to its disposition and how it behaves in a roleplaying or combat situation. For example, a chaotic evil monster might be difficult to reason with and might attack characters on sight, whereas a neutral monster might be willing to negotiate.

The alignment specified in a monster's stat block is the default. Feel free to depart from it and change a monster's alignment to suit the needs of your campaign. If you want a good-aligned green dragon or an evil storm giant, there's nothing stopping you.

Some creatures can have any alignment. In other words, you choose the monster's alignment. Some monsters' alignment entries indicate a tendency or aversion toward law, chaos, good, or evil. For example, a berserker can be any chaotic alignment (chaotic good, chaotic neutral, or chaotic evil) as befitting their wild nature.

Many creatures of low intelligence have no comprehension of law/chaos nor good/evil. They don't make moral or ethical choices, but rather act on instinct: these creatures are unaligned.

5 - ARMOR CLASS

A monster that wears armor or carries a shield has an Armor Class (AC) that takes its armor, shield, and Dexterity into account. Otherwise, a monster's AC is based on its Dexterity modifier and natural armor, if any. If a monster has natural armor, wears armor, or carries a shield, this is noted in parentheses after its AC value.

AC, hit points, and resistances are the determining factors for a monster's defensive capabilities. These defensive capabilities are calculated with the creature's damage output to determine its Challenge Rating.

Creatures with higher AC often serve well as tanks, especially when they Dodge and take cover, making it even harder for their enemies to hit them.

6 - HIT POINTS (AND HIT DICE)

A monster usually dies or is destroyed when it drops to 0 hit points.

A monster's hit points are represented both as a die expression and as an average number. For example, a monster with 2d8 hit points has 9 hit points on average (2 × 4½). A monster's size determines the die used to calculate its hit points.

Additionally, the monster's Constitution modifier also affects the number of hit points it has. Its Constitution modifier is multiplied by the number of Hit Dice it possesses, and the result is added to its hit points. For example, if a monster has a Constitution of 12 (+1 modifier) and 2d8 Hit Dice, it has 2d8 + 2 hit points (average 11).

AC, hit points, and resistances are the determining factors for a monster's defensive capabilities. These defensive capabilities are calculated with the creature's damage output to determine its Challenge Rating.

Creatures with higher hit points are useful in close combat situations, serving as Brutes or Tanks.

7 - SPEED

A monster's speed tells you how far it can move on its turn.

All creatures have a walking speed, simply called the monster's speed. Creatures with no form of ground-based locomotion have a walking speed of 0 feet. Some creatures have one or more of the following additional movement modes: fly, swim, etc.

The monster's speed and movement modes can help you determine the types of environments in which the creature should fight and where to place them at the start of combat.

Slow-moving creatures are those whose primary forms of movement are 25 feet or less. These creatures will have more difficulty getting close to their targets than those with movement speeds of 30 or more. Make sure to start these creatures closer to their targets.

Fast-moving creatures are those whose primary forms of movement are 35 feet or greater. These creatures can serve as Lurkers or Skirmishers. Assuming that most characters have a movement speed of 30 feet, placing these creatures just outside of that range keeps them safe from most melee attacks during the first round of combat.

Burrowing creatures usually need soft earth to dig through. Certain creatures can also burrow through rock and stone with no penalty to their movement. Nearly all burrowing creatures have the tremorsense feature, allowing them to detect creatures on the surface while they are underground.

Climbing creatures, especially those with the Spider Climb trait, function best in environments with hard-to-read vertical passages, cliffs, and other difficult terrain.

Flying creatures need a lot of space to maneuver, especially if they have a fast flying speed (30 feet or greater).

Swimming creatures need water to move around effectively.

8 - ABILITY SCORES

Every monster has six ability scores (Strength, Dexterity, Constitution, Intelligence, Wisdom, and Charisma) and corresponding modifiers.

A monster's ability scores provide hints into how they should be run during combat.

Strength. Creatures with high Strength scores relative to their size often fight as brutes, especially if they have relatively poor Dexterity scores to match.

Dexterity. Creatures with high Dexterity scores perform best as Artillerists, Lurkers, and Skirmishers. They might also perform well as tanks if their Dexterity modifier lends itself to its AC.

Constitution. Creatures with high Constitution scores usually perform better as melee combatants, such as Brutes or Tanks, as they typically have a high number of hit points.

Intelligence. For the purposes of combat, a creature's Intelligence score measures its grasp of strategy and tactics. Creatures with extremely low Intelligence scores (3 or less) may not be sentient and have no sense of self-preservation.

Wisdom. A creature's Wisdom score helps the creature understand its surroundings and gauge its chances of survival. It also helps determine the creature's morale. Creatures with low Wisdom scores (9 or lower) are more likely to miss small details and become easily distracted. They also have a poor sense of when to enter or exit combat, sometimes fleeing when they should stay and fight or vice versa.

Charisma. A creature with a high Charisma score is more likely to negotiate or deceive its targets versus one with a low Charisma score. A high Charisma score can also represent a creature with a strong sense of self and/or willpower.

9 - SAVING THROWS

The Saving Throws entry is reserved for creatures that are adept at resisting certain kinds of effects. For example, a creature that isn't easily charmed or frightened might gain a bonus on its Wisdom saving throws. Most creatures don't have special saving throw bonuses, in which case this section is absent.

Low CR creatures with excellent saving throw proficiencies (especially in Dexterity, Constitution, or Wisdom) are usually elite creatures, such as the bandit captain. There are a few low CR creatures whose saving throw proficiency offsets its low ability score modifier, such as the zombie's +0 Wisdom saving throw modifier.

Most high CR creatures, particularly elites and solo monsters, have excellent saving throw proficiencies to protect them from spells and other effects.

Magic Resistance and similar features that grant advantage on saving throws against certain types of attacks or effects serve the same function as excellent saving throw proficiencies.

10 - SKILLS

The Skills entry is reserved for monsters that are proficient in one or more skills.

Only certain skills, such as Athletics, Perception, and Stealth, have actual combat functionality. Below is a brief overview of how each skill helps you understand how to run a creature both in and out of combat properly.

Acrobatics helps dexterous creatures avoid and escape grapples and avoid certain hazards.

Animal Handling is for creatures who often work alongside beasts.

Arcana is mostly for flavor and is usually found alongside spellcasters or creatures with magical knowledge. Creatures with proficiency in Arcana might be able to identify and avoid certain spells faster than others.

Athletics helps strong creatures avoid and escape grapples and avoid certain hazards. It also helps creatures without climbing speeds climb.

Deception is useful for creatures who prefer to con their way out of combat situations.

History covers a wide range of information in the game. From a combat standpoint, a creature with proficiency in History will understand tactics better and will have made preparations before combat begins.

Insight helps a creature understand their targets better, allowing them to predict the moves that their opponents will make in combat and social situations.

Intimidation is a social skill that allows targets to force their allies to do what they want. Usually, these creatures act like bullies.

Investigation allows a creature to spot minute details and relate them to the bigger picture. These creatures might spot traps or ambushes before they're sprung on them.

Medicine allows a creature to identify and treat injuries, illnesses, and other health concerns. Creatures with proficiency in Medicine may tend towards the support role.

Nature grants a creature an understanding of its surroundings, even if it isn't their natural environment, allowing them to use the terrain to their advantage.

Perception represents how well a creature utilizes its senses. It's especially helpful in spotting hidden creatures or objects.

Performance is a measure of how well a creature executes a particular task while being observed by other creatures.

Persuasion is a social skill that is less focused on deception or intimidation and more on using logic and reason to convince targets to see the creature's way of thinking.

Religion is an Intelligence skill that lets the creature better understand organized religions, cults, and sometimes fiends and undead. A creature with proficiency in Religion may know how to motivate certain creatures more than others (such as cultists or priests) and know how to work with or counter fiends and undead.

Sleight of Hand allows a creature to palm small objects and perform actions that require manual Dexterity. Certain creatures might use Sleight of Hand to steal items from the enemy or hide important objects where the enemy can't see them.

Stealth allows a creature to hide or move silently during combat, usually contested by the opposition's active or passive Wisdom (Perception) checks.

Survival not only helps a creature survive in a difficult environment outside of their typical terrain (such as a scout in the forest), but also allows the creature to track its targets.

11 – VULNERABILITIES, IMMUNITIES, AND RESISTANCES

Some creatures have vulnerabilities, resistances, or immunities to certain types of damage. Some creatures are even resistant or immune to damage from nonmagical attacks (a magical attack is an attack delivered by a spell, a magic item, or another magical source). In addition, some creatures are immune to certain conditions.

A creature with damage vulnerabilities but a high Wisdom score should actively try to avoid the thing they're vulnerable to; for example, a treant will avoid fire whenever possible, and a rakshasa may not enter combat with a good-aligned creature armed with a magic weapon. Creatures with damage vulnerabilities but a low Wisdom score, such as skeletons, may not be aware that the vulnerability is present until it is too late.

Intelligent and wise creatures with damage immunities and resistances carefully consider their targets when they enter combat. If there is an enemy that deals a damage type to which the creature is not resistant or immune, the creature may either focus their attacks on that enemy, removing them from play completely, or they might avoid that creature altogether.

Creatures with damage immunities may operate solely in environments filled with hazards related to their damage immunity. For example, a red dragon might fight near a volcano, where ash, lava, and extreme heat will pose additional risk to adventurers. Similarly, animated armor can fight in an area affected by *cloudkill*, where its blindsight and natural immunity to poison allow it to operate unimpeded.

Condition immunities further dictate a creature's surroundings and the type of creatures it works alongside. For example, creatures immune to the poisoned condition can fight in poisonous environments, while creatures with immunity to petrification can fight alongside basilisks and medusas without fear of being turned to stone.

12 - SENSES

The Senses entry notes a monster's passive Wisdom (Perception) score, as well as any special senses the monster might have. The section "Senses in Combat" goes into further detail.

13 - LANGUAGES

The languages that a monster can speak are listed in alphabetical order. Sometimes a monster can understand a language but can't speak it, and this is noted in its entry. A "--" indicates that a creature neither speaks nor understands any language.

Telepathy is a magical ability that allows a monster to communicate mentally with another creature within a specified range. Creatures that rely on verbal communication may have to shout their tactical advice to their allies on the battlefield, whereas those that have telepathy do not.

14 - CHALLENGE

A monster's challenge rating tells you how great a threat the monster is. An appropriately equipped and well-rested party of four adventurers should be able to defeat a monster that has a challenge rating equal to their Average Party Level (APL) without suffering any deaths. For example, a party of four 3rd-level characters should find a monster with a challenge rating of 3 to be a worthy challenge, but not a deadly one.

Monsters that are significantly weaker than 1st- level characters have a challenge rating lower than 1. Monsters with a challenge rating of 0 are insignificant except in large numbers; those with no effective attacks are worth no experience points, while those with attacks are worth 10 XP each.

Some monsters present a greater challenge than even a typical 20th-level party can handle. These monsters have a challenge rating of 21 or higher and are specifically designed to test players' skills.

The formula for determining a monster's challenge rating is the average of two parts: its offensive capabilities and defensive capabilities.

15 - SPECIAL TRAITS

Special traits (which appear after a monster's challenge rating but before any actions, bonus actions, or reactions) are characteristics that are likely to be relevant in a combat encounter and require some explanation. Usually, these are passive features which are always in effect, such as Fiery Aura, Legendary Resistance, or Magic Resistance, that do not require an action, bonus action, reaction, or Legendary Action to trigger.

Note that older versions of Fifth Edition monster stat blocks sometimes list bonus actions and spells under the special traits section.

16 - ACTIONS

When a monster takes its action, it can choose from the options in the Actions section of its stat block or use one of the actions available to all creatures, such as the Dash or Hide action.

17 - BONUS ACTIONS

If the monster has any special features that allow it to take bonus actions in combat (such as the ability to cast the *shield* spell), it is listed under bonus action.

Note that older versions of Fifth Edition monster stat blocks sometimes list bonus actions and spells under the special traits section.

18 - REACTIONS

If a monster can do something special with its reaction, that information is contained here. If a creature has no special reaction, this section is absent.

19 - LEGENDARY ACTIONS

Certain monsters are considered Legendary, which means that they can take special actions outside of their normal turn and reactions. Usually, a monster with Legendary Actions is limited to only three such actions per turn and may only do so after another creature takes its turn. Legendary Actions not only improve the creature's action economy, but help them protect themselves before taking their actual turn in combat.

20 - LAIR ACTIONS AND REGIONAL EFFECTS

Legendary creatures sometimes have Lair Actions and regional effects, too. Typically, a Lair Action allows a creature in its lair to perform a special action on initiative count 20, improving their action economy and helping them protect themselves before taking their actual turn in combat. Regional effects are usually passive effects that affect the area surrounding the creature's actual lair. However, some monsters have Regional Effects that offer assistance in combat, such as the effect a mummy lord has on divination magic in its lair.

UNDERSTANDING THE OVERALL GAME DESIGN OF 5E

Fifth Edition, at its core, is a resource management board game blended with elements of tactical skirmish and storytelling. Resource management games grant the players a finite number of resources that they apply towards completing tasks and earning points. The resources also measure the amount of time a character has to complete these tasks and earn points before they must rest. A character's resources include their hit points, spell slots, arrows, 1/day-use abilities, consumable magic items, and anything else with a limit to the number of times it can be used before the character must rest, purchase more goods, etc.

While there are plenty of ways to deplete resources in the Fifth Edition game, they are primarily used to fight monsters. Monsters' attacks remove hit points. Characters must use arrows, spell slots, and 1/day abilities to harm monsters. And so forth. Monsters also provide experience points, which, in most games, are used to improve the characters' abilities and increase their resources and ability to accomplish tasks.

CAMPAIGN DESIGN

Although there is no real way to "win" a game like Fifth Edition fantasy, for many players, the goal is to earn experience, find treasure, and improve their characters. Characters in Fifth Edition have levels from 1 to 20. It takes 355,000 experience to reach the 20th level in Fifth Edition. Assuming that the typical session lasts four hours and a character earns one-third of the experience needed to reach the next level per session, it takes roughly 200 to 225 hours of gameplay to reach that milestone. Naturally, this can't be done in one sitting (not without copious amounts of caffeine, at least); therefore, most Fifth Edition players and gamemasters create campaigns, a series of interconnected game sessions during which the characters earn experience and gain rewards.

SESSION DESIGN

A session is a single play of Fifth Edition fantasy, usually three to four hours in length. If you use the Adventuring Day XP structure set forth in the Fifth Edition guide for gamemasters, characters who encounter 6-8 Medium or

Hard encounters will earn one-third of the experience required to reach the next level. The only exception to this rule is it usually takes only a single adventuring day to reach 2nd level, one to reach 3rd level, and two more to reach 4th. This means that it takes approximately 52 sessions to reach 20th-level—so if you run one session per week using these metrics, the characters will go from 1st-level to 20th-level in a single year.

ADVENTURING DAY DESIGN

According to the Fifth Edition guide for gamemasters, the typical party has enough resources between long rests to handle 6 to 8 Medium or Hard challenge encounters in a day. This concept is known as "Adventuring Day Experience." Check out the gamemaster guide for more information. At the 1st and 2nd levels, the Adventuring Day Experience per day per character is the exact same as the experience points required to reach the 2nd and 3rd levels, respectively. It then takes two days of Adventuring Day Experience to go from 3rd to 4th. After that, it's approximately three days per level until 20.

The rules for session-based experience in the Fifth Edition guide for gamemasters take this into consideration. That way, if you want to run a game where the players don't earn experience through just killing monsters, but also gain experience for using non-violent solutions, disarming traps, solving puzzles, etc., you can use the session-based system and still have them gain experience at roughly the same rate they would if they were killing everything in sight.

MONSTER DESIGN

Now that we understand campaign design, session design, and how adventuring days work, we can reasonably estimate that medium or hard challenge encounters cause the party to use up one-sixth to one-fourth of the characters' resources. Easier encounters will use less, while more difficult encounters will use more.

MONSTER CHALLENGE RATINGS

A monster's challenge rating tells you how great a threat the monster is. An appropriately equipped and well-rested party of four adventurers should be able to defeat a monster that has a challenge rating equal to their Average Party Level (APL) without suffering any deaths. For example, a party of four 3rd-level characters should find a monster with a challenge rating of 3 to be a worthy challenge, but not a deadly one.

Monsters that are significantly weaker than 1st- level characters have a challenge rating lower than 1. Monsters with a challenge rating of 0 are insignificant except in large numbers; those with no effective attacks are worth no experience points, while those with attacks are worth 10 XP each.

Some monsters present a greater challenge than even a typical 20th-level party can handle. These monsters have a challenge rating of 21 or higher and are specifically designed to test players' skills.

The formula for determining a monster's challenge rating is the average of two parts: its offensive capabilities and defensive capabilities.

OFFENSE AND DEFENSE

A creature's offensive capabilities are an aggregate measure of the damage output it does in a single round of combat, the probability of its attacks hitting, and the probability of a character failing its saving throw against one of the creature's spells or special features.

A creature's defensive capabilities are a measure of its hit points and the probability of it avoiding the characters' attacks and spells.

Certain traits, spells, and other features on the monster stat block may alter the rating for the monster's defensive and offensive capabilities. For example, a monster that can fly is difficult for a low-level party to hit. Therefore, flying monsters with challenge ratings of 10 have marginally better defensive capabilities than their hit points and armor class would suggest. Similarly, a monster that can Hide on each of its turns as a bonus action is likely to hit more targets and deal more damage, warranting a higher offensive rating.

If a monster's feature or trait does not lend itself to improving the monster's offensive or defensive capabilities, then no adjustment is necessary.

ENCOUNTER EXPERIENCE VERSUS ACTUAL EXPERIENCE

The Fifth Edition guide for gamemasters refers to two types of experience points.

Actual experience points are the experience points that individual monsters reward after they have been defeated. For example, a goblin is a CR 1/4 creature that awards 50 experience. So long as you use the typical rules for awarding experience, a party that defeats that goblin earns 50 experience points regardless of how many other creatures are present in the encounter.

Encounter experience is a numerical value used for measuring encounter difficulty. It is the product of the monster's actual experience multiplied by the encounter multiplier and any applicable party size multipliers. For example, for a single goblin that fights a party of three, four, or five characters, the encounter is worth 50 encounter experience points.

50 (goblin's actual XP) x 1 (encounter multiplier) x 1 (party size multiplier) = 50

However, if there are two goblins in the encounter, then the two goblins are worth a total of 150 encounter experience.

50 (goblin's actual XP) x 2 (# of goblins) x 1.5 (encounter multiplier) x 1 (party size multiplier) = 150

The idea here is that more creatures in an encounter have more action economy than a lone goblin, and are therefore more likely to expend the party's resources. Similarly, a larger party of characters will have more action economy of their own, which will make certain encounters easier, and vice versa for a smaller party.

Encounter experience is used to determine the relative level of difficulty for the party. Regardless of the encounter's subjective difficulty, the party should only ever earn the actual experience awarded by the monster. Despite two goblins having encounter experience of 150, they still only reward 100 experience divided evenly by the party.

Check out the Fifth Edition guide for gamemasters for more information about relative difficulty, encounter multipliers, and party size multipliers.

ENCOUNTER DIFFICULTY RATINGS

There are four difficulty ratings for encounters.

Easy encounters are ones that don't tax the characters' resources nearly as much as the other levels of encounters. An easy encounter uses approximately one-eighth of the characters' resources.

Medium encounters might have one or two scary moments but usually aren't that dangerous for a well-prepared and well-rested party. A medium encounter uses approximately one-sixth of the characters' resources. A single monster whose challenge rating equals the party's average level (assuming a group of four characters) is always a Medium encounter.

Hard encounters are riskier than medium encounters and may even result in a major injury or death, especially if the party isn't well-rested or prepared. A hard encounter uses approximately one-fourth of the characters' resources.

Deadly encounters are even more lethal than hard encounters and could result in one or two deaths or even a total party kill (TPK) for a party that isn't well-rested or prepared for the encounter. Deadly encounters use approximately one-third of the characters' resources.

ENCOUNTER DIFFICULTY SUBJECTIVITY

It is important to recognize that an encounter's difficulty is subjective to how well-rested and how prepared the party is when the combat begins. For example, a well-rested party with all of their hit points, spell slots, and limited-use features active may not feel that a deadly encounter is "deadly" at all, especially if there are no casualties. However, the encounter may have forced the fighter to use its Action Surge, the wizard to burn their highest-level spell slots, or the paladin to use up most of their Lay on Hands pool. The deadly encounter softened the party up, and they might not even realize it until they enter another combat. Once the party experiences three such deadly encounters back-to-back without rest, they will start to feel the pressure. At that point, even easy encounters will feel difficult.

SINGLE-ENCOUNTER SESSIONS

Fifth Editon's core design is built on the idea of the Adventuring Day Experience format. It assumes that a well-rested and prepared party will fight eight easy encounters, six medium encounters, four hard encounters, or three deadly encounters (or any combination thereof) before they complete a long rest and regain their expended resources. However, not every gamemaster or group has time for so many combat encounters in a single session. Moreover, higher-level characters with access to teleportation magic and spells like *magnificent mansion* can rest more frequently. This makes nearly every combat—even deadly ones—feel relatively easy due to the encounter difficulty subjectivity paradox mentioned above. Only at early levels, 1st, 2nd, and sometimes 3rd, will a deadly encounter actually feel deadly for a well-rested party.

Unfortunately, there are no rules given in the official core rulebooks on how to make a single session encounter feel more difficult. However, we can approximate such encounters based on creatures with higher-challenge ratings than what should be reasonable even for a well-rested party to face.

For example, the tarrasque is a CR 30 monster, which awards 155,000 experience points when it is defeated. Assuming that a party of four 20th-level characters fight the epic monster, they each would earn 38,750 experience points; that's three times as much as a deadly encounter for a 20th-level party would award. However, a 20th-level character's Adventuring Day Experience total is 40,000.

Therefore, it stands to reason that a single-session encounter should offer an encounter experience equal to the party's adventuring day XP. However,

SINGLE SESSION ENCOUNTER EXPERIENCE

Party Level	Max CR	3 Characters	4 Characters	5 Characters	6 Characters
1st	2	300	400	500	600
2nd	3	600	800	1,000	1,200
3rd	4	1,200	1,600	2,000	2,400
4th	5	1,500	2,000	2,500	3,000
5th	10	5,250	7,000	8,750	10,500
6th	11	6,000	8,000	10,000	12,000
7th	13	7,500	10,000	12,500	15,000
8th	14	9,000	12,000	15,000	18,000
9th	16	11,250	15,000	18,750	22,500
10th	17	13,500	18,000	22,500	27,000
11th	20	23,625	31,500	39,375	47,250
12th	21	25,875	34,500	43,125	51,750
13th	21	30,375	40,500	50,625	60,750
14th	22	33,750	45,000	56,250	67,500
15th	23	40,500	54,000	67,500	81,000
16th	23	45,000	60,000	75,000	90,000
17th	26	75,000	100,000	125,000	150,000
18th	27	81,000	108,000	135,000	162,000
19th	28	90,000	120,000	150,000	180,000
20th	30	120,000	160,000	200,000	240,000

this doesn't work for every level, especially those that don't have the ability or resources to resurrect the dead.

The Single Session Encounter Experience table suggests guidelines for single-session encounters based on the aforementioned arithmetic and playtesting. The Max CR table suggests the maximum challenge rating that the party should encounter at the respective level. This will prevent low-level parties from being destroyed in one or two hits (for example, the CR 6 mage can cast *fireball*, which can easily decimate a 1st-level party).

Using the Single Session Encounter Experience table, a gamemaster that wanted to run an encounter that took place during a single session for a well-rested party for three 11th-level characters would have 23,625 encounter experience to work with. The highest CR monster in the encounter is 20. So a party of three 11th-level characters can reasonably fight an ancient white dragon or a pit fiend. It will be an extremely difficult encounter, mind you, and the party will need to rest afterwards, but they will likely feel that it is actually a "deadly" challenge.

CREATING ENCOUNTERS

Now that we understand the "hows" and "whys" of monster statistics and how they work towards creating challenges for the party, we can discuss building actual encounters.

Here are the basic steps to encounter design:

1. Determine if the encounter is a single-session encounter or a part of a series of adventuring day encounters.
2. Determine your encounter budget.
3. Determine how many hostile creatures are in the combat encounter.
4. Use the Encounter Budget Multiplier to adjust your encounter budget based on the total number of hostile creatures participating in the encounter.
5. Use the encounter budget to "purchase" monsters for the encounter.

STEP 1 - SINGLE-SESSION OR PART OF A SERIES

The first step in building an encounter is to determine whether or not the encounter is a single-session encounter or part of a series of adventuring day encounters.

A single-session encounter assumes that the characters start the combat well-rested and will have the opportunity to rest again after the encounter.

An encounter that is part of a series of adventuring day encounters will only use a fraction of the character's resources, allowing them to fight multiple encounters between long rests.

STEP 2 - DETERMINE THE ENCOUNTER BUDGET

Next, determine the budget for your encounter.

If the characters will face a single-session encounter, use the Single-Session Encounter Experience table on page 30 to determine the budget. Make a note of the max CR, too, which will come in handy in Step 4.

If the encounter is one encounter in a series of adventuring day encounters, use the XP Thresholds by Character Level table in the Fifth Edition guide for gamemasters to determine your encounter budget. Don't forget to multiply the number listed there by the number of characters participating in combat.

STEP 3 - DETERMINE THE NUMBER OF HOSTILE CREATURES

Once you have your budget, determine how many hostile creatures will participate in the combat. This can be any number you want, although I never recommend more than 10 as it tends to slow down combat, especially at higher levels.

STEP 4 - MULTIPLY THE BUDGET BY THE ENCOUNTER MULTIPLIER

With the number of hostile creatures in mind, take the budget you determined in step 2 and multiply it by the encounter multiplier listed on the table below.

ENCOUNTER BUDGET MULTIPLIER

Hostile Creatures	2 Characters	3-5 Characters	6+ Characters
1	0.67	1.00	1.50
2	0.50	0.67	1.00
3-6	0.40	0.50	0.67
7-10	0.33	0.40	0.33
11-14	0.25	0.33	0.25
15 or more	0.20	0.25	0.20

STEP 5 - "PURCHASE" MONSTERS

Once you know your encounter budget, use the budget to "purchase" monsters using their actual experience value. Careful not to add or subtract too many monsters beyond the number you selected in Step 3, as it may cause you to use a different Encounter Budget Multiplier.

ENCOUNTER BUILDING EXAMPLE

Here is an example of designing an encounter. Bob wants to create an encounter for his group of five 5th-level characters.

- **Step 1.** He only has two hours to run the session, so he estimates that all they will have time for is a single-session encounter.
- **Step 2.** Reviewing the Single-Session Encounter Experience table, Bob sees that a single-session encounter for five 5th-level characters has a working budget of 8,750 encounter experience with a max CR of 10.
- **Step 3 and 4.** Bob wants to throw three monsters at his party. Reviewing the Encounter Budget Multiplier table, Bob sees that he needs to multiply his budget by 0.50. That leaves him with 4,375 encounter experience with which he can purchase monsters.
- **Step 4.** Bob decides to "purchase" one succubus (1,100 XP), one barbed devil (worth 1,800), and one lamia (1,100 XP). That leaves 375 encounter experience for this single-session encounter. Bob could add in another creature worth 200 encounter experience without having to adjust any modifiers, but he decides that the three monsters are challenging enough for his well-rested party.

TACTICAL BASICS

This chapter covers basic tactics, breaking down combat into three distinct sections: pre-combat, during-combat, and post-combat. It also lists the ten basic fighting styles for monsters and how to identify and use each effectively.

MONSTER FIGHTING STYLES

Although the monster stat blocks and Fifth Edition's core rulebooks don't explicitly state that there are fighting styles for monsters, upon closer inspection, we can see that certain monsters share similarities to other monsters. There are ten primary fighting styles: artillerist, brute, controller, elite, lurker, minion, skirmisher, solo, support, and tank. This chapter explains each fighting style and general tips for running such creatures in combat. The next chapter organizes the game's most common monsters—those presented in the Fifth Edition manual of monsters—and reveals their fighting styles and how to run them based on that information. For monsters that don't appear in this book, this chapter also gives tips on understanding a monster's fighting style based on its stat block alone.

While one can arguably play a monster any way they like—using a skirmisher as a tank or a minion as a solo creature—the assigned fighting style for a given monster emphasizes its strengths and downplays its weaknesses.

ARTILLERIST

An artillerist monster relies heavily on ranged attacks. Examples include barbed devils, drow, and goblins.

HALLMARKS

Most artillerists have the following features in common:

- A spell or weapon with a range of more than 30 feet
- Special senses that allow the monster to view its targets from a range
- Stealth skills or unique forms of movement that allow the monster to hide between the shots it takes
- Relatively poor defensive capabilities compared to other monsters of its Challenge Rating

- Relatively poor melee capabilities compared to its ranged attacks

Optimal Terrain

The artillerist wants to fight in wide open areas with clear lines of sight (at least from its point-of-view) with plenty of cover. Placing difficult terrain and other obstacles in the path of their targets helps keep them safe, too.

Basic Tactics

While every monster is different, here are some basic tactics to keep in mind when using an artillerist.

Keep Your Distance. The artillerist should always keep their distance, at least 40 feet or more, between themselves and their targets. If possible, place difficult terrain and obstacles between the artillerist and their targets to slow down fast movers.

Use Your Senses. Because an artillerist only needs to see their enemy and not vice versa, consider placing the artillerist in a dark place with a clear line of sight to an illuminated area where the targets will stand. Certain creatures, like drow, have better-than-usual darkvision, often allowing them to see their targets and not vice versa.

Take Defensive Action. Artillerists usually have relatively poor defensive capabilities. Make sure to place your artillerist behind cover between shots. Don't forget that you can fire and still move. Also, you can drop prone without expending any of your action economy, giving enemy artillerists disadvantage on ranged attacks made against you.

Key Pairings

Artillerists perform best when they work with creatures capable of distracting their foes. Brutes, minions, and tanks perform well in this role.

BRUTE

A brute is a creature that relies primarily on its ability to deal heavy damage as a melee fighter, often putting itself in jeopardy to do so. Examples of brutes include bulettes, frost giants, and ogres.

Hallmarks

Most brutes have the following features in common:

- Strong melee attacks that deal considerable damage

- Relatively low defensive capabilities (particularly AC) compared to other creatures of the same Challenge Rating
- Proficiency in Intimidation
- A lack of strong ranged attacks

Optimal Terrain

Brutes want to get into close combat as soon as possible. If they don't start combat within reach, ensure there isn't a lot of difficult terrain or obstacles in their path unless those obstacles do not affect them.

Basic Tactics

While every monster is different, here are some basic tactics to keep in mind when using a brute.

Get Close Fast. If your movement speed is 30 or less, start within reach of your targets whenever possible. If your movement speed is greater than 30, consider starting right at the edge of your movement range—the slight difference in spaces may keep you safe from melee combatants who get to act in initiative order before you do. When combat begins, move within reach of as many targets as possible.

Bash, Bash, Bash. Brute tactics are relatively straightforward—hit the enemy until they stop moving. If you are a relatively intelligent creature, focus your attacks on targets where you have advantage on your rolls. Brutes have relatively poor defensive capabilities; therefore, it's imperative that you down your enemies before they have a chance to down you.

Create a Distraction. If you are working alongside other creatures, make sure to use your damage output, intimidation, and large size to draw attention away from your weaker allies, particularly artillerists, lurkers, and skirmishers.

Key Pairings

You want to work alongside creatures that help give you advantage on your attack rolls, making it easier for you to remove enemies from the battlefield before they can remove you. Work alongside controllers who have effects that can knock targets prone, restrain, or blind the enemy. Other creatures like artillerists, lurkers, and skirmishers will benefit from the distraction you cause while you are on the battlefield.

CONTROLLER

Controllers are specialist monsters whose primary job is to alter the battlefield to their side's advantage. They also help their allies gain advantage on attack rolls by imposing conditions on the enemy. Examples of controllers include chain devils, gibbering mouthers, and water elementals.

Hallmarks

Most controllers have the following features in common:

- Traits, spells, or attacks that impose conditions on targets
- Relatively poor defensive capabilities compared to creatures of other challenge ratings
- Rudimentary attacks compared to their special traits

Optimal Terrain

Most controller traits, spells, and attacks have a limited range, which requires them to get closer to their targets than an artillerist would. However, they don't want to be within melee range of the enemy either. Place controllers close and behind cover, using other monsters to serve as distractions whenever possible.

Basic Tactics

While every monster is different, here are some basic tactics to keep in mind when using a controller.

Work with Others. Your controller powers often impose conditions on enemies, which give you and others on your side advantage on attack rolls made against those targets. Typically, your own attacks are too weak to benefit from this setup.

Keep Out of Reach. You probably have poor defensive capabilities; therefore, it's wise to keep out of the enemy's reach. Not only are you relatively weak, but a single hit could disrupt your concentration.

Take Defensive Measures. Once you utilize your controller powers, take cover and consider Dodging, especially if you need to maintain concentration. You might even put some distance between yourself and the controlled enemies.

Key Pairings

Controllers perform poorly on their own. Work alongside brutes, minions, and tanks who can serve as a distraction while you keep your distance and use your controller features. The other creatures will benefit from your presence.

ELITE

Elites are versatile creatures who can reasonably fill a variety of fighting styles but don't quite possess the action economy to fight as solo monsters. Examples of elites include archmages, driders, and medusas.

Hallmarks

Most elites have the following features in common:

- Strong defensive and offensive capabilities
- Better-than-average action economies
- Effective melee and ranged attacks
- Multiple types of movement speeds
- Controller or support powers

Optimal Terrain

The elite's optimal terrain depends on the fighting style you assign it. See the other fighting styles for details.

Basic Tactics

Your tactics depend on the fighting style that you are emulating and the other types of creatures present during the combat.

Key Pairings

As versatile creatures, elites work well alongside all monster types, filling whatever void there is in the group's dynamic. Artillerists, controllers, lurkers, skirmishers, and support usually need someone to fill the role of brute or tank to distract the enemy. Brutes, minions, and tanks need artillerists, controllers, and support.

- Artillerists and controllers need brutes, minions, or tanks.
- Brutes, minions, and tanks need artillerists, controllers, or support.
- Controllers and support need brutes
- Lurkers and skirmishers need brutes or tanks.

LURKER

Lurkers are ambushers designed to surprise foes, deal damage quickly, then escape before the enemy can strike back. Examples include behirs, green hags, and mimics.

Hallmarks

Most elites have the following features in common:

- High stealth proficiency or a feature that allows the creature to hide in plain sight
- Fast movement speed or unusual modes of movement (like burrowing or climbing speeds)
- High damage output
- Auto-grapple attacks
- Defensive attacks

Optimal Terrain

More so than any other creature, lurkers benefit the most from fighting in their optimal terrain. The terrain in which you should fight should complement your natural ability to hide and avenues of escape that complement any unusual modes of movement.

Basic Tactics

While every monster is different, here are some basic tactics to keep in mind when using a lurker.

Stay Hidden. Start combat hidden and don't attack until a target comes within reach of your main mode of attack.

Kill and Grab. If you have an auto-grapple feature, use it to grapple an opponent. Keep an eye out for enemies that are two size categories smaller than you, too, since they won't slow down your movement. If you don't have an auto-grapple feature, try to drop your target in one hit, then grab it as part of your movement.

Escape. Immediately after you attack the target, escape, regardless of whether or not you successfully grabbed the target. Use whatever mode of movement you possess that your enemies lack—i.e., climb up a sheer wall with your climbing speed or phase through a wall with your Incorporeal Movement trait.

Optimal Pairings

You are built to ambush and then flee. Any creatures that can help distract your targets while you make your escape are valuable companions indeed. Work alongside brutes and minions who make great distractions.

MINION

Minions are weaker-than-normal creatures who are usually not very challenging individually and perform best when in large groups, supported by monsters of other fighting styles. Examples include cultists, guards, and kobolds.

Hallmarks

Most minions have the following features in common:

- Low challenge rating
- Poor action economy
- Lack of strong ranged attacks
- Features that benefit from the presence of other creatures (such as Pack Tactics)

Optimal Terrain

Minions want to be close to the targets. However, they don't want to gather in clumps, as it may increase the risk for area of effect attacks. Use minions in areas where they can spread out but still serve as obstacles to the enemies' goal or other creatures under your control.

Basic Tactics

While every monster is different, here are some basic tactics to keep in mind when using a minion.

Spread Out. As a minion, you will probably fight with other minions. If you gather in clumps, you increase the risk of getting hit by an area of effect spell or effect. Additionally, you want to threaten as much area as possible.

Look for Advantage. Minions often have poor offensive capabilities. Look for ways to gain advantage on attack rolls against your targets, either through features like Pack Tactics or conditions imposed by controllers working on your side.

Be Annoying. If your job as a minion is to slow down the enemy, do whatever it takes to keep them occupied. Take the Dodge action to make it harder for them to hit you, waiting until they move through the area you threatened to make attacks of opportunity. Grapple and knock prone foes with poor Strength and Dexterity scores relative to your own. Draw enemies into traps.

Key Pairings

In addition to working well with other minions, minions also perform well when they have controllers working with them, setting them up for attacks with advantage. Supporters also help boost minions and keep them alive longer, further amplifying their obnoxiousness.

SKIRMISHER

Skirmishers are fast-moving creatures that primarily utilize hit-and-run tactics. Examples include air elementals, bone devils, and chimeras.

Hallmarks

Most skirmishers have the following features in common:

- Fast movement speed
- Long reach attacks
- Defensive features and attacks that prevent attacks of opportunity

Optimal Terrain

The skirmisher's success depends on its ability to move unimpeded, make an attack, and move away before the attacker has a chance to reciprocate. Unless the target has a flying speed, avoid areas with difficult terrain, as it will slow your chance to escape. However, areas with cover or concealment are good to include, as it gives you a place to escape from attacks.

Basic Tactics

While every monster is different, here are some basic tactics to keep in mind when using a skirmisher.

Strike First. Start combat with enough distance between you and your opponent that they can't reach you in one turn. Don't charge until the distance between you and your opponent is equal to or less than half your full movement speed.

Use Reach. Use reach weapons to maintain a safe distance between yourself and your targets, making it impossible for them to make an attack of opportunity against you. Alternatively, use effects like Flyby to escape without receiving an attack of opportunity.

Knock 'em Prone. Many skirmishers possess attacks that allow them to knock their opponent prone on a hit and a failed saving throw. Although you may not be able to benefit from the advantage the prone condition grants melee attackers, as the target will likely stand up on their next turn, it at least makes it harder for them to follow you.

Key Pairings

The last thing a skirmisher wants is to get hit with a well-timed attack of opportunity, especially one that could reduce its movement. Your skirmishers should work alongside creatures that can distract your foes, like brutes and tanks, or even burn up the enemy's reactions, like minions.

Solo

Relatively few and far between, solo creatures are often high CR creatures who have enough action economy to fight without support from other creatures. Examples include aboleths, ancient dragons, and storm giants.

Hallmarks

Most solo creatures have the following features in common:

- High action economy
- Strong offensive and defensive features
- Controller or support powers

Optimal Terrain

The majority of solo monsters in the Fifth Edition manual of monsters come with Lair Actions and Regional Effects. As such, these creatures should always fight in these settings. If a solo monster is caught outside of its lair (or it lacks such special actions), it should still favor terrain that complements its statistics and gives it plenty of space to move, hide, take cover, and make attacks.

Basic Tactics

While every monster is different, here are some basic tactics to keep in mind when using a solo creature.

Slow Them Down. Nearly all solo monsters have at least one Lair Action which they can use on initiative count 20 that allows them to grapple, blind, or otherwise alter the battlefield. Use these to slow them down before they can take their turn. If you lack Lair Actions, instead, put plenty of distance between you and your targets, making it impossible to target you during the first round of combat.

Divide and Conquer. Use your special features to separate individual enemies from each other, then deal as much damage as possible against the divided target. If you lack special features, use skirmisher tactics to draw out the "heroes", using their own desire to defeat you against them.

Defense, Then Offense. So long as you have the action economy for it, use your main action to protect yourself, using Dodge to impose disadvantage on attacks made against you. Skirmish and keep your distance, taking cover whenever possible. Then, when the perfect opportunity presents itself, attack. Once you've significantly weakened a group of foes, burning half their resources, switch to offense.

KEY PAIRINGS

By design, solo creatures don't typically need additional support. However, you might work alongside a few minions, having them serve as obstacles and minor annoyances for the party. So long as the minions' Challenge Rating is relatively low compared to your own Challenge Rating and your foes' levels, then they should have no effect on your encounter experience budget.

SUPPORT

Creatures that qualify as support are those who possess spells, features, and traits that allow them to boost their allies in some way. Most mounts are also considered support creatures. Examples include acolytes, nightmares, and unicorns.

HALLMARKS

Most solo creatures have the following features in common:

- Features or abilities that boost the abilities of other creatures
- Relatively low offensive capabilities
- Poor action economy or few attacks
- The ability to carry a rider as a mount

OPTIMAL TERRAIN

Like controllers, support creatures need to be close enough to the targets of their support ability, but far enough away to avoid attacks from dangerous foes. Areas with cover and concealment can help you hide between your turns. If you have a quick movement speed, wide open spaces without difficult terrain also help.

Basic Tactics

While every monster is different, here are some basic tactics to keep in mind when using a support creature.

Keep Your Distance. Never start combat within reach of melee attackers or within the view of artillerists. Typically, support creatures have relatively low defensive capabilities, so it's not hard for an enemy to remove you from combat on the very first round.

Determine Optimal Targets. Decide who among your allies will benefit the most from your support features.

Use Defensive Maneuvers. Whether you're a spellcaster boosting your allies with spells like *bless* or *healing word*, or you're a flying mount granting your rider a boost to their flying speed, you want to make sure that you stay alive to continue to protect them. Whenever you aren't using your action to protect your allies, use Dodge, Dash, or Disengage to keep yourself safe.

Key Pairings

Like controllers, support creatures require the presence of other creatures. The types of creatures you pair with depend on your mode of support, but typically, you should support creatures that fight in close combat, such as brutes, minions, or tanks.

Tank

A tank is a creature with higher-than-normal defensive capabilities, particularly armor class, whose primary job is to absorb attacks from their foes. Examples of tanks include azers, nobles, and shield guardians.

Hallmarks

Most tanks have the following features in common:

- High Armor Class and/or multiple damage resistances and immunities
- Poor action economy or few attacks
- Passive damage-dealing features

Optimal Terrain

Tanks, like brutes and minions, want to engage targets as quickly as possible. If the tank can't start combat within reach of its targets, make sure that there isn't any difficult terrain or obstacles standing in the tank's way.

Basic Tactics

While every monster is different, here are some basic tactics to keep in mind when using a tank.

Defense! As a tank, your job is to draw the enemy's attacks in any way possible. This helps burn their action economy and keep your allies safe. But you need to stay safe, too—use Dodge, the Parry reaction, and whatever other features you have at your disposal to make it difficult for enemies to hit you.

Threaten Attacks of Opportunity. Ensure you engage with as many targets as possible, getting them within your reach. This makes it difficult for them to move away from you without either using the Disengage action or provoking attacks of opportunity.

Block the Way. Make sure that your allies are safe from attacks by putting yourself in the enemies' path. Even a Small or Medium creature with a 5-foot reach effectively threatens a 15-foot-square area, making it difficult for enemies to slip past without engaging them first.

COMMON MONSTER COMBINATIONS

When you create encounters, consider the different fighting styles mentioned above. These will help you determine which monsters to feature in combat. Try to create combinations that have good synergy and balance out each other's strengths and weaknesses. Below are some common fighting style combinations.

Artillerists and Brutes. The brute monster draws the targets' attention while artillerists keep their distance and take shots from behind cover.

Controllers and Skirmishers/Lurkers. The controller uses their spells and traits to impose negative conditions on the targets, allowing lurkers and skirmishers to attack and escape without taking hits.

Elites and Support. The elite fills whatever role is necessary while support creatures boost and protect them.

Solo and Minions. Solo creatures usually don't need much help, but if you decide to give them some assistance, toss in a few minions to eat up the enemy's action economy.

Tanks and Minions. The tank distracts the party and absorbs blows while the minions move in and make attacks.

PRE-COMBAT

Before combat begins, there are a few considerations you must make to

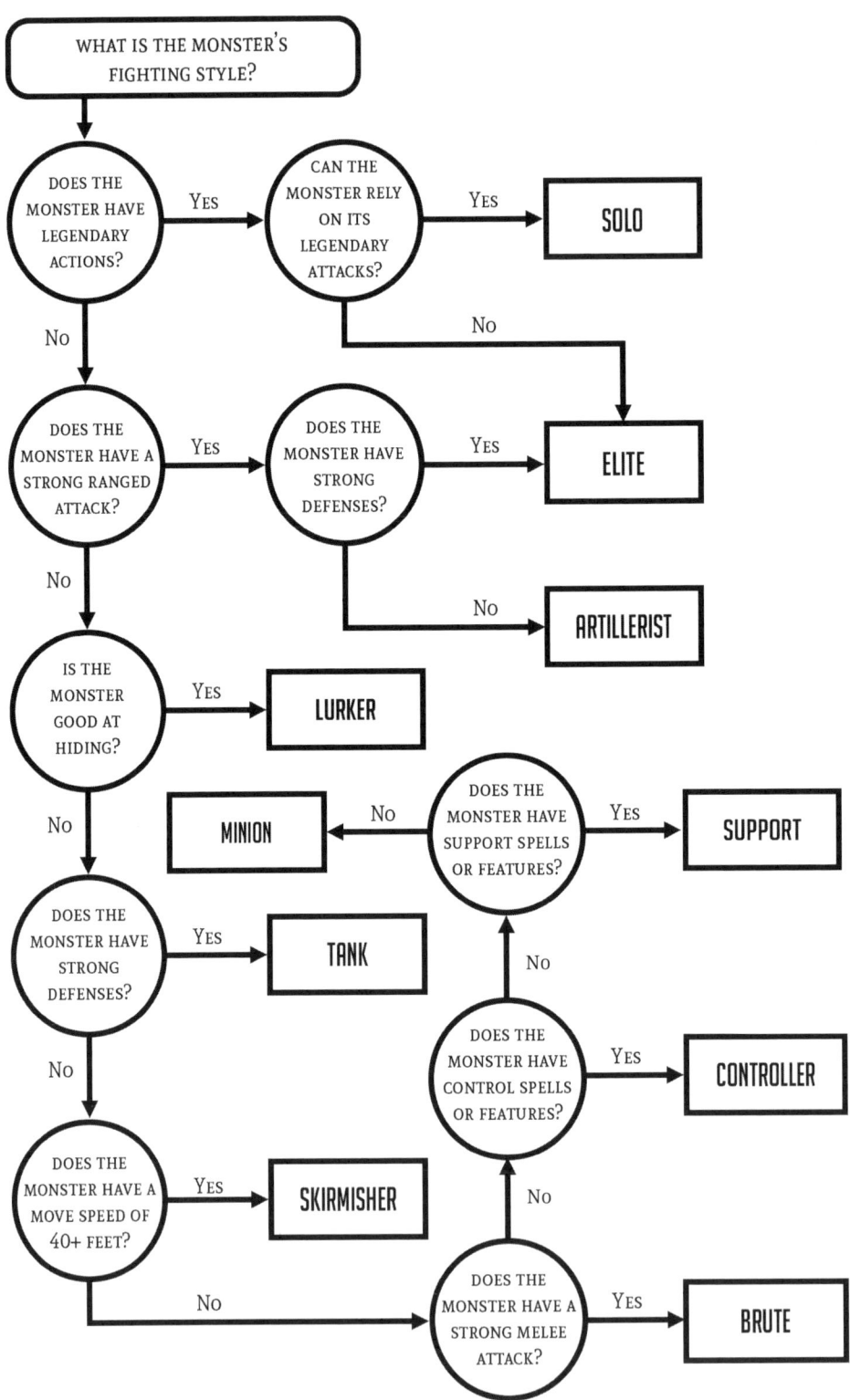

ensure that your monster is set up for battle—even if it's surprised.

WHAT ARE THE MONSTERS' MOTIVATIONS?

Not every monster wants to fight. Some don't want to be bothered. Others are wise enough to recognize when they're in danger. And not all monsters that work together actually like each other. Subordinates might follow their leader's instructions until the characters kill the leader—at which point they surrender or switch sides.

Before combat begins, decide what the monsters' motivations are. This will help guide the course of combat, especially when you need to decide whether or not the monsters would surrender or flee.

A few ideas for motivations include but aren't limited to::

Conquering. The monster desires to destroy and subjugate others. It's likely that such a creature only picks on the weak and will avoid difficult combat situations. Alternatively, the monster could see the characters as potential allies and ask them to join forces.

Hunting. The creature is actively looking for food, or waiting for an easy meal to fall into their lap.

Questing. The creature is searching for a specific item or person in the area or is answering the call to adventure. They might see the characters as potential allies or competitors.

Recovering. The creature is resting after another battle and may not want to engage.

Sanctuary. The monster just wants to find a safe place and will only fight to defend itself.

Slaying. The creature is hunting for one of its rivals. The rival could be another creature in the area or even the characters. If the latter, the creature might already know the characters' strengths and weaknesses and plan accordingly.

Sneaking. The creature is avoiding danger, either its enemies or another horrible creature in the area—possibly even the characters.

HOW IS THE BATTLEFIELD SET UP?

It is rare that the characters will ever encounter hostile creatures in a place that is a 180-foot-square featureless flat plain. Difficult terrain, obstacles, hazards, obscuration, and other features all lend themselves to interesting locations. And if the characters encounter a creature on its own turf or within its lair, it's likely that the location is designed to complement the creature's fighting style and features.

Difficult Terrain

Combat rarely takes place in bare rooms or on featureless plains. Boulder-strewn caverns, briar-choked forests, treacherous staircases—the setting of a typical fight usually contains difficult terrain.

Every foot of movement in difficult terrain costs 1 extra foot. This rule is true even if multiple things in a space count as difficult terrain.

Low furniture, rubble, undergrowth, steep stairs, snow, and shallow bogs are examples of difficult terrain. The space of another creature, whether hostile or not, also counts as difficult terrain.

Creatures that benefit the most from difficult terrain are those who want to keep their distance from their enemies (artillerists, controllers, and support) or those whose movement modes and features allow them to avoid it.

Cover

Walls, trees, creatures, and other obstacles can provide cover during combat, making a target more difficult to harm. A target can benefit from cover only when an attack or other effect originates on the opposite side of the cover.

There are three degrees of cover. If a target is behind multiple cover sources, only the most protective degree of cover applies; the degrees aren't added together. For example, if a target is behind a creature that gives half cover and a tree trunk that gives three-quarters cover, the target has three-quarters cover.

A target with half cover has a +2 bonus to AC and Dexterity saving throws. A target has half cover if an obstacle blocks at least half of its body. The obstacle might be a low wall, a large piece of furniture, a narrow tree trunk, or a creature, whether that creature is an enemy or a friend.

A target with three-quarters cover has a +5 bonus to AC and Dexterity saving throws. A target has three-quarters cover if about three-quarters of it is covered by an obstacle. The obstacle might be a portcullis, an arrow slit, or a thick tree trunk.

A target with total cover can't be targeted directly by an attack or a spell, although some spells can reach such a target by including it in an area of effect. A target has total cover if an obstacle completely conceals it.

Creatures with relatively low defensive capabilities benefit the most from cover, especially if they need to keep their distance. Artillerists, controllers, and support should always hide behind cover whenever possible, ducking in and out between shots. Skirmishers and lurkers can use cover between their attacks. Even close combat fighters should consider positioning themselves so there is cover between them and enemy artillerists.

Hazards

Spiderwebs, dangerous molds and slimes, molten lava, pools of acid, and other dangers offer deadly features that force the combat participants to consider their movement and actions carefully.

Hazards don't always have to deal damage, either. Bad weather creates hazards, too, limiting vision and imposing disadvantage on ranged attack rolls.

Creatures fighting in optimal conditions might use these hazards to challenge the characters further and potentially boost themselves. When you set up the battlefield, look at the monster's damage immunities and special features. For example, fire giants are immune to fire, so they don't suffer from the hazards of an active volcano—but their enemies probably do. Most undead and constructs are immune to poison, so you have nothing to worry about placing them in an area consumed by a toxic cloud.

Obscured Areas

The most fundamental tasks of adventuring—noticing danger, finding hidden objects, hitting an enemy in combat, and targeting a spell, to name just a few—rely heavily on a character's ability to see. Darkness and other effects that obscure vision can prove a significant hindrance.

A given area might be lightly or heavily obscured. In a lightly obscured area, such as dim light, patchy fog, or moderate foliage, creatures have disadvantage on Wisdom (Perception) checks that rely on sight.

A heavily obscured area—such as darkness, opaque fog, or dense foliage—blocks vision entirely. A creature effectively suffers from the blinded condition when trying to see something in that area unless it has a special form of vision that allows it to see through the cause of obscurity. Blindsight sees through opaque fogs and mists, while tremorsense can help a creature detect targets so long as they are touching the same ground as they are.

The presence or absence of light in an environment creates three categories of illumination: bright light, dim light, and darkness.

Bright light lets most creatures see normally. Even gloomy days provide bright light, as do torches, lanterns, fires, and other sources of illumination within a specific radius.

Dim light, also called shadows, creates a lightly obscured area. An area of dim light is usually a boundary between a source of bright light, such as a torch, and surrounding darkness. The soft light of twilight and dawn also counts as dim light. A particularly brilliant full moon might bathe the land in dim light. A creature with darkvision can see in dim light as if it were bright light.

Darkness creates a heavily obscured area. Characters face darkness outdoors at night (even most moonlit nights), within the confines of an unlit dungeon or a subterranean vault, or in an area of magical darkness. A creature with darkvision can see in darkness as if it were dim light. Don't forget that dim light creates a lightly obscured area; therefore, creatures with darkvision have disadvantage on Wisdom (Perception) checks made to see in total darkness.

Traps

Traps can be found almost anywhere. One wrong step in an ancient tomb might trigger a series of scything blades, which cleave through armor and bone. The seemingly innocuous vines that hang over a cave entrance might grasp and choke anyone who pushes through them. A net hidden among the trees might drop on travelers who pass underneath. In a fantasy game, unwary adventurers can fall to their deaths, be burned alive, or fall under a fusillade of poisoned darts.

Intelligent creatures that have a chance to set up the battlefield terrain in their favor often set up traps for their enemies as part of an ambush. Kobolds, goblins, and other small creatures are famous for doing this, drawing their foes (or prey) deeper and deeper into their trap-filled hovels.

What will the monster do if it wins (or loses) initiative?

Initiative is one of the most important parts of the battle, especially for the monsters, as initiative order can mean the difference between life and death. If the monster's initiative check result is high, it will be able to move and act before its enemies do. But if the result is low, the monster could get killed before it even has a chance to bare its fangs.

Unless the monster is surprised or isn't particularly intelligent, always set up your monsters under the assumption that they will come last in initiative. If they have relatively poor defensive capabilities, place them far enough away from the party that melee strikers can't reach them on their first turn, not without using the Dash action, at least. Put them behind cover and place difficult terrain and other obstacles in the way. Place stronger creatures within reach of its targets so it forces them to engage with it.

Consider the monster's reactions, too, since an unsurprised creature can still use its reaction before its turn begins. Place the monster in a spot that threatens attacks of opportunity. If it has a special reaction, treat that as a potential "pre-turn" action that it might get to use. For example, the knight has the Parry feature, granting the knight a +2 to its AC against melee attacks that would hit it. Place the knight close to its enemies, encouraging them to use their attacks against it, thereby protecting the knight's allies.

WHAT EFFECTS/SPELLS ARE ALREADY AFFECTING THE MONSTER?

Plenty of creatures have spells and other special features that they can use outside of combat. The mage probably already has *mage armor* cast on itself since the spell has a duration of 8 hours and doesn't require concentration. Likewise, archmages with time to prepare for combat may have *mage armor, mindblank, stoneskin*, and even *invisibility* up and running before combat starts.

Before you run the combat, review the creature's special features and spells. Look for those that have durations of 10 minutes or longer, particularly those that don't require concentration. Assume that the creature will use whatever it has to enhance its abilities during combat further.

WHAT TACTICS WILL THE MONSTERS EMPLOY?

Finally, determine the creature's overall game plan. Beasts and other creatures with bestial Intelligence scores (5 or less) rely purely on instinct, often fleeing at the sign of danger. More intelligent creatures, especially those with proficiency in their weapons, will at least devise simple tactics based on their fighting styles. And highly intelligent creatures who've had time to research their foes might even build their tactics around the strengths and weaknesses of their foes.

Try to get a sense of the creature's basic tactics by either reviewing the 10 Fighting Styles section starting on page 34 or reviewing the specific creature's tactics in the next chapter, Individual Monster Tactics.

DURING-COMBAT

Once combat begins, all of your decisions become turn-based. The key, then, is to determine in advance the tactics you'd like to employ and stick with them unless there is no doubt that they won't work (i.e., you plan to use firebolt against your enemies, but they're suddenly all immune to fire damage, etc.).

DETERMINE SURPRISE

Before combat begins and initiative is determined, you must determine whether anyone involved in the combat encounter is surprised. While it's possible for characters to surprise the enemy, it's relatively rare thanks to noisy suits of armor and martial characters with poor Dexterity. Monsters surprising the characters are much more common. Here are a few ways that you can surprise characters.

Deception. A creature that seems non-hostile to the characters might use Deception to hide its motives, especially if they have proficiency in

Tactical Basics

Deception and lack a monstrous appearance. Before combat begins, have each character make a Wisdom (Insight) check contested by the creature's Charisma (Deception) check. Each character whose check is lower than the creature's check starts combat surprised.

Disguises. Certain creatures have special features and powers, such as False Appearance and change shape, that allow them to hide in plain sight. Previous iterations of these powers granted automatic surprise to the disguised creature; however, new versions of these abilities grant advantage on initiative checks and allow the creature's targets to make an Intelligence (Investigation) check to discern the creature's true nature.

Illusions. Spellcasting creatures may use illusions to hide, creating objects to duck behind or altering the landscape in some way that prevents their targets from seeing them. This functionality works similarly to disguises (see above).

Obscured Area. Another way to earn surprise is to hide within an area obscured by an effect such as magical darkness or natural phenomenon like a fog cloud. Arguably, this should only work if you can see through the obscured area yourself. So a drow could surprise a human wandering around in the dark without any light, but the drow couldn't surprise the same human if both of them were in the area of a fog cloud.

Stealth. Perhaps the most common way to gain surprise is to use the Dexterity (Stealth) skill to hide from targets. Any target whose passive Wisdom (Perception) is lower than the result of your Dexterity (Stealth) check starts combat surprise.

Sudden Appearance. A creature that suddenly appears near its targets, and it is already aware of its targets, might gain surprise on its attacks. A gelatinous cube falling from the shaft above the party or a mage using *dimension door* to get the jump on the party are two such instances.

ESTABLISH POSITIONS

Once you know who is surprised and who isn't, decide where all the characters and monsters are located. Given the adventurers' marching order or their stated positions in the room or other location, the gamemaster figures out where the adversaries are—how far away and in what direction.

STARTING DISTANCE

The main thing to consider with your monsters when establishing their positions is the distance they start away from the characters. There are two factors to help you determine this: the monster's fighting style and its movement speed.

By Fighting Style. Monsters with fighting styles that lend themselves better to melee combat—such as brutes, minions, and tanks—want to start as close as possible to their targets. Meanwhile, targets with poor defensive capabilities and/or ranged attacks and abilities—such as artillerists, controllers, and support—need to keep their distance. The table below shows you some quick-and-easy rules for using the monsters' fighting styles to guide how you place them.

By Movement Speed. Another key factor in determining your monster's starting position is its movement speed. This is especially important for creatures that need to get within melee range of targets as soon as possible while also keeping them safe until it's their turn.

Most characters have movement speeds of 30 feet. So, if your monster

STARTING DISTANCE BY FIGHTING STYLE

Fighting Style	Starting Distance
Artillerist	Start at least 40 feet away up to the maximum range of your ranged weapon.
Brute	Start within reach of your foes or at the maximum range of your movement speed.
Controller	Start at least 40 feet away up to the maximum range of your controller spells/features. Based on the fighting style you emulate.
Elite	Start within reach of your foes.
Lurker	Start within reach of your foes or at the maximum range of your movement speed.
Minion	Start within reach of your foes or at the maximum range of your movement speed.
Skirmisher	Start at least 40 feet away up to the maximum range of your movement speed.
Solo	Based on the fighting style you emulate.
Support	Start at least 40 feet away up to the maximum range of your support spells/features.
Tank	Start within reach of your foes or at the maximum range of your movement speed.

has a movement speed of 40 feet or more, you can start them at the far end of their movement range. That way, the character with 30 feet of movement speed won't be able to reach your monster without taking the Dash action or some other movement-boosting feature, such as Cunning Action or the *expeditious retreat* spell.

If your monster doesn't have a movement speed greater than 30 feet, consider placing the monster within 5 feet of as many targets as possible. While there's the possibility that your monster will take damage before its turn, its presence and the threat of attacks of opportunity will tie up its opponents during the first round of combat.

Skirmishers function a little differently, as they are designed to move, hit, then retreat all in the same round. Place the skirmisher up to half of its full movement speed away from its targets, especially if its movement speed is greater than 60 feet or it uses an unusual form of movement, such as flying or swimming.

ROLL INITIATIVE

Next, everyone involved in the combat encounter rolls initiative, determining the order of combatants' turns. While it's usually impossible to predict where you'll fall in the initiative order, having surprise and placing your monsters in the proper positions on the battlefield will help you avoid the enemy's attacks during the first round of combat.

BEFORE YOUR FIRST TURN

So long as you aren't surprised, you can take reactions before the start of your turn. This is important for brutes and tanks, especially if they are within reach of targets, as their presence may threaten attacks of opportunity. Certain monsters have Legendary Actions and Lair Actions, too, which allow them to take actions before their first turn. The best use for such actions is to alter the battlefield to your advantage, control your foes, or reposition yourself to reduce the risk of injury before your first turn begins.

YOUR FIRST TURN

What you do on your first turn depends on your fighting style. Fighting styles that focus on dealing damage, such as artillerists, brutes, and skirmishers, choose their optimal targets and start making attacks. Defensive fighting styles, like minions and tanks, take the Dodge action and turn themselves into obstacles. Controllers and support utilize the most useful spell or feature they have at their disposal. Elites and solo creatures determine the fighting style they wish to emulate and begin performing actions relevant to that choice. Finally, lurkers make their opening attack and escape (hopefully with a tasty meal in their clutches).

Action Economy. During your turn, consider your action economy. Action economy measures how much a given creature can accomplish in one round. Almost all creatures in Fifth Edition can move up to their full movement speed and take one action. A creature may also interact with an object as part of its movement without expending an action. Many creatures can make additional attacks, use bonus actions to perform additional actions, and take reactions when available. Legendary creatures have Lair Actions and Legendary Actions, too, allowing them to operate outside of their turn. It's important to understand your creature's action economy before you begin their turn; that way, you can benefit from every option available to them.

Movement. Almost all creatures have movement speeds, but not all of them need to move. Creatures designed for close combat should limit their movement, only moving when absolutely necessary. Skirmishers are designed to move, hit, and retreat, breaking up their movement speed during their turn. Similarly, lurkers are designed to surprise targets, attack, then move out of reach. Creatures with relatively poor defensive capabilities who aren't designed for close combat should use their movement to keep their distance, taking cover or dropping prone whenever possible.

Actions. While the most obvious actions for a target to take on its turn is the Attack or Cast a Spell actions, consider the value of the other actions available to your monsters.

Attack. If you are playing with creatures who are built to deal damage, then attack seems the most obvious option, especially if they have features like multiattack, which allow them to make multiple attacks.

Cast a Spell. Creatures that rely on spellcasting for their attacks, control features, or support options must use the Cast a Spell action to do so.

Dash. Use Dash when you need your creatures with poor defensive capabilities to put more distance between themselves and their targets. Dash is also useful for lurkers escaping with prey (or simply escaping). You can also use Dash to distract and draw away faster-moving enemies from their groups.

Disengage. Like Dash, use Disengage to help creatures with poor defensive capabilities escape. Keep in mind, however, that if you Disengage and your movement speed is no greater than the enemy's, it might be difficult to escape their reach.

Dodge. Tanks use Dodge to decrease the likelihood of getting attacked, effectively burning the enemy's action economy. Creatures with Legendary Actions, bonus actions, or extra reactions can also use their main action to Dodge while using their secondary action economy to perform actions.

Help. The Help action allows a creature to aid a friendly creature in attacking a creature within 5 feet of it; the ally gains advantage on the next attack roll that they make so long as it's made before the end of your next turn. The best time to use this is when the creature offering Help has a poor to-hit modifier and deals relatively poor damage compared to the creature it assists.

Hide. Creatures that benefit from using Hide during combat are artillerists who may gain advantage on their attack roll thanks to the unseen attacker rule, lurkers who want to escape without being seen, and other creatures whose defensive abilities aren't strong enough to withstand attacks. Remember that you can Hide and still concentrate on spells, too, so controllers and support casters may benefit from the Hide action more than they would by making an attack and exposing themselves.

Ready. Ready can be extremely useful, allowing you to transform your action into a reaction. However, before you use the Ready action, consider its effect on the action economy, especially if you are using a creature that can deal more than one attack per turn, as you can't Ready a multiattack. When the enemy starts its turn outside of your creatures' reach/range, use Ready to Attack them when they get close enough.

Search. While Search is somewhat expensive from an action economy standpoint, it is useful for pinpointing the locations of hidden targets, especially if the one who finds the target can tell others where they are.

Use an Object. All creatures can interact with an object as part of their turn. However, a creature that needs to interact with a second object, or needs to use an object that is more complicated, uses this action. This action is subjective to the combat situation, but may come in handy for readying both a sword and shield, pulling a lever to trigger a trap, or closing and locking a door.

Other Actions. Many monsters have special actions that require them to use an action. Whether or not the monster should use this action depends on what the action does and their fighting style.

Bonus Actions. If your monsters have bonus actions, first, assess whether or not the bonus action can only be used at the expense of the monster's full action economy. For example, a priest that wishes to cast *spiritual weapon* won't be able to cast another spell other than a cantrip with their main action. If there is no conflict with the creature's action economy and the use of the bonus action, then use the bonus action where appropriate.

IN BETWEEN TURNS

Although the monster's turn is over, it may still have reactions, Legendary Actions, and Lair Actions available to it.

Reactions. Certain special abilities, spells, and situations allow you to take a special action called a reaction. A reaction is an instant response to a trigger of some kind, which can occur on your turn or on someone else's. The opportunity attack, described later in this chapter, is the most common type of reaction.

When you take a reaction, you can't take another one until the start of your next turn. If the reaction interrupts another creature's turn, that creature can continue its turn right after the reaction.

Special Reactions. Before you run the monster in combat, make sure you know if the monster has any special reactions available to it, such as a knight's Parry reaction or a mage's *shield* spell. Then, determine the instances in which your monster would use that reaction.

Attacks of Opportunity. You can make an opportunity attack when a hostile creature that you can see moves out of your monster's reach. To make the opportunity attack, you use the monster's reaction to make one melee attack against the provoking creature. The attack occurs right before the creature leaves your reach. Before making the attack of opportunity, consider if it is more valuable to make an attack with your reaction or to use another special reaction or Readied action.

Readied Actions. If you used your action to ready an action, look out for the reaction's triggers, whatever it is.

Lair Actions. Some legendary monsters encountered in their lairs come with special actions that they can use on initiative count 20. These special actions are useful for securing a position at the top of the queue, allowing the monster to reposition itself or control the battlefield before most creatures in combat can take their first turn. Some Lair Actions deal damage, too; if the creature is in an optimal position, use these. Otherwise, it's usually best to favor those that help the monster control the battlefield, effectively acting as a "bonus controller."

Legendary Actions. Special monsters come with Legendary Actions, which allow them to take a special action immediately after another creature takes its turn. Usually, a monster has a limit to the number of Legendary Actions it can take in a round, typically three. And some Legendary Actions cost more than one action to use. Carefully consider the Legendary Actions you wish to use before using them. Also, consider your position in initiative order relevant to the other creatures on the battlefield before using them. For example, if you have a creature that can move as a Legendary Action, you might use this Legendary Action right before your turn begins, setting yourself up for a melee attack.

SUBSEQUENT TURNS

The monster's fighting style dictates its actions in subsequent turns. Melee combatants continue to stay as close to the enemies as possible, moving only to engage more targets and threaten more spaces. Artillerists, controllers, and support continue to keep their distance. Skirmishers move, make melee attacks, and retreat. Elites and solo creatures consider their side's status in combat before determining what to do next. Only lurkers are different, as they may immediately end combat after the first turn, repositioning themselves for a future surprise attack.

ENDING COMBAT

How combat ends depends on the monster's motivations, how they are faring in combat overall and their fighting style.

Ambushers. Lurkers are designed to ambush, attack, and retreat. The ideal situation for a lurker involves them escaping without a scratch. If they wish to continue the combat, they only do so after they find another place to stage an ambush.

Fight to the Death. Fanatical creatures, such as cultists, or those more afraid of their masters than their foes, such as low-tier demons and devils, will usually fight until destroyed. Traditionally, creatures that aren't native to the Material Plane, such as celestials, fiends, and elementals, return to their home plane when they are destroyed. Creatures that lack sentience, such as constructs and low CR undead, will fight until destroyed unless commanded otherwise by their creators. Creatures with poor Wisdom scores may also stay in combat since they aren't experienced enough to know when it is the right time to flee.

Flee/Surrender. Creatures with poor motivation to fight may escape combat or surrender as soon as their hit points are reduced by half or more, or they lose half or more of their allies. Creatures with bestial Intelligence and with average or better Wisdom scores will usually flee, so long as they aren't under the effects of enchantment or backed into a corner.

Mission Accomplished. Sometimes, creatures have different reasons for starting combat than "destroying the foe." Goals such as forcing the foe to surrender, getting past an obstacle, or stealing a special object on the battlefield may not require the creatures to continue the combat unless absolutely necessary.

AFTER COMBAT

Even when combat ends, there's plenty to consider.

Did the characters kill the monsters? If so, can they loot the bodies and find treasure? Or did killing the monster make the adventure more difficult for the characters? Perhaps the monsters had important information that the characters needed. Or maybe the monsters' allies will now seek revenge on the characters. Maybe the characters are in a place of pure evil, and the monsters will rise again as vengeful revenants. Sometimes, monsters even play dead, hoping the characters don't notice. Dead bodies smell, too. Maybe the body will attract bigger, uglier monsters. At the very least, a swarm of insects might eventually appear, creating a horrible cloud through which the characters must pass to leave the area.

Or did the monsters escape? Was the monster a lurker who prefers to make hit-and-run attacks? And if so, where will the lurker set up its next ambush? Maybe the monster ran away to fetch its allies. Or perhaps it wants to set up or trigger a trap for the characters.

What happens if the monster surrenders? Does the monster share what it knows in exchange for its life? Or does the monster continue to shout obscenities at its captors? Maybe the monster uses Deception to trick the characters into another trap or encounter. The monster might even join the party, working tirelessly to earn their trust—until it stabs them while they're sleeping at the inn, of course.

INDIVIDUAL MONSTER TACTICS

The following pages list monster tactics in alphabetical order as they appear in the Fifth Edition *Monster Manual*. The legend below details the various iconography.

MONSTER TYPE	FIGHTING STYLES
Aberration	Artillerist
Beast	Brute
Celestial	Controller
Construct	Elite
Dragon	Lurker
Elemental	Minion
Fey	Skirmisher
Fiend	Solo
Giant	Support
Humanoid	Tank
Monstrosity	
Ooze	
Plant	
Undead	

ABOLETH

 CR 10

Four long tentacles writhe from this three-eyed fish-like creature's flanks, and its green body glistens with thick, clear slime.

Aboleths are ancient alien horrors from the Elemental Plane of Water. They plot endlessly from their murky subterranean pools, sending their countless thralls to do their bidding.

Fighting Style: Solo. Although aboleths are rarely without minions to assist them, they do have the capacity to take on a party by themselves, especially when they are in their lairs.

Set-up: Subterranean Pool. Aboleths rarely leave their lairs, which they make within murky subterranean pools. The pool should have plenty of space for you to swim around and be deep enough that you can hide from targets if necessary. Aboleths have 120 feet of darkvision, so you don't need lights.

Weaknesses: Dexterity Saving Throws. Aboleths have poor Dexterity scores and no proficiency in Dexterity saving throws. Plus, they don't come with Magic Resistance. Make sure to keep them in cover whenever possible, Dodging when you can't find any. Target spellcasters that force Dexterity saving throws as much as you can.

Pair With Minions or Soldiers. Team up with tanks and minions, especially those that can grapple and/or restrain targets, allowing you to hit and run without reprisal. Chuuls are perfect as brutes or tanks, while grimlocks, zombies, and other low CR creatures function perfectly as minions.

Tactics: Dodge and Use Lair or Legendary Actions. Aboleths are swimmers, so make sure they always stay in the water. The water should be sufficiently disgusting thanks to its mucous cloud and provide full cover when it dives down. They also have darkvision out to 120 feet, so always stay at the edge of the enemy's darkvision.

As a legendary creature, the aboleth has Legendary Actions that allow it to perform actions out of its initiative order. Plus, it has some relatively powerful controller Lair Actions. Because the aboleth is relatively weak and has poor Dexterity saving throws, it should use its main action to Dodge while it uses its Legendary Actions and Lair Actions to soften up the party.

Open combat with your Pools of Water lair action to draw weaker targets into the pool. Use this as often as possible, as you have the home-field advantage while in water. If you have minions, have them grapple targets and drag them toward you.

Try to draw enemies to you into the water, Dodging, moving, and staying out of sight as you do.

Once you have three or more targets within 80 feet of you, you can use your turn to move within 60 feet of all of them, still Dodging as you do. Then, when initiative count 20 comes back around, hit them with either phantasmal force (especially if they're not in the water yet) or your rage conduit.

Aboleths are intelligent and patient, so you must be, too—you must sufficiently weaken your foes before you dare get close enough to start making melee attacks. However, if one of your minions manages to pull a target close enough to you, you can let them have it with your full Multiattack. But only do this if you are out of range of the rest of your enemies.

ACOLYTE

Acolytes are priests in training and more or less represent a 1st-level cleric as an NPC.

Fighting Style: Support. Acolytes are marginally more durable than commoners and exist solely to help out their fellow teammates. Without frontline fighters, an acolyte will likely surrender in the face of danger.

Set-up: Cover and Range. The two support spells you'll want to start with have a 30-foot range. Once you cast those, retreat into cover and use your *sacred flame*. If your allies need healing, they should come to you, not the other way around.

Weaknesses: Glass Cannons. It doesn't take much to drop an acolyte to 0 hit points. Make sure to keep them behind cover with at least 30 feet or more between them and melee attackers.

Pair With Brutes or Tanks. Team up with creatures that will tie up the enemy while you cast spells from the backline.

Tactics: Support First, Attack Second. Pre-cast *sanctuary* on yourself or one of your allies and *bless* your three best attackers before combat begins. If you can't get these spells off before the start of combat, then give *bless* priority. As soon as you get this support spells off, move out of the charging range of the melee attackers and take cover. Use *sacred flame* on targets with low Dexterity (the ones in heavy armor), moving and repositioning whenever necessary.

ANGEL, DEVA

 CR 10

This tall, human-like creature has long, feathery wings and a gentle inner radiance that makes it difficult to look at directly.

Devas are divine messengers with various roleplaying-friendly features such as Change Shape, a high Insight modifier, and healing powers.

Fighting Style: Skirmisher. Devas come with a dizzying flying speed of 90 feet and resistance to various damage types. Plus, they have 120 feet of darkvision.

Set-up: Dark, Open Spaces. Devas are fliers with 120 feet of darkvision. Keep them in the air and in the dark.

Weaknesses: Controllers. Watch out for targets that can grapple or restrain you. Losing your ability to fly severely weakens you and leaves you open to reprisal from the entire party.

Pair With Tanks. Your attack style works best when your enemies are busy targeting another creature. Team up with something that can Dodge and is willing to take hits while you perform hit-and-run maneuvers. You can heal that creature in lieu of making attacks, too, but if you're in danger, focus on taking out your opponents.

Tactics: Hit and Run. Make sure to start combat with plenty of distance between you and your enemies, preferably out of sight. Spend a moment determining who the most dangerous target is, and then position yourself, so you're within 45 feet of that target while still out of reach of the target's allies. Once you get within 45 feet of the target, fly down and hit the target with your Multiattack. Then fly back out of range. Use the cover of darkness to reposition yourself, staying just out of the enemy's vision.

As a lawful good creature, you won't kill non-evil creatures, dealing non-lethal damage whenever possible.

ANGEL, PLANETAR

 **CR 16**

Muscular, bald, and tall, this humanoid creature has emerald skin and two pairs of shining, white-feathered wings.

Planetars serve as weapons of the gods and only appear when something or someone needs to be smitten.

Fighting Style: Solo. Planetars come with various features and attacks that allow them to face their enemies alone if the need arises. The trick is to fight the enemy in two phases. First, weaken them with your spells from a distance. Then smash them with hit-and-run attacks until they surrender or you render them unconscious.

Set-up: Dark, Open Spaces. Planetars are fliers with 120 feet of truesight. Keep them in the air and in (magical) darkness.

Weaknesses: Controllers. Beware of any creature that can remove your ability to move, especially strong grapplers.

Pair With Minions. Planetars are strong enough that they won't need much support, but a few minions to eat up spellcasters' slots while you deal with more challenging targets never hurts.

Tactics: Weaken, Then Attack. Start combat 60 to 120 feet away from your targets or at least out of the range of their vision. You have 120 feet of truesight, so you can see them even when they can't see you. Consider making yourself invisible before combat begins.

Open combat with *insect plague*. As soon as you cast it, move far out of range and let the spell do its work. After the party finds a way to escape the *insect plague*, switch to *blade barrier*, cutting off ranged attackers with the ringed wall option. While concentrating on *blade barrier*, pummel targets with *flame strike*. Always stay just out of their line of sight high in the air.

After you exhaust your *flame strike* spells, employ hit-and-run tactics, targeting creatures that lack a way to grapple you as a reaction—move 60 feet towards the target, hit it with your Multiattack, then fly out of range. If the party starts to get smart, use *invisibility* to reposition yourself. Let their impatience get the best of them.

ANGEL, SOLAR

 **CR 21**

This towering humanoid creature has shining topaz eyes, metallic skin, and three pairs of white wings.

Solars serve gods as their faithful right hands. Even demon princes fear these powerful celestials.

Fighting Style: Solo. Few creatures are more terrifying than a solar in terms of their attacks, spells, and features.

Set-up: Dark, Open Spaces. Solars are fliers with 120 feet of truesight. Keep them in the air and in the dark (magical darkness, if possible).

Weaknesses: Roleplaying. It's hard to find a weakness in the solar's build. They're armed with some of the best-ranged attacks in the game, come with Legendary Actions, have Magic Resistance, and have impressive statistics across the board. However, they are still lawful good creatures, which means—as villains are so fond of saying—"their compassion is their weakness."

Pair With Minions. Solars are fully capable of handling entire armies by themselves. However, having a few minions around never hurts to draw the enemy force's action economy.

Tactics: Weaken, Then Attack. Start combat with plenty of distance between you and the targets, ideally invisible. Open with *blade barrier,* dividing the ranged attackers from the melee attackers. Use your slaying longbow to eliminate targets with low hit points and poor Constitution saving throws (the solar is wise enough to tell who's who).

Between attacks, keep your Teleport Legendary Action in reserve in case a target gets too close, or you need to get out of the range of a ranged attacker. If you happen to draw out all melee attackers, use Teleport to get behind the backline so you can nail them with Blinding Gaze. But only do this just before your turn starts again; that way, none of the melee attackers have a chance to come back to you before you can return to the skies.

ANIMATED OBJECT, ARMOR

 **CR 1**

This empty suit of armor clangs as it moves, making an awful sound as it approaches.

Animated suits of armor are simplistic constructs designed to blend in with their surroundings, attacking whenever a trespasser gets in range.

Fighting Style: Brute. While animated armors have excellent AC for their relatively low CR, they aren't smart enough to Dodge or use other defensive tactics. As simple automatons, they punch their foes until they or their foe is destroyed.

Set-up: Disguised. Animated armor comes with the False Appearance trait, which allows them to blend into their surroundings. Most players know that a suit of armor is rarely a suit of armor, so you might put a few red herrings in the way before they encounter the actual animated armor.

As a bonus, consider placing it in an area of magical darkness where it will benefit from its blindsight.

Weaknesses: Stupid. Animated armor has Intelligence and Charisma scores of 1 and a Wisdom score of 3. They have zero grasp of tactics and only perform whatever simple actions for which they were programmed.

Pair With Artillerists or Skirmishers. Animated armor packs a mean punch, especially at low levels, quickly drawing the attention of most of the party. Keep the enemies busy while your allies attack from range.

Tactics: Slam Slam Slam. So long as the party doesn't suspect the armor is animate, it should surprise them in the first round of combat thanks to False Appearance. It then moves and attacks whatever target is closest to it.

ANIMATED OBJECT, FLYING SWORD

This longsword flies around the room as if possessed by some unseen vengeful spirit.

Flying swords are relatively simple constructs that lie dormant until a target comes close enough for it to attack.

Fighting Style: Brute. While the flying sword possesses features that would otherwise qualify it as a lurker or skirmisher, its low Intelligence, Wisdom, and Charisma scores dictate that it should fight as a brute.

Set-up: Disguised. Flying swords function best in armories, trophy rooms, or treasure chambers where their False Appearance will allow them to hide in the open. They can fly, so consider putting lots of difficult terrain in the area to slow down attackers. Also, they have blindsight out to 60 feet, so they function unhindered in areas of magical darkness.

Weaknesses: Stupid. Flying swords have Intelligence and Charisma scores of 1 and a Wisdom score of 5. They have zero grasp of tactics and only perform whatever simple actions for which they were programmed.

Pair With Artillerists and Skirmishers. Keep enemies distracted with ranged allies fire from afar, and skirmishers perform hit-and-run attacks.

Tactics: Slash, Slash, Slash. Too simple for advanced tactics, you remain hidden until a target comes within 50 feet of you. So long as the target doesn't suspect that you're an animated object, you should surprise them. Continue to attack whatever target is closest until you are destroyed, or they are.

ANIMATED OBJECT, RUG OF SMOTHERING

 **CR 2**

What looked like an ordinary rug only moments ago springs to life and attacks.

Rugs of smothering are animated objects that literally pull the characters' feet from out under them. Because they are so limited in their scope, they function more like traps than creatures.

Fighting Style: Brute. The rug of smothering is too simple to do anything beyond smothering a target, doing so until it or its target is destroyed.

Set-up: Disguised. The rug of smothering blends effortlessly into any interior environment and draws much less attention to itself than other animated objects. It has blindsight out to 60 feet, so it functions best in areas of magical darkness.

Weaknesses: Stupid. Rugs of smothering have Intelligence and Charisma scores of 1 and a Wisdom score of 3. They have zero grasp of tactics and only perform whatever simple actions for which they were programmed.

Pair With Artillerists or Skirmishers. While you distract the party, smothering one of them to death, artillerists pop off shots from afar while skirmishers employ hit-and-run tactics.

Tactics: Wait and Smother. Stay hidden until a target steps on you, then surprise it with a Smother attack. Continue to smother the target until it is dead or you are destroyed. Don't forget that attacks made against you also harm the target. Furthermore, the target doesn't gain any cover from you while you're smothering it.

ANKHEG

 CR 2

This burrowing, bug-like monster scuttles about on six legs, drooling noxious green ichor from its clacking mandibles.

Ankhegs resemble massive praying mantises covered in hard, chitinous plates. They wait below the surface of the earth before they strike.

Fighting Style: Lurker. Ankhegs stay hidden in the ground until a target triggers their tremorsense. From there, they leap out and attack, hoping to grapple a creature with its bite so it can drag it back underground.

Set-up: Dark, Earthy Areas. Ankhegs tunnel belowground but can't penetrate rock. Keep them hidden in loose soil 10 feet below the surface. They have darkvision out to 60 feet, so likely they only attack at night.

Weaknesses: Animalistic. Ankhegs aren't intelligent creatures but have enough Wisdom to preserve themselves. If an ankheg finds itself faced with prey that it can't easily bite and drag off in one or two rounds, it likely escapes.

Pair With Artillerists. Use artillerists to attack targets that you grapple with your bite. Duergars or drow might train the ankhegs to serve as lurkers, attacking enemies from behind while they attack from a distance.

Tactics: Grab and Dash. Wait 10 feet below the surface in one of your tunnels. When a target comes within 15 feet of you, emerge. You should catch the target by surprise, allowing you to bite it with advantage. Once you grapple with the target, drag it back into your tunnel. If you fail to grab the target or too many other enemies follow you, use your Acid Spray to cover your escape.

ARCHMAGE

 **CR 12**

Archmages are old and powerful spellcasters, representing 18th-level wizards (or even sorcerers). Extremely intelligent, they rarely enter combat; when they do, they're always prepared.

Fighting Style: Elite. The archmage's spell list and features allow it to take on various roles, playing whatever role is missing from its group. However, it does not have enough defensive features or action economy to fight a party solo.

Set-up: Wide Open Areas. An archmage should always fight on its own turf, using the battlefield to its advantage. Start combat with plenty of distance between yourself and the enemy, at least 60 feet. There should be plenty of places for you to take cover between spells.

Weaknesses: Glass Cannon. Archmages have pitifully low defensive capabilities, especially against melee and nonmagical ranged attacks. Make sure to keep plenty of distance between the attackers and yourself, and always take cover.

Pair With Brutes and Tanks. Assuming that you fill the artillerist or controller role in the group (the archmage's strengths), use tough defenders and frontline damage dealers to keep the enemy occupied while you attack. Try to use companions that are immune to cold damage, so they won't get hurt while you cast *cone of cold*.

Tactics: Divide and Conquer. These tactics assume that you will be the artillerist in the group. Before combat begins, protect yourself with *mage armor, mind blank, mirror image*, and *stoneskin*. None of these spells require concentration. So long as you have these spells up, you won't need to use *time stop*—save that 9th-level slot for an upcast *cone of cold*. Potentially start combat invisible, so your enemies can't target you. Keep at least 60 to 120 feet between yourself and your opponents.

On your first turn, cast *wall of force* in its dome shape to trap ranged attackers or enemies with high movement speeds. You have resistance to damage from spells, Magic Resistance, *mind blank*, and high Intelligence and Wisdom saving throws, so you have nothing to worry about when it comes to spellcasters. However, you might cordon off spellcasters to protect your allies.

After casting *wall of force*, hit as many targets as possible with upcast *cones of cold*; use your 6th or 9th-level spell slots for it. Save the 7th-level slot in case you need to escape with *teleport* and your 4th-level slots in case you need to use *wall of force* again.

Once you use all your high-end slots for *cone of cold*, switch to *lightning bolt* or *fire bolt*. Remember: your *fire bolt* deals 22 (4d10) damage on a hit.

If things start to go badly for you, find a way to escape, casting *invisibility* if necessary.

ASSASSIN

CR 8

Assassins are essentially high-level rogues designed to swiftly kill targets, escaping before anyone notices they are there.

Fighting Style: Lurker. Assassins come with exceptional Stealth skill and a variety of features that benefit from their advantage on their attack. Once the assassin makes its opening attack, it likely flees, even if the initial attack isn't successful.

Set-up: Hidden With Escape Routes. Hide somewhere within 80 feet of the target. If you don't have darkvision, ensure the target is illuminated. Make sure there are plenty of ways to escape after you take your shot.

Weaknesses: Getting Caught. Under no circumstances should you ever get caught. Not only is it bad for business (your employers will be pretty mad if they hear you got captured), but you aren't built for ordinary combat. Always plan an escape.

Pair With Controllers. While most assassins probably work alone, if you decide to team up with some other creatures, collaborate with those who can give you advantage on the attack—restraining, blinding, or even using the Help action.

Tactics: Shoot and Run. From your hiding spot, fire your light crossbow at your target. So long as you surprise the target, you can use your Assassinate and Sneak Attack features against it. This combination allows you to roll a grand total of 2d8 + 22d6 + 3 damage dice (average of 89 damage), enough to kill most creatures. After you score the shot, flee the area. If you're determined to kill more targets, find another hiding spot and start the process over again.

AWAKENED SHRUB

 **CR 0**

This ambulatory shrub moves like an intelligent creature.

Awakened shrubs are ordinary shrubs given sentience and mobility thanks to the *awaken* spell or other magic.

Fighting Style: Minion. Awakened shrubs are slow, have pitiful AC, and barely deal any damage with their attack. Their purpose is to slow down targets for their allies.

Set-up: Natural Outdoors Environment. Awakened shrubs have the False Appearance trait, which allows them to blend in wooded areas. Alternatively, you could have one stand in a pot with soil indoors.

Weaknesses: Weak. Awakened shrubs have low statistics across the board (no pun intended), hence their measly challenge rating of 0.

Pair With Artillerists or Skirmishers. Place plenty of awakened shrubs around the board to slow down attackers while artillerists fire from afar and skirmishers perform hit-and-run attacks.

Tactics: Surprise and Distract. Start combat hidden with your False Appearance trait. Make sure to space them out 10 feet apart to threaten attacks of opportunity. Dodge until targets come in range to minimize your losses.

AWAKENED TREE

CR 2

This tall tree moves and behaves like an intelligent creature.

Awakened trees are ordinary trees given sentience and mobility by the *awaken* spell or other magical effects.

Fighting Style: Brute. Awakened trees are big and slow but pack a mean punch. They will keep enemies occupied while their allies attack from a distance.

Set-up: Natural Outdoors Environment. The awakened tree functions best in any environment where one might encounter a tree, allowing it to benefit from its False Appearance trait.

Weaknesses: Fire. Awakened trees have some strong resistances and decent defensive capabilities. Unfortunately, they are also vulnerable to fire damage. A spellcaster will make quick work of you.

Pair With Artillerists and Skirmishers. The threat of your powerful attacks will distract your foes while artillerists fire from afar and skirmishers employ hit-and-run tactics.

Tactics: Surprise and Slam. Use False Appearance to remain undetected until a target comes within 10 feet; this should allow you to surprise your foe. Continue to slam it while your allies assist. Beware of fire!

AZER

Heat ripples the air near this squat, brass-skinned humanoid. Its head and shoulders blaze with a mane of fire.

Azers are the "dwarves" of the Elemental Plane of Fire. As lawful neutral creatures, they uphold order without concern for good or evil.

Fighting Style: Tank. Azers have exceptional AC for their challenge rating and deal passive damage when hit. Use defensive maneuvers to draw your opponents and protect your allies.

Set-up: Fiery and/or Poisonous Environments. Azers come with fire and poison immunities, allowing them to operate within toxic environments. They only need to defend themselves while they let the hazards surrounding them do all the work.

Weaknesses: Charisma Saving Throws. As creatures that aren't native to the material plane, azers are vulnerable to the *banishment* spell. Their relatively poor Charisma scores compound this flaw.

Pair With Artillerists or Skirmishers. Your job is to stand still and defend while artillerists fire from cover and skirmishers perform hit-and-run maneuvers.

Tactics: Dodge and Wait. So long as you have other ways to damage the enemies—companions or environmental hazards—start combat within 30 feet of your foes. Take the Dodge action and draw them to you. Try to threaten as much space as possible to score attacks of opportunity whenever possible. Using your movement, draw targets towards hazards that hurt them but not you.

BANDIT

Bandits are low-level fighters or rogues that often serve as fodder for more vital NPCs.

Fighting Style: Artillerist. The one thing that sets bandits apart from other low-CR humanoids is their light crossbow, which allows them to keep plenty of distance between themselves and their targets.

Set-up: Wide Open Spaces with Cover. Traditionally, bandits ambush their targets, surprising them in dark alleys or shady forests. Make sure there are clear lines of sight for your ranged attacks with plenty of cover for you to hide.

Weaknesses: Squishy. The only thing that separates bandits from minions is their light crossbow. Otherwise, they are relatively weak targets that drop after one or two hits. Make sure to keep plenty of distance between yourself and your enemies.

Pair With Brutes or Tanks. Use a brute or tank to distract your enemies while you fire at them from 60 to 80 feet away. Bandit captains easily fill either role.

Tactics: Keep Your Distance. Start combat 60 to 80 feet away from the targets behind at least half-cover. On your turn, fire at the most dangerous-looking targets, particularly other ranged attackers or controllers. Return to cover when possible, and consider dropping prone to impose disadvantage on attacks made against you.

BANDIT CAPTAIN

 **CR 2**

Bandit captains lead gangs of bandits. They come with various talents and features that make them formidable low-level villains.

Fighting Style: Elite. While the bandit captain doesn't have quite enough action economy to fight a group solo, their versatility lends itself well to fighting as elites. They fill whatever role is needed of them, particularly those that require it to get close and personal.

Set-up: Close and Personal. Set yourself within 30 feet of the enemy so you can use your powers of negotiation to distract the party while your allies get into position. When combat begins, take defensive action to draw attacks.

Weaknesses: Grappling. If you fight as a tank, grappling is your worst enemy since it will stop you from being able to Dodge and move. Fortunately, you have an Athletics modifier of +4. If you get grappled, switch to Brute tactics to harm those foolish enough to challenge you.

Pair With Artillerists. Work alongside ranged attackers that can pick off your foes from afar while you draw their attacks. Bandits are the most obvious pairing.

Tactics: Dodge and Parry. You come with a 15 AC, which is already pretty good, and have a decent number of hit points. Take the Dodge action to reduce the chance of your enemies hitting you, and save your Parry reaction to use against targets that hit hard, such as a barbarian wielding a great axe. If you get grappled, or the party doesn't fall for your tactics, switch to Brute tactics and go after the weakest-looking member of the party in range.

BANSHEE

 **CR 4**

This beautiful, ghostly elven woman glides through the air, her lengthy hair flowing around a face knotted into a mask of rage.

Banshees are the spirits of vain elves cursed to eternal sorrow. They are extraordinarily dangerous against low-level parties and even valuable against high-level parties thanks to their devastating wail.

Fighting Style: Skirmisher. As incorporeal undead, banshees can fly and move through solid objects. Plus, they come with a wide array of damage resistances, which means they have little to fear from nonmagical attacks.

Set-up: Lots of Cover. Incorporeal creatures perform best in places with lots of full cover into which they can retreat. Buildings with multiple walls and rooms, forests with large trees, and other cramped areas are your best bet.

Weaknesses: Magic. Banshees come equipped with many defensive features, but magical weapons, and spells that cause radiant or force damage, will quickly end your existence. Target these creatures first, ignoring those that aren't capable of dealing severe damage to you.

Pair With Undead Brutes or Tanks. Your wail can harm any creature that hears it, including your allies. However, constructs and undead are immune. Use strong undead creatures to draw attacks from your foes while you move and strike.

Tactics: Wail, Fear, Strike. Start combat 40 feet away from the party, ideally behind full cover. On your first turn, move within 30 feet of as many targets as possible, then use your wail. Quickly duck back behind full cover. On your next turn, use your visage to frighten any targets that weren't dropped by your wail attack. After using these two features, switch to hit-and-run tactics, targeting any creature that could harm you. Failing that, target any creatures that were reduced to 0 hit points.

BASILISK

CR 3

This squat, reptilian monster has eight legs, bony spurs jutting from its back, and eyes that glow with pale green fire.

Basilisks are slow, lumbering creatures whose Petrifying Gaze will make quick work of those who don't know better than to close their eyes. And if that doesn't work, they have a nasty poisonous bite, too.

Fighting Style: Brute. The basilisk's gaze is too dangerous to keep active on the field, forcing your enemies to engage you before they attack other creatures.

Set-up: Close and Personal. Your gaze only works against targets that are within 30 feet of you. Make sure you start combat close but obscured so the party will have trouble knowing what they're up against until it's too late.

Weaknesses: Slow. Basilisks are painfully slow creatures, both in terms of speed and Dexterity. Your gaze will slow down a lot of targets, but ranged attackers will make quick work of you.

Pair With Artillerists. Keep your enemies occupied while ranged attackers fire at the enemies from a safe distance (i.e., they can't see your eyes). If you need to work alongside creatures that fight in close range, ensure they have immunity to petrification.

Tactics: Bite Whatever Comes Near. You have an Intelligence score of 2, so you don't have a grasp for tactics. Plus, your Wisdom score is probably too low to recognize the danger until it's too late. Move towards whatever is within range and bite it until it stops moving.

BEHIR

CR 11

This slithering, multilegged blue reptile has a fearsome head crowned with two large, curling horns.

Behirs are monstrosities that favor rocky environments where they can climb and hide, patiently waiting for prey to come close enough to grab.

Fighting Style: Lurker. You have a +7 to Stealth, a climbing speed of 40 feet, and an attack that lets you auto-grapple your foes. As such, you should grab and dash whatever target comes near.

Set-up: Difficult Terrain. Hide in a place with lots of difficult terrain and high-up spots, making it difficult for enemies to follow you after you grab one of their allies. Canyons, caves, cliffs, and other rocky terrain works exceptionally well.

Weaknesses: Mental Saving Throws. While you have better-than-average Strength, Dexterity, and Constitution, your low Intelligence, Wisdom, and Charisma scores leave you wide open against enchantments that could stop you in your tracks. Arguably, you aren't intelligent enough to recognize a spellcaster until it actually targets you with a spell.

Pair With Controller or Minions. As a lurker, you need to grab your target as quickly as you can and then escape. Although you don't understand tactics, you probably know that particular creatures in your environment help distract your prey's allies while you escape.

Tactics: Grab and Dash. Start combat hidden up high. You know that the weakest and easiest-to-catch members of groups usually walk in the center of the rear, so let the targets wearing metal go first. Once your target comes within 10 feet of you, reveal yourself, constrict it, and bite it. Then, climb with the target in your clutches to a safe area. On the next round, try to swallow the target to subdue it. If the target's allies are pursuing you, use your lightning breath to slow them down.

BERSERKER

 CR 2

Berserkers are powerful outlanders that function similarly to low-level barbarians.

Fighting Style: Brute. You deal a lot of damage with your reckless, quickly drawing the attacks of your enemies while your allies fight from a distance.

Set-up: Up Close and Personal. You want to make sure that you have a way to reach your enemy as quickly as possible so you can start swinging your greataxe.

Weaknesses: Poor Mental Saving Throws. With low Intelligence, Wisdom, and Charisma saving throws, you are vulnerable to enchantments. You probably aren't smart enough to recognize a spellcaster immediately but know you should target them as soon as they start casting.

Pair With Artillerists and Skirmishers. Keep your targets occupied with your devastating attacks while your allies make attacks from the safety of cover, and skirmishers employ hit-and-run tactics.

Tactics: Charge and Swing. There isn't much nuance to your tactics; get within range of your enemy as fast as possible, go reckless, and start swinging.

BLINK DOG

 CR 1/4

This sleek canine has a coarse, tawny coat, pointed ears, and pale eyes. A faint blue nimbus seems to dance upon its fur.

Blinks dogs are intelligent fey creatures who take their name from their ability to teleport in and out of existence.

Fighting Style: Skirmisher. Your blink power lets you move, bite, and teleport to a safe distance every other turn.

Set-up: Lots of Cover. As a skirmisher, you perform best when you have plenty of places to hide and take cover while waiting for your teleport to recharge.

Weaknesses: Mental Saving Throws. Although you are relatively intelligent compared to beasts and monstrosities, you still don't have good saving throws against enchantment effects or effects that hold you in place.

Pair With Brutes and Tanks. Use brutes and tanks to distract your foes while you make hit-and-run attacks and hide between teleport charges.

Tactics: Hit-and-Run and Hide. Start combat hidden with your +5 to Stealth. When a target comes within 20 feet of you, emerge, engage, and bite. Then, teleport 20 to 30 feet away near full cover. Use the rest of your movement to hide behind the cover. If your teleport recharges on your next turn, repeat these tactics. If there isn't a target close enough to you to use these tactics or if your teleport doesn't recharge, take the Hide action.

BUGBEAR

 CR 1

This ugly creature resembles a wild thing of flared black and brown fur whose pelt juts out from its body at freakish angles. Its ears are large and floppy, draping shoulder-length.

Bugbears are the largest of the primary goblinoid races, a lumbering brute that stands at least a head taller than most humans. Despite their large frame, they are extraordinarily stealthy lurkers.

Fighting Style: Lurker. Despite your large frame, you perform best as a lurker, using your Stealth and Survival to track and ambush your targets.

Set-up: Hidden with Escape Routes. Bugbears, like goblins, have expertise in Stealth. Start combat hidden with plenty of ways for you to escape. Fight in the dark whenever possible to give disadvantage to Perception checks made to detect you.

Weaknesses: Mental Saving Throws. You have poor Intelligence, Wisdom, and Charisma saving throws, which makes you vulnerable to enchantment spells. Although you aren't very intelligent, you're arguably wise enough to recognize a spellcaster by their robes or spellbook. Take them out as soon as possible.

Pair With Controllers or Minions. You function best when you make a single attack and then flee the scene. Use controllers or minions to slow down targets while you reposition.

Tactics: Ambush. Start combat hidden. When a target comes within 5 feet of you, emerge and attack it with your morningstar. So long as you surprise the target, you should deal bonus damage from your Surprise Attack. Immediately flee the scene while your enemies scramble to understand what happened. So long as your enemies don't follow you, find another place to hide and repeat these tactics. Use your Survival skill to track targets that try to avoid you.

Bugbear Chiefs. Bugbear chiefs use the same tactics as common bugbears but come with additional features that save them from being enchanted. Plus, they have two attacks, allowing them to damage their surprised prey even more.

BULETTE

 **CR 5**

This armor-plated creature's toothy maw gapes wide as a fin-like dorsal plate rises between its shoulders

Sometimes called a "land shark," bulettes are massive burrowing creatures with legendary ferocity.

Fighting Style: Brute. Bulettes deal excessive damage with their Deadly Leap and Bite. Unlike some burrowing creatures, you're tough enough to withstand hits while you try to devour your prey.

Set-up: Earthy Areas. As a burrowing creature, you have a burrow speed of 40 feet and tremorsense up to 60 feet. You want to fight in areas with loose soil where you can remain hidden until something delicious-looking approaches.

Weaknesses: Saving Throws. You have poor Dexterity, Intelligence, Wisdom, and Charisma saving throw modifiers, which makes you vulnerable against most magical attacks. You also aren't smart enough to identify a spellcaster. However, you probably have enough Wisdom to escape when targeted by damaging spells.

Pair With Artillerists. While you aren't smart enough to manage a group of targets, other creatures might train you to serve as their brutish pet. Artillerists should give you a wide berth since you're just as likely to eat them as your other targets.

Tactics: Surprise and Crush. Start combat 10 feet underground, using your tremorsense to detect when prey comes near. Once targets come within 40 feet of you, emerge from the ground and leap onto them. If you scored a high initiative, you should get to attack at least one or two prone foes on your next turn, biting them with your mighty jaws. Continue to attack targets until you successfully kill at least one; that one is dinner.

CAMBION

This red-skinned, demonic humanoid has a forked tongue, and a pair of black horns sprout from its brow.

Cambions are the offspring of humanoids and fiends, inheriting qualities from both parents. Strong and versatile, they make great low-tier villains.

Fighting Style: Elite. You come packed with a variety of powerful features both in the offensive and defensive categories, as well as a handful of controller powers. You can fill any role.

Set-up: Open Spaces. How you set up depends on whether or not you're working alone. Either way, it doesn't hurt to give yourself plenty of room to fly around.

Weaknesses: Wisdom Saving Throws. Despite having excellent saving throws everywhere else, you have a relatively lousy Wisdom saving throw and no immunities to conditions. Get rid of spellcasters as fast as possible.

Pair With Minions. As an elite, you can fill any necessary role, so you work well with all combatants. However, minions will help distract targets on the ground while you pick them off from above.

Tactics: Fly and Fire Ray. As a flying creature, you must stay in the sky as often as possible, putting you out of reach of pesky paladins. Start combat using your charm action to gain an ally among your enemies. Then use your ranged attack to target spellcasters.

CENTAUR

CR 2

This creature has the sun-bronzed upper body of a seasoned warrior and the lower body of a sleek warhorse.

Centaurs are highly-territorial nomads with excellent offensive capabilities but relatively poor defenses.

Fighting Style: Artillerist. Although playing centaurs in close-quarters combat is fun, you would be wise to keep your distance and target foes with your longbow. The longbow ensures that foes can't hit you with melee attacks and even helps you avoid most ranged attacks.

Set-up: Wide Open Spaces. You want to ensure that you have plenty of distance between you and your foes and can still see them. Since you lack darkvision, you should only fight during the day unless your foes are well-illuminated by a campfire or similar light source.

Weaknesses: Defensive Capabilities. You have relatively poor AC and hit points for a CR 2 creature, which means it doesn't take much for evenly-matched foes to knock you down to 0 hit points. Keep your distance.

Pair With Brutes or Tanks. Team up with monsters that can distract your foes while you keep plenty of distance.

Tactics: Keep Your Distance. Start combat 100 to 150 feet away from targets, ideally in some cover. Use your longbow to target foes that can hit you with ranged attacks, particularly spellcasters. If you have to fight at close range, use hit-and-run tactics. Your pike's 10-foot reach allows you to hit a target without provoking an attack of opportunity.

CHIMERA

CR 6

This winged monster has the body of a lion, though two more heads flank its central feline one—a dragon and a horned goat.

Despite possessing bestial Intelligence, chimeras are instinctually chaotic evil creatures, bred to cause harm to those who enter their lairs or areas their masters tasked them to protect.

Fighting Style: Skirmisher. With only an Intelligence score of 3, you rely purely on instinct to fight your enemies. Fortunately, you are a creature born with wings; therefore, it stands to reason that you would know how to fight as a skirmisher, employing hit-and-run tactics.

Set-up: Wide Open Places. You are a flying creature; therefore, you should fight in areas with lots of room to maneuver. Additionally, you are a nocturnal creature. Fight in the dark whenever possible.

Weaknesses: Low Intelligence. Despite being a deadly predator, you have relatively low Intelligence compared to other CR 6 creatures. You aren't smart enough to identify spellcasters until it's too late. However, you are wise enough to retreat when things start to go badly for you.

Pair With Tanks. Team up with creatures willing to stand and take hits while you use your flight and hit-and-run tactics to harm your enemies.

Tactics: Hit-and-Run. Start combat 30 feet away from your targets in the air. On your turn, move towards the nearest group of creatures, getting within 5 feet of just one of them. Use fire breath to hit as many targets as possible, then use your claws and bite against the nearest target. Retreat to the sky. ets as possible, then use your claws and bite against the nearest target. Retreat to the sky. Don't worry about getting hit with an attack of opportunity—one attack of opportunity is better than four regular attacks.

CHUUL

 CR 4

This lobster-like creature has a thick armored shell. A pair of tiny eyes gleams above a mouth full of writhing tentacles.

Chuuls are the ancient servants of aboleths designed to track, attack, and capture spellcasters.

Fighting Style: Brute. Although you should grab-and-dash like a lurker, you are better equipped to fight as brutes.

Set-up: Near Water. You have a swim speed of 30 feet, which will help you escape without your prey's allies pursuing you. Plus, the water will help you hide at the start of combat.

Weaknesses: Poor Mental Saving Throws. While you are physically hardy, your mental saving throws leave something to be desired. Enchantment magic will quickly end your quest to grab a spellcaster. Fortunately, aboleths created you to sense and subdue spellcasters, so you will still target them first.

Pair With Minions. When you acquire your target, you need companions to distract your quarry's allies until you can return the water. Team up with low-cost minions such as zombies or grimlocks to distract your foes while you escape.

Tactics: Grab-and-Dash. Start in water, ideally in the dark. Wait until a target spellcaster is within 10 feet of you to spring your attack; emerge from the water and use your multiattack against the target. Try to stay in the water if possible. If you grab the target, you can use your tentacles to paralyze them. Paralyzed or not, drag them to the water, where your swimming speed will give you the advantage.

CLOAKER

 **CR 8**

This ray-like creature opens a toothy maw and leers with glaring red eyes. Behind it whips a menacing tail of segmented bone.

Cloakers are horrific aberrations that lurk and hunt in subterranean realms. They are too smart to challenge a strong group and will only attack if the opportunity is right.

Fighting Style: Lurker. You have the False Appearance trait and a decent Stealth modifier. You hide until a creature comes near, then spring your attack. Once you grab a target, you retreat with it, using your tail, moan, and phantasms to ward off the prey's allies.

Set-up: Dark Places with High Ceilings. You need a place to hide where a random cloak lying on the ground won't seem out of place. Once you grab a target, you must escape upward with it, moving to an area the others can't reach.

Weaknesses: Bright Light. You dread bright light, which gives you disadvantage on your attack rolls and Wisdom (Perception) checks. Don't attack targets carrying torches or lanterns. Instead, target weak-looking prey that relies on darkvision.

Pair With Minions. Use minions to keep your prey distracted before you attack and to keep them busy after you escape with your prey.

Tactics: Grab and Dash. Start combat hidden using your False Appearance trait. Wait until a weak-looking target comes near you, then reveal yourself and attack it with your bite. So long as your bite hits, you attach to the target., and if you have advantage, you blind the target and suffocate it. If the target is Small or smaller, you can fly away with it. Otherwise, you must use your tail, moan, and phantasms to defend yourself while biting the target.

COCKATRICE

 CR 1/2

This hideous avian creature has the body of an emaciated rooster, the wings of a bat, and a long, scaly tail.

Cockatrices are chicken-like creatures whose bite can temporarily turn targets to stone. Although they subsist on small, easy-to-swallow creatures, they will fight anything that enters their territory.

Fighting Style: Skirmisher. You have a flight speed of 40 feet and decent hit points for a CR ½ creature. Use instinctual hit-and-run tactics to fight your foes.

Set-up: Dark, Open Spaces. As a flying creature, you need room to move. Plus, you have darkvision, which means you perform better at night or underground.

Weaknesses: Low Intelligence. You have an Intelligence score of 2, which means you have no concept of tactics. You attack whatever comes close to you.

Pair With Controllers. Although you aren't intelligent enough to create your own group (other than with other cockatrices, of course), others might use your petrifying bite to distract your foes. Controllers capable of blinding or restraining targets can lend you advantage on attacks, increasing your chance of petrifying your targets.

Tactics: Hit-and-Run. Start combat 20 feet away from your targets. On your turn, fly towards the nearest enemy and bite it. Then retreat 20 feet away back into the air. Continue this tactic, constantly moving in, attacking, then moving away. Don't worry about attacks of opportunity—one hit from your target is better than multiple hits from the target and its allies.

COMMONER

 CR 0

Commoners represent the basic NPC in a fantasy world, covering the vast majority of humanoids that the characters will encounter.

Fighting Style: Minion. You aren't trained to fight. In fact, you probably don't want to fight at all. But sometimes, you have to. When you do, you do your best to hurt your foes, looking for attacks of opportunity rather than outright assault. You're also not above fleeing.

Set-up: Lots of Allies. You are relatively weak compared to most adventurers, so you won't get into a fight unless you have numbers in your favor or there's a trained fighter on your side. Otherwise, you will likely flee or surrender.

Weaknesses: Leaving the House. You have AC 10, 4 hit points, and no special defenses or attacks. Your only weapon is your club (or frying pan, log, barstool, or whatever other items you could grab). It doesn't take much to take you out of the fight.

Pair With Anyone. As a minion, your job is to distract the targets and go for attacks of opportunity whenever possible. All other fighting styles benefit from your minion fighting style.

Tactics: Spread Out and Defend. Start combat with yourself and the other minions 10 feet apart, threatening attacks of opportunity whenever possible. Take the Dodge action on each of your turns, making it harder for the enemies to hit you. If you get hit and manage to survive, you should probably run away or surrender if you get hit and survive.

COUATL

 CR 4

This great serpent has multicolored wings and eyes that glimmer with intense awareness.

Couatls are servants of lawful and good deities, though some operate independently of any greater being. Overall, couatls function best as roleplaying encounters. Still, you never know when you might have to toss one in a fight.

Fighting Style: Support. You come with various helpful spells and attacks that subdue targets rather than kill them.

Set-up: Open Areas. You have a flying speed of 90 feet, so you'll want a lot of room to maneuver. However, you still want to be close to your allies while not drawing attacks yourself, so look for spots with cover. Finally, you have truesight, so you suffer no penalties while fighting in magical darkness.

Weaknesses: Magic Weapons. Spells are ineffective against you, thanks to your high saving throws and immunity to psychic damage. However, magical weapons surpass your bludgeoning, piercing, and slashing immunities. Keep away from anyone carrying one of these weapons.

Pair With Brutes, Minions, or Tanks. Team up with melee attackers who will keep the party busy while you run support from a distance. You can also serve as a battlefield general, using telepathy to communicate with the other group members.

Tactics: Lead the Battle. Unless you're fighting alone, you should serve as the battlefield commander. Start combat 60 feet in the air away from everyone, high enough that you can see everything that's happening. Before combat, use *sanctuary* to defend yourself or your strongest tank. Then use *bless* to boost your three biggest melee attackers. From there, use hit-and-run tactics against deadly enemies with poor Constitution saving throws, such as artillerists and spellcasters.

You are a lawful good creature, so unless the enemy is unrepentantly evil, you want them to surrender. Failing that, you will try to knock them unconscious.

CRAWLING HAND

 CR 0

With a jolt, this severed hand springs to life, its fingers propelling it forth at great speed like a deformed spider.

Crawling hands are efficient killing tools employed by necromancers and other vile masters of the dark arts to assassinate specific targets.

Fighting Style: Minion. You aren't very strong, and your attack deals very little damage. Unless you plan on attacking targets in their sleep, you'll need backup.

Set-up: Dark Places. You are a Tiny creature, so you can hide in small spots such as holes in the wall, inside a jar of flour, or even under bed covers. If fighting alongside other creatures, you might hide in a purse or large pocket.

Weaknesses: Squishy. With only 2 hit points and an AC of 12, it only takes one decent roll to kill you.

Pair With Controllers. You only have a +3 to hit, so any creature that can offer you help in the form of blinding, restraining, knocking targets prone, or supplying the Help action will help you score more hits.

Tactics: Wait for Help. Start combat hidden in full cover. Then, when a target is blinded, falls prone, or becomes restrained, emerge and attack, hoping for a critical hit.

CULT FANATIC

 CR 2

Cult fanatics serve as cult leaders and function as low-level evil clerics or warlocks dedicated to dark deities.

Fighting Style: Controller. Your spell list includes *command* and *hold person*. Both spells help your allies make attacks with advantage against your foes.

Set-up: Cover and Escape Routes. During combat, you don't want to be caught out in the open, especially while you concentrate on *hold person*. Make sure to fight in a place with a lot of cover for you to duck behind between castings.

Weaknesses: Constitution Saving Throws. Your best spell, *hold person*, requires you to maintain your concentration. So whenever you get hit with an attack, there is a chance that your concentration will break, and unfortunately, you have a pretty low Constitution modifier. Stay away from enemies who can hit you, and keep behind cover.

Pair With Minions. Your best spells are designed to help your allies. Make sure to team up with plenty of low-CR creatures—cultists make the most obvious choice.

Tactics: Control, Then Attack. Start combat 60 feet away from the enemy with your minions between you and them. On your turn, cast *hold person* on obvious melee attackers. Make sure to duck back behind cover after you cast it. If the casting fails, continue casting *hold person* until you stop someone, then direct your minions to attack the restrained targets. If you successfully capture someone with *hold person* or you run out of 3rd-level spell slots, switch to offensive tactics. You can cast *sacred flame* the same round that you cast *spiritual weapon*. When targets get too close to you, move away and use *command* to slow them down.

CULTIST

CR 1/8

Cultists are low-level fighters devoted to a dark purpose. Although they are minions, their fanaticism drives them to risk their lives fighting enemies of the cult.

Fighting Style: Minion. You are a darkly devoted killing machine; you are here to drown foes of the cult in your blood!

Set-up: Up Close and Personal. You come equipped with a scimitar and no ranged weapons; therefore, you must start combat as close to the enemy as possible. Try to spread 10 feet apart from the other cultists with you so you can threaten more attacks of opportunity and reduce losses caused by an area of effect spell.

Weaknesses: Poor Defenses. With only 9 hit points and AC 12, it only takes a few hits to take you down. Make sure to spread out from the rest of the cultists so you don't get hit with an area of effect spells.

Pair With Controllers. Your attack modifier is a relatively low +3, so you need as much help as possible. Work alongside controllers like cult fanatics who can restrain or trip your foes, giving you advantage on attacks.

Tactics: Kill the Heretics! Start combat spaced 10 feet apart from the other cultists in your group. Wait for the controllers to use their effects to give you advantage on attacks. Potentially ready your attack for such occurrences. You're devoted to your cause, so there's no chance you will flee unless magically forced to do so.

CYCLOPS

 **CR 6**

A single huge eye stares from the forehead of this nine-foot-tall giant. Below this sole orb, an even larger mouth gapes like a cave

Cyclopes are dull-witted, superstitious creatures that prefer to be left alone. However, they're not above eating pesky adventurers who try to plunder their wealth.

Fighting Style: Brute. Neither intelligent nor wise, you prefer to use your brute strength to crush your foes to a pulp.

Set-up: Close and Personal. You're relatively slow for a giant, so you want to ensure that you start combat as close to your targets as possible. Although you can throw rocks, you have disadvantage on attack rolls made against targets more than 30 feet away.

Weaknesses: Poor Mental Saving Throws. With an abysmally low Wisdom score of 6, you easily succumb to enchantment spells. Furthermore, you aren't intelligent enough to recognize spellcasters until it's too late.

Pair With Artillerists and Skirmishers. Although you prefer to fight alone, sometimes a little help is nice. Work alongside targets that fight from a distance or use hit-and-run tactics while you distract the foes with your greatclub.

Tactics: Dash and Bash. Start combat within 35 feet of your enemies. On your turn, move to the nearest target and hit it with our greatclub. If you can't reach a target, throw rocks until you can reach them.

DARKMANTLE

 **CR 1/2**

As this creature falls from the cavern roof, it opens like a hideous octopus, its thin, hook-lined tentacles connected by a fleshy web.

Darkmantles are bizarre predators that disguise themselves as natural rock formations on cavern ceilings. When a target comes near, they create a sphere of darkness and descend.

Fighting Style: Lurker. You have the False Appearance trait and can create magical darkness through which you can see, thanks to your blindsight. As such, you perform best as a lurker.

Set-up: Caverns. Since your False Appearance disguises you as a natural rock formation, you prefer to hide in caverns among other rock formations.

Weaknesses: Silence. Your blindsight relies on your ability to hear; if you lose that, you lose the ability to track your targets in the darkness.

Pair With Other Lurkers. Your ability to create darkness works well alongside other creatures with blindsight—team up with other lurkers who benefit from your features.

Tactics: Hide, Darkness, Crush. Start combat disguised as a stalactite on a ceiling no higher than 15 feet. When your targets move under you, use your darkness aura to blind them. Then, on your next turn, attack. If your targets disrupt your concentration, fly away; lurkers only want easy meals.

DEATH DOG

CR 1

This black-furred, two-headed dog is as large as a pony and has midnight-black eyes. Tiny worms crawl on its mangy hide.

Death dogs are two-headed dogs native to subterranean realms. Despite their animalistic intelligence, they hate humanoids and attack explorers and humanoids on sight.

Fighting Style: Lurker. Your bite delivers a terrible disease that weakens targets and causes them to waste away until they are cured. Thanks to your multiattack, you can attack with this bite twice on your turn. However, you aren't tough enough to take on an entire group yourself. Instead, inflict your disease, then track the prey as it wastes away over the next few days.

Set-up: Up Close and Personal. Likely, you'll spot potential prey while wandering around the subterranean realms. However, you won't launch your attack until you're at least within 40 feet of your targets, using your Stealth to get close.

Weaknesses: Low Armor Class. Although you have decent hit points, your AC 12 makes it relatively easy for targets to hit you.

Pair With Minions. Although you aren't terribly intelligent, you at least have enough sense to attack targets while they're distracted. Wait for your prey to encounter swarms of insects, stirges, or other simple creatures of the subterranean realm, then sneak in an attack.

Tactics: Bite and Dash. Start combat hidden. When a target comes within 20 feet of you, charge and bite the target twice. Assuming that you surprised the target and it didn't see you, both attacks should be with advantage. After biting the target, flee, using your fast movement speed to escape. Patiently wait for the target to rot away, tracking it through the subterranean realms.

DEATH KNIGHT

 CR 17

At first glance, this darkly armored warrior appears to be a paladin; however, the glowing red eyes and pallid skin reveals that it is some sort of undead horror.

Death knights were usually paladins in life who failed to fulfill their oath. Cursed to an undead state, they are evil creatures who loathe the living.

Fighting Style: Elite. You fill whatever role is needed. There isn't much that you can't do; you have strong offensive and defensive abilities and even several controller spells. Plus, your presence alone gives all undead within 60 feet of you advantage on saving throws against features that turn undead.

Set-up: Dark, Open Battlefield with Undead Minions. Pick a dark battlefield where you can stand just out of range of your target's darkvision. Your darkvision is 120 feet, which means you can see them even when they can't see you. Plus, your ranged orb attack has a 120-foot range, meaning you can impose disadvantage on Dexterity saving throws made to avoid it, thanks to the unseen attacker rule.

Weaknesses: Clerics and Paladins. Although you are relatively strong, clerics and paladins have a variety of spells sure to make quick work of your hit points unless you're careful. Use your orb attack to weaken these enemies, then keep them busy with your minions.

Pair With Minions. Fill the battlefield with both undead and living minions to slow down your enemies while you use your control magic. Don't use exclusively undead minions, as it only takes one sound effect that turns undead to destroy them all.

Tactics: Start Long Range, Then Close. Start combat 60 to 120 feet away from your targets. Send forth your minions to distract your targets, and then hit as many enemies as possible with your ranged orb attack. Step into view to use your control spells like *banishment*, *hold person*, and *command*, then return to the safety of the dark. When enemies close in on you, switch to aggressive brute tactics, attacking whatever target poses the biggest threat. Save your Parry against attacks landed by paladins, as those will destroy you quickly. If you still have minions working for you, use Dodge to avoid attacks while the minions deal damage.

DEMILICH

 CR 18

Glittering jewels encrust this leering skull as it floats up on a swirling vortex of dust and shimmering magic.

Liches that fail to eat souls eventually lose their bodies, which turn to dust, leaving only their skulls.

Fighting Style: Solo. You are a terrifying enemy capable of reducing your enemies to ash. You have a flying speed, which helps you keep your distance, and you're armed with both Legendary Actions and Lair Actions.

Set-up: Labyrinthine Tunnels. You are an extraordinarily patient creature who knows that combat with tomb raiders is often a battle of attrition. Make sure you are always encountered within your lair to gain full advantage of your Lair Actions and traits. Furthermore, make sure that your lair is nearly inescapable. Even if your foes destroy you, your enduring existence lets you return a few days later, fully rejuvenated.

Weaknesses: Being Restrained. Mobility is your ally; if you lose the ability to fly, it won't take long for your enemies to destroy you temporarily. Always keep your distance and save your Legendary Resistances for magical effects that halt your movement.

Pair With Minions. Minions distract enemies and help you heal yourself with your life-draining options.

Tactics: Hit and Run. Start combat hidden until targets come within 30 feet of you. First, use your antimagic Lair Action to disarm the strongest caster, ideally getting others. Then, on your turn, use your Howl to reduce as many as possible to 0 hit points. Quickly retreat into the air, taking full cover. Before the start of your next turn, use your legendary Flight to reposition yourself. On the next initiative count 20, prevent targets that fell victim to your life drain attack from healing with your Lair Action. When your actual turn comes up, use Howl again if it recharged. Otherwise, Dodge, staying 30 feet away in the air as you do. If you need to escape, use your Legendary Actions to do so. Otherwise, use your curse legendary action to disable a target. If you take too much damage from a single hit, flee the scene and return after you've had a chance to recover.

DEMON, BALOR

 **CR 19**

This winged fiend's horned head and fanged visage present the perfection of the demonic form, fire spurting from its flesh.

Balors are the biggest and baddest of the demons, ruling as generals over demonic armies.

Fighting Style: Brute. Most demons lack ranged attacks and prefer to fight up close and personal; you're no different. But you're not a dumb brute by any stretch. You know how to draw out your opponents and get to the backline to cause the most damage possible.

Set-up: Dark, Wide Open Spaces. You have a flying speed of 80 feet and truesight out to 120 feet. Make sure your battlefield has plenty of space to move around. Whenever you can, fight in areas of magical darkness, using your truesight to see your enemies while they're blind to your presence.

Weaknesses: Magic Weapons. Thanks to your excellent saving throws, you're well-protected against most types of magic. However, melee attackers armed with magic weapons—especially paladins—will quickly deliver a lot of damage. Avoid getting hit by these creatures at all costs.

Pair With Minions. Use lots of low-cost minions to keep the enemies' melee attackers busy while you pick off the backline. Make sure to space them out 10 feet apart; this will help reduce the risk of area-of-effect magic and increase their threat range for attacks of opportunity.

Tactics: Draw Out Melee Attackers. Start combat 60 to 80 feet away from your targets. Draw out melee attackers (taunting them with roleplay), holding a Teleport action as you do. Once the melee attackers are close, Teleport 30 feet behind the enemy's backline. Use your whip to pull targets to you so you can hit them with your longsword. When frontline attackers return, return to the skies. Continue to use these tactics to divide and conquer.

DEMON, DRETCH

CR 1/4

This creature's bloated frame shudders with each heaving step, yet despite its shape, the thing moves with surprising quickness.

Dretches are, for lack of a better term, "fart demons." Although they're easy to kill, they're a relatively affordable way to slow the party down while bigger, uglier bad guys get into position.

Fighting Style: Minion. You are slow, weak, and have lousy to-hit modifiers. However, your Fetid Cloud is a wonderful tool for reducing the efficiency of well-armed foes.

Set-up: Close and Personal. Your job is to get close and drop your Fetid Cloud, poisoning as many targets as possible. Make sure to space yourself 10 feet apart from other minions to minimize the damage caused by area-of-effect spells and threaten more attacks of opportunity.

Weaknesses: Poor Armor Class. You have an AC of 11, offset only slightly by your resistances. It won't take much to kill you. Hopefully, you'll poison a few enemies before you're sent back to the Abyss.

Pair With Brutes and Tanks. Your poison cloud imposes disadvantage on your enemy's attack rolls and slows targets down, robbing them of their valuable action economy. This hindrance gives allied brutes and tanks a chance to score a few extra hits, potentially turning the tide of battle. Just make sure those brutes and tanks are immune to poison.

Tactics: Get Close and Fart. Start combat within 20 feet of your targets. Move as close as possible to the enemy and use Fetid Cloud, poisoning as many as possible.

DEMON, GLABREZU

CR 9

Four arms grace the torso of this towering monstrosity. The monster's eyes shine with a mix of intelligence and cruelty.

Glabrezus are the tempter demons, content to use their charm—and aggressive attitudes—to get what they want out of foolish mortals. If that doesn't work, they're also pretty good at killing people.

Fighting Style: Elite. You have enough features to fill any role necessary on the battlefield (except maybe an artillerist). You're strong enough to tank, have controller spells, and can deal much damage as a brute.

Set-up: Close and Personal. Regardless of your role, you'll want to be within 30 feet of your foes at the start of combat. Plus, your at-will *darkness* functions better when there's nowhere for the enemies to run.

Weaknesses: Magic Weapons. With four strong saving throws and Magic Resistance, you're well-protected against spells. However, magic weapons, especially those wielded by paladins, pose a significant risk to you. The best way to thwart these attacks is to keep those attackers in the dark, confused, or stunned.

Pair With Minions. Team up with minions that can see in the dark as well as you can and who will benefit from your controller spells and features. Grimlocks, bats, and insects all come with blindsight.

Tactics: Control and Attack. Start combat as close to your enemies as possible. Immediately cast *darkness*, centered on yourself, and attack with your pincers, focusing on the most dangerous opponent. On your next turn, recast *darkness* if you need to and attack the same target. If *darkness* is still up, use *power word stun*, instead against whatever target looks like it will suffer the most from it—clerics and other spellcasters make good targets, especially if they're concentrating on spells or they can see through your *darkness*. Switch to four attacks with your pincers and fists once you no longer need to cast spells, still targeting the most dangerous creature present first.

DEMON, HEZROU

 CR 8

This fiend's armored flesh is scaly and moist. Its large, toothy mouth gapes below a pair of hungry, reptilian eyes.

Hezrous are frog-like demons that smell like they've been rolling around in an otyugh's breakfast. Like most demons, their tactics are pretty straightforward—hit the enemy until it stops moving.

Fighting Style: Brute. Your Stench poisons targets within 10 feet of you, and you have three attacks via your multiattack that require you to be within 5 feet of the enemy. You are a true brute.

Set-up: Up Close and Personal. You want to get as close to your targets as possible from the start of combat. Lore-wise, demons have nothing to fear from being destroyed outside their home plane; therefore, you'll fight until you're destroyed.

Weaknesses: Magic Weapons. You have excellent saving throw proficiencies, damage resistances out of the wazoo, and Magic Resistance. However, melee attackers armed with magic weapons—especially paladins—pose a significant threat. Get rid of them first.

Pair With Artillerists and Skirmishers. Your Stench and attacks will make you the enemy's primary target; this allows ranged allies and skirmishers to make attacks while you distract their targets.

Tactics: Stink and Slash. Start combat within 30 feet of your enemies. When it's your turn, get as close to as many targets as possible to affect them with your Stench. You aren't intelligent enough to understand tactics, so attack whatever creature hurts you the most with its attacks.

DEMON, MARILITH

CR 16

This snake-bodied fiend has a six-armed woman's torso, pointed ears, and glittering, otherworldly eyes.

The dreaded mariliths serve demon lords as governesses, advisors, and even lovers, yet their brilliance as tacticians makes them most sought after as generals and commanders of armies.

Fighting Style: Elite. You come equipped with excellent offensive and defensive capabilities and one of the most robust features in the game, Reactive, which allows you to take a reaction every turn in combat.

Set-up: Dark, Open Places. A big part of your tactics involves using your Teleport action to get behind enemy lines. Plus, with your 120 feet of truesight, you can stand outside the enemy's darkvision range and taunt them without fear of reprisal from their artillerists. Difficult terrain will also help slow down melee attackers.

Weaknesses: Magic Weapons. You have four excellent saving throw proficiencies, resistance to most elemental damage types, and Magic Resistance. Therefore, you don't have much to worry about in the way of spellcasters. However, melee attackers armed with magic weapons—especially paladins—may cause trouble. Get them away from the backline.

Pair With Controllers. You earn the title of elite only because you can easily switch between brute and tank fighting styles; however, you don't have any features that let you control your enemies. Work alongside low-level controllers like cult fanatics to gain advantage on your seven attacks. Or use creatures capable of casting/creating *darkness*, like glabrezus or darkmantles.

Tactics: Draw Out Melee Attackers. Start combat 60 to 120 feet away in the dark, just outside the enemy's vision. Hold the Teleport action until the enemy gets within 10 feet of you, then Teleport behind the enemy's backline. When your next turn begins, attack whatever target is closest to you with all your attacks. If you don't kill the target, grapple it with your tail and pull it away. Continue to attack your grappled target until the melee attackers come back to join the rest of the party. Then, teleport away again, repeating these tactics. Don't forget that you can Parry every turn.

DEMON, NALFESHNEE

CR 13

A towering, corpulent beast, this fiend has the hideous head of a boar and arms ending in fatty, four-fingered hands.

Nalfeshnees are demonic commanders with a knack for logistics, thanks to their higher-than-usual Intelligence scores. They are often described as one of the most horrific-looking demons, hence their Horror Nimbus feature.

Fighting Style: Elite. You have excellent defensive and offensive capabilities, the ability to fly and teleport, truesight, and a power that inflicts the frightened condition. Excluding an artillerist, you can fill any role necessary.

Set-up: Dark, Open Spaces. Your tactics involve using your Teleport action to draw out melee attackers, so you want to make sure there's lots of runway for them to chase you. Difficult terrain will also help you slow them down and won't affect your movement since you can fly and Teleport. With 120 feet of truesight, you can stand at the edge of the enemy's field of vision without worrying about reprisal from ranged attacks.

Weaknesses: Magic Weapons. Your excellent saving throws, elemental damage resistances, and Magic Resistance feature will protect you from your enemy's spells. However, melee attackers armed with magic weapons—especially paladins—pose a severe threat. Make sure to disable these foes quickly.

Pair With Controllers. Once you draw melee attackers away from their backline, you want to keep them occupied. Use controllers to *entangle*, blind, restrain, etc. the frontline attackers while you decimate the other side's artillerists and controllers. Cultists and cult fanatics are good options.

Tactics: Draw Out Melee Attackers. Start combat 60 to 100 feet away from the enemy's backline targets. Provoke them (through roleplaying) to engage you while you Ready the Teleport action. When the targets get near, Teleport behind the backline. Then, on your turn, use your Multiattack to attack the targets. When the melee attackers return to face you, use Horror Nimbus to frighten them off, then fly or Teleport away. Repeat these tactics for as long as you're able.

DEMON, QUASIT

CR 1

Ram horns curl back from the twisted head of this tiny winged demon, and its body is thin and wiry.

The quasit is perhaps the least powerful demon, yet it is not the least respected. Their small size and ability to change shape and turn invisible make them effective servants and pawns against mortals.

Fighting Style: Lurker. You can turn invisible at will, have excellent Stealth, and have far too few hit points to consider fighting a protracted battle.

Set-up: Lots of Distractions. You wouldn't dare engage in combat unless you were sure that you could make an attack and escape without the enemy reciprocating. Make sure that your targets are busy dealing with other creatures or otherwise distracted in some way.

Weaknesses: Squishy. You have relatively low hit points compared to other demons, even when you factor in your resistances. It only takes a few well-placed hits to send you back to the abyss. Make your attack and escape as quickly as possible.

Pair With Minions or Tanks. Use minions or tanks to distract the enemy while you position yourself for the perfect attack.

Tactics: Lurk, Then Attack. Start combat invisible in your bat form (unless you're underwater, use your toad form). Choose a target that's easy to hit—whichever one isn't wearing a lot of clunky metal armor—and then emerge, attack, and fly away. Keep your distance behind full cover and turn invisible again as soon as possible. Once the enemy stops searching for you, repeat these tactics.

DEMON, SHADOW

Only this shadowy bat-winged demon's teeth and claws have any sense of physicality to them—the rest is lost in darkness.

Shadow demons are incorporeal demons cobbled together from the souls of hateful murderers. They function similarly to other shadows.

Fighting Style: Lurker. As an incorporeal creature that can take the Hide action as a bonus action, you perform best when you catch your enemies by surprise. However, if you stay too long, you'll get subjected to a volley of deadly spells and attacks with magical weapons.

Set-up: Dark Places with Lots of Cover. You want to stick to shadowy areas where you can benefit from your stealth. Additionally, your tactics rely on phasing through objects and hiding between attacks. Pick claustrophobic areas with plenty of cover and absolutely no light.

Weaknesses: Light. As a shadow creature, you dread light in any form—and you especially hate radiant damage, to which you're vulnerable. Avoid targets carrying torches, lanterns, or other illuminated objects.

Pair With Brutes and Tanks. Use melee attacker allies (almost every demon ever) to keep your enemies distracted while you use your hit-and-run tactics.

Tactics: Lurk, Then Attack. Start combat hidden behind full cover. When a target comes within 5 feet of you, emerge and attack it, then fly through the nearest cover—you can go through walls, ceilings, or floors—and take the Hide action. Continue to perform hit-and-run tactics like this, spacing them out, so the enemy temporarily forgets you exist.

DEMON, VROCK

CR 6

A cloud of spores and a trail of feathers surrounds this twisted cross between a man and a gigantic vulture.

Vrocks are simplistic vulture demons that love to cause pain and chaos wherever they go.

Fighting Style: Skirmisher. With a flying speed of 60 feet and plenty of resistances, you perform best as a hit-and-run attacker.

Set-up: Dark, Open Spaces. You have darkvision out to 120 feet, which means you can stand at the edge of the enemy's darkvision and still see them. You're a flier, so you want to have a lot of room to maneuver. Make sure there's plenty of difficult terrain to slow down melee attackers.

Weaknesses: Magic Weapons. You have resistance to most elemental damage, decent saving throw proficiencies, and Magic Resistance. Therefore, you don't have to worry about spellcasters nearly as much. However, melee attackers armed with magic weapons—especially paladins—pose a viable threat. Try to keep away from them while you attack their allies.

Pair With Minions. Your screech can stun all non-demons within 20 feet of you; this allows weaker allies, such as dretches, a chance to score attacks against the enemy. Make sure to space your minion allies apart so they don't risk being obliterated by area-of-effect magic.

Tactics: Screech, Poison, Then Attack. Start combat 45 to 60 feet away from your targets. If you have minions working alongside you, fly close and hit all the targets you can with your Stunning Screech. If you've already used your Screech or don't have minions, use your Spores attack. Then, return to the sky, keeping out of range of low-range spells, auras, and reach weapons. If your spores recharged the next turn and didn't affect many targets the last time you used it, try again. Otherwise, get close to a poisoned target and attack it with your multiattack. Make sure to fly out of range at the end of each of your turns.

DEVIL, BARBED

CR 5

From the tip of its lashing tail to the serrated features of its fang-filled visage, this fiery-eyed sentinel bristles with barbs.

Barbed devils are lesser devils that serve as diabolical jailers and bodyguards to greater devils.

Fighting Style: Artillerist. Although your spikey hide would suggest you should fight up close and personal, your impressive darkvision range and ability to Hurl Flame 150 feet positions you better as an artillerist.

Set-up: Dark Spaces with Lots of Cover. You have 120 feet of darkvision, which means you can usually see your foes in the dark even when they can't see you. Plus, your Hurl Flame has a normal range of 150 feet, letting you set fire to targets. Make sure there's some cover for you to hide behind, too.

Weaknesses: Magic Weapons. Your impressive saving throw proficiencies, Magic Resistance, and damage resistances and immunities help you avoid most spells. However, a melee attacker with a silver or magic weapon—especially a paladin—poses a severe threat. Stay far away from melee attackers.

Pair With Brutes and Tanks. Use formidable allies to distract your foes while you pummel them with flames from 150 feet away in the dark.

Tactics: Keep Your Distance. Start combat 60 to 120 feet away from your enemies behind cover. Use your multiattack to Hurl Flame twice, targeting enemies that pose the most significant threat to your frontline. Move just enough to make it hard for your enemies to pinpoint your location and take cover once more. If enemies get close, move to put more distance between yourself and them.

DEVIL, BEARDED

CR 3

This seething devil deftly wields a vicious, saw-toothed glaive while below its toothy maw writhes a hideous, twitching beard.

Bearded devils are the frontline soldiers in the unending war between devils and demons.

Fighting Style: Brute. Your beard deals poison damage, and your glaive causes grievous injuries that cause your targets to bleed until they receive medical attention.

Set-up: Up Close and Personal. You want to get into melee combat as fast as possible. And like other devils, you have devil's sight, so try to fight in areas of magical darkness whenever possible.

Weaknesses: Magic Weapons. Your impressive saving throw proficiencies, Magic Resistance, and damage resistances and immunities help you avoid most spells. However, a melee attacker with a silver or magic weapon—especially a paladin—poses a severe threat. Remove these targets as fast as possible.

Pair With Controllers. As a brute, your style complements most fighting styles; however, controllers capable of restraining or grappling your enemies help you inflict hits with your 10-foot reach glaive without giving the target chance to reciprocate.

Tactics: Make 'Em Bleed. Start combat within 30 feet of your targets. When it's your turn, target enemies that pose the biggest threat to you and your allies or attack a target against which you have a clear advantage.

DEVIL, BONE

CR 9

Merging the most horrifying features of a carrion-fed insect and a withered cadaver, this bony devil moves in unsettling lurches.

Bone devils are the highest-ranking lesser devils and often come to the material complain to tempt and make one-sided deals with foolish mortals. Basically, they're hell's sales representatives.

Fighting Style: Skirmisher. You have a flying speed of 40 feet, and both your primary attacks (as well as your optional polearm attack) have a 10-foot reach.

Set-up: Dark, Open Spaces. As a flying creature, you want to fight in areas with open sky or high ceilings. Incorporate difficult terrain to slow down melee attackers and magical darkness to make it hard for your enemies to reciprocate.

Weaknesses: Magic Weapons. Your impressive saving throw proficiencies, Magic Resistance, and damage resistances and immunities help you avoid most spells. However, a melee attacker with a silver or magic weapon—especially a paladin—poses a severe threat. Avoid these creatures.

Pair With Controllers. Use controllers to slow down enemies by poisoning, restraining, or blinding them with magical darkness. Tanks, brutes, and minions are also valuable, helping you keep the enemy preoccupied while you make hit-and-run attacks.

Tactics: Hit-and-Run. Start combat 25 feet away from your targets. On your turn, move within 10 feet of a target, hit it with your multiattack, and then return to the sky.

DEVIL, CHAIN

CR 8

Wickedly barbed chains adorn this lean figure, and gaps in the bindings reveal deathly pale flesh etched with jagged scars.

These diabolical priests are known to raise hell (get it?), serving as the evangelists of the lower realms.

Fighting Style: Controller. You can animate four chains, giving you a total of six attacks per turn that automatically grapple and restrain on a hit. Plus, the chains deal damage at the start of each of the targets' turns.

Set-up: Dark Areas with Lots of Chains. Your Animate Chains feature requires chains to work, so make sure you fight in a place with plenty of chains. You have devil's sight, so try to fight in places with magical darkness. Even if you can't fight in magical darkness, you have 120 feet of darkvision, so you can stand at the edge of your enemy's darkvision field and still see them. Difficult terrain is also helpful in slowing down melee attackers.

Weaknesses: Magic Weapons. Your impressive saving throw proficiencies, Magic Resistance, and damage resistances and immunities help you avoid most spells. However, a melee attacker with a silver or magic weapon—especially paladins—poses a severe threat. Use your chains to keep these foes away from you.

Pair With Brutes and Minions. Your job is to grapple and restrain the enemy, allowing your companions to attack with advantage against them as you do.

Tactics: Keep Your Distance. Start combat 40 to 60 feet away from your targets. Animate chains as soon as possible. Spread the chains out, so they threaten as big an area as possible (a chain effectively threatens a 25-foot diameter sphere centered on itself). When a target tries to get close to you, use your Unnerving Mask to stop them in their tracks. When your turn comes around, grapple as many targets as possible, inflicting damage. While your chains operate on your behalf, take cover or move into complete darkness to avoid the enemy's ranged attacks.

DEVIL, ERINYES

 **CR 12**

Some calamity has befallen this angelic warrior. Wings stained black shear the air as her merciless eyes search for a target.

Erinyes are fallen angels that function as assassins and executioners for the archdevils. Although they are just as clever as their fellow greater devils, they prefer action over diplomacy.

Fighting Style: Elite. You have excellent defensive and offensive capabilities, and you come equipped with a longbow that permanently poisons targets on a failed saving throw. Other than controller or support, you can fill any role your allies need.

Set-up: Dark, Open Places. As a flier, you want an open sky or high ceilings above you. Fight in dark places—magically dark, if possible—with lots of difficult terrain to slow your enemies down. Try not to offer your enemies too much cover, as you'll want to weaken them with your longbow.

Weaknesses: Magic Weapons. Your impressive saving throw proficiencies, Magic Resistance, and damage resistances and immunities help you avoid most spells. However, a melee attacker with a silver or magic weapon—especially paladins—poses a severe threat. Keep your distance from these foes, saving them for last.

Pair With Controllers. Although you're strong enough to absorb a few hits from your targets' attacks of opportunity, it never hurts to restrain, blind, or stun them, granting you advantage on your attacks of opportunity. Chain devils make an excellent pairing.

Tactics: Fire From a Distance. Unless you're tasked to function as a brute or tank, keep 100 to 120 feet of distance between yourself and your targets. Use your longbow to poison as many targets as you can. Once you've poisoned a few targets, focus on one target with all your attacks until it is dead. Try to keep just out of your enemy's darkvision range to give yourself advantage on your attacks.

DEVIL, HORNED

CR 11

Bristling with terrible spines and a crown of deadly horns, this leering winged terror wields a whirling barbed chain.

These elite killing machines fight at the forefront of the ceaseless demon/devil wars, second only to archdevils.

Fighting Style: Elite. You come equipped with excellent offensive and defensive capabilities. You can fight at a range, tossing balls of flame at your enemies, or fight up close, inflicting infernal wounds with your tail. Furthermore, both melee attacks have a 10-foot reach, allowing you to operate as a skirmisher.

Set-up: Dark, Wide Open Spaces. As a flying creature with ranged attacks, you perform best when there's an open sky or high ceilings above you and nowhere for your enemies to hide. Because your darkvision range is more significant than most of your enemies, you can position yourself to see them and not vice versa.

Weaknesses: Magic Weapons. Your impressive saving throw proficiencies, Magic Resistance, and damage resistances and immunities help you avoid most spells. However, a melee attacker with a silver or magic weapon—especially a paladin—poses a severe threat. Keep your distance and rely on your flames.

Pair With Controllers. While your Hurl Flame attack is helpful, you are especially deadly in close combat with your tail. Team up with a creature that can blind, restrain, stun, etc., your targets so you may attack them at advantage.

Tactics: Keep Your Distance. Start combat 60 to 120 feet away in total darkness. Open with Hurl Flame, targeting whatever creature poses the biggest threat to you and your allies. Then move, so your targets can't pinpoint your location. If your allies manage to subdue most of your enemies, move in close and attack with your tail and fork. Even at this close range, stick to the skies to avoid melee attacks.

DEVIL, ICE

CR 14

A pair of frozen, multifaceted eyes coldly judge all before this towering, insectile monstrosity.

Ice devils rise from the frozen hellscapes to lead lesser devils in combat. Extraordinarily intelligent, they help archdevils plan world-ending plots.

Fighting Style: Elite. You come packed with powerful offensive and defensive capabilities, which lets you work as a tank or brute. Your speed and reach help you fight as a skirmisher. And you can create unlimited walls of ice, making you a controller.

Set-up: Dark, Cramped Spaces. All of your attacks require you to fight up close and personal. Furthermore, your Wall of Ice attack lets you divide and conquer your foes. Try to fight in places where your Devil's Sight and blindsight give you advantage over your enemies, such as areas of magical darkness or those obscured by fog clouds or the *cloudkill* spell.

Weaknesses: Magic Weapons. Your impressive saving throw proficiencies, Magic Resistance, and damage resistances and immunities help you avoid most spells. However, a melee attacker with a silver or magic weapon—especially a paladin—poses a severe threat. Use your wall of ice to subdue these targets.

Pair With Artillerists. Since you will likely fill the role of brute, tank, or skirmisher, work alongside artillerists like barbed devils who can attack your foes from a distance.

Tactics: Divide and Conquer. Start combat 45 to 60 feet away from your targets. Use your Wall of Ice action to put a dome over dangerous melee attackers, leaving only one or two targets outside the dome. When your turn comes back around, use the Wall of Ice again (assuming it recharges) to further divide the party or re-up your walls. Otherwise, move close to attack targets that weren't caught in the wall. If the melee targets break out of your wall, take the Dodge action and move away until you can use the Wall of Ice again.

DEVIL, IMP

CR 1

Fiendish wings and a whipping scorpion-like tail lash behind this diminutive, red-skinned nuisance.

Although relatively weak compared to other devils (lemures excluded), imps often work on behalf of greater devils to establish negotiations and infernal deals with mortals. They also work alongside evil spellcasters as familiars.

Fighting Style: Lurker. You can turn invisible at will and have excellent Stealth skills. With relatively low hit points, you don't want to participate in combats that go for more than a single round.

Set-up: Lots of Distractions. You don't want to attack your targets unless they're busy dealing with another problem or creature. Also, make sure there are lots of places for you to hide or escape after you make your attack.

Weaknesses: Squishy. Despite your resistances and immunities, you only have 10 hp and 13 AC. It only takes a few good hits to send you careening back to hell.

Pair With Brutes, Minions, or Tanks. Team with melee attackers so that they can keep your targets distracted while you position yourself for the perfect attack.

Tactics: Lurk, Then Attack. Start combat invisible in your raven form, which has a better flying speed than you usually do. While invisible, sneak up beside a target. Then, attack the target with your sting at the start of the next available turn. Immediately retreat and take cover somewhere they can't easily reach you. Turn invisible as soon as you get a chance. Once the enemies stop looking for you, repeat these tactics.

DEVIL, LEMURE

A roiling wave of flesh gushes forward. Amid the fatty surge, wriggle half-formed limbs and a dripping tumorous face.

The least of devilkind, lemures roil forth from the ranks of souls damned to Hell, shapeless masses of quivering flesh. Other devils use hordes of these creatures to overwhelm their foes.

Fighting Style: Minion. You are barely more than a bag of hit points designed to slow down the foes of your masters. Plus, destroying you outside of hell isn't the end—you simply get sent home. Not that that's any better, mind you.

Set-up: Spaced Out. You and the rest of the lemures present should spread out at least 10 feet apart to reduce the risk of area-of-effect spells and encourage attacks of opportunity. Unfortunately, you're probably not smart enough to realize this and will likely linger wherever your wobbly flesh takes you.

Weaknesses: Stupid. You have an Intelligence score of 1 and a Charisma score of 3, which means you are barely sentient. Your Wisdom score is an 11, which means you're at least wise enough to realize being destroyed by mortals is better than angering your infernal masters.

Pair With Artillerists or Skirmishers. Your job is to surround your foes, blocking any method of escape that they might try. Meanwhile, artillerists and skirmishers fighting your side can attack without fear of reprisal.

Tactics: Waddle and Punch. Start combat as close as you can to the enemy. When you get near them, hit them. Continue to do this until your enemy dies or your masters tell you to stop.

DEVIL, PIT FIEND

CR 20

A pair of gigantic, flame-seared wings and eyes smoldering like embers give this towering devil a truly horrific appearance.

Pit fiends are among the deadliest of devils and usually function as high lords of hell, only a step below their archdevil masters. All other devils fear or respect pit fiends and do their bidding without question.

Fighting Style: Elite. You come loaded with impressive offensive and defensive capabilities, control spells, and effects, flying speed, and even infinite *fireballs*. You can play whatever role is needed of you.

Set-up: Anywhere. As one of the most versatile devils, you can fight anywhere. Of course, you prefer wide open spaces where you can benefit from your flying speed and dark areas that let your 120 feet of truesight see enemies before they see you. *Wall of fire* and your fear aura allow you to fight in close quarters.

Weaknesses: Magic Weapons. Your impressive saving throw proficiencies, Magic Resistance, and damage resistances and immunities help you avoid most spells. However, a melee attacker with a silver or magic weapon—especially a paladin—poses a serious threat. Keep away from melee attackers using your ranged attacks or *wall of fire*.

Pair With Minions. You're an incredible fighter, so you don't really need assistance. However, a few minions like lemures are useful for burning your enemies' action economy and spell slots.

Tactics: Ranged Then Close. Start combat 60 to 120 feet away from your enemy, just out of the range of their darkvision. If the enemy comes with many artillerists, create a ringed *wall of fire* around them to block their vision. Otherwise, chuck *fireballs* at the entire group from your long range. Continue to do this until you've eliminated targets that aren't resistant or immune to fire damage. Start moving closer, using any remaining walls of fire to separate dangerous melee attackers (like paladins) from the rest of the party. If you run out of *walls of fire*, switch to *hold monster*, targeting specific melee attackers. Use your multiattack against any targets left standing.

DOPPELGANGER

 **CR 3**

This grayish humanoid creature seems almost unfinished, with a narrow head, gaunt limbs, and a sinister, noseless face.

With their ability to assume any humanoid form and read the thoughts of others, doppelgangers are the best spies around. Plus, they hit pretty hard, too!

Fighting Style: Lurker. You're pretty strong but even more dangerous when you surprise your foes. Fortunately, you come with a lot of different ways to do that.

Set-up: Crowded Places. You want to fight in places where it's easier to hide after you make an attack; pick spots with lots of humanoids, so it's easy for you to blend in and get lost. Failing that, you still have a +4 to Stealth, so you can hide in dark areas if you need.

Weaknesses: Truesight. Watch out for enemies that can see through your disguises. If you can't surprise your foes, you lose many of your special features.

Pair With Minions. You want to keep your foes distracted so you can make an attack and escape without the enemy following you. Team up with creatures who can threaten attacks of opportunity if your targets try to chase after you.

Tactics: Surprise, Slam, and Escape. Start combat as close as possible to your enemies, disguised as someone else. Use Read Thoughts to ensure they don't recognize you as an enemy. If you surprise the enemy, you get an advantage on your attack and deal extra damage. Hit the target twice with your slam, then escape. Find a place to hide using your Stealth skill or polymorphed into another humanoid. Wait until they lose interest in you before trying to attack them again.

DRAGONS, TRUE

True dragons come in many different shapes, sizes, and colors. In fact, there are 40 different variants in the Fifth Edition monster book, and that doesn't even include lich dragons, dragon turtles, fairy dragons, etc. Fortunately, for the purposes of writing this book—and saving your brain from exploding—dragons mostly have the same tactics for each of their age groups. All wyrmlings fight the same, all ancient dragons fight the same way, and so forth. Of course, this doesn't mean that you should roleplay the same or put them in the same environments.

This section organizes dragons by their age groups, giving general tactics for each group. I left notes where there are noticeable differences between the different colored dragons.

DRAGON WYRMLINGS

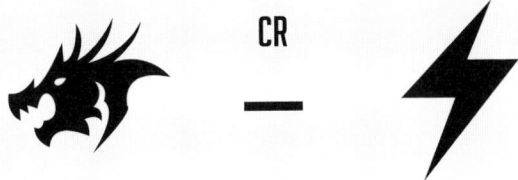

Aged 5 years or fewer, wyrmlings are the youngest category of true dragons.

Fighting Style: Skirmisher. You have a flying speed of 60 feet, regardless of your color, and a breath weapon that's either a cone or line.

Set-up: Dark, Open Spaces. You have two types of vision: blindsight and darkvision. Therefore, you want to fight in heavily obscured spaces whenever possible. Make sure there's plenty of room for you to fly around, too, because you don't want to get hit by melee attackers while waiting for your breath weapon to recharge. Consider placing difficult terrain everywhere to slow down attackers and prevent them from escaping.

Weaknesses: Melee Combat. Your natural weapons are relatively weak compared to your breath weapons. Unfortunately, your breath weapon only recharges on a roll of 5 or 6. Stay away from foes and be patient; rely on your wings and breath weapon.

Pair With Brutes or Tanks. You want our enemies to stay distracted while you lurk in the skies waiting for your breath weapon to recharge. Consider teaming with creatures that can restrain your foes and have a natural immunity to your breath weapon.

Tactics: Rely on Your Breath Weapon. Start combat 30 feet away from your targets in the air. On your first turn, fly within your breath weapon's range and hit as many targets as possible. Then retreat to the sky. Continue to fly and Dodge until your breath weapon recharges, then return for another hit-and-breathe attack.

DRAGON, YOUNG

CR —

Young dragons are between 6 and 100 years old and are Large creatures. They are similar in fighting style to wyrmlings, albeit much stronger.

Fighting Style: Skirmisher. You have a flying speed of 80 feet and a breath weapon with a longer ranger or area. Stick to the skies and blast targets with your breath.

Set-up: Dark, Open Spaces. You have two types of vision: blindsight and darkvision. Therefore, you want to fight in heavily obscured spaces whenever possible. Make sure there's plenty of room for you to fly around, too, because you don't want to get hit by melee attackers while waiting for your breath weapon to recharge. Consider placing difficult terrain everywhere to slow down attackers and prevent them from escaping.

Some dragons have special movement speeds, which give them additional benefits (green dragons can swim, blue dragons can burrow, etc.) When possible, fight in areas with terrain that compliment your tertiary movement methods.

Weaknesses: Melee Combat. Entering melee combat makes you an easy target for your enemies, especially if they have ways to grapple or restrain you. Don't enter melee combat until you've downed at least half of your targets with your breath weapon.

Pair With Brutes or Tanks. You want our enemies to stay distracted while you lurk in the skies waiting for your breath weapon to recharge. Consider teaming with creatures that can restrain your foes and have a natural immunity to your breath weapon.

Tactics: Rely on Your Breath Weapon. Start combat 40 feet away from your targets in the air. On your first turn, fly within your breath weapon's range and hit as many targets as possible. Then retreat to the sky. Continue to fly and Dodge until your breath weapon recharges, then return for more hit-and-breathe attacks until you eliminate at least half of your targets. Switch to your multiattack to clean up the rest while waiting for your breath weapon to recharge.

DRAGON, ADULT

   CR
—

Adult dragons are aged 101 to 800 years and qualify as legendary creatures, which means that they benefit from Lair Actions. These dragons always fight on their turf whenever they can.

Fighting Style: Solo. You are loaded with offensive and defensive capabilities and plenty of action economy, which means you can take on entire groups of enemies by yourself.

Set-up: The Dragon's Lair. Fight in your lair, giving you access to your Lair Actions. Your lair should have high ceilings (or open skies), hazards and traps that don't affect you (i.e., hot lava if you're a red dragon, ice and snow if you're a white dragon, etc.) You have 60 feet of blindsight, so effects that obscure vision, such as smoke, heavy snowfall, etc., are welcome additions.

Weaknesses: Losing Your Action Economy. You are a legendary dragon that comes stacked with plenty of options to take on your turn and outside of it. Beware of enemies that can stun or paralyze you, especially spellcasters. Save your Legendary Resistances for these effects, and always try to escape with your Wing Attack when you're in danger of getting caught.

Pair With Minions. As a solo creature, you can fight an entire group by yourself. But a few low-CR minions are always fun to keep your enemies distracted.

Tactics: Keep Your Distance. Start combat 40 feet away from your enemies. Start combat using one of your Lair Actions, whichever one will give you advantage against the most targets, especially if your breath weapon forces Dexterity saving throws. If you need to put distance between yourself and your targets before your first turn begins, use Wing Attack to reposition yourself. Otherwise, use your breath weapon to hit as many targets as possible, then use your wings to keep distance between yourself and your enemies. On the next initiative count 20, use your next best controller Lair Action or a damage-dealing Lair Action to disrupt a caster's concentration. If your breath weapon recharges, repeat the same tactics as before, moving in to attack, then retreating to the sky. Otherwise, take the Dodge action and rely on your Legendary Actions to make attacks against any targets that get within 15 feet of you.

DRAGON, ANCIENT

 CR
—

Ancient dragons are Gargantuan terrors over 800 years old. Having led a successful life, they rarely have any reason to leave their lairs and massive hordes.

Fighting Style: Solo. You are loaded with offensive and defensive capabilities and plenty of action economy, which means you can take on entire groups of enemies by yourself.

Set-up: The Dragon's Lair. Fight in your lair, giving you access to your Lair Actions. Your lair should have high ceilings (or open skies), hazards and traps that don't affect you (i.e., hot lava if you're a red dragon, ice and snow if you're a white dragon, etc.) You have 60 feet of blindsight, so effects that obscure vision, such as smoke, heavy snowfall, etc., are welcome additions.

Weaknesses: Losing Your Action Economy. You are a legendary dragon that comes stacked with plenty of options to take on your turn and outside of it. Beware of enemies that can stun or paralyze you, especially spellcasters. Save your Legendary Resistances for these effects, and always try to escape with your Wing Attack when you're in danger of getting caught.

Pair With Minions. As a solo creature, you can fight an entire group by yourself. But you can use a few minions to keep enemies distracted.

Tactics: Keep Your Distance. Start combat 40 feet away from your enemies. Start combat using one of your Lair Actions, whichever one will give you advantage against the most targets, especially if your breath weapon forces Dexterity saving throws. If you need to put distance between yourself and your targets before your first turn begins, use Wing Attack to reposition yourself. Otherwise, use your breath weapon to hit as many targets as possible, then use your wings to keep distance between yourself and your enemies. On the next initiative count 20, use your next best controller Lair Action or a damage-dealing Lair Action to disrupt a caster's concentration. If your breath weapon recharges, repeat the same tactics as before, moving in to attack, then retreating to the sky. Otherwise, take the Dodge action and rely on your Legendary Actions to make attacks against any targets that get within 20 feet of you.

DRAGON TURTLE

 **CR 17**

This long-tailed aquatic beast resembles a massive snapping turtle with draconic features.

Although dragon turtles aren't "true dragons," they possess many similar qualities to their winged counterparts.

Fighting Style: Elite. You're stacked with defensive and offensive capabilities and have a breath weapon that has a 60-foot range. The only thing that prevents you from fighting as a pure solo creature is your lack of action economy.

Set-up: Submerged. You have a swim speed of 40 feet, twice your land speed. Plus, water will help protect you from attacks made against you.

Weaknesses: Fighting on Land. Your slow land speed makes you a sitting duck outside of water. Without mobility, you're forced to fight as a brute. Of course, you're good at that, too (as well as tanking).

Pair With Artillerists. As the biggest target on the field, you'll keep the enemy busy while it tries to penetrate your massive shell. Work alongside artillerists that can pick off your foes from the safety of cover.

Tactics: Move and Blast. Start combat 40 feet away from your targets in the water. Use your Steam Breath to hit as many targets as possible. Then, swim back just enough to get out of the enemy's darkvision range, drawing out melee fighters as you do. If there are still a lot of foes on the field, Dodge until your Steam Breath recharges. If you've reduced your enemy's numbers enough, or if your Steam Breath is ineffective, move in close and attack with your Multiattack. You can swim away after attacks like a skirmisher, as your AC 20 and 341 hp will keep you safe from most attacks of opportunity.

DRIDER

 CR 6

This terrifying creature has the armored body of a drow warrior from the waist up and the abdomen, thorax, and legs of a massive spider from the waist down.

Driders were drow warriors transformed into their spider-humanoid state after failing their dark goddess,

Fighting Style: Elite. You possess strong offensive and defensive capabilities, which allows you to play the role of tank or brute. You also carry a longbow and have darkvision out to 120 feet, which makes you the perfect artillerist. As a spellcaster, you can serve as controller or support.

Set-up: Dark, Difficult Terrain. Assuming you play the role of artillerist or lurker, you want to start in dark places that are hard for non-spiders to traverse. Vertical passages, thick webbing, rocky floors, etc., work great. Your 120 feet of darkvision means that you can usually see your foes long before they can see you, which gives you a massive advantage in combat.

Weaknesses: Mental Saving Throws. Although you're pretty tough, your mental saving throws are relatively low for a CR 6 creature, which leaves you vulnerable to enchantment magic. Try to stay back 60 feet to avoid the majority of those spells.

Pair With Minions. As an elite, you can take care of yourself in combat. However, having a few minions to distract the characters while you pick them off with your bow from a distance never hurts.

Tactics: Keep Your Distance. Start combat 60 to 120 feet away in cover. Fire your longbow from that range, targeting foes that can't see you. If the foes come near, reposition, so you always keep at least 60 feet between you and them. If the targets can see you, use *faerie fire* on the entire group to give yourself advantage. Use *darkness* to cover your escape if necessary.

Drider Spellcasters. A variant of drider gives you a better Wisdom score and a variety of helpful support and control spells. If you use this variant, your tactics will change to suit the controller role. Use *silence* to shut down spellcasters, mainly to protect you and others from enchantment magic from the other side. Protect your best defender with *sanctuary* and use *hold person* against whatever melee attacker stands to cause the most damage.

DRUID

CR 2

Druids are forest-themed spellcasters who function as controllers or artillerists (or both).

Fighting Style: Controller. You have the *entangle* spell, which you can use three times per long rest; this is your most potent combat spell and lets you keep 90 feet between yourself and your enemies.

Set-up: Forests with Lots of Cover. Although you can fight in any terrain (*entangle* isn't terrain dependent), lore-wise, it makes more sense for you to fight in the wild. Just make sure you have plenty of distance between yourself and the enemies.

Weaknesses: Melee Combat. You are relatively weak for a CR 2 creature in terms of defense and offense—especially when compared to a dryad, which more or less fills the same role but does it better. Always keep your distance, using spells like *thunderwave* and *entangle* to slow down enemies.

Pair With Artillerists. Your *entangle* spell will restrain everyone in a 20-foot square and create an area of difficult terrain for the duration. You don't want melee allies to get caught in it, so instead, work alongside artillerists who also benefit from the restraints.

Tactics: Restrain and Take Cover. Start combat 60 to 90 feet away from your enemy in cover. When your turn begins, use *entangle* to capture as many enemies as possible. Alternatively, use it to create an area of difficult terrain to slow them down. From there, hide. If you're fighting alone or the enemy defeats all your allies, flee or surrender.

DRYAD

 CR 1

This strange, beautiful woman has flesh that seems made of wood and vibrant hair that resembles leaves and blossoms.

Dryads are fey forest guardians bound to a specific tree. They serve as guides and watchers and often work with other sylvan creatures.

Fighting Style: Controller. You have the *entangle* spell, which you can cast three times per day, and also can charm creatures to do your bidding.

Set-up: Heavily Wooded Areas. Your Tree Stride feature lets you use trees as "teleporters." Additionally, you can Speak with Beasts and Plants. There's rarely a reason for you ever to be encountered anywhere but in the wilderness.

Weaknesses: Roleplaying. You are relatively well-balanced for a CR 1 creature, with above-average defensive and offensive capabilities and useful controller powers. However, the forest is your weakness; enemies who threaten it might force your hand.

Pair With Minions. You can charm up to three beasts per day in addition to one humanoid. Plus, you can speak to them. Therefore, it seems reasonable that these animals come with you from the start. Pick animals with valuable features, such as wolves with their Pack Tactics and trip ability or spiders with their webs and climb speeds.

Tactics: Control and Move. Start combat 60 to 90 feet away from your enemies, preferably hidden. Cast *entangle*, restraining as many foes as possible. Send your minions forward to attack entangled creatures. Then, step into the nearest tree and emerge in a tree closer to the enemy, but behind full cover where they can't see you. On your next turn, use your fey charm on the closest, low-Wisdom target (go for particularly dopey-looking melee attackers who didn't get entangled), and command your new ally to protect you and your allies at all costs. Step back through your tree to a different location, still protected by full cover. Let your charmed minions do the work while you Dodge and wait. If you lose control of any of your minions or one dies, pick new targets to control with your charm.

DUERGAR

CR 1

This bald, long-bearded dwarf has dull gray skin, low arching brows, and eyes that seem to absorb rather than reflect the light.

The dwarves of subterranean realms, duergar, are highly disciplined warriors who come with various bizarre powers and features, making them highly versatile in combat.

Fighting Style: Elite. You have excellent offensive and defensive capabilities, which makes you a capable tank or brute. And your Invisibility allows you to lurk in the dark and surprise your foes, making you a lurker. Also, you have a javelin, which gives you a long range of 120 feet, perfectly complementing your 120 feet of darkvision. You and other duergar can work as a cohesive unit, each filling a different role.

Set-up: Dark Areas. As an elite, you can fight in any environment so long as it's dark. Your 120 feet of darkvision allows you to see most of your enemies before they can see you, granting advantage on your attack rolls thanks to the unseen attacker rule.

Weaknesses: Sunlight. Relatively strong for a CR 1 creature, your only real weakness is sunlight, which imposes disadvantage on attack rolls and Wisdom (Perception) checks that rely on sight.

Pair With Controller. Although you are a highly versatile fighter, the one thing you lack is the ability to control your foes. Team up with other creatures who can restrain, charm, blind, etc., your foes, granting you advantage on attack rolls against them.

Tactics: Surprise and Organize. Start combat enlarged 60 to 120 feet away from your enemies. Before your enemies come within 60 feet of you, throw your oversized javelins at them. If they can't see you because of darkvision disparity, the advantage given by the unseen attacker rules overrules the disadvantage of fighting at long distances. Continue to use ranged attacks until the enemy gets within 25 feet of you. Then, switch to melee tactics with a portion of the duergar in your group (assuming that you're fighting in a group) taking the role of brute while the rest play the role of tanks. Use Invisibility to flank or escape.

ELEMENTAL, AIR

 **CR 5**

This cloud-like creature has dark hollows reminiscent of eyes and a mouth, and a howling wind whips it into ominous shapes.

Air elementals are fast, flying creatures made of living air. Primitive and territorial, they resent being summoned or doing the bidding of mortals and much prefer to spend their time on the Plane of Air, swooping and racing through the endless skies.

Fighting Style: Skirmisher. You have a flying speed of 90 feet and a wide range of defensive capabilities, allowing you to make quick attacks and escape without fear of reprisal.

Set-up: Open Spaces. You're a flier, so you need lots of room to move. Areas with difficult terrain will slow your foes but not you.

Weaknesses: Magic. You are naturally resistant to most attacks, but spells and magic weapons harm you and put you at risk for charmed or frightened conditions. You're probably not smart enough to recognize spellcasters immediately, but as soon as they start casting, go after them.

Pair With Tanks. Use tanks to distract your foes while you employ hit-and-run tactics. Controllers are also helpful to help give you advantage on attack rolls.

Tactics: Hit-and-Run. Start combat 45 feet away from your enemies in the air. On your first turn, move into the same space of as many creatures as you can. Then, use your Whirlwind attack. Immediately leave the area. Remember, a few attacks of opportunity are better than having mid-tier melee attackers get their full array of attacks against you. If your whirlwind recharges, repeat these tactics. Otherwise, keep your distance, Dodging as you do. Don't forget to target any casters capable of hurting you.

ELEMENTAL, EARTH

 **CR 5**

This hulking, roughly humanoid creature of dirt and stone explodes up from the earth, faceless save for two glowing gemstone eyes.

Earth elementals are plodding, stubborn creatures made of living stone or earth. Despite their lumbering appearance, their features make them surprisingly dangerous ambushers.

Fighting Style: Lurker. While your AC, hit points, and attacks might suggest tank or brute, you perform best as a lurker. Your earth glide feature allows you to slip away after you make attacks, repositioning yourself as you go.

Set-up: Earthen Terrain. Your earth glide allows you to move through nonmagical unworked earth and stone. Make sure there's plenty of it around so you can capitalize on this feature.

Weaknesses: Magic. You are naturally resistant to most attacks, but spells and magic weapons harm you and put you at risk for charmed or frightened conditions. You're probably not smart enough to recognize spellcasters immediately, but as soon as they start casting, go after them.

Pair With Controllers. Use controllers to help you gain advantage on attacks against your enemies. Plus, your tremorsense functions even when you can't see, so magical darkness is your friend.

Tactics: Lurk, Then Attack. Start combat at least 10 feet underground, using your tremorsense to detect potential targets. Emerge on your turn and attack with your Multiattack. Then, dip back into the earth using your earth guide feature. Don't worry about attacks of opportunity, as one attack of opportunity is always preferable to the enemies' full range of attacks. Reposition yourself and perform these tactics again. Beware of controllers and grapplers, as they'll quickly end these tactics.

ELEMENTAL, FIRE

CR 5

This creature looks like a living, mobile bonfire, with tongues of flame reaching out in search of things to burn.

Fire elementals are quick, cruel creatures of living flame. They enjoy frightening beings weaker than themselves and terrorizing any creature they can set on fire.

Fighting Style: Brute. You are one of the few creatures capable of dealing passive damage simply by moving. Toss in a couple of touch attacks—which also sets targets on fire—and you can inflict a lot of damage quickly.

Set-up: Up Close and Personal. You love nothing more than setting things on fire. The closer your targets are, the better.

Weaknesses: Magic. You are naturally resistant to most attacks, but spells and magic weapons harm you and put you at risk for charmed or frightened conditions. You're probably not smart enough to recognize spellcasters immediately, but as soon as they start casting, go after them. However, you will recognize water and know better than to go near it.

Pair With Artillerists. When you're on the field, all your flammable enemies are focused on getting rid of you; this gives artillerists the perfect opportunity to attack without fear of reprisal. Skirmishers wouldn't dare come near you, fearful they might catch on fire, too.

Tactics: Set Everything on Fire. Start combat within 40 to 50 feet of your enemies. When your turn begins, charge the enemy and move through their spaces, setting as many of them on fire as possible with your Fire Form. Then, make two touch attacks against whatever targets look the most flammable (that fellow on the robes looks like he'd make a pretty bonfire). Continue this until your enemies are ash or you're destroyed.

ELEMENTAL, WATER

CR 5

This translucent creature's shape shifts between a spinning column of water and a crashing wave.

Water elementals are patient, relentless creatures made of living fresh or salt water.

Fighting Style: Controller. Your most devastating attack is your Whelm, which allows you to grapple targets that fail Strength saving throws automatically. While grappling targets, you damage each target at the start of your turn. As a Large creature, you can hold up to four such creatures simultaneously. Whelm is an excellent tool for splitting up the enemy.

Set-up: Dark Water. Your swim speed is three times that of your walking speed; ensure you always fight in or near water. Even while grappling creatures, you can move 45 feet per turn. And with darkvision out to 60 feet, it doesn't hurt to fight with the lights out.

Weaknesses: Magic. You are naturally resistant to most attacks, but spells and magic weapons both harm you and put you at risk for charmed or frightened conditions. You're probably not smart enough to recognize spellcasters immediately, but as soon as they start casting, go after them, especially if they use cold magic.

Pair With Minions. Use minions to distract targets and slow down pursuers after you grapple targets. Just make sure you don't Whelm them, too.

Tactics: Grab and Dash. Start combat in water within 45 feet of your targets. On your turn, enter the spaces of as many enemies as possible and use your Whelm. If you successfully grapple one or two targets, use the rest of your movement to flee with them in your grasp. So long as these targets remain in your Whelm, use your Multiattack against them. If the creatures in your grasp escape—or die—target another group of creatures with another Whelm attack, repeating the above-mentioned tactics.

ELF, DROW

 **CR 1/4**

This dark-skinned elf stands in a battle-ready pose, her hair silver and eyes white and pupilless.

The elves of the subterranean realms, drow, are highly-disciplined fighters who use their dark, spider-ridden environments to their advantage.

Fighting Style: Artillerist. Although your hand crossbow has a relatively short range, you have darkvision out to 120 feet, which means you can often see your enemies while they can't see you.

Set-up: Dark Areas with Lots of Cover. You want to put at least 60 feet of distance between your enemies and you and ensure that the area is dark so you can benefit from your 120 feet of darkvision. Make sure there are places to take cover between shots, making it harder for your enemy to retaliate.

Weaknesses: Being Seen. So much of your tactics rely on your ability to stay hidden in the dark. Enemies with darkvision ranges equal to or greater than your own pose a threat as you lose your primary combat advantage.\

Pair With Brutes or Controllers. Use melee attackers to distract your enemies while you pick them off from a distance. Alternatively, use controllers like giant spiders (or web hazards in general) to restrain your targets, giving you even more chances at making attacks with advantage.

Tactics: Fire from the Dark. Start combat 60 to 120 feet away from your targets behind cover. Fire from the darkness at the targets that can't see you; you will have advantage on the attack, canceling out the disadvantage warranted by your weapon's long range. If your foes can see you, use your *faerie fire* spell to light them up, granting you a different method to get advantage. Take cover or drop prone between each of your shots to prevent the other side's artillerists from firing at you.

Drow Elite Warrior. The boost in defense and damage output better suits drow elite warriors as tanks or brutes, relying on their hand crossbow only in exceptional circumstances. These drow Dodge or inflict damage while the rank-and-file drow serve as artillerists.

Drow Mage. Drow mages are elites that function best as lurkers or controllers. If you use your drow mage as a lurker, use *greater invisibility* to set up devastating castings of *lightning bolt*. And if you act as a controller, disable as many enemies as possible with your *black tentacles, cloudkill,* or *web* spells. Finally, disrupt the concentration of enemy spellcasters with your *magic missile* or *ray of frost*.

Drow Priestess. These drow come equipped with controller and support spells. Before combat begins, protect yourself and your essential allies with *protection from poison* and *freedom of movement*; neither of these spells requires concentration. When combat starts, open with *web, faerie fire,* or *insect plague*. Alternatively, *conjure animals* or summon a demon. After you've cast your concentration spell or effect, switch to support spells to boost your allies.

ETTERCAP

CR 2

This hideous purple creature walks upright like a man, but its face is that of a spider, and its hands are sickle-shaped claws.

Ettercaps are often solitary creatures who rely on traps they set to catch their prey.

Fighting Style: Lurker. Your defensive capabilities are relatively poor for a CR 2 creature, so you're better equipped to grab and dash with targets.

Set-up: Dark Areas with Lots of Webs. As a lurker, you want to hide in areas that hinder your prey and give you a comfortable place to hide. Make sure there are vertical passages into which you can escape after you grab a target.

Weaknesses: Squishy. You only have 44 hit points, an AC of 13, and no resistances or immunities. Evenly matched targets will make quick work of you if you allow them. Keep your distance and only target weak-looking targets.

Pair With Brutes or Minions. Use melee attackers like brutes and minions to distract your prey's allies while you escape with them into vertical passages. Controllers that can restrain your foes are also valuable to your group.

Tactics: Grab and Dash. Start combat hidden. When a weak-looking target comes by (those that aren't wearing metal are usually the weakest, in your experience), emerge and attack with your Web or Web Garrote (if using that variant). Once the target is restrained, drag it upward into a vertical passage where its allies can't reach you. If you fail to capture a target or can't escape the pursuers, abandon your quarry and flee to a safe place.

ETTIN

CR 4

This lumbering, filthy, two-headed giant wears tattered stripes of clothing and clutches a battleaxe in one fist and a morningstar in the other.

Ettins, or two-headed giants, are vicious and unpredictable hunters that stalk the night. Their two heads give them unparalleled powers of perception, making them excellent guards.

Fighting Style: Brute. Although you don't have much in the way of AC, the damage dealt by your dual weapons causes considerable damage that will keep your enemies preoccupied.

Set-up: Up Close and Personal. You want to get into combat as swiftly as possible so you can bash them with your battleaxe and morningstar, which is excellent because you're not intelligent enough to employ other tactics.

Weaknesses: Poor AC. Your natural armor provides very little resistance to attacks. Just hope that you manage to kill your targets before they kill you.

Pair With Artillerists and Skirmishers. As the most significant damage dealer on the battlefield, you'll keep your enemies busy while your companions fire from a distance or employ hit-and-run tactics.

Tactics: Bash, Bash, Bash. Start combat within 40 feet of your targets. Move toward the nearest enemy and hit it with your weapons until it stops moving. Then, pick a new target. Repeat.

FAERIE DRAGON

 CR 1-2

A pair of brightly colored butterfly wings sprouts from the back of this miniature dragon.

Faerie dragons are whimsical, playful pranksters that spend most of their time relaxing in cool forest glades or engaging in some sort of prank.

Fighting Style: Controller. You come with various spells and features that give you control over targets, leveling the playing field for your allies.

Set-up: Lots of Distractions. Thanks to your ability to remain invisible—even while casting spells and making attacks—you're a lurker and controller. However, the last thing you want is to get targeted by an area-of-effect spell that will make quick work of your 15 measly hit points. Make sure your targets are distracted before you try to join the fray.

Weaknesses: Squishy. You are fast and can fly, but you only have 14 hit points. It won't take much to put you down. Make sure to stay invisible as often as possible and stay far away from your targets.

Pair With Brutes or Minions. Use brutes and minions to deal damage on your behalf while you flitter about, confusing your targets with your breath. weapon

Tactics: Lurk, Then Breathe. Start combat invisible within 30 feet of your targets. If you have the *color spray* spell, use it, as it has the potential to affect more creatures and doesn't break your concentration. Otherwise, use your breath weapon to confuse a single target at a time. Then, move 30 feet away and take full cover if possible to avoid area-of-effect spells. On your next turn, if your breath weapon recharges, repeat these tactics. Otherwise, take the Dodge or Hide action until your breath weapon recharges.

FLUMPH

CR 1/8

This pale, jellyfish-like creature floats gently in the air, two long eyestalks extending from either side of its puckered mouth.

Come from distant stars to protect unprepared worlds from cosmic horrors, flumphs are jellyfish-like creatures that float in the air and hunt with acidic spikes growing from their undersides.

Fighting Style: Controller. Your Stench Spray coats your enemies in a foul-smelling liquid that poisons them for 1 to 4 hours. Plus, any creature within 5 feet of the coated creature is also poisoned; no saving throw is allowed. Unfortunately, you can only use this powerful feature once per day.

Set-up: Easy Escape Routes. You have a flying speed of 15 feet, and you're relatively weak; as soon as you use your tendrils or Stench Spray, you want to escape somewhere your enemies can't reach.

Weaknesses: Squishy. You are laughably weak and can actually get knocked upside-down if someone knocks you prone. Make sure to keep plenty of distance between yourself and your targets.

Pair With Brutes or Minions. Once you use your Stench Spray or tendrils, you want your allies to distract your enemies while you fly away, occasionally sneaking back to make attacks with your tendrils.

Tactics: Spray, Then Flee. Start combat 15 feet away from your enemies in the air. When it's your turn, hit as many creatures as possible with your Stench Spray, then fly out of their reach—be careful not to incur attacks of opportunity. When you see an enemy burn its reaction, use that opportunity to move to it, hit it with your tendrils, and escape without suffering an attack of opportunity.

FUNGUS, VIOLET

This mushroom grows from a bed of tentacular roots. Deep violet tendrils slither out of the dozens of fissures in its pointed cap.

Violet fungi are fearsome ambulatory plants that leave horrific scars on the few who survive their rotting touch.

Fighting Style: Minion. Barely sentient and painfully slow-moving, other creatures use you as a hazard capable of distracting enemies. And you don't care—you're not smart enough to care.

Set-up: Spread Out in Total Darkness. You aren't smart enough to chase targets or employ tactics. However, you grow and root in areas where you're likely to find food without fighting other violet fungi. Put at least 15 feet of distance between yourself and other fungi. Although you don't know, this also helps you minimize the risk of area-of-effect attacks while simultaneously threatening more territory. You also have blindsight, allowing you to fight in areas of total darkness.

Weaknesses: Slow and Barely Sentient. Your Intelligence score is 1, and your Charisma score is 1. You aren't even aware that you exist. Plus, you only move 5 feet on a turn, 10 if you dash. Just stay still and hope something tasty comes your way.

Pair With Artillerists. You'll keep the enemy distracted while artillerists—who you're probably not even aware of—fire from the safety of cover. Not that you can tell friends from foe anyways. You also work well with darkmantles, whose darkness aura won't impede your vision, making it easier for you to hit targets with your Rotting Touch.

Tactics: Attack Whatever Comes Near. Start combat 15 feet away from other violet fungi in the area. When a target comes within reach, use your Rotting Touch against them. Make attacks of opportunity against any targets that try to sneak past you.

GARGOYLE

CR 2

Seemingly carved from a dark gray stone, this sinister crouching humanoid resembles a horned, winged demon.

Gargoyles are dreadful, winged creatures from the elemental plane of earth. They gleefully serve as tormenters and kidnappers for their dark masters.

Fighting Style: Skirmisher. You have a flying speed of 60 feet and plenty of natural resistances, which make you perfect for carrying out hit-and-run attacks.

Set-up: Wide Open Spaces with Statues. Your False Appearance gives you the perfect camouflage for areas where statues are common, like cemeteries, gothic cathedrals, and the roofs of city buildings. You want plenty of room to maneuver so you can escape after your attack.

Weaknesses: Magic. You have damage resistance against most nonmagical attacks, making you a formidable opponent against unprepared enemies. However, foes armed with magic or adamantine weapons and spellcasters will have no trouble penetrating your rocky hide.

Pair With Minions. Keep your enemies distracted with plenty of minions. Just make sure to space them apart, so they don't get wiped out with a quick area-of-effect spell.

Tactics: Surprise, Then Hit-and-Run. Start combat within 30 feet of your enemies in your motionless/statue state. Surprise the enemy, then swoop down into range and hit them with your multiattack. Quickly escape before their allies can attack you, ducking behind cover if possible. Remember: one attack of opportunity made against you is always preferable to having multiple enemies hitting you with their weapons and spells.

GENIE, DJINNI

 **CR 11**

This creature stands nearly twice as tall as a human, although its lower torso trails away into a vortex of mist and wind.

Djinn are the genies of air. They are often servants, believing it is their fate to be commanded by others, although they don't necessarily enjoy it.

Fighting Style: Controller. Your most potent spell action option allows you to create a massive whirlwind that can dispose of enemies with poor Strength saving throws—so basically, an entire backline. This tactic leaves only strong melee attackers to contend with, who you can easily vanquish using hit-and-run tactics.

Set-up: Wide Open Spaces. You have a flying speed of 90 feet, and your whirlwind remains as long as you can see it. You want to fight your enemies out in the open whenever possible.

Weaknesses: Weak Relative to CR. Your offensive and defensive capabilities are relatively weak compared to other CR 11 monsters (including other genies). If you engage enemies equal to your challenge (such as 11th-level characters), the enemy will quickly destroy you unless you keep your distance and use your Create Whirlwind to divide the group.

Pair With Minions. Keep your enemies distracted with plenty of minions. Just make sure to space them apart, so they don't get wiped out with a quick area-of-effect spell.

Tactics: Divide and Skirmish. Start combat invisible 120 feet away from your enemies in the air. On your turn, use Create Whirlwind to trap as many enemies as possible. Likely, a few will escape, but you should catch enough to make things even. If you fail to catch any the first time, move the whirlwind to catch more. Otherwise, send the restrained target as far away as possible. Once you have the enemies divided, start making hit-and-run attacks. Move 45 feet toward an enemy, hit it three times with your scimitar, then retreat to the sky. Don't worry about attacks of opportunity, as getting hit once by a single attack is preferable to getting hit multiple times by multiple targets. Continue to move the whirlwind every turn so long as you can see it.

GENIE, EFREETI

This muscular giant has crimson skin, smoldering eyes, and small black horns. Smoke rises in curls from its flesh.

Efreetis are the polar opposites of djinn. Spiteful, hateful, and determined to enslave anyone they can, they're the tyrannical rulers of the Elemental Plane of Fire.

Fighting Style: Artillerist. You come equipped with Hurl Flame, which you can use twice with your multiattack. It lets you keep plenty of distance between yourself and your enemy. You also have the *wall of fire* spell, which can further slow down pests.

Set-up: Dark Places with Clear Lines of Sight. You want to fight in a dark place where your 120 feet of darkvision will give you an advantage over creatures with a darkvision range of only 60 feet. Ideally, this place shouldn't have a ton of cover, giving you a clear view of your targets. Fire hazards are a plus since you're immune, and most enemies won't be.

Weaknesses: Dexterity Saving Throws. You're strong, tough, and have excellent mental saving throws; however, you only have a +1 to Dexterity saving throws. This poor modifier leaves you a sitting duck for many spells and magical effects.

Pair With Brutes and Minions. Use brutes and minions to keep your enemies occupied. So long as you can keep your distance from the enemy and they can't see you in the dark, conjure a fire elemental to keep them preoccupied.

Tactics: Keep Your Distance. Start combat 60 to 120 feet away from your enemies, behind cover, or invisible if possible. Cast *wall of fire* to section off melee attackers from ranged attackers and spellcasters. On your next turn, maintain concentration and use Hurl Flame to hit foes on the side of the wall facing you. If you lose your *wall of fire*, conjure a fire elemental to keep your foes distracted while you continue to Hurl Flames. Move frequently so ranged attackers can't pinpoint your position.

GENIE, MARID

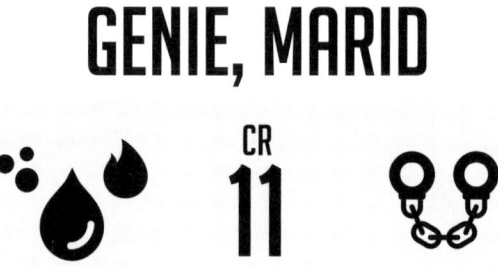

This being resembles a mighty giant with hairless blue-green skin, deep blue eyes, striking eyebrows, and pearlescent teeth.

Marids are chaotic genies from the elemental plane of water. They believe all creatures—including other genies—to be inferior.

Fighting Style: Controller. You come with various spells and actions that let you control the enemy on the battlefield, setting up your minions for success.

Set-up: Near Water. You have a swim speed of 90 feet and can *control water*. While you can still fight well outside of water—you can fly 60 feet, too—the faster you can move, the better.

Weaknesses: Dexterous Foes. Your jet attack relies on Dexterity saving throws, which is excellent against heavily armored and/or slow-moving foes. However, it doesn't help against Dexterous foes, particularly those with evasion. Utilize your *control water* spell against these targets as it forces a Strength saving throw.

Pair With Minions. Your ability to control the battlefield and your enemies give your allies considerable advantage against your enemies. Since you will probably fight in or near water, use those with swim speeds and can breathe underwater.

Tactics: Divide and Conquer. Start combat invisible in water 60 feet or more away from your enemies. At the start of combat, use your control water spell to restrain as many targets as possible, specifically targeting those with poor Strength saving throws and high Dexterity saving throws (you're wise enough to know who's who). Use your jet attack to target as many creatures as possible while maintaining your concentration on your whirlpool. Once you remove the stronger targets from the battlefield, use *fog cloud* to blind the previously restrained targets. You have blindsight out to 30 feet so you can move through *fog cloud* unhindered. Make hit-and-run attacks against targets. Careful of those who have blindsight, too (like high-level rogues).

GHAST

 CR 2

This humanoid creature has long, sharp teeth, and its pallid flesh is stretched tightly over its starved frame.

Ghasts are ghouls with more ties to the abyssal plane, making them a little more cunning than ordinary ghouls.

Fighting Style: Brute. Your claw attack averages 10 damage per hit and can stun targets with weak Constitution scores. Plus, your Stench will poison targets until they succeed in a saving throw against it. Your enemies will try to get rid of you quickly.

Set-up: Close and Personal. You want to start combat as close as possible to your targets so you can quickly affect them with your Stench and paralyze them with your claws.

Weaknesses: Relatively Squishy. You only have an AC of 13 and 36 hit points, despite being a CR 2 monster. Fortunately, your Stench makes it harder for enemies to hit you. Make sure to attack hard and fast and surprise the enemy whenever possible.

Pair With Artillerists and Controllers. Enemies will be preoccupied with trying to remove you from the battlefield, allowing your artillerist allies to attack without fear of reprisal. Consider working alongside controllers, too, who can give you advantage on your attack rolls, making it easier to deal damage and paralyze.

Tactics: Dash and Slash. Start combat within 30 feet of your enemies. On your turn, get as close as possible to as many targets as possible, so they all have to make saving throws against your Stench. Attack weaker-looking targets (i.e., the ones that aren't wearing heavy armor or the big buff barbarian), hoping to paralyze them. If you successfully paralyze a target, your desire to eat flesh will force you to use your bite against them. It looks like meat's back on the menu, boys!

GHOST

CR 4

This spectral, horrifying figure glides silently through the air, passing through solid objects as if they didn't exist.

Ghosts come in various shapes, sizes, and situations. Some might be benevolent spirits that aren't even aware they're dead. Others are hateful apparitions determined to make the living hurt.

Fighting Style: Lurker. You have a flying speed of 40 feet, the Incorporeal Movement trait, and can flee to the Ethereal Plane if necessary. These traits are the perfect combination of lurker features.

Set-up: Spooky, Dark Buildings. Your incorporeality functions best when you have lots of full cover to phase through and hide behind.

Weaknesses: Magic Weapons. As an incorporeal creature, you are resistant or immune to most forms of damage. However, melee attackers armed with magic weapons and spellcasters with force and radiant damage spells won't take long to blast their way through your 45 hit points. Don't get hit!

Pair With Brutes and Minions. As a lurker, you want to keep your enemy distracted while you make your smash-and-dash attacks. Consider working alongside ghouls, ghasts, skeletons, or zombies.

Tactics: Emerge, Attack, Vanish. Start combat behind full cover, such as behind the wall in another room. When the targets come within 10 to 20 feet of you, phase through the cover and use your Horrifying Visage to terrify as many as possible (and potentially age them a few decades). Then fly back through the cover, taking cover. While the enemies try to catch up to you, find another hiding place. Then, strike again with your Possession feature or Withering Touch when the moment is right. Once more, slip through a wall, ceiling, or floor to take cover. Continue these tactics until someone deals serious damage to you or uses turn undead. Immediately go ethereal when this happens.

GHOUL

 CR 1

This humanoid creature has long, sharp teeth, and its pallid flesh is stretched tightly over its starved frame.

Ghouls are corporeal undead that are marginally more intelligent than zombies. They live (or unlive?) to eat flesh.

Fighting Style: Minion. Relatively weak for a CR 1 monster and armed with mediocre attacks, you serve more as a distraction than you make a credible threat, especially for higher-level opponents. However, enemies who fail to remove you from the battlefield quickly might soon find themselves paralyzed while you eat their face.

Set-up: Up Close and Personal. You want to get into combat as soon as possible so you can start paralyzing and biting. Space yourself at least 10 feet away from the other minions to reduce the risk of area-of-effect spells and to threaten a larger area.

Weaknesses: Relatively Squishy. You only have AC 12 and 22 hit points, which puts you on par with CR 1/8 creatures. Make sure you strike hard and fast, paralyzing whoever you can before they have a chance to retaliate.

Pair With Artillerists and Controllers. Enemies will be preoccupied with trying to remove you from the battlefield, allowing your artillerist allies to attack without fear of reprisal. Consider working alongside controllers, too, who can give you advantage on your attack rolls, making it easier to deal damage and paralyze.

Tactics: Dash and Slash. Start combat within 30 feet of your enemies. On your turn, charge the nearest target (you're probably not smart enough to be picky) and start slashing it, hoping you can paralyze them. Once you paralyze a target, your desire to eat living flesh overpowers your tactical sense, and you switch to your bite.

GIANT EAGLE

 CR 1

This giant eagle stands about 15 feet tall, has a wingspan of approximately 30 feet and resembles its smaller cousins in nearly every way except size.

With higher Intelligence and Charisma scores and the ability to speak their own language, giant eagles stand apart from other beasts.

Fighting Style: Skirmisher. You have a flying speed of 80 feet, so you're perfectly equipped to make hit-and-run attacks.

Set-up: Lots of Open Space. As a flier, you need open skies or high ceilings to withdraw into after you make your attacks.

Weaknesses: Squishy. You have relatively low AC and hit points for a CR 1 creature. Make sure to keep plenty of distance between yourself and your enemies.

Pair With Brutes, Minions, or Tanks. Use allies that rely on melee attacks to keep your enemies preoccupied while you stick to the skies.

Tactics: Hit-and-Run. Start combat 40 feet away from your targets. On your turn, fly close and make two attacks with your Multiattack. Then, retreat 40 feet back into the air. Don't worry about attacks of opportunity—getting hit once with an attack of opportunity is better than getting hit multiple times on the enemies' turns.

GIANT ELK

 CR 2

This massive elk is roughly 10-12 feet long, and its antlers span 10 feet or more.

Like giant eagles and vultures, giant elk stand apart from other beasts thanks to their higher-than-usual Intelligence and Charisma scores and ability to speak their own language.

Fighting Style: Skirmisher. You have a charge attack which lets you deal extra damage and knock targets prone. Your ram attack also has a 10-foot reach, which means you can make the attack and (usually) escape without suffering from attacks of opportunity.

Set-up: Room to Charge. You need at least 20 feet to charge a target and hit it with your ram attack to knock it down. Make sure there's room to move without any obstructions.

Weaknesses: Relatively Squishy. You have relatively low defensive capabilities for a CR 2 monster, so you must keep out of reach of attackers, employing hit-and-run tactics.

Pair With Brutes and Minions. Your charge attack makes you a pseudo-controller, knocking targets prone when they fail their saving throw against it; this allows your companions to make attacks with advantage against the downed target. Plus, they'll keep the enemy distracted while you make hit-and-run attacks.

Tactics: Hit-and-Run. Start combat 20 to 40 feet away from your target. On your turn, move in a straight line to your target and hit it with your ram. If you knock the target prone, make sure any minions present grapple the target (to keep it prone). Move back 20 feet and select a new target to charge on your next turn. Alternatively, if your last victim doesn't stand, return and use your hooves against it.

GIANT SPIDER

 CR 1

A spider, the size of a horse, crawls silently from the depths of its funnel-shaped web.

Although they are beasts of low Intelligence, giant spiders deserve a call out due to their unique build and frequent appearances in underground-themed adventures.

Fighting Style: Lurker. Giant spiders have Stealth +7, climb speeds, and the ability to create webs. They set up traps with their webs, then wait to attack, doing so quickly.

Set-up: Lots of Webs. Your Web Sense and Web Walker features demand you lair in dark caverns covered in webs. Employ many vertical shafts to escape into after wrapping your prey up in your webs.

Weaknesses: Relatively Squishy. You have an AC of 14 and 26 hit points, which makes you relatively easy to kill for a CR 1 monster. Make sure to use Stealth and speed to capture and subdue foes before they have a chance to reciprocate.

Pair With Brutes or Minions. Use allies to distract your enemies while you sneak up behind them. Try to use brutes or minions who don't suffer from your webs, such as swarms of spiders or giant wolf spiders.

Tactics: Grab and Dash. Start combat hidden within your webbed nest. When a target comes within 15 feet of you, use your web to restrain and grapple it. Try to grab Small or smaller targets since they don't hinder your movement when you carry them. After webbing your foe, carry it away further into your nest, ideally into a vertical shaft or similar hard-to-read area. Bite your prey as you go, potentially poisoning and paralyzing it.

GIANT VULTURE

 CR 1

A wickedly hooked beak and an immense bald head draw attention from this enormous scavenger's vast wingspan.

Giant vultures are somewhat intelligent evil creatures capable of understanding the Common language, setting them apart from other beasts. They are vicious creatures who enjoy tormenting wounded creatures.

Fighting Style: Skirmisher. You have a flying speed of 60 feet and are relatively squishy, meaning you must employ hit-and-run tactics.

Set-up: Open Skies. You're a flier, so make sure you have plenty of space to move around above your enemies and out of their reach.

Weaknesses: Fighting Alone. As a creature with Pack Tactics, you benefit from having others assist you in combat. If you can't team up with allies, look for targets engaged in combat with brutes or minions.

Pair With Brutes and Minions. You have Pack Tactics, which gives you advantage on attack rolls made against targets within 5 feet of an ally. While more giant vultures might seem like the perfect combination, it means at least one of you will have to stay near the target. Therefore, teaming up with ground-based brutes or minions is your best bet.

Tactics: Hit-and-Run. Start combat 30 feet away from your enemies in the air. If fighting alongside ground-based creatures, wait until those creatures get within 5 feet of your enemy before you move and attack. Otherwise, move 30 feet toward your enemy, attack it with your Multiattack, then return to the sky.

GIANT, CLOUD

 **CR 9**

This towering giant has finely chiseled features. Her skin is pale and smooth, and her long wispy hair flutters like a breeze.

Cloud giants are the wealthiest of all the 'true" giants, accustomed to living in breathtaking palaces built into the clouds far above. They're also the trickster giants; good cloud giants love to use their sly wit and silver tongue to negotiate, while evil cloud giants turn towards deceit and vicious pranks.

Fighting Style: Controller. You have a variety of spells that allow you to control the battlefield and your enemies, benefiting your allies.

Set-up: Close… But Not Too Close. You want to be close enough to your enemies to use your controller spells against them (and maybe pop them with a few of your rocks) but not so close that they can chop you down. Consider placing difficult terrain or other obstacles in the way to prevent easy access.

Weaknesses: Low AC. Although you have plenty of hit points and great saving throws, you still only have an AC of 14, which is hardly a challenge for high-level enemies. Keep your distance and watch out for ranged attackers.

Pair With Brutes and Tanks. Use brutes and tanks to keep your enemies preoccupied while you use controller spells and chuck rocks from a safe distance. Allies with blindsight are precious since they can see through your *fog cloud*.

Tactics: Control, Then Throw Rocks. Start combat within 60 feet of your targets. When combat begins, use *telekinesis* to dispose of troublesome artillerists who can target you and make short work of any minions you have with you. Alternatively, use *fog cloud* on the enemies, especially if you're working alongside creatures with blindsight. While holding them, throw rocks at other targets that could reach you.

GIANT, FIRE

 **CR 9**

This lumbering giant has short stumpy legs and powerful, muscular arms. Its hair and beard seem to be made of fire.

Deceptively intelligent, ruthless, and filled with malevolent creativity, fire giants pose a considerable threat to anyone brave—or foolish—enough to go against them.

Fighting Style: Brute. Although your high AC and hit points qualify you as a tank, the considerable damage you deal with your great sword makes you a powerful brute, bound to draw the attention of all enemies on the battlefield.

Set-up: Up Close and Personal. You want to get within 10 feet of your enemies as soon as possible, so make sure there aren't many obstacles. Consider fighting in areas with intense heat, lava, or fire, as you won't suffer from the effects, but your targets might.

Weaknesses: Weak Mental Saving Throws. You have a Wisdom saving throw modifier of +2 and no immunities to the charmed or frightened condition, which leaves you a sitting duck for enchanters. Make sure to rid the battlefield of spellcasters as soon as possible.

Pair With Artillerists and Skirmishers. When you're on the battlefield, all eyes are on you, giving ranged attackers and those who employ hit-and-run tactics the opportunity to make attacks without fear of reprisal.

Tactics: Dash and Slash. Start combat within 35 feet of your foes. Target spellcasters first, moving through Medium and smaller enemies if you must. Use your greatsword to deal as much damage as possible. If fiery hazards are nearby (such as lava pools), consider using your extremely high Athletics score to grapple foes and dunk them.

GIANT, FROST

CR 8

This monstrous giant has pale blue skin and frost-white hair. It wears the furs of multiple animals around its shoulders and back.

Frost giants are the brute northern "true giants" who live a more tribal lifestyle than the other giants of the Ordning. Unlike fire giants and stone giants, who are consummate craftsmen, frost giants believe that giants should make war and not goods.

Fighting Style: Brute. You aren't nearly as durable as fire giants or storm giants, but you still deal considerable damage with your multiattack.

Set-up: Up Close and Personal. You want to reach your targets as soon as possible, so the fewer obstacles, the better. Consider fighting in areas with freezing temperatures and cold hazards, such as blizzards, icy lakes, etc.

Weaknesses: Relatively Squishy. You are a CR 8 creature but have the defensive capabilities of a CR 5 monster. Your damage output balances this out, but unless you're careful, it's easy for enemies to take you down. Strike hard and fast and get rid of the enemy's biggest damage dealers first.

Pair With Lurkers. Keep the enemy distracted while lurkers use the wintery conditions to surprise foes, particularly those capable of dealing much damage to you, like spellcasters and artillerists.

Tactics: Dash and Bash. Start combat within 40 feet of your enemy. When your turn begins, move up and start swinging with your greataxe. If you spot a spellcaster or one particular enemy starts hurting you more than the others, make that one your target.

GIANT, HILL

 **CR 5**

This hunched giant exudes power and a crude, stupid anger, its filthy fur clothing bespeaking a brutish and backwoods lifestyle.

Hill giants are the perhaps the least respected of the true giants, somewhat resembling larger-than-normal ogres. Their insatiable appetites are the stuff of legend.

Fighting Style: Brute. Consumed by neverending hunger and painfully stupid, hill giants are the least respected members of the Ordning. Regardless, they are not a threat to be taken lightly.

Set-up: Up Close and Personal. Although you can chuck rocks, you prefer to bash enemies with your greatclub, which you can do twice on your turn. Fight in areas where there are few obstacles between you and your enemies.

Weaknesses: Dumb. You are less intelligent than most great apes and have inferior Wisdom. Not only does this make you a poor tactician, but it leaves you open for spell attacks. And unfortunately, you're not intelligent or wise enough to recognize spellcasters.

Pair With Artillerists or Skirmishers. Your Huge size and aggressive nature will keep enemies distracted, allowing your allies to make ranged or skirmisher attacks without fear of reprisal.

Tactics: Dash and Bash. Start combat within 40 feet of your enemy. When your turn begins, move up and start swinging with your greatclub. You're hungry, so you might stop fighting as soon as you knock a target unconscious, stuffing it into your bag or pants. However, if enemies continue to attack, you might destroy them just to make them stop.

GIANT, STONE

 **CR 7**

This giant has chiseled, muscular features and a flat, forward-sloping head, looking almost as if it were carved of stone.

Stone giants are graceful athletes and artisans who prefer to be left alone to their own devices. However, they believe that the real world is nothing more than a dream and suffer no qualms about causing harm or other creatures.

Fighting Style: Lurker. You have advantage on Dexterity (Stealth) checks made to hide in rocky terrain. This feature lets you hide and observe foes before deciding whether they're worth attacking. And when you do attack, you usually do so with surprise on your side.

Set-up: Dark Caverns. Your stone camouflage allows you to blend perfectly with your natural surroundings, lending itself to your lurker status. Use darkness to impose disadvantage on your foes' Wisdom (Perception) checks.

Weaknesses: Poor Stealth Skill. Although your stone camouflage is helpful, it's offset by a relatively low Stealth modifier of only +2. Make sure to hide only in dark areas with rocky terrain. Bright lights will help your enemies pinpoint your location, too.

Pair With Brutes, Minions, and Tanks. Use melee attackers to draw attention away from your hiding space so you can surprise your foes. Even a startled swarm of bats serves as a useful distraction.

Tactics: Lurk, Emerge, and Bash. Start combat hidden in a dark, rocky area. You have advantage on the Dexterity (Stealth) check made to hide, and targets relying solely on darkvision with have disadvantage on their Wisdom (Perception) checks to spot you. When a target comes within 15 feet of you, emerge and attack it, bashing it with your club twice.

GIANT, STORM

 **CR 13**

This giant is a towering, muscular human of heroic proportions with bronze skin, dark hair, and sparkling green eyes.

Storm giants prefer to live far removed from mortals, content to spend their long lives meditating on ancient prophecies and strange omens.

Fighting Style: Solo. Despite not having the typical action economy required to fight as a solitary creature, you have a lightning strike attack with a 500-foot range (yes, really) that deals an average of 54 damage per round. So long as you keep plenty of distance between yourself and your attackers and they keep within a few squares of each other, you can hold your own for quite a while. Even if your enemies get within reach, your multiattack deals a whopping 60 damage per turn.

Set-up: Underwater. You have a swim speed of 50 feet and an attack that lets you keep 500 feet away from your enemy. Unless the enemy comes with some good teleportation magic, it's going to be tough to reach you underwater.

Weaknesses: Dimension Door. Your lightning strike attack lets you stay 500 feet away from your enemies. Very few spells or attacks in the game will let your enemy hit you from that distance. However, a *dimension door* can help your enemy move closer to you, making you have to fight melee. Fortunately, you're good at that, too.

Pair With Brutes, Minions, and Tanks. As an artillerist, you perform best while your targets are distracted. Stick a few brutes, minions, or tanks in the way

Tactics: Stay Back and Zap. Start combat 400 to 500 feet away from your enemies. Use your lightning strike attack, targeting a point to hit the most targets possible. If your Lightning Strike recharges on your next turn, use it again. Otherwise, Dodge until it recharges. If the enemies try to catch up to you, swim far enough away that you keep a distance between them. And if they somehow get within your reach, continue to make attacks against those within 10 feet of you while swimming away from them.

GIBBERING MOUTHER

 **CR 2**

This horrid mass of eyes, mouths, and formless flesh stares in all directions, its countless maws yammering ceaselessly.

Like something out of a Lovecraft novel, gibbering mouthers are dangerous amoeboid creatures borne of failed magical experiments, exposure to chaotic planes, and other horrific situations. Parties unprepared to face them will quickly suffer from their devastating controller attacks and gruesome bites.

Fighting Style: Controller. Although most people wouldn't guess it by looking at you, you can control the battlefield through your passive effects and your blinding spittle. And if your foes are foolish enough to get close to you, your bite deals a ton of damage and knocks targets prone, too.

Set-up: Claustrophobic Areas. Place yourself in an area where targets will find it hard to avoid you, such as small chambers, narrow corridors, or areas flanked by deadly hazards or obstacles.

Weaknesses: Poor AC. You have no natural armor and a low AC, which means enemy artillerists will focus on removing you; which isn't necessarily bad for your allies.

Pair With Artillerists. Smart artillerists will train you to stand in the way while they hide behind you, using your controller features to prevent melee attackers from reaching them. Plus, your presence will tie up other artillerists who'll be anxious to remove you from the battlefield.

Tactics: Stand and Deliver. Start combat in the middle of a tight space, so it's impossible to maneuver around you. Ready your blinding spittle to hit any target that comes within 15 feet of you. Arguably, you aren't smart enough to take the Dodge action, so when you don't have blinding spittle ready, move closer to the enemy to continue pushing them backward. Bite anything that comes near.

GLADIATOR

CR 5

Gladiators represent mid-tier fighters (approximately level 7 or 8) with various features that allow them to keep enemies occupied for extended periods.

Fighting Style: Elite. Your attacks and features allow you to cover a broad spectrum of fighting styles. Your AC and Parry make you a tank, while your Brute and Multiattack features make you a brute (go figure). You also have a spear for ranged attacks and can even control enemies with your Shield Bash.

Set-up: Close and Personal. Although you can take on the artillerist role, you're ultimately built for close combat. Make sure to position yourself so that you're in between the enemy and your allies.

Weaknesses: Wisdom Saving Throws. Although you have advantage on saving throws against being frightened, your relatively poor Wisdom modifier leaves you vulnerable to other forms of enchantment magic, particularly charm effects. Make sure to remove these spellcasters from the battlefield as fast as possible.

Pair With Artillerists, Lurkers, or Skirmishers. As one of the most versatile fighters on the battlefield, you'll keep your enemies distracted. These tactics allow artillerists to make ranged attacks and lurkers and skirmishers to surprise foes with hit-and-run attacks without fear of reprisal.

Tactics: Dash and Bash. Start combat within 30 feet of your enemy. On your turn, move towards our primary target (spellcasters if you can tell who they are) and use your multiattack. Shield Bash until you successfully knock them down, then switch to your spear attack. Save your Parry against targets that deal heavy damage with melee weapon attacks, such as paladins and barbarians. If the enemy surrounds you and you have allies working alongside you, switch to Dodge to tank and tie up the enemies while your companions strike.

GNOLL

 CR 1/2

Hunched and feral, this furred, hyena-headed humanoid stands slightly taller than the average human.

Gnolls are vicious, ravenous creatures of limited intelligence who delight in eating their foes while they're still alive. They should strike fear in the hearts of their enemies.

Fighting Style: Minion. Although you have many attacks and features, you're too chaotic and unintelligent to use competent tactics. Your longbow only serves to slow enemies down, as you prefer getting up close and hitting with your spear or bite attack.

Set-up: Up Close and Personal. The faster you can get to your enemy and knock them down, the sooner you get to eat their face.

Weaknesses: Unintelligent. You have poor Intelligence, Wisdom, and Charisma scores, which leaves you wide open for spell attacks. Plus, your unpredictable nature keeps you from utilizing sound fighting maneuvers.

Pair With Controllers. With only a +4 to hit targets with your melee attacks and a +3 with your ranged attacks, work alongside controllers who can help you make attacks with advantage against your foes.

Tactics: Dash and Stab. Start combat within 30 feet of your targets. Use your bow if you can't reach them in the first round. Otherwise, ditch the bow for your spear and shield, move towards the enemy, and hit with your spear. You might even ditch the shield to use your spear with two hands. As soon as you knock an enemy to 0, use Rampage to go after the next nearest target.

Gnoll Fang. Gnoll fangs are fiendish gnolls who serve as brute fighters, thanks to their Multiattack and venomous bite. Use them to keep the enemy distracted.

Gnoll Pack Lord. Pack lords are marginally stronger gnolls with a feature that allows them to incite the Rampage feature in other gnolls, making them support. The pack lords are smart enough to stay 30 feet away from their allies, using the rampage-inciting feature whenever possible, then deferring to their bow while it recharges.

GNOME, DEEP

CR 1/2

This bald gnome has rocky gray skin and a wiry physique. Its pale eyes are overly large and expressive.

Also called "Svirfneblin," deep gnomes are subterranean humanoids who act as gemstone harvesters and friends of earth elementals.

Fighting Style: Lurker. You have Stone Camouflage, Stealth +4, and *nondetection*, which you can cast at will. You attack from hiding and escape before the enemy can reciprocate.

Set-up: Dark Places with Lots of Cover. You have darkvision 120 feet and a ranged weapon, meaning you want to fight in dark places with enough obstacles to hide behind and take cover.

Weaknesses: Slow. You have a plodding movement speed of 20 feet, which means it isn't easy for you to escape. Make sure you remain hidden and far out of reach so enemies can't catch you.

Pair With Brutes, Minions, and Controllers. Work alongside melee attackers to keep foes distracted while you toss darts from hiding. And use controllers to restrain, blind, etc., your foes, giving you advantage on our attack rolls.

Tactics: Toss Darts From the Dark. Start combat 60 to 120 feet away, outside the enemy's darkvision range, if possible. Make sure to hide behind cover and have escape routes planned. Toss a dart at a target. Although it's outside your normal range, you won't make your attack with disadvantage so long as you can see your foes, but they can't see you, thanks to the darkvision disparity.

GOBLIN

CR 1/4

This creature stands barely three feet tall, its scrawny, humanoid body dwarfed by its broad, ungainly head.

Stubborn and foul-tempered but surprisingly clever, goblins delight in ambushing unprepared enemies. Their lairs are riddled with traps, alarms, and tunnels too small for their enemies to chase them.

Fighting Style: Artillerist. You come with Nimble Escape, a powerful feature that lets you Disengage or Hide as a bonus action on each of your turns. You also have a +6 to your Dexterity (Stealth) checks, making you a deadly artillerist.

Set-up: Lots of Cover. Your Nimble Escape demands that you fight in areas with lots of places for you to Hide and take cover between shots. Forests, caverns with small holes, rocky canyons, etc., are great places to stage an ambush.

Weaknesses: Squishy. You only have 7 hit points, so it doesn't take much to knock you out of combat. Keep your distance and always stay behind cover.

Pair With Brutes and Tanks. Team up with brutes or tanks that can keep your enemies busy while you fire from the safety of cover.

Tactics: Move, Shoot, Hide. Start combat hidden behind cover. When an enemy comes within 80 feet of you, reveal yourself and attack with your shortbow. So long as they didn't spot you, you have advantage on the attack roll. After making an attack, move to a different spot and use Nimble Escape to hide again. Drop prone if necessary to impose disadvantage on the enemy artillerists' return attacks.

Goblin Boss. Goblin bosses have a better AC than their lessers and can redirect attacks made against them to hit goblins standing near them. How this helps the other goblins is a mystery and seems to be played more for comedic effect than anything.

GOLEM, CLAY

CR 9

This lumbering figure is sculpted from soft clay. It wears filthy rags and crude jewelry, and its face is vaguely humanoid.

Clay golems might seem like lumbering hunks of clay, but they're surprisingly fast, thanks to their Haste effect. They serve as defenders and harbingers of retribution on behalf of their creators.

Fighting Style: Brute. As a golem, you're already pretty durable, thanks to a wealth of damage immunities. You're immune to most mental conditions, too, and have Magic Resistance. But your real strength lies in your ability to deal considerable damage with your 1-4 attacks per turn, depending on how fast your Haste recharges.

Set-up: Up Close and Personal. You move slowly, so you want to make sure that you start as close as possible to your targets so you can deal damage. Acid damage heals you, so consider fighting in areas with acid hazards or even naturally acidic creatures like oozes.

Weaknesses: Magic Weapons. Although you have plenty of defenses against spells and magical effects, magic and adamantine weapons cut through your damage immunities. With only 133 hit points, it doesn't take long for an enemy to reduce you to a pile of lifeless clay.

Pair With Artillerists and Controllers. As the primary brute in the combat, your enemies will spend many of their turns trying to reduce you to 0 hit points. Meanwhile, artillerists can attack you without fear of reprisal. Consider teaming up with controllers, too, who can help give you advantage on your attack rolls. As a bonus, work alongside creatures that deal acid damage, such as oozes, black dragons, and ankhegs.

Tactics: Move and Mash. Start combat within 20 feet of your targets. Haste immediately, then move and use your bonus action to make an extra attack. Then, on your next turn, use your Multiattack against a target and another bonus attack. After that, if your Haste recharges, repeat these tactics. Otherwise, rely on just your Multiattack until it returns. You are not self-aware; therefore, you feel no desire to preserve yourself.

GOLEM, FLESH

A hideous monstrosity crafted from body parts stitched together with thick string, wire, and metal staples lurches to horrific life.

Pulled from classic novels like Frankenstein, flesh golems are sturdy, hard-hitting creatures with a little higher Intelligence than other golems.

Fighting Style: Tank. Your offensive capabilities are only so-so for your CR, but you have a lot of immunities for a CR 5 creature, making you a natural tank despite your lousy AC.

Set-up: Up Close and Personal. You want to get as close to the enemy as soon as possible so you can start wailing away at them. Hopefully, you're allied with creatures smarter than you, so they can direct you toward the ones that need bashing the most.

Weaknesses: Magic Weapons and Fire. Blessed with Magic Resistance and a bucket full of immunities, you have only two real fears. Magic weapons can cut through your defenses and make short work of your AC 9 and 93 hit points. And you have a natural aversion to fire. Beware of well-armed groups, especially those that use fire magic.

Pair With Artillerists and Controllers. Your job is to keep enemies distracted while your artillerist allies fire ranged weapons from afar. Use controllers to enhance your ability to hit targets. Also, consider working alongside creatures with natural lightning weapons, such as blue dragons, behirs, or will-o-wisps.

Tactics: Dash and Bash. Start combat within 30 feet of your enemies. When your turn begins, move towards the closest targets—or whichever one your allies tell you to attack—and start hitting it. Beware of fire, though. Fire bad!

GOLEM, IRON

 CR 16

This iron automaton stands twice as tall as a normal human. Its heavy footfalls shake the ground with bone-jarring force.

Iron golems are the largest and deadliest of the four most common golem types, built to withstand intense punishment while simultaneously dolling it.

Fighting Style: Brute. Although you can deal a lot of damage to your foes, your defensive capabilities and extremely high AC make you a formidable tank, capable of withstanding punishment for multiple rounds at a time. And if that's not enough, fire damage heals you, effectively rendering a wide variety of popular spells useless.

Set-up: Warm, Cramped Places. You're built to take damage, so there's no issue with you getting close and personal right away. Plus, you want natural fire hazards around to give you "passive regeneration" each turn. Finally, your poison breath demands that you trap as many targets as possible.

Weaknesses: Magic Weapons. Your Magic Resistance, condition immunities, and Fire Absorption traits make many spells useless against you. However, a strong combatant armed with magic weapons could make short work of your 210 hit points. Hopefully, your handler is nearby to direct you to take defensive maneuvers on each of your turns, extending your lifespan.

Pair With Artillerists and Controllers. You will be a major distraction on the battlefield, allowing ranged targets to pick off your foes from the safety of cover. Team up with controllers who can further slow the targets and make it easier for you to hit them.

Tactics: Up Close and Personal. Start combat within 30 feet of your enemies. Open combat with poison breath, hitting as many targets as you can. Take the Dodge action (if you have a handler you listen to nearby) on subsequent turns, increasing your natural defenses against weapon attacks until your poison breath recharges.

GOLEM, STONE

CR 10

This towering stone automaton bears the likeness of an archaic, armored warrior. It moves with ponderous but inexorable steps.

Stone golems are relatively tough constructs that come with all the typical defensive capabilities of the other common golems while also possessing some unique defensive capabilities.

Fighting Style: Tank. You have excellent AC and hit points, damage and condition immunities, and Magic Resistance. Plus, you have a Slow ability that reduces the effectiveness of attackers.

Set-up: Up Close and Personal. You want to get within 10 feet of all your foes as soon as possible to hit them with your Slow attack.

Weaknesses: Magic Weapons. Your Magic Resistance and condition immunities keep you safe from most spells, but you have no resistance or immunity to magic weapons. Use your Slow to keep well-armed enemies from cutting through your hit points, and take the Dodge action (assuming someone commands you) to make it harder to hit you.

Pair With Artillerists and Brutes. Your Slow effect will leave multiple enemies as sitting ducks for your allies with melee attacks and enemies firing from cover.

Tactics: Get Close and Slow. Start combat within 30 feet of your enemies. On your turn, get within 10 feet of as many targets as possible, then use your Slow to weaken them. If you weaken most melee attackers, use offensive maneuvers against whatever target your handlers tell you to attack. Otherwise, take the Dodge action until your Slow recharges.

GORGON

CR 5

This bull-like creature seems to be made of interlocking metallic plates. Faint plumes of green smoke puff from its mouth.

Gorgons are foul-tempered bull-like magical creatures feared for their petrifying breath.

Fighting Style: Brute. You are a simple creature whose devastating trampling charge and Petrifying Breath make you the number one target for most enemies you face.

Set-up: Enough Room to Charge. You want a clear path to your targets, but you don't want them to spread out before you can breathe your petrifying breath onto them.

Weaknesses: Animal Intelligence. Despite your excellent defenses and attacks, you still have the Intelligence of a cow with no natural immunities to protect you. Hopefully, your allies will keep you safe while you plow through the enemy ranks.

Pair With Artillerists and Controllers. Likely, you aren't intelligent enough to recognize friends from foes, and your Petrifying Breath is a considerable threat for most creatures that encounter it, including allies. Artillerists and controllers can keep their distance while you tear up the battlefield.

Tactics: Charge, Trample, and Breath. Start combat within 20 feet of your targets. Use your trampling charge to knock your target prone and stomp on it. On your next turn, use your Petrifying Breath on as many targets as possible. If there is a target restrained by your Petrifying Breath within charging range, charge that target. Otherwise, continue attacking the closest target until your breath weapon recharges again.

GRICK

CR 2

This pallid, slimy, worm-like creature is the size of a human, its mouth a sickening tangle of tentacles and hooked jaws.

Gricks are subterranean worms whose naturally rocky exterior allows them to blend in with their surroundings.

Fighting Style: Lurker. Although you aren't proficient in the Stealth skill, you have Stone Camouflage, which gives you advantage on Dexterity (Stealth) checks made to hide in rocky areas. Plus, you have a climbing speed of 30 feet. You evolved to strike fast from the shadows and then retreat.

Set-up: Dark, Rocky Areas. Your Stone Camouflage demands that you hide in rocky terrain. Additionally, you know that light makes it easier for your prey to see you (remember that Perception checks made to see using only darkvision has disadvantage). Hide in areas with vertical passages so you can attack your prey quickly and flee with it locked in your mouth.

Weaknesses: Magic. Your resistances won't work against magical weapons or spells. When pitted against such harmful things, you're likely to flee and hide.

Pair With Minions. Although you aren't intelligent enough to work alongside other creatures, you can at least deduce that it's easier to attack from hiding when your prey is distracted. Hunt near areas with bats, stirges, and other simple creatures who'll keep your targets preoccupied while you sneak up on them.

Tactics: Lurk, Attack, Dash. Start combat hidden in a dark, rocky place. When a target comes within 5 feet of you, emerge from hiding and attack with your tentacles. If your tentacles hit, you can make a bite attack. If the creature dies, grab it with your tentacles and climb away. If the creature survives your initial attack, try again the next turn unless you see that the creature and its allies pose too serious a threat. Retreat when this happens.

Grick Alpha. Bigger, uglier, and faster, grick alphas use the same tactics as their lessers, except they also get a tail attack.

GRIFFON

CR 2

This majestic beast has the body of a lion, the head and forelegs of a great eagle, and a massive pair of feathered wings.

These awesome, mountain-dwelling creatures sometimes serve as mounts for humanoids. They're fiercely territorial.

Fighting Style: Skirmisher. With a flying speed of 80 feet, you're best equipped to use hit-and-run tactics against your targets.

Set-up: Wide, Open Spaces. Your flying speed works best when you have plenty of room to maneuver.

Weaknesses: Animal Intelligence. You have bestial intelligence, which means you rely solely on instinct and can't formulate tactics beyond what comes naturally to you, given your abilities.

Pair With Brutes and Minions. Although you aren't intelligent enough to know how to work alongside other creatures, you do know that a distracted target is easier to attack than one focused on you.

Tactics: Hit-and-Run. Start combat 40 feet away from your targets in the air. On your turn, fly 40 feet toward the target, use your Multiattack against it, then fly 40 feet away from it.

GRIMLOCK

 **CR 1/4**

A muscular humanoid stares with dark, eyeless sockets. It fingers a spiked club and emits a low growl.

Grimlocks are aggressive, territorial, and often despicably evil humanoids that dwell in the darkest parts of the subterranean realms.

Fighting Style: Minion. With AC 11, only 11 hit points, and a single weapon attack, you function best as a minion, distracting the enemy and slowing them down.

Set-up: Dark, Rocky Areas. You have blindsight out to 30 feet, proficiency in Stealth, and the Stone Camouflage feature, which gives you advantage on Dexterity (Stealth) checks made to hide in rocky areas. You and other minions working alongside you use these areas to stage ambushes, keeping yourself spread out to reduce the risk of area-of-effect attacks.

Weaknesses: Squishy. You have very few hit points and no other defenses to protect you against attacks and magic.

Pair With Artillerists and Controllers. While you're distracting enemies with your club attacks, artillerists can fire at the enemy from the safety of cover. Meanwhile, controllers can boost your effectiveness by creating areas of magical darkness (which won't affect you) or finding other ways to give your attacks advantage.

Tactics: Lurk, Then Attack. Start combat hidden using your Stone Camouflage feature. When targets come within reach, emerge and attack.

GUARD

CR 1/8

Guards represent 1st-level fighters who serve as protectors, rank-and-file soldiers, or actual city guards.

Fighting Style: Minion. Although you have better AC than most creatures with the same CR as you, you're still relatively weak and only have one attack per turn. You work best in large numbers.

Set-up: Spread Out and Close. As a trained soldier living in a world of magic, you know better than to clump up in large groups. You're armed with a spear, but its normal range is only 20 feet. Make sure to start combat as close to the enemy as possible.

Weaknesses: Poor Attack Rolls. Your AC is relatively good, and you have decent hit points for a CR 1/8 creature. However, you only have a +3 to attack.

Pair With Artillerists and Brutes. You'll keep the enemy preoccupied and stuck in their position while artillerists make ranged attacks against them. Since you have a relatively good AC, you should also pair up with brutes who'll deal damage while you defend.

Tactics: Look for Opportunities. Start combat at least 10 feet apart from your allies to reduce the risk of area-of-effect attacks and to threaten as much as possible. If working alongside artillerists or brutes, use the Dodge action to keep the enemy preoccupied. Otherwise, divide into two groups: attackers and defenders. The defenders use the Dodge action and look for attacks of opportunity, while the attackers stay behind the defenders and throw their spears.

HAG, GREEN

CR 3

Knots of dark, moldering hair spill over the features of this sickly, thin, green-skinned crone.

Green hags are gruesome fey creatures who lurk in foreboding swamps and dark forests. They delight in tempting and corrupting mortals.

Fighting Style: Lurker. You have many features and spells that allow you to surprise and trick your foes, such as *minor illusion, dancing lights*, Illusory Appearance, and Invisible Passage. A patient creature, you have no qualms about making quick attacks and then vanishing to reset the ambush.

Set-up: Dark, Treacherous Places. You want to fight on your turf where you can lure unsuspecting enemies into traps, hazards, and the lairs of other creatures, making it easier for you to overtake them. Consider fighting near water, too, as you're amphibious.

Weaknesses: Mental Saving Throws. You're relatively strong for a CR 3 creature, with excellent AC 1 and decent hit points. However, you don't have the most outstanding mental saving throws and no natural immunity to the charmed and frightened conditions. This weakness makes you vulnerable to enemy controllers.

Pair With Brutes and Minions. Use brutes and minions to distract your foes while you lurk and make hit-and-run attacks.

Tactics: Lurk, Attack, Flee. Start combat disguised as another creature, invisible, hidden, or underwater. When a creature comes within 5 feet of you, attack it with your claws. Then, use your whole movement to escape and take cover. Don't worry about attacks of opportunity; you're strong, and one hit is better than sticking around for multiple attacks. When your turn comes back around, turn invisible and find a new place to stage another ambush.

HAG, NIGHT

 **CR 5**

Grisly fetishes and the rags of once fine clothes hang off the corpse-thin frame of this horrifying, sharp-fanged crone.

Night hags are among the most feared and respected creatures in the cosmos. Popular in the soul trade, they often work alongside other fiends, making their homes in dismal extraplanar lairs.

Fighting Style: Artillerist. You can cast *magic missile* at will, an incredibly powerful feature. So long as you keep your distance and remain in cover, you give targets a run for their money.

Set-up: Dark Places with Lots of Cover. You have darkvision out to 120 feet, which means you can often see your enemies even when they can't see you. Make sure the location has lots of cover, too, so you can hide between attacks with your *magic missile*.

Weaknesses: Magic Weapons. You have Magic Resistance and multiple damage resistances, which protects you against most spells. However, magic weapons can break through your resistance. Make sure that melee attackers armed with magic weapons don't get too close to you.

Pair With Brutes and Minions. Use minions and brutes to distract your enemies while you pick them off from a distance with your *magic missiles*.

Tactics: Shoot From Cover. Start combat more than 60 feet away from your targets, hidden behind cover. Use your *magic missile* to target the creatures that pose the biggest threat to you, such as clerics, paladins, or enemy artillerists armed with magic weapons. If a melee attacker gets too close to comfort, consider popping into the ethereal plane and repositioning; failing that, *plane shift* away. *Ray of enfeeblement* is almost totally useless against melee attackers who will probably have excellent AC and will be able to make the follow-up Constitution saving throws.

HAG, SEA

 **CR 2**

Hair like rotting seaweed drapes this ancient witch. Loose, algae-colored skin sags off her starved frame.

Sea hags are the "ugliest" of the hags, so much so that merely looking at one is enough to kill you. Typically chaotic evil, they are even closer to demons in nature than the fiendish night hags.

Fighting Style: Controller. Your horrific appearance forces creatures to succeed on a saving throw or become frightened. Combine this with your death glare that reduces targets to 0 hit points, and it won't take long for you to take command of the battlefield.

Set-up: Near Water. You have a swim speed of 40 feet and can breathe underwater. Use the water to hide and escape the reach of deadly targets.

Weaknesses: Relatively Squishy. You only have 52 hit points and no natural immunities or resistances, which makes you relatively squishy for a CR 2 monster. Make sure to keep your distance and use cover whenever possible.

Pair With Brutes and Minions. You don't want your foes getting too close, so make sure to employ strong and/or expendable allies in the way. Try not to use humanoids, as they will have to make saving throws against your Horrific Appearance, too.

Tactics: Reveal and Glare. Start combat within 30 feet of your targets (but not too close) with difficult terrain or water in the way. Hold a Dash action to move in case targets try to charge you. Hopefully, they will fail their saving throws against your Horrific Appearance before the start of your next turn. On your next turn, get within 30 feet of a frightened target and hit it with your Death Glare. Continue to keep distance between your targets and you, only closing in once you've dropped half or more of the group. Then, move in to use your claws. If too many powerful targets are left on the battlefield, and they're all temporarily immune to your Horrific Appearance, consider escaping.

HALF-RED DRAGON VETERAN

CR 5

Introduction Text: Half-red dragon veterans are the example creature used for the half-dragon template in the Fifth Edition monster book. Veterans are already deadly, so adding dragon features makes them even better in combat.

Fighting Style: Brute. Your defensive capabilities leave something to be desired for a CR 5 creature. Still, you have a wide array of attacks that make you a formidable opponent on the battlefield, particularly in close combat.

Set-up: Up Close and Personal. Although you have a heavy crossbow, all of your best attacks demand that you get as close to the enemy as possible so you can use your multiattack. You have blindsight out to 10 feet, too, so consider fighting in heavily obscured areas.

Weaknesses: Few Hit Points. Although you have AC 18, you only have 65 hit points, which is pretty low for a CR 5 monster.

Pair With Artillerists and Controllers. Your job is to keep the enemy distracted while your artillerist allies fire from afar. Work alongside controllers, especially those that can cast *fog cloud* or *darkness*, so you can benefit from your blindsight.

Tactics: Dash and Bash. Start combat within 30 feet of your foes. Get close and hit as many targets as possible with your breath weapon (at least 3 or more). Use it again if your breath weapon recharges on your next turn and it proved effective last time. Otherwise, rely on your multiattack to remove deadly foes from the battlefield.

HARPY

 CR 1

Save for the tattered wings and taloned feet, this creature resembles a feral woman with a wild look about her.

Harpies are elven-bird hybrid creatures feared for their luring songs and brutal demeanors.

Fighting Style: Controller. Your luring song is one of the most potent charm effects in the game, affecting every humanoid and giant that can hear it within 300 feet of it. Plus, you can club your targets while they're charmed without disrupting the enchantment.

Set-up: Wide Open, Deadly Terrain. You have a flying speed of 40 feet, and your luring song has a range of 300 feet. There's no reason why you should start combat anywhere near your targets.

Weaknesses: Relatively Squishy. You have poor AC and few hit points, making it easy for enemy attackers to kill you. Make sure to keep plenty of distance from foes, relying on your luring song to bring them to you.

Pair With Brutes and Minions. Work alongside non-humanoid, non-giant brutes and minions to gang up on targets while they're in their charmed state. These allies will also keep foes from reaching your location.

Tactics: Sing, Sing, Sing. Start combat more than 200 feet away from your enemies in a hard-to-reach place. When combat begins, start your song, trying to charm as many targets as possible. When targets inevitably reach your location, club them to death. If the targets snap out of it and try to get to you, escape.

HELL HOUND

 **CR 3**

This creature resembles a thin, lanky wolf with reddish-brown fur, white claws, and burning, fiery red eyes.

Hellhounds are monstrous, fire-breathing dogs hailing from the most uninhabitable planes in the cosmos. Gifted with relatively high intelligence, they're cunning enough to recognize the pain and torment they cause.

Fighting Style: Skirmisher. Your defensive capabilities are relatively poor for a CR 3 creature, but you have a fast movement speed. Use hit-and-run tactics to keep yourself from being hit by melee attackers.

Set-up: Hazardous, Open Environments. You have immunity to fire, which means you won't suffer from lava, fiery rain, or other hazards common in the lower planes or around volcanoes. You also want plenty of space to move to skirmish against your enemies.

Weaknesses: Relatively Squishy. Although your AC is decent, you only half 45 hit points, less than half what other creatures of the same CR have. Don't let melee attackers gang up on you.

Pair With Minions and Tanks. You have Pack Tactics, which grants you advantage on attacks made against targets so long as one of your allies is within 5 feet of the target. Work alongside allies who like to get up close and personal so you can benefit from the distraction. Bonus points if they have immunity to fire damage, so they don't get hit by your fire breath.

Tactics: Hit-and-Gang-Up. Start combat 25 feet away from your targets. On your turn, get close to your enemies and use your Fire Breath, trying to hit as many as possible (at least 2). Then back away. If your fire breath recharges and it proved effective last turn, use these tactics again. Otherwise, choose a target within 25 feet of you engaged with one of your allies and bite it. Remember to always back away after you make attacks. Don't worry about attacks of opportunity; one attack of opportunity made against you on your turn is better than multiple regular attacks made between your turns.

HIPPOGRIFF

CR 1

This large, brown, horse-like creature has hawk's wings, talons, and a hooked beak.

Hippogriffs are magical monstrosities combining elements of horses and eagles—not to be confused with griffons, who are lion/eagles.

Fighting Style: Skirmisher. You have a flying speed of 60 feet and relatively poor defensive capabilities for your challenge rating. Keep your distance between attacks.

Set-up: Wide, Open Spaces. As a flier, you need plenty of space to maneuver. You probably live in the mountains, too, so plenty of difficult terrain for non-fliers wouldn't seem too out of place.

Weaknesses: Squishy. You have AC 11 and 19 hit points, which makes it easy for your enemies to reduce you to 0. Avoid attacks as often as possible.

Pair With Brutes and Minions. Although you aren't intelligent enough to organize tactics with other creatures, you at least recognize that a distracted target is easier to grab than one focused on killing you.

Tactics: Hit-and-Run. Start combat 30 feet away in the air. Move 30 feet towards your enemy and attack it with your multiattack. Then, escape back to the sky. Don't worry about attacks of opportunity—one attack from a single foe is always preferable to multiple attacks from multiple foes.

HOBGOBLIN

CR 1/2

Standing as tall as a human, this heavily armored, muscular orange-skinned creature peers about with tiny, observant eyes.

Hobgoblins are the most disciplined and authoritative of the three primary goblinoid races. As such, they understand strategy and tactics better than their cousins.

Fighting Style: Elite. Although you have the relatively poor hit points and attack rolls of a minion, your versatility makes you a flexible combatant capable of fulfilling artillerist, brute, minion, or tank roles.

Set-up: Organized. As an elite, you can fight in any terrain. And so long as you're working alongside other hobgoblins, you can organize your group members to take on different roles, increasing your effectiveness.

Weaknesses: Few Hit Points. You have excellent AC, and your Martial Advantage feature makes it possible to deal lots of damage with a single hit, but it only takes one good attack roll made by an enemy to harm you.

Pair With Controllers and Support. You cannot usually give yourself advantage on attack rolls except with the Help action. Work alongside creatures who can improve your attack rolls and impose disadvantage on your foes. Hobgoblin captains and warlords are obvious choices since they come with the Leadership feature.

Tactics: Organize and Attack. Start combat 30 feet away. If you're fighting alone, use the same tactics an artillerist would—keep your distance and fire from cover. If you're working alongside multiple hobgoblins, determine ahead of time who will play the role of artillerists and who will serve as tanks. Start the tanks within 30 feet of the enemy. Their job is to get close and take the Dodge action, making it harder to push past their defenses. Don't forget to space them out to reduce the risk of ranged attacks. The artillerists remain behind cover and target foes within 5 feet of their allies to get bonus damage from Martial Advantage.

Hobgoblin Captain. Captains work as support and tanks for the hobgoblins, using their leadership ability to boost their allies' attack rolls and saving throws. Use the Dodge action to remain on the battlefield for as long as possible.

Hobgoblin Warlord. These elite warriors have the Leadership ability, which they should use immediately to boost their allies. Plus, they can function as controllers, thanks to their Shield Bash, or tanks, using their Parry.

HOMUNCULUS

 **CR 0**

This vaguely humanoid creature is about the size of a cat but looks more like a toothy, winged devil.

Cobbled together from clay, ash, manure, etc., homunculi are extremely squishy creatures with one of the best low-cost attacks in the game, capable of poisoning and knocking targets unconscious.

Fighting Style: Minion. A single homunculus isn't scary—but an entire swarm of them is extraordinarily deadly. Work alongside as many of your kind as possible to improve your chances of poisoning and knocking targets unconscious.

Set-up: Spread Out. Although you are a Tiny creature, you want to keep at least 10 feet between you and your allies to ensure that you all don't get taken out with a single area-of-effect attack. Plus, it lets you threaten a greater area for potential attacks of opportunity.

Weaknesses: Squishy. You only have 5 hit points, so it doesn't take much to kill you. Regardless, try to get in as many attacks as possible before the enemy eliminates you.

Pair With Brutes. Your poison/unconscious effect makes you a pseudo-controller, setting up melee attackers capable of dealing much damage for great critical hits.

Tactics: Swarm and Bite. Start combat within 40 feet of your target, ideally in cover. When combat begins, move in and start biting, hoping to score a hit, so your targets have to make Constitution saving throws against your poison. You're smart enough (or at least your creator is smart enough) to recognize the value in poisoning as many targets as possible. Therefore, once you target a creature, move on to the next one until all your enemies are poisoned.

HYDRA

 **CR 8**

Multiple angry crocodile-like heads rise from this terrifying monster's sleek, serpentine body.

Straight from Greek mythology, hydras are terrifying, multi-headed monstrosities capable of dealing insane amounts of damage to ill-prepared heroes.

Fighting Style: Brute. You are one of the game's most well-balanced CR 8 creatures, with your defensive and offensive statistics right where they should be. Combine that with the fact that you can make extra attacks of opportunity between turns and regrow your heads, and you're a pure damage dealer.

Set-up: Up Close in Water. You have a swim speed of 30 feet and can hold your breath for 1 hour. Plus, water diminishes the risk of taking damage from your opponents, allowing you to survive for more extended periods.

Weaknesses: Fire. Fire is the only thing that prevents your heads from regrowing, so stay far away. Fight underwater if necessary and remove foes wielding fire as fast as possible. Unfortunately, you're not smart enough to recognize spellcasters until they start using spells.

Pair With Artillerists and Controllers. Although you aren't smart enough to organize groups, other creatures with ranged attacks and spells know that you are an incredible distraction while on the battlefield. Hopefully, they know you have a weakness to fire and will remove those targets as quickly as possible.

Tactics: Get Close and Bite. Start combat 30 to 35 feet away from your targets in the water. When combat begins, swim close and attack with your heads. Focus your attacks on any target that demonstrates that it's capable of burning you.

INTELLECT DEVOURER

 **CR 2**

Devoid of a head or any features save for four short, clawed legs, this creature's body looks like a giant, glistening brain.

Capable of extracting and replacing the brains of humanoids, intellect devourers are fearsome creatures few parties are ready to face.

Fighting Style: Lurker. You are a Tiny creature with excellent Stealth and the ability to detect living creatures from 300 feet away, regardless of barriers. Plus, you have blindsight, which means you can hide in obscured areas undetected.

Set-up: Dark Places with Cover. You're Tiny and have blindsight out to 60 feet, so you want to hide in dark areas where you can quickly spring an ambush on unsuspecting travelers.

Weaknesses: Squishy. You have AC 12 and only 21 hit points, which makes you easy to kill. Make sure to strike your foes fast to steal control of a body before getting caught.

Pair With Brutes, Minions, and Tanks. Use melee attackers to keep your foes preoccupied while you devour the intellect of your foes from hiding.

Tactics: Attack from Hiding. Start hidden in a dark place, ideally with full cover. Pick a rather dumb-looking target (you can tell) and drain its intelligence from the safety of your hidey-hole. Once you eliminate its intelligence, steal its body. You can devour intelligence and steal bodies from hiding without revealing your location (although this might drive your players nuts if you do).

INVISIBLE STALKER

CR 6

You can detect no proper form, yet a sense of force and hulking malevolence is undeniable in this creature's presence.

Invisible stalkers are air elemental creatures conjured to serve as trackers and assassins. They remain invisible even while they attack.

Fighting Style: Skirmisher. You are an invisible creature with 50 feet of flight. Plus, you come equipped with damage resistance and immunity to most conditions. You can efficiently perform hit-and-run maneuvers without the worry of reprisal.

Set-up: Open Spaces. As a flying creature, you perform best when you have room to move. Include difficult terrain in the setting to further impede your foes.

Weaknesses: Being Seen. The majority of your advantages stem from your ability to remain unseen. Foes with truesight, the *see invisibility* spell, or a spell that reveals hidden creatures like *faerie fire* or *moonbeam* can rob you of this benefit.

Pair With Brutes, Tanks, and Minions. Work alongside close combat creatures to draw attention away from you as you perform your hit-and-run attacks.

Tactics: Hit-and-Run. Start combat hidden, ideally somewhere high above your targets. When an enemy comes within 25 feet of you, swoop down and attack it with your multiattack. Then, retreat to the air. Your foes can't make attacks of opportunity against you if they can't see you. Try not to linger in a single area for too long, as it'll make it easier for foes to hit you with area-of-effect spells.

JACKALWERE

 CR 1/2

This armored humanoid has a jackal's head, bulging muscles, and a gaze that makes the world drift away.

Jackalweres win the award for lowest challenge creature with immunity to non-magical attacks not made with silvered weapons, which makes them an extraordinary threat for low-level characters. Plus, they have a sleep attack that relies on Wisdom saving throws rather than hit points totals.

Fighting Style: Controller. You have a variety of robust features that makes you a versatile combatant. Your natural immunities make you a capable tank, your Pack Tactics and speed allow you to skirmish, and your Sleep Gaze helps you control the battlefield.

Set-up: Plenty of Cover. You want to start combat hidden, and you want to take cover between your attacks. Crowded bazaars, dungeons with lots of debris and furniture, or even forests make great battlegrounds.

Weaknesses: Magic. Your immunities are one of your best features; take those away, and you're in danger. Be wary of spellcasters and targets armed with magical weapons.

Pair With Brutes, Minions, or Tanks. As a controller with skirmisher capabilities, you perform best when you work alongside melee attackers who can keep your foes distracted. Plus, you have advantage on attack rolls against targets so long as you have at least one ally within 5 feet of the same target.

Tactics: Ambush, Gaze, Skirmish. Start combat hidden with your +4 to Stealth. When a particularly dopey-looking target comes within 30 feet of you, use your Sleep Gaze attack to subdue it, especially if it's armed with a magic weapon. Avoid using your Sleep Gaze on foes that look like apparent spellcasters, as they probably have enough willpower to avoid falling victim to it. Instead, use skirmisher tactics against these targets, dashing in, making attacks with your sword, and fleeing before they can attack back. Make sure that your targets have an ally within 5 feet of them so you can get advantage on the attack roll thanks to your features.

KNIGHT

CR 3

Knights are mid-tier fighters or paladins who can nearly hold their own in combat, with their only major drawback being their lack of action economy.

Fighting Style: Elite. You can fight as a tank, brute, artillerist, and even support. You fill whatever role is needed.

Set-up: Close to Your Allies. You have the Leadership trait, which gives your allies a d4 bonus to add to their attack rolls and saving throws so long as you remain alert.

Weaknesses: Dexterity Saving Throws. Although you have excellent AC and can parry melee attacks, you are vulnerable to attacks that force you to make Dexterity saving throws. Make sure to address spellcasters as soon as possible.

Pair With Brutes and Minions. Your job is to draw the attention of melee combatants while simultaneously boosting as many of your allies as possible. The more helpers you have, the better, especially since your Leadership effectively increases the challenge of each one within 30 feet of you.

Tactics: Fight at the Frontlines. Start combat within 30 feet of your allies but just a little outside the enemy's charging range. Open with Leadership. On your turn, take the Dodge action and press forward toward the enemy with your allies. Continue to protect yourself so long as your allies remain. Otherwise, switch to using your greatsword against the most dangerous targets—probably spellcasters.

KOBOLD

CR 1/8

This short, reptilian humanoid has scaled skin, a snout filled with tiny teeth, and a long tail.

Kobolds are tiny, sun-sensitive creatures that fight in packs, utilizing cramped lairs littered with traps to torment their foes.

Fighting Style: Minion. As one of the squishiest creatures in the game, you perform better when you've got a mess of friends to back you up.

Set-up: Claustrophobic and Filled with Traps. You must take the fight into your territory, where small tunnels laced with traps will cause more damage than you're worth. Your traps don't have to be deadly—obnoxious hazards do the trick, too.

Weaknesses: Squishy. You have AC 12 and 5 hit points. It only takes one hit to knock you out of the fight. Make sure to work with plenty of allies and keep as far away from the enemies' weapons as possible.

Pair With Brutes and Tanks. Join forces with creatures more formidable than you to distract your enemies. Your Pack Tactics feature works with your ranged weapons, too, so your bigger friends double your combat effectiveness.

Tactics: Follow Me! Start combat hidden somewhere in your lair with your pals. When enemies enter the lair, lead them into trapped areas, into the reach of allies or hazards, or into small tunnels where they'll have trouble fighting you. Use Dodging kobolds to burn attacks of opportunity, allowing others to skirmish and to grant other kobolds with sling attacks held with Ready advantage.

Kobold, Winged. Winged kobolds are just marginally stronger kobolds with a flying speed. Instead of using a sling to hurl rocks, they drop them onto the heads of their foes from above. Otherwise, their tactics are basically the same.

KRAKEN

CR 23

This tremendous leviathan resembles a vast squid with draconic features, yet its body's markings are strangely unsettling.

Fifth Edition's krakens are manipulative, cunning beasts whose machinations are felt across the entire world.

Fighting Style: Solo. Your defensive and offensive features are exceptional, you have excellent saving throws, built-in freedom of movement, and you can make attacks with your lair and Legendary Actions.

Set-up: Big, Wet Areas of Difficult Terrain. You have a swim speed of 60 feet and truesight out to 120 feet. Plus, you have a lightning storm attack that allows you to make attacks against three creatures up to 120 feet away from you. Finally, your freedom of movement feature allows you to ignore difficult terrain.

Weaknesses: The Power of Love? You have 472 hit points, 18 AC, and a cornucopia of devastating attacks at your disposal, which you can use before, during, and after your turn. Basically, you don't have any weaknesses.

Pair With Minions. Although you hardly need them, having a few minions serving as speed bumps for your foes never hurts.

Tactics: Keep Your Distance and Zap. Start combat underwater within 60 feet of your targets. Use your lightning vulnerability Lair Action to affect as many creatures as possible. Use your lightning storm effect as a Lair Action as soon as possible—specifically, target creatures with long-range attacks that can hurt you. Then, on your turn, use your lightning storm effect again, then swim 60 feet away from your enemies. Before your next Lair Action comes up, reserve your tentacle attack to hit any target that gets within 30 feet of you. If too many targets come within 60 feet of you, use your strong current Lair Action to push them backward. Otherwise, make them vulnerable to your Lightning Storm again, and use your Legendary Actions to zap your foes again. If you grappled a particularly pesky foe with your tentacle attack, use a Lair Action to fling it away or swallow it with your bite attack on your turn. Otherwise, continue to hold the extra Legendary Action for other pesky targets that get too close, and use your turn to zap more targets.

LAMIA

 CR 4

This creature's upper torso is that of a comely woman with cat's eyes and sharp fangs, while her lower body is that of a lion.

Lamias are usually depicted as depraved, vain predators who use pleasure to dominate and control others. Skillful at Deception, they make excellent low-level villains.

Fighting Style: Controller. Nearly all of the spells on your spell list allow you to control foes, whether through mind control (*charm person*, *geas*, and *suggestion*) or via illusions (*disguise self*, *major image*, and *mirror image*). Plus, your Intoxicating Touch attack gives disadvantage to Wisdom saving throws and all ability checks, making it even easier for you to affect simple minds.

Set-up: Create a Web of Lies. A big part of your tactics lies in your ability to create convincing illusions, luring your foes into traps. Make sure you have ample space filled with traps that you can disguise with major illusion.

Weaknesses: Mental Saving Throws. Ironically, despite your specialization in such magic, you have no natural defense against effects that charm or frighten you. Watch out for spellcasters.

Pair With More Controllers. Your Intoxicating Touch is a powerful attack, but you only have two spells that can benefit from it, both of which require concentration, and you can only use each one three times per day. Work alongside other controllers with similar features to further confuse and torment the enemies.

Tactics: Misdirect and Enchant. Start combat hidden behind one of your illusions, potentially behind a trap or some other obstacle. You might even assume a disguise capable of confusing the targets, such as a familiar NPC, victim, or dangerous enemy. Use your *charm* or *suggestion* spells early in combat to remove low-Wisdom targets from the combat. Continue to take cover and avoid spellcasters who have enough Wisdom to resist your enchantments. Continue to create new and more convincing illusions, continually cursing and compromising the enemy forces.

LICH

Once fine robes hang in tatters from this withered corpse's frame. A pale blue light shines from where its eyes should be.

Perhaps one of the most popular bad guys in the game, liches are spellcasters so obsessed with gaining knowledge that they use dark rituals to extend their lifespan.

Fighting Style: Elite. Although you have Legendary and Lair Actions, you are far too weak to fight alone. All it takes is one lousy initiative check, and you're toast. Having said that, you have a wide range of spells and special abilities. You can control enemies, support your allies, or make ranged attacks.

Set-up: Create Distance and Obstacles. You don't want your enemies getting too close to you, so you want to fight in places that put plenty of distance between you and them. Make sure there's difficult terrain, hazards, minions, and other valuable obstacles. You also have truesight out to 120 feet, so consider fighting in areas of magical darkness.

Weaknesses: Magic Weapons. Your Legendary Resistances, saving throw proficiencies, resistances, and *globe of invulnerability* will keep you safe from most spells. However, a melee attacker—especially a paladin—armed with a potent magic weapon will cut through your 135 hit points like butter. Avoid them and remove them as soon as possible.

Pair With Minions. Use minions to slow down the enemy and benefit from the controller effects you use. Minions with blindsight and immunity to poison, such as animated objects, are especially effective when they fight within the area of a *cloudkill* spell.

Tactics: Keep Your Distance and Control. You are one of the most intelligent creatures in the game; therefore, it stands to reason that you will be prepared to face your targets before they even reach your lair. Start far from your enemies, outside their spell range and your own. Taunt the enemy to force their melee attackers to charge you. You want your foes to come at you one at a time. Ready whatever spell will work best against the charging attacker (see the "Tactics for Player Builds" section for details). Your best choices are *dominate monster* (if you want a new friend) or *power word stun* if you want to completely eradicate the enemy using the disintegrate spell on your next available turn. Alternatively, use *ray of frost* to slow the target down since the movement reduction stacks. If you dominate the foe, turn it back against its allies. And if you stun it, use *disintegrate* against it on your next available turn—stunned creatures automatically fail their Dexterity saving throws. If *disintegrate* doesn't kill it, use *power word kill* on the next round. Even a high-level barbarian won't survive that barrage of attacks.

Continue to perform this trick, always staying far outside enemy artillerists' ranges, waiting with Readied spells to catch enemies. Then, when initiative 20 happens, use your spell slot regain feature to recover spent spells. Once you've eliminated all close-range targets, bring up your *globe of invulnerability* and take the fight to the spellcasters.

LIZARDFOLK

 **CR 1/2**

This reptilian humanoid has green scales, a short and toothy snout, and a thick alligator-like tail.

Lizardfolk are territorial swamp and forest creatures who don't care too much for outsiders.

Fighting Style: Lurker. You have expertise in Stealth, a swim speed of 30 feet, and the ability to hold your breath for an hour. Like your alligator ancestors, the game built you to stalk and snatch.

Set-up: Wetlands. You perform best when you have watery terrain where you can lurk and hide, waiting to surprise your prey.

Weaknesses: No Darkvision. You have decent defensive and offensive abilities for a CR 1/2 creature, and your swim speed and Stealth skill make you a successful hunter. Unfortunately, you have no darkvision, so you must relegate your hunting to the daytime hours.

Pair With Brutes and Minions. Use melee combatants to distract foes while you set up an ambush against them.

Tactics: Lurk, Emerge, Attack. Start combat hidden in the water. When a target comes within 5 feet of you, emerge, potentially surprising them, and attack them with your multiattack. If you successfully subdue them, drag their body underwater. If you fail to subdue them, escape the area to prevent retribution.

Lizard King/Queen. These fiendish lizardfolk leaders are stronger and deadlier than their lessers but more or less use the same tactics. The major difference is that they come with a skewer attack that allows them to deal extra damage with their tridents and regain temporary hit points.

Lizardfolk Druid. Lizardfolk druids are lizardfolk with a few levels in the druid class, allowing them to cast controller spells. Work alongside other lizardfolk, using your spells to slow and control your enemies. Unfortunately, you can only cast one at a time (they're almost all concentration spells), so pick the ones likely to have the greatest effects. For example, use *entangle* against creatures with poor Strength scores, *heat metal* on well-armored targets, and *spike growth* against fast-moving targets.

LYCANTHROPE, WEREBEAR

 **CR 5**

This humanoid is covered in shaggy fur and carries a heavy axe in one of his clawed hands.

Werebears are one of the few "good" lycanthropes in fantasy Fifth Edition, serving as guardians of forested areas and helping those in need.

Fighting Style: Tank. Although your AC isn't great, your high hit points and damage immunities more than makeup for it. Lower-level enemies will have difficulty getting past your immunities without magic, and higher-level enemies will still fear your brutal multiattack.

Set-up: Up Close and Personal. You're built specifically for close combat. Don't fight in places where you'll have trouble getting close to your foes.

Weaknesses: Magic. You have damage immunities against nonmagical attacks, which makes you nearly impossible to kill. However, your saving throws aren't great against spell attacks, and your AC is pitifully low. Take out spellcasters and creatures with magic weapons first. Failing that, avoid them.

Pair With Artillerists and Controllers. Your job is to keep enemies distracted while your allies armed with ranged attacks pick them off from cover. Work alongside controllers, too, to help give you advantage on attacks against your targets and to dispose of unwelcome spellcasters.

Tactics: Dash and Slash. Start combat within 30 feet of your enemies. Consider staying in humanoid form so your targets don't suspect you're a lycanthrope until it's too late. Use your greataxe against the target that poses the biggest threat to you and your allies. If serving as a defender, take the Dodge action instead, allowing your artillerist allies to deal damage on your behalf.

LYCANTHROPE, WEREBOAR

 **CR 4**

This potbellied creature has the body of a man and the head of a crazed boar. Large tusks jut from his upper jaw.

Wereboars are typically heinous creatures who delight in punishing their prey. They're also described as one of the few lycanthropes that delight in infecting others.

Fighting Style: Brute. You are an aggressive fighter whose charge attack can deal a lot of damage to targets caught off guard. You're Relentless, so don't let up on them until you convert them to one of your kind or they die.

Set-up: Charging Room. You want enough space to charge but not enough for your enemies to escape quickly. Choose large rooms or clearings in forests to stage combat.

Weaknesses: Magic. You have damage immunities against nonmagical attacks, which makes you nearly impossible to kill. Plus, the Relentless feature keeps you standing even after you drop to 0 hit points. However, your saving throws aren't great against spell attacks, and your AC is pitifully low. Take out spellcasters and creatures with magic weapons first. Failing that, avoid them.

Pair With Artillerists and Controllers. Your charge attack allows you to knock targets prone when you hit them. Work alongside grapplers who can continue to hold your target down, making it easier for you to attack them on following rounds.

Tactics: Charge and Crush. Start combat in hybrid form to get the best of both worlds and 15 feet away from your target. Charge your target, knock it prone, and then use your maul against it. Continue to attack the same target until you infect or kill it. Then choose another viable target within 15 feet of you.

LYCANTHROPE, WERERAT

CR 2

This hunched creature looks like a human in studded leather, but fur covers its body. Its face is rat-like, and it has a long, naked tail.

Wererats are the lowest CR lycanthrope listed in the Fifth Edition monster book but perhaps one of the more versatile, thanks to their ranged weapons.

Fighting Style: Artillerist. You come armed with a hand crossbow which you can fire twice per turn so long as you are in humanoid or hybrid form. Although you have plenty of damage immunities, why tempt fate? Keep your distance and shoot, shoot, shoot!

Set-up: Distance and Cover. Fight in dark areas with lots of places to hide and take cover. You also want a few escape routes in case your enemies come prepared to fight lycanthropes.

Weaknesses: Magic. You have damage immunities against nonmagical attacks, which makes you nearly impossible to kill. However, your saving throws aren't great against spell attacks, and your AC is pitifully low. Take out spellcasters and creatures with magic weapons first. Failing that, avoid them.

Pair With Brutes and Tanks. Use brutes and tanks to draw the enemies' attacks while you fire from cover.

Tactics: Take Cover and Fire. Start combat 20 feet or more away from your targets behind cover. If working with other wererats or minions, spread out in case the enemy charges you. On your turn, target spellcasters with your hand crossbows. If the enemy comes prepared to fight lycanthropes, switch to lurker tactics, firing as you move and hide.

LYCANTHROPE, WERETIGER

 CR 4

This tiger-like humanoid stands a full head taller than most full-grown humans. It wields a mighty longbow and wears a slick-looking scimitar on its hip.

Weretigers are fiercely territorial creatures that lurk in jungles and other remote parts of the world.

Fighting Style: Elite. Thanks to your immunities, you can tank enemies. Alternatively, you can fight as a brute, too, relying on your Pounce and Multiattack combination to deal considerable damage in a short period. And you also have a longbow, which allow you to put plenty of distance between yourself and your targets.

Set-up: Lots of Cover. You're relatively wise; therefore, you won't take your chance against unknown enemies; keep your distance and use cover to fire from afar before engaging in close combat.

Weaknesses: Magic. You have damage immunities against nonmagical attacks, which makes you nearly impossible to kill. However, your saving throws aren't great against spell attacks, and your AC is pitifully low. Take out spellcasters and creatures with magic weapons first. Failing that, avoid them.

Pair With Brutes and Tanks. Use melee fighters to keep your targets distracted while you fire at them from up to 150 feet away with your longbow.

Tactics: Take Cover and Shoot. Start combat between 120 to 150 feet away from your targets behind cover. Use your longbow, targeting the foes that pose the biggest threat, likely spellcasters. Move between shots to make it harder for targets to reciprocate.

LYCANTHROPE, WEREWOLF

 CR 3

With fur as dense as a midnight forest, this fearsome creature stands on two legs, its eyes glowing an otherworldly yellow that chills the soul. Its elongated snout reveals razor-sharp teeth, and as it throws back its head to howl at the moon, you feel a primal dread that speaks to something ancient within you.

Perhaps the most famous of all lycanthropes, werewolves are typically despicable evil creatures content to toy with their prey before they attack and kill them.

Fighting Style: Skirmisher. You have relatively low hit points compared to the other lycanthropes around your CR; this means you prefer to attack targets much weaker than you. It also means you prefer to use hit-and-run tactics.

Set-up: Lots of Cover. You want to fight in your wolf form and have places where you can hide after you make attacks. Unlike ordinary wolves, you don't benefit from features that give you Pack Tactics or knock targets prone; therefore, there's no reason to stick around.

Weaknesses: Magic. You have damage immunities against nonmagical attacks, which makes you nearly impossible to kill. However, your saving throws aren't great against spell attacks, and your AC is pitifully low. Take out spellcasters and creatures with magic weapons first. Failing that, avoid them.

Pair With Brutes and Minions. Work alongside targets that will keep your foes distracted while you dash in and out of cover. Dire wolves, winter wolves, and mundane wolves all make good choices.

Tactics: Hit-and-Run. Start combat in wolf form hidden behind cover. When a target comes within 5 feet of you, emerge and attack it with your multiattack. Then, retreat to cover. Your immunities should keep you safe from attacks of opportunity, and even if they don't, one attack of opportunity is better than standing around like a sitting duck. Repeat these tactics.

MAGE

CR 6

Mages are 9th-level wizards with a fantastic combination of default spells that, when played correctly, can devastate an unprepared group of foes.

Fighting Style: Lurker. You have the *greater invisibility* spell and a whole bunch of spells capable of decimating a group of unprepared enemies. Stay hidden, stay safe!

Set-up: Cover and Room to Maneuver. You'll want to stay invisible during the combat, so make sure you've got plenty of room to move between spells and have cover to duck behind in case the enemy tries to fish you out with area-of-effect spells.

Weaknesses: Being Seen. Your most outstanding defense is your *greater invisibility* spell, which keeps you hidden even when you make attacks. But if the enemy possesses truesight or blindsight or is under the effect of the *see invisibility* spell, it won't take long to find you. Strike hard and fast.

Pair With Minions. Use minions to tie up and distract yours while you attack from hiding. Ensure they're immune to the damage types of your area of effect spells, lest you remove them from the board.

Tactics: Turn Invisible and Blast 'Em. Try to cast *greater invisibility* before the start of combat if you can. Otherwise, make it the first spell you cast. Immediately move to a location that provides at least half-cover. You might Hide for a turn or two to make your enemies think you've run away. Then, when ready, use your area of effect spells (*cone of cold*, *fireball*). Make sure to move between shots, always taking cover when possible. Save your 4th-level spell slots if you have to cast *greater invisibility* on yourself again (it only lasts 1 minute).

MAGMIN

Built of fire and magma, this short humanoid radiates intense heat that causes the air around it to shimmer.

Magmins are stumpy elemental humanoids from the region where the elemental planes of earth and fire meet. They love to make fire wherever they go.

Fighting Style: Minion. You're small and relatively squishy and have no fear of death since it merely sends you back to your home plane. And, as a bonus, you explode when you die, setting more things on fire.

Set-up: Hot, Up Close, and Personal. Setting things on fire is your favorite thing to do. So the less time you waste getting to your target, the better. Team up with others of your kind to get as close to your targets as possible, creating obstacles they can't ignore. Since you're immune to fire, consider fighting in areas with plenty of natural fire hazards like volcanoes or forest fires.

Weaknesses: Squishy. You have only 9 hit points. Even with your damage resistances, it doesn't take much to destroy you. But you want to die anyways because it sets more things on fire, plus it's funny.

Pair With Controllers. Team up with creatures capable of slowing or restraining your targets, making it easier for you to reach them and set them ablaze.

Tactics: Burn, Baby, Burn. Start combat within 30 feet of your targets. On your turn, get close and use your touch, setting them ablaze on a hit. Consider provoking attacks of opportunity, so you get hit and explode.

MANTICORE

 **CR 3**

This creature has a vaguely humanoid head, a lion's body, and dragon's wings. Its tail ends in long, sharp spikes.

Ugly, mean, and crafty, manticores are dangerous for low-level targets. They also speak Common, which makes them all the eerier.

Fighting Style: Artillerist. Your tail spike attack lets you stick to the skies and make three ranged attacks per turn. You only have 24 spikes, so after eight rounds, you're spent.

Set-up: Wide Open Spaces. As a flier, you want to ensure that you have a lot of space to maneuver, either the open sky or high ceilings. You're clever enough to understand the value of cover, too, so incorporate that when possible.

Weaknesses: Mental Saving Throws. The quickest way to ground you is through magic, and unfortunately, you don't have excellent saving throw proficiencies beyond your base modifiers. Especially be careful around spellcasters who use enchantment magic. As soon as a target reveals the ability to cast spells, make it your primary target.

Pair With Brutes and Minions. Keep enemies on the ground preoccupied with targets that fight up close and personal, so you don't have to worry about the enemy firing back at you.

Tactics: Fly and Shoot. Start combat up to 100 feet away from the enemy in the sky. Fire your spikes at whatever target looks the "softest" (aka, no armor). If one of the enemies starts casting spells or shooting back at you, go after that one instead.

MEDUSA

 **CR 6**

This slender, attractive woman has strangely glowing eyes and a full head of hissing snakes for hair.

Extraordinarily deadly and versatile, medusas represent a deadly challenge even for higher-level groups.

Fighting Style: Elite. You have decent defensive capabilities, strong melee attacks, and even better-than-average Stealth. Your longbow allows you to serve as an artillerist, and let's not forget our controller feature—the dread gaze of the medusa. You can fill any necessary role.

Set-up: Wide Open Spaces with Lots of Hiding Spaces. You are an effective combatant no matter the range—close, medium, or far. However, you want your enemies to start far from you so you can engage them in three separate stages. Make sure you have a large lair where you can start combat hidden, filled with difficult terrain and hazards that make reaching you an arduous affair.

Weaknesses: Mental Saving Throws. Cover and distance should protect you from most damage-dealing spells, but enchantment magic will quickly disrupt your tactics. You're smart enough to know that most enchantment spells only have a range of 60 feet, so keep your distance until you can eliminate spellcasters.

Pair With Brutes and Minions. Work alongside brutes and minions that are either blind (like grimlocks) or immune to petrification (like most elementals). These creatures won't suffer from your Petrifying Gaze and will help keep your targets locked up while you target them with your ranged attacks and Gaze.

Tactics: Start Far Away, Then Move Closer. Start combat between 60 and 150 feet away from your targets behind cover. Use your longbow to remove spellcasters first. Hide that you're a medusa until it's too late for your enemies to react appropriately. When a target comes within 30 feet of you, use your gaze against it. Keep using your bow, moving behind cover after each shot. Once you remove those who pose the biggest threat to you, close in so you can use both your Petrifying Gaze and attacks at the same time.

MEPHIT, DUST

CR 1/2

This small humanoid creature has thin wings, small horns, and a mischievous smile. It appears to be made from dust.

Perhaps it's because they're composed of earth and air, but dust mephits are imp-like elementals obsessed with death.

Fighting Style: Controller. You can cast the *sleep* spell once per day and have a blinding breath attack that requires a Dexterity saving throw. Plus, when you die, you can blind targets as you go.

Set-up: Enough Space to Move Around. Although you aren't afraid of death (elementals simply return home after being destroyed), you still want to cause as much chaos as possible while on the material plane. Fight in places where your flight speed can keep you away from your enemies.

Weaknesses: Relatively Squishy. You have relatively low hit points for a CR 1/2 creature, making it relatively easy to stop you. Additionally, you have vulnerability to fire, a favorite damage type for most spellcasters. If you get destroyed, ensure it's while you're within 5 feet of another creature so you can blind them.

Pair With Brutes and Minions. Use brutes and minions to keep enemies distracted while you fly around using your Blinding Breath and claws. Working with creatures unaffected by blindness is helpful, but you're too malevolent to care either way.

Tactics: Sleep, Blind, Skirmish. If using the summoning variant, try calling additional dust mephits before combat starts. Start combat within 60 feet of your targets, preferably hidden. On your turn, use your *sleep* spell to target as many enemies as possible. Fly closer and take cover. When your next turn comes up, move close enough to hit any targets still standing with your Blinding Breath. Don't worry about getting so close that the targets might get an attack of opportunity against you; getting destroyed gives you one last chance to blind your foes. If you survive until the third round, attack blinded targets with your claws. If there are no blinded targets around, reuse your Blinding Breath if it recharged, attack unconscious foes, or attack whoever is nearest to you.

MEPHIT, ICE

This small humanoid creature has thin wings, small horns, and a mischievous smile. It appears to be made from solid ice.

Ice mephits are lethargic, cruel elementals who enjoy delivering pain to living creatures.

Fighting Style: Lurker. You have the False Appearance feature, Stealth +3, and can cast fog cloud. Create ambushes to surprise your foes.

Set-up: Cold, Dark Places. Your False Appearance trait allows you to disguise yourself as a shard of ice. Make sure you pick fights where you can benefit from this feature.

Weaknesses: Relatively Squishy. Although you have 21 hit points, your AC is only 11, and you have vulnerabilities to fire and bludgeoning, two popular damage types. Fortunately, death isn't permanent for you so long as you're not on your home plane. And you explode when you die, so make sure you're at least within 5 feet of some foes when you inevitably explode.

Pair With Brutes and Minions. Work alongside brutes and minions, particularly those with blindsight, so that they can see in your *fog cloud*. They'll keep your enemy preoccupied while you lurk in your *fog cloud*, waiting for your frost breath to recharge.

Tactics: Surprise, Breath, Hide. If using the summoning variant, try calling additional ice mephits before combat starts. Start combat hidden with your False Appearance feature. When a few targets come within 15 feet of you, surprise them and use your Frost Breath, hitting as many as possible. Then fly high where they can't reach you (especially enemies with bludgeoning weapons). On your next turn, use your Frost Breath again if it recharges, or cast *fog cloud* to give yourself a place to hide while waiting for it to recharge. Once the Frost Breath recharges, pop out of your fog cloud and attack again. Otherwise, take the Dodge action until it's ready.

MEPHIT, MAGMA

CR 1/2

This small humanoid creature has thin wings, small horns, and a mischievous smile. It appears to be made from magma.

Magma mephits are dull and stubborn creatures composed of molten earth.

Fighting Style: Lurker. Your False Appearance trait allows you to hide as an ordinary lump of magma. Plus, you have a +3 to Stealth. Set up ambushes whenever possible.

Set-up: Hot Spots. Your False Appearance feature works best when you have other mounds of magma around to hide among. Plus, with immunity to fire damage, you can duck into lava or step into burning buildings without fear of taking damage.

Weaknesses: Cold. You have decent hit points for a CR 1/2 creature but have a vulnerability to cold damage. It doesn't take a high Intelligence score to recognize that "cold puts out fire." Be wary of spellcasters.

Pair With Brutes and Minions. Use brutes and minions to distract your foes while you lurk in hiding, waiting for your fire breath to recharge or your *heat metal* spell to run its course.

Tactics: Series of Ambushes. If using the summoning variant, try calling additional magma mephits before combat starts. Start combat hidden using your False Appearance trait. When a target wearing metal armor comes within 60 feet of you, emerge and use your *heat metal* spell against it. Then, fly away and find a new hiding spot using your False Appearance trait. Continue to concentrate on *heat metal*, dealing as much damage as possible. When the targets come near you again, emerge and use Fire Breath, then fly away again. Repeat the same tactics as before, finding a new hiding place and allowing your Fire Breath to recharge.

MEPHIT, STEAM

This small humanoid creature has thin wings, small horns, and a mischievous smile. It appears to be made from hot steam.

Steam mephits consider themselves the leader of all mephits and love bossing other creatures around.

Fighting Style: Skirmisher. You have a flying speed of 30 feet and can cast *blur* to protect yourself from hits. Focus on making hit-and-run attacks with your Steam Breath and claws.

Set-up: Plenty of Room to Maneuver. You want to have ceilings or an open sky above you to make it easier for you to make hit-and-run attacks while under the effects of the *blur* spell.

Weaknesses: Relatively Squishy. Although you have 21 hit points and immunity to fire, your AC is only 10. Make sure to get blur up as soon as you can and try to maintain concentration on it. Once you do, start fighting as close as possible to your enemies to encourage them to explode you.

Pair With Artillerists. Work alongside artillerists who can fire at the enemy while you distract the enemy with hit-and-run tactics.

Tactics: Attack! If using the summoning variant, try calling additional steam mephits before combat starts. Additionally, try to cast blur before you start combat. Start combat within 15 feet of your foes in the air. On your turn, fly towards the enemies and use your Steam Breath to hit as many as possible. Move away, relying on your blur to keep you safe. If your Steam Breath recharges on your next turn, use it again. Otherwise, make hit-and-run attacks using your claws. Don't worry about attacks of opportunity—if you die, you explode, damaging foes as you go.

MERFOLK

 CR 1/8

This blue-skinned aquatic creature has the torso, arms, and head of a humanoid but the lower half and tail of a fish. It moves through the water with ease.

Merfolk are often the dominant humanoid species of the sea. They typically live in small, nomadic tribes or great kingdoms below the waves.

Fighting Style: Minion. Your defensive capabilities and offensive capabilities are both relatively low. The only feature that makes you stand out is your quick swim speed of 40 feet. It's best to work in groups.

Set-up: Wet Environments. So long as you're fighting land dwellers, you want to fight on your turf, below water, where your swim speed will give you an edge over non-swimmers. Make sure never to fight alone unless absolutely necessary.

Weaknesses: Fodder. You have low AC, 11 hit points, and a weak weapon attack. Without backup, you and others in your tribe won't fare well against well-prepared groups.

Pair With Brutes, Tanks, and Controllers. Use other melee support to draw attacks away from you while you provide support. And controllers can help by creating situations for you to gain advantage on your attacks.

Tactics: Spread Out and Keep Your Distance. Start combat in water 40 feet away from the enemy. On your turn, ready your spear to throw at any enemy that comes within 20 feet of you. On your next turn, use your swimming speed again to put at least 40 feet of distance between you and your enemies, readying more spears in c

ase they get close. Space yourself from the other minions you're working with to reduce the risk of area-of-attack spells.

MERROW

 CR 2

This giant has pale green, scaled skin, large, webbed hands, and a fish tail instead of legs. On either side of its neck are slotted gills.

Merrows are essentially the merfolk equivalent of ogres. They swell in undersea caves where they store treasure stolen from coastal dwellers and sailors.

Fighting Style: Controller. Your defensive capabilities are relatively low, but you pack a mean punch thanks to a multiattack. Typically, this would qualify a creature like you as a brute, but you also come equipped with a "get over here!" style harpoon attack, helpful in singling out backline targets.

Set-up: Lots of Room to Move Underwater. As an amphibious creature with a swim speed of 40 feet, you always want to fight underwater. Not only are you four times as fast there, but your foes are probably not great swimmers.

Weaknesses: Relatively Squishy. Although you are a CR 2 creature, you have the defensive capabilities of a CR 1/4 creature. Avoid targets with strong melee attacks, and always fight underwater where ranged attacks are less effective.

Pair With Brutes, Minions, and Tanks. Work alongside foes built for melee combat who can distract your foes while you use your harpoon to cherry-pick enemies.

Tactics: Hook 'Em and Bite 'Em. Start combat underwater 20 feet away from your targets. On your turn, fire your harpoon at a weak-looking target within 20 feet of you, then reel it towards you and bite it. Continue to attack this creature while your minions (if there are any) keep the target's allies busy.

MIMIC

 CR 2

What appeared to be a chest filled with treasure comes to life as it grows long, glistening tentacles and many sharp teeth.

As everyone's favorite treasure-chest-shaped terror, mimics have long been a fun tool for GMs to keep their players on their toes.

Fighting Style: Lurker. You can take on the appearance of any object that you like. While in this form, you wait for foes to come by, then your adhesive coating to grab them and bite them.

Set-up: Enticing Offers. The best way to surprise prey is to disguise yourself as an enticing object, such as a treasure chest or drinking fountain, or something that gets used a lot without thought, such as a door, ladder, or section of floor.

Weaknesses: Stereotypes. Most of your enemies will know better than to approach a lonely treasure chest in an empty room without inspecting it first. Avoid suspicion by taking the form of "less obvious" mimic-friendly objects.

Pair With Artillerists. Your adhesive will literally keep foes stuck to you, keeping them distracted, allowing artillerists to pick them off from the safety of cover.

Tactics: Lurk and Strike. Take the form of an everyday object found in your environment. If the target touches you, it adheres to you. Once stuck to you, you can bite it with advantage. Otherwise, use your pseudopod to grapple it and then bite on the next round.

MINOTAUR

 CR 3

The glazed bovine eyes of this bull-headed humanoid betray a feral cunning. With the torso of a muscular human, this beast is covered with thick, shaggy fur from the waist down. Its gnarled and callused hands grip the haft of a massive axe, the edge stained from the blood of its previous victims. With a furious snort and a stamp of its hooves, it lowers its deadly horns.

This a-MAZE-ing monster lurks within labyrinths and other subterranean areas filled with dizzying corridors and endless chambers.

Fighting Style: Brute. You more or less have the same build as a mid-level barbarian (Reckless), but even better, thanks to your Charge feature. You can also play the lurker role, thanks to your Labyrinthine Recall and relatively quick speed.

Set-up: Room to Charge. You want to start combat with your charge, but you don't want your foes to escape. Naturally, you should fight in a narrow corridor—good thing there's a whole bunch of those in labyrinths.

Weaknesses: Poor Dexterity. Although you have relatively good Strength, Con, and Wisdom, your Dexterity is pretty low, making you an easy target for spells that force Dex saves. Watch out for spellcasters.

Pair With Artillerists. As a brute, you will keep the foes distracted as they try to remove you from the battlefield.

Tactics: Charge and Gore. Start combat 40 feet away from your target. When combat begins, use your Reckless feature and Charge, potentially knocking your target backward. On subsequent turns, Charge when possible. Otherwise, rely on your greataxe.

MUMMY

 **CR 3**

Wrapped from head to toe in ancient strips of moldering linen, this humanoid moves with a shuffling gait.

Mummies are classic tomb-dwelling undead creatures wrapped in bandages. They often serve more powerful undead as guardians of the site's treasure stash.

Fighting Style: Controller. You can use your Dreadful Glare every turn, frightening enemies with low Wisdom scores, and your Rotting Fist is a strong enough attack to make your foes keep plenty of distance.

Set-up: Up Close and Personal. Although you're a controller, you move relatively slowly, and your weakness to fire makes you a sitting duck against spell attacks. Get the drop on your foes fast, and ensure you've got an unobstructed path so you can use your glare without issue.

Weaknesses: Magic (Especially Fire). You have resistance to nonmagical attacks, but magic weapons and spells—especially fire—will cut through your 58 hit points pretty quickly, especially considering that you have poor AC, Dexterity, and Wisdom. Unfortunately, you're probably not Intelligent enough to recognize spellcasters without help from a more competent commander.

Pair With Artillerists. You'll be up close and personal, paralyzing and inflicting curses, keeping foes distracted. Meanwhile, your allies can fire their ranged weapons from the safety of cover.

Tactics: Dash and Bash. Start combat within 20 feet of your foes. On your turn, use your Dreadful Glare to target whatever enemy is closest to you. Then, use your Rotting Fist on the same target. On subsequent rounds, continue to use your Dreadful Glare either on the same target (if it failed its last saving throw against it) or against a new target if the current one is immune. Continue to attack the same target with your rotting fist until it's dead.

MUMMY LORD

 CR 15

Dirty linen strips swathe this emaciated, once-noble figure from head to toe. Its eyes burn with unholy light.

Much more Intelligent than their lesser counterparts, mummy lords are the revived corpses of priests, kings, spellcasters, and other figures of import. Their presence is enough to double the dangers inherent in their lairs.

Fighting Style: Controller. You come with a plethora of controller spells and features, almost overwhelmingly so. Your job is to stand back and use this magic on your foes while your undead minions do the dirty work.

Set-up: Behind Minions. Make sure that you fight your foes with some minions at your side. If you don't have any, you can use your "undead GPS" Lair Action to summon a few. You want to keep your distance, especially since you have relatively low hit points for a CR 15 (16 in your lair) creature.

Weaknesses: Magic Weapons and Fire. You have four good saving throws and Magic Resistance. However, your immunity to bludgeoning, piercing, and slashing quickly disappears when foes show up with magic weapons. Keep plenty of distance between yourself and these targets, using your spells if necessary. Additionally, you have no bonus to your Dexterity saving throws. If a spellcaster uses *fireball* or a similar fire-based spell that forces a Dex save, you will have difficulty avoiding it.

Pair With Minions. You have a Lair Action that lets you give all undead within the lair the ability to detect living creatures for a round; use this to call minions every other turn (1d6 mummies should do the trick). Use these minions to attack targets while you use your spells and Legendary Actions to subdue your foes.

Tactics: Control and Summon. Before combat begins, cast *guardian of faith* to give yourself an extra line of defense, placing it between you and your enemies. Start combat at least 60 feet away from your foes. If you don't have minions present already, use your Lair Action to call some to you. Otherwise, use the Lair Action that lets you shut down spellcasters. Before your turn begins, save your Whirlwind of Sand Lair Action to make a quick escape if your enemies get too close. You can also use your Dreadful Glare

Lair Action to target individual creatures who attempt to reach you. When your turn begins, cast *silence*, targeting as many spellcasters as possible. So long as *silence* is effective, alternate between your Lair Action that allows you to summon other undead and the one that shuts down spells (just in case). If you lose *silence*, recast it. Otherwise, use your *command* spell to give advantage to your minions. Consider targeting weakened spellcasters with harm, especially if minions are near them—combo this with your Channel Negative Energy feature to prevent downed heroes from healing.

NAGA, GUARDIAN

 **CR 10**

A contemplative humanoid face framed by a cobra-like hood adorns the body of this long, brightly-colored serpent.

Guardian nagas are typically wise and good defenders of sacred places and items of magical power. They prefer non-violent solutions whenever possible.

Fighting Style: Controller. You have a diverse spell list that focuses on subduing and removing enemies from your lair rather than hurting them (although you can hurt them if it comes to that).

Set-up: Plenty of Room to Move. You want lairs that make it difficult for creatures to reach you but still grant you enough room to cast your enchantment and abjuration spells to defend yourself and your treasure.

Weaknesses: Relatively Few Hit Points. Although you possess a wide range of defensive features, such as AC 18 and five saving throw proficiencies, you have relatively low hit points. Melee attackers with a lot of action economy could give you trouble. Make sure to keep them away from you.

Pair With Controllers or Support. As a primarily non-violent creature, you want to work alongside other creatures who share the same compassionate response to combat as you. Most celestials are helpful in this regard.

Tactics: Diffuse and Remove. Before combat begins, protect yourself and your allies with *freedom of movement*. Learn as much as you can about your enemies with *clairvoyance*. Start combat 60 feet away from your enemies. Use *calm emotions* to diffuse the situation. If that fails, use subsequent turns to convince targets to remove the area using *banishment* or *hold person* to deal with the biggest troublemakers.

If you have to fight, use flamestrike, which you can use up to three times (burning your 5th and 6th level slots). Continue to use either banishment or *hold person*, and bite or spit poison at anyone who comes too close.

NAGA, SPIRIT

CR 8

Yellowed, venom-dripping fangs fill the human-like mouth of this sinister serpentine monstrosity.

Standing in stark contrast to the benevolent guardian nagas, spirit nagas are gloomy, hateful monstrosities that constantly bemoan and plot against creatures that they feel wronged them.

Fighting Style: Controller. Although you come with a variety of spells, your relatively poor defensive capabilities beg that you control your targets as much as possible before you start throwing *lightning bolts* at them.

Set-up: Room to Maneuver. You're relatively quick, so you want a lair with plenty of room to move around. Choose those with lots of cover, too, to ensure that enemy artillerists and spellcasters can't target you between your attacks.

Weaknesses: Relatively Poor Defenses. You are a CR 8 creature but have the defenses of one much lower. A melee attacker with a lot of action economy will make quick work of your measly 75 hit points. Keep plenty of distance between yourself and your foes and stay out of sight.

Pair With Brutes, Minions, and Tanks. You don't want the targets reaching you, so make sure that you've got some melee helpers out in front taking blows while you slither between areas of cover.

Tactics: Cast and Move. Start combat hidden within 60 feet of your targets but not too close. On your turn, emerge from hiding and cast *dominate person* against the target you suspect will lose its saving throw (you're wise enough to tell the difference). Then, duck behind cover, and use your telepathic connection to that creature to turn it against the others. Use its skills and features to target those it can harm the most. If you failed to capture that target or its allies ended the condition on it, try again on a different target. Continue to keep your distance, taking cover between castings. *Dimension door* to a safer spot if necessary. When you catch three or more targets standing in a line, use *lightning bolt* against them, especially if the enemies look bad at Dexterity saving throws (i.e., heroes wearing heavy armor or spellcasters).

NIGHTMARE

CR 3

This eerie horse-like creature's skin is an inky blackness. Fire spurts from its hair and nostrils, and its hooves spray sparks.

These fiendish dread steeds serve as steeds for creatures of exceptional evil.

Fighting Style: Support. A creature riding you gains a wide variety of benefits: a flying speed of 90 feet, fire resistance, and the ability to enter the Ethereal plane and vice versa at will. Plus, you can make attacks at the same time that they do.

Set-up: Open Spaces. You and your companions will want to fight in places where you can fly around without too many obstacles in your way, essentially turning you and your rider into skirmishers. Failing that, use the Ethereal Plane to escape into a sideways dimension so you can fight as lurkers.

Weaknesses: Bright. Your ability to fly and lurk in the Ethereal Plane are handy features for you and your allies. Unfortunately, you burn like a bonfire, making it hard for you to sneak up on foes.

Pair With Artillerists. Although any evil creature can ride you, you work best with Artillerists, allowing them to fly and attack while you weave in and out of the Ethereal Plane.

Tactics: Lurk, Then Appear. Since you are an intelligent creature, you and your rider take your own turns. Start combat within the normal-range distance of your rider's ranged attack. If your rider goes first, it fires at the targets. If you go first, enter the Ethereal Plane with your rider. Use a turn or two to reposition yourself and choose a target you want to hurt. Your rider should Ready an attack to use against the chosen target. On your next turn, reenter the material plane. Your rider fires its attack at your target, and then you fly 90 feet away to avoid follow-up attacks. Before you return to the Ethereal Plane, your rider makes additional attacks (if possible). Continue these tactics, using the Ethereal Plane to keep both of you safe every other turn.

NOBLE

Nobles are usually influential members of society, representing monarchs, wealthy elites, and other beings of status.

Fighting Style: Tank. Despite your relatively low hit point total and low CR, you have better-than-average AC for your challenge and the Parry reaction. Use these to draw attacks while your lackeys make attacks.

Set-up: Up Close and Personal. If you plan to get into combat—and not flee in fear of a swift death—make sure you start combat as close to the enemy as possible with plenty of minions to help you.

Weaknesses: Few Hit Points. Although you have a lot of extraordinary defensive abilities, you still only have 9 hit points. It only takes one or two good hits to knock you down, so make your time on the battlefield count.

Pair With Artillerists and Minions. Use minions to attack your foes while you have them distracted. Meanwhile, your artillerists fire from the safety of cover.

Tactics: Dodge and Parry. Start combat within 30 feet of your enemies, and make sure your sword is drawn. Take the Dodge action and start goading your enemy into making attacks against you. Use your reaction to Parry attacks or to hit targets when they provoke attacks of opportunity.

OGRE

 CR 2

This creature's python-thick arms and stumpy legs conspire to drag its dirty knuckles through the wet grass and mud. The stooped giant blinks its dim eyes, and an excess of soupy drool spills over its bulbous lips. Its misshapen features resemble a man's face rendered in watercolor, then distorted by a careless splash. It snarls as it charges, a sound the offspring of bear and man might make, showing flat black teeth well suited for grinding bones to paste.

Ogres are "lesser" giants, standing only ten to twelve feet tall. They frequently work alongside creatures of other species serving as muscle and protection.

Fighting Style: Brute. No creature better represents the brute fighting style in Fifth Edition than you, the ogre. With intelligence too low for complicated tactics, you prefer to get close and bash.

Set-up: Up Close and Personal. You don't want a lot of obstacles in the way of your targets, nor do you want a way for them to escape.

Weaknesses: Poor Defensive Capabilities. You only have 59 hit points and an AC of 11. And unfortunately, your offensive capabilities don't balance the CR equation. It doesn't take long for your foes to drop you to 0 hit points.

Pair With Artillerists and Support. Keep the enemies distracted while your artillerist allies fire from the safety of cover. Use support to keep you standing while your foes pick away at your hit points.

Tactics: Dash and Bash. Start within 40 feet of your enemies. On your turn, charge the nearest target and start hitting it with your club. Continue doing this until it stops moving, or you do.

OGRE, HALF

CR 1

This being resembles a somewhat ugly human. It wears tattered skins over a suit of hide armor.

Functioning as a "lower challenge ogre," the half-ogre is a little weaker than their giant ancestors but marginally more intelligent.

Fighting Style: Brute. Regardless of your minor bump in intelligence over full ogres, you still prefer to dash and bash.

Set-up: Up Close and Personal. Your job is to hit things until they stop moving. Make sure there aren't a lot of obstacles in the way of your targets.

Weaknesses: Poor Defensive Capabilities. Your AC 12 and 30 hit points are terrible, especially considering that you're a CR 1 creature. Fortunately, the damage you deal and your to-hit modifier help balance it out a little.

Pair With Artillerists and Support. Keep the enemies distracted while your artillerist allies fire from the safety of cover. Use support to keep you standing while your foes pick away at your hit points.

Tactics: Dash and Bash. Start within 30 feet of your enemies. On your turn, charge the nearest target and start hitting it with your greataxe. Continue doing this until it stops moving, or you do.

ONI

Clad in beautiful armor, this exotically garbed giant roars, its tusks glistening and its eyes afire with murderous intent.

Fifth Edition onis are ogre mages. They are far more intelligent and clever than their distant cousins and extraordinarily dangerous.

Fighting Style: Lurker. You come with various spells and abilities that allow you to ambush your foes, such as the *darkness* and *invisibility* spells and your ability to change shape at will.

Set-up: Hidden and Close. Place yourself in an environment where you can easily hide using one of your spells or the Change Shape feature. Make sure there's plenty of cover and escape routes to retreat into after you make your attacks.

Weaknesses: Losing Mobility. Losing your ability to move will severely limit your combat options. While your Magic Resistance and Strength modifier are enough to avoid most spells that can restrain you, a strong grappler with a high Athletics modifier might get ahold of you. When this happens, use *gaseous form* to escape.

Pair With Brutes or Minions. You want to work alongside creatures that can keep your foes distracted while you stay mobile and make attacks from range.

Tactics: Lurk, Attack, Escape. Start combat hidden using *darkness*, *invisibility*, or Change Shape, ideally 30 feet away. Use your flight to distance yourself and your foes if necessary. Open with *cone of cold*, targeting as many foes as possible. Then retreat into full cover. Use *invisibility* or *darkness* to cover your escape, then find a new area to stage an ambush.

OOZE, BLACK PUDDING

 **CR 4**

This black, amorphous blob piles up on itself, a quivering mound of midnight sludge that glistens darkly before surging forward.

Black puddings are shadowy blobs capable of eating flesh, wood, metal, and bone. Only stone remains behind them, including valuable gems.

Fighting Style: Brute. Although you are painfully slow and have a pitiful AC, most opponents loathe your attacks as they quickly destroy valuable weapons and armor.

Set-up: Surprise. You aren't fast or intelligent or wise—or even sentient, for that matter. But sometimes, you luck into spots that keep you fed, such as right around a corner, in an area of magic darkness (your blindsight lets you see through it), or at the bottom of a pit.

Weaknesses: Poor AC. Although you have decent hit points and plenty of damage immunities, you only have AC 7. And without fire immunity, spellcasters with fire-based magic will quickly stop your blobby ways.

Pair With Artillerists. You aren't intelligent enough to tell friends from foes (and you're content to eat, either), but wise creatures might use you to distract the foes while they fire their weapons from the safety of cover.

Tactics: Wobble and Bop. Start within 60 feet of your foes, where you can see them. Move towards the nearest target. Smack it with your pseudopod. Repeat.

OOZE, GELATINOUS CUBE

CR 2

Bits of broken weapons, coins, and a partially digested skeleton are visible inside this quivering cube of slime.

Gelatinous cubes are strange creatures who serve as guardians and housekeepers in dungeons, using their full girth to slither down hallways, cleaning it of dust, dropped goods, and adventurer corpses.

Fighting Style: Lurker. You are transparent, which lets you "sneak up" on targets. Of course, if you've recently eaten and have bits of skeleton and armor floating around in your mass, your foes might realize they're in trouble.

Set-up: Narrow Hallways. You take up 1,000 cubic feet of space. Move through narrow passageways 10 feet wide and 10 feet high so that you can gobble up anything in your path. Alternatively, sit at the bottom of a pit that perfectly fits your dimensions.

Weaknesses: Slow. You have an AC 6, 15 feet of movement, and a -4 on your Dexterity saving throws. Make sure you surprise foes whenever possible; otherwise, they'll remove you from the battlefield before you even get close.

Pair With Controllers. Although you aren't intelligent enough to coordinate with other monsters, spellcasters might use controller spells to slow down your targets, making it possible for you to mow them down.

Tactics: Clean Up. Start combat within 10 feet of your foes (assuming you surprised them). Use your Engulf feature to gobble up as many as possible. Continue on your way while they struggle inside of you.

OOZE, GRAY

CR 1/2

A seemingly mundane puddle, a patch of moist stone, or glistening rock is suddenly revealed to be more as a terrible pseudopod lashes out.

Although the gray ooze is seemingly the "weakest" of the oozes, it is also one of the quickest-moving ones (although that's still not saying much) and capable of dealing psychic damage using the psychic gray ooze variant.

Fighting Style: Lurker. You have a False Appearance trait that makes you look like an ordinary puddle so long as you remain motionless. Plus, you have a positive Stealth bonus, which allows you to hide.

Set-up: Rocky, Wet Places. Your False Appearance trait disguises you as a wet rock or an oily pool, so make sure to lurk within areas that fit that description.

Weaknesses: Slow. Like most oozes, you are painfully slow, possessing only a movement speed of 10 feet, AC of 8, and a Dexterity score of 6. Make sure that you wait in hiding until a creature comes near.

Pair With Controllers. If you're a psychic, you might recognize the benefit of working alongside creatures that can slow or stop your targets. But if you aren't psychic, you aren't intelligent enough to recognize this. Either way, controllers have spells and features that can help you reach your enemies before they can escape.

Tactics: Lurk, Then Attack. Start combat disguised as an oily pool or wet rock. When a target comes within 5 feet of you, reveal yourself and attack. If you have psychic powers, instead attack from hiding. It isn't clear if this reveals your location, so you might be able to make psychic attacks while remaining undetected.

OOZE, OCHRE JELLY

 CR 2

This yellow-orange amoeboid creature slithers across the ground, pseudopods grasping ahead of its slow approach.

Ochre jellies serve as the lower CR counterpart to black puddings thanks to their curiously similar builds. One thing that makes ochre jellies stand out is that they're marginally more intelligent than the other oozes in the Fifth Edition monster book, having Intelligence scores on par with beasts like birds and horses.

Fighting Style: Brute. Although you are a touch more intelligent than other oozes, you're still a slow-moving blob. You're built to get close and hit things with your pseudopod.

Set-up: Lurking Just Out of Sight. Although you aren't Dexterous enough to hide, you know it's always better to hide just around the corner, at the bottom of pits, or even stuck to the ceiling. With a speed of 10 feet, you don't want to start combat too far from your targets.

Weaknesses: Slow. You have a movement speed of 10 feet, AC of 8, and a Dexterity score of 6. Make sure you get as close to your targets as possible before initiating combat.

Pair With Controllers. Having limited intelligence, you might recognize that working near or alongside creatures that can blind, slow, grapple, or stun your targets keeps you well-fed.

Tactics: Wobble and Bop. Start combat within 10 feet of your foes. Charge the nearest target and hit it with your pseudopod. Repeat.

ORC

This muscular, gray-skinned humanoid wears armor made from thick furs and brandishes a large, blood-stained greataxe.

Orcs are strong, hardy humanoids and masters of war. Although they live tribal lifestyles and tend towards the chaotic end of the spectrum, they are well-organized and quite clever.

Fighting Style: Brute. Your greataxe deals considerable damage and hits with a +5 modifier and your "Aggressive" bonus action (likely to be renamed with the forthcoming edition update) allows you to Dash as a bonus action.

Set-up: Room to Charge. Although you're a brute, your Aggressive bonus action allows you to clear 60 feet of distance and still make an attack. Allow this space to prevent the enemy from reaching you first, and ensure there isn't difficult terrain or obstacles in your path.

Weaknesses: Low Armor Class. Despite having excellent attack capabilities, you have only AC 13 with only 15 hit points to keep you safe. It doesn't take a lot to take you out.

Pair With Artillerists and Controllers. Your allies with ranged attacks will fire from the safety of cover while you keep the enemy distracted. Use controllers to blind, disarm, slow, etc., your foes, keeping you safe and granting advantage on your attacks.

Tactics: Dash and Slash. Start combat 40 to 60 feet away from the enemy. On your turn, move and use your bonus action to Dash to reach your targets. Attack with your greataxe.

Orc Eye. Orc Eyes are the priests of orc tribes, functioning as support and controllers. It uses *bless* to amplify the best fighters. And it uses *command* to grant advantage to them.

Orc War Chief. War chiefs are more robust and more intelligent orcs whose Battle Cry grants advantage on attacks to those who hear it. Beyond this feature, the war chief fights the same way as other orcs.

Orog. Orogs are larger, more vicious orcs and can sometimes play the role of tanks thanks to their plate mail.

OTYUGH

 CR 5

This three-legged freak is mostly mouth. Three tentacles, two tipped with barbs and one with eyes, extend from its sides.

Otyughs are everyone's favorite impossible-to-pronounce monster, notable for lurking in sewers, eating filth and rotting things. Despite their off-putting appearance, they're actually somewhat intelligent (roughly the same as great apes) and even have their own language.

Fighting Style: Brute. Your tentacles and bite both deal tremendous damage, the latter infecting targets with a debilitating disease. Once you have multiple targets grappled, you can slam them against hard surfaces.

Set-up: Dark, Dirty Places. Otyughs thrive in environments that are perpetually dark and filled with filth. They also have darkvision out to 120 feet, which means they can usually see foes before foes can see them.

Weaknesses: Mental Saving Throws. You're tough, but you don't have any natural protections against enchantments, which leaves you vulnerable to spellcasters. Unfortunately, you aren't intelligent enough to recognize spellcasters until they use flashy spells that deal damage.

Pair With Artillerists and Controllers. Artillerist allies can fire from the safety of cover while you distract enemies. Meanwhile, controllers can use magic and unique features to grant you advantage on your attacks.

Tactics: Grab, Bite, and Slam. Start combat 30 feet away from your targets. On your turn, move towards them and grab up to two creatures with your tentacles. Then, bite the one that seems most tender (i.e., not wearing any armor). If the targets prove difficult, use your slam against them next turn to soften them up and stun them.

OWLBEAR

 CR 3

An amalgam of fur and feathers, this bizarre half-bear, half-owl monstrosity raises its huge, ursine claws in anger.

Owlbears are cranky, aggressive creatures that lurk in forests and caverns. Fiercely territorial, they attack anything within their line of sight, especially if their young are near.

Fighting Style: Brute. You have a brutal Multiattack, letting you deal up an average of 24 damage per round.

Set-up: Up Close and Personal. You don't want to have a lot of obstacles or difficult terrain in the way of your enemies.

Weaknesses: Poor Defensive Capabilities. You're strong and deadly but you only have AC 13 and 59 hit points, roughly the same as a CR 2 ogre (who also has poor ratings for its CR). You have to ensure that you destroy your enemies before they destroy you.

Pair With Artillerists and Controllers. Although you're too aggressive and not smart enough to organize tactics with other creatures, others will find the benefit of you distracting foes. Controllers can use their magic to slow down enemies and set up advantage for your attack rolls.

Tactics: Dash and Slash. Start combat 40 feet away from your enemies. Charge the nearest target and start attacking it with your beak and claws.

PEGASUS

This magnificent horse has great bird-like wings upon its back and moves with quiet and proud grace.

Pegasi are another staple of Greek mythology that rears its head in the Fifth Edition monster book. They serve well as mounts for good-aligned creatures.

Fighting Style: Support. Assuming that someone is using you as their mount, you offer your rider a flying speed of 90 feet. Otherwise, your fighting style is more similar to skirmishers.

Set-up: Wide, Open Spaces. As a flying creature, you perform best when you have a lot of room above you to maneuver.

Weaknesses: Few Options. Although you add an outstanding flying speed to your rider's stat block, you don't offer much else to them (as opposed to a nightmare, for example).

Pair With Artillerists and Skirmishers. Your flying speed lets you keep plenty of distance between you and your foes. Work with riders who can make attacks with reach or range. Choose those with limited action economies since they'll rely primarily on their Ready action to make attacks.

Tactics: Dash Back and Forth. Start combat 90 feet or more away from your targets in the air. Your rider should Ready an attack for when you get within their reach or normal range. If the rider uses a weapon with a reach greater than 5 feet, move just outside of the target's reach so you don't provoke an attack of opportunity. Then, use your action to Dash back to your starting position or another area far from the enemies.

PERYTON

 CR 2

This creature has a stag's body, a hawk's wings and talons, and the head of a slavering wolf with a rack of sharp antlers on its brow.

Evil, intelligent, and brimming with unnatural hunger, perytons are a terror to anyone unprepared to face one in combat.

Fighting Style: Skirmisher. You have a flying speed of 60 feet, a Dive Attack that deals extra damage, and a feature that lets you fly out of an enemy's reach without provoking attacks of opportunity.

Set-up: Wide Open Spaces. You want plenty of space to maneuver and make hit-and-run attacks as a flier. A little cover is a good idea, too, so consider fighting in forests or canyons.

Weaknesses: Relatively Squishy. Your offensive capabilities are excellent, but you only have AC 13 and 33 hit points, far below the standard for your challenge rating. Make sure to skirmish and vanish behind cover as soon as possible.

Pair With Brutes and Controllers. Use brutal melee attackers to distract foes while you perform hit-and-run attacks. Controllers are helpful, too, limiting the action economy of your targets and setting you up for advantage.

Tactics: Hit-and-Run. Start combat 30 feet away from your targets, ideally hiding in cover. On your turn, move 30 feet straight toward a target and hit it with your multiattack. If the attack hits, you deal extra damage from your Dive Attack. Immediately retreat 30 feet into the sky. Because of your flyby feature, enemies can't reciprocate.

PHASE SPIDER

CR 3

This sizable spider-like monster has eerie, translucent skin revealing its internal organs. Its entire body shimmers and shifts, as if its presence in your reality isn't permanent.

Phase spiders are foul creatures that live on the Ethereal Plane and can move between the two realms in a wink of an eye.

Fighting Style: Lurker. Your Ethereal Jaunt ability allows you to step into the Ethereal Plain from the Material Plane or vice versa as a bonus action. This useful feature helps you ambush and escape enemies.

Set-up: Webbed Spaces. As a spider creature, you have both Spider Climb and Web Walker, the latter allowing you to move through webbing without restriction. Since it's unlikely that your foes will have similar protections (unless they use the *freedom of movement* spell or something similar).

Weaknesses: Relatively Squishy. Thank goodness for your ability to step into the Ethereal Plane because your AC and hit points are abysmally low for a CR 3 creature.

Pair With Brutes and Controllers. Use brutes to keep your enemies distracted while you make hit-and-phase attacks. Controllers are helpful, too, taking control of the foes, thereby improving your chances of making attacks with advantage.

Tactics: Hit-and-Phase. Start combat in the Material Plane, 30 feet away from the targets and hidden (you have Stealth +6). On your turn, climb towards the nearest target and bite it. Then, use your bonus action to escape to the Ethereal Plane. On your next turn, while still on the Ethereal Plane, reposition yourself into another hiding place that overlaps with the Material Plane. Then, repeat the same maneuver as before.

PIXIE

This tiny, whimsical-looking humanoid darts about swiftly on wildly colored gossamer wings.

These benevolent, diminutive fey creatures work alongside other good creatures, using their magic to diffuse situations. Even when faced with evil creatures, they'd instead prank the villains than cause harm.

Fighting Style: Controller. You're loaded with a bevy of spells that confuse, trap, or render foes unconscious.

Set-up: Secret and Safe. Although you can use your magic while invisible, you still don't want to give foes a chance to reciprocate with area-of-effect spells or random swings of the sword. Take cover.

Weaknesses: 1 Hit Point. You only have 1 hit point. Not good.

Pair With Other Controllers. As a non-violent creature, you don't want to work alongside other creatures who "hit first, ask questions later." Work with other controllers—including other pixies—to handle your foes in a non-violent manner.

Tactics: Control From Hiding. Start combat within cover, full cover if possible, and invisible. Spend a moment identifying the enemies you're up against, using *detect thoughts* or *detect evil and good* if necessary. Once you know the types of creatures you will face, choose the most effective spell to cast against them:

- Use *sleep* against multiple foes with few Hit Dice.
- *Entangle* foes that have poor Strength scores.
- Target an unintelligent individual with *phantasmal force*.
- Cast *confusion* against groups with poor Wisdom scores.
- Cast *polymorph* against an individual with a poor Charisma score.

All of the spells require concentration, so choose wisely. Once you cast it, duck back behind full cover for the spell's duration.

PRIEST

 CR 2

Priests are mid-tier clerics, usually leading temples or other spiritual groups.

Fighting Style: Elite. Your diverse spell list allows you to perform many different roles. You can use *guiding bolt* and *sacred flame* to act as an artillerist; *spirit guardians* and *spiritual weapon* to tank; and *sanctuary*, *cure wounds*, and *lesser restoration* (and *guiding bolt*, too, actually) to provide support.

Set-up: Lots of Cover and Obstacles. You want to keep your distance and avoid ranged attacks, so ensure you've got some cover to duck behind. Additional obstacles and difficult terrain between you and your foes aren't bad ideas either.

Weaknesses: Poor Defensive Capabilities. You only have AC 13 and 27 hit points. Plus, you're relatively slow, with a movement speed of 25 feet (for whatever reason). Although your Divine Eminence feature says you should fight up close and personal, don't. It won't take much for an enemy to remove you from the battlefield. Even if you play the tank role, take the Dodge action on each of your turns, relying on your *spirit guardians* and *spiritual weapon* to deal damage.

Pair With Brutes, Minions, and Tanks. Use melee attackers to keep enemies distracted while you take shots with *guiding bolt* and *sacred flame* from the safety of cover. Use *sanctuary* on whatever target will be tanking—just ensure they don't disrupt the spell by making attacks.

Tactics: Keep Your Distance. Assuming that you will fight as artillerist/support, start combat 60 feet away from your enemies behind cover. If possible, cast *sanctuary* on the ally performing the tank role in your group before combat begins. On your turn, target a foe with low AC using your *guiding bolt* spell. Don't forget that *guiding bolt* gives advantage on the next attack roll against the same target, so make sure you have an ally that can follow up with their own attack. If you don't plan to use 2nd or 3rd-level slots, use those to amplify your *guiding bolt*. Otherwise, switch to *sacred flame* (it does 2d8 damage thanks to your spellcaster level) with *spiritual weapon*.

PSEUDODRAGON

This housecat-sized miniature dragon has fine scales, sharp horns, wicked little teeth, and a tail tipped with a barbed stinger.

These tiny, good-natured dragons frequently serve as quiet, defensive familiars for mages.

Fighting Style: Lurker. You have decent Stealth, a flying speed of 60 feet, and blindsight. And unfortunately, you only have 7 hit points. Stay out of sight.

Set-up: Lots of Hiding Places. You're a tiny creature with a flying speed that doesn't want to get hit with an attack, so make sure you only fight in places with plenty of small areas for you to take cover and hide. With blindsight, you can fight in places of magical darkness or heavily obscured by *fog cloud* without suffering any penalties.

Weaknesses: Squishy. You have AC 13 and only 7 hit points. Don't get hit!

Pair With Brutes, Controllers, and Minions. Work alongside creatures who will keep your enemies distracted while you make quick attacks from hiding.

Tactics: Lurk, Attack, Hide. Start combat hidden in full cover or heavily obscured. When a target comes within reach, attack with your sting, then flee to another hiding space that provides full cover. Hide until the foes can't find you. Repeat these tactics.

PURPLE WORM

 **CR 15**

This enormous worm is covered with dark purple plates of chitinous armor. Its giant, tooth-filled mouth is the size of an ox.

Purple worms are massive burrowing monsters who can burrow their way through solid rock like it was difficult terrain. They're known for leaving behind gems and other valuables in their waste.

Fighting Style: Lurker. Despite overwhelmingly excellent defensive capabilities, you're a simple creature who only wants a quick meal. You are content to wait underground until foes come near, emerge, bite them, and then leave.

Set-up: Earthy Area. You're a burrowing creature with tremorsense, so you want to fight in areas where you can easily wait for food to come near. Although you can tunnel through solid rock, you prefer softer earth since you can use your full burrow speed versus half.

Weaknesses: Mental Saving Throws. You have poor Intelligence, Wisdom, and Charisma saving throws, which leaves you highly vulnerable to enchantment spells, especially those cast by high-level spellcasters.

Pair With Controllers. Although you aren't smart enough to coordinate attacks with other monsters, other monsters may use you as a worthy distraction for your foes. Artillerists can fire at foes while they chase you, and controllers can help you by slowing, blinding, restraining, etc., your targets.

Tactics: Lurk, Emerge, Devour, Leave. Start combat 15 feet below the surface, using your tremorsense to detect foes. When a target walks over you, burrow through the earth and attack it with your bite attack. If you successfully swallow the target, escape with the target in your gullet.

RAKSHASA

 **CR 13**

This figure's backward-bending fingers and bestial, snarling visage leave little doubt about its sinister nature.

These tiger humanoid fiends make excellent bad guys pulling the strings from behind the curtain. The characters in your campaign might feel their machinations without ever truly knowing who is behind them.

Fighting Style: Controller. You come with a wide range of enchantment and illusion spells explicitly designed to confuse, control, and disorient your foes.

Set-up: Misdirection. You are an illusionist and an enchanter, so your chosen battleground should reflect this. Use areas with lots of traps, secret doors, and other unique hazards to draw your foes into while you use your magic to confuse and disorient.

Weaknesses: Magic Weapons. You are virtually immune to spells and nonmagical forms of attack. However, a creature armed with a magic weapon—especially if it's a good-aligned creature—poses a severe threat to you. Make sure you make such foes your number-one targets.

Pair With Minions. You're clever enough to fight alone, using misdirection and enchantment to get the best of your foes. However, a few minions serving as speed bumps never hurts.

Tactics: Illusions and Enchantments. Start combat invisible or altered with *disguise self*. Use *major image* to confuse and divide your foes, especially the less intelligent ones who can't tell what's real and what's fake. Move and frequently hide, dividing them as best you can, especially if the enemy has support present. Once you get a foe of low Wisdom and high value alone, use *dominate person* to control them. Then, send them back to combat the others while you continue to hide. If the *dominate person* fails, resort to *charm person* instead. Remember to remove and corrupt good-aligned foes wielding magic weapons as soon as possible. If you can't control them, keep your distance, as they are your only weakness.

REMORHAZ

CR 11

An immense centipede-like beast erupts from the snow, rows of chitinous plates on its back glowing red-hot.

Remorhazes are giant arctic bugs with surprisingly high Intelligence for an insect; think "clever girl."

Fighting Style: Lurker. You have a burrow speed of 20 feet and tremorsense, which means you like to hide under the snow and soft earth for foes to come near before you strike.

Set-up: Cold Places with Deep Snow. You like to burrow through snow and know it often slows your prey. You can't burrow through solid rock, so make sure the snow is deep, and the earth below is soft.

Weaknesses: Slow Burrower. You only have a burrow speed of 20 feet, which makes it relatively easy for creatures to follow you once you grab one of their own. Since you're relatively intelligent for an insect, consider leading the allies of your prey into more dangerous areas, such as frozen waters or geothermal hot spots.

Pair With Controllers. When you emerge, you want to ensure that you can grab your prey as quickly as possible and escape without being attacked by its allies. You're clever enough to recognize other creatures who can slow down and torment your prey while you sneak up on them.

Tactics: Lurk, Attack, Escape. Start combat 10 feet below the surface of deep snow or soft earth, using your tremorsense to track foes. When a target comes within reach of the ground directly above you, emerge and bite it. Your bite automatically grapples the target, so dive back into the snow or earth. On your next turn, swallow the creature, then continue burrowing away.

Young Remorhazes. Young remorhazes use the same tactics as their elders, except they can't swallow their targets and must gnaw on them instead. Fortunately, they have plenty of hit points, allowing them to hang around for a few turns while they gobble their prey.

REVENANT

CR 5

This shambling corpse is twisted and mutilated. Fingers of sharpened bone reach out with malevolent intent.

Revenants are relentless, undead creatures fueled by hatred and revenge. Destroying one is almost impossible, as they continue to regenerate and rejuvenate until they serve vengeance.

Fighting Style: Brute. You are an unstoppable killing machine, but you aren't here to help others. Your job is to find the one who wronged you and pummel it with your foes until it stops moving so you can finally rest.

Set-up: Inconvenient Appearances. You strike whenever and wherever you can, with little care for the terrain. You know that even if the enemy destroys you, you'll be back in 24 hours, ready to track them again.

Weaknesses: One Track Mind. You only care for revenge, so damn those who will prevent you from enacting justice. Beyond that, little slows you down save for a *wish* spell or perhaps burying one of their undestroyed bodies in an unmarked grave, preventing them from escaping.

Pair With Controllers. If you are going to work with someone, you want it to be someone who'll make capturing your quarry much easier. Work with controllers whose spells can subdue your targets, allowing you to pummel them unimpeded.

Tactics: Surprise, Mofo! Start combat within 30 feet of your target. Open with Vengeful Glare to ensure that you can paralyze the target. Even if paralyze fails, move within 5 feet of the target to make it difficult for it to escape. On your next, if you're not yet within reach of the target and it isn't paralyzed, use your glare again. Otherwise, start bashing it. You can automagically grapple the target, too, so if there's a hazard nearby—a pit filled with spikes, bonfire, lumber mill saw, etc.—toss the foe into the hazard.

ROC

This immense raptor unleashes a shrill cry as it bares its talons, each large enough to carry off a horse.

These humongous birds are hard to train and see everything—including giants—as potential prey.

Fighting Style: Skirmisher. You have a flying speed of 120 feet, which means very few things can stop you from appearing, grabbing a target, and dashing away.

Set-up: Wide, Open Spaces. As a flier, you want plenty of skies to maneuver around.

Weaknesses: Low Intelligence. Although you are a true terror in the sky, you aren't very intelligent, making it easy for foes to outwit and trap you.

Pair With Artillerists or Brutes. Those clever enough to train you and ride you gain the advantage of your tremendous flying speed and ability to grapple targets with your massive talons automatically.

Tactics: Hit-and-Run. Start combat in the sky within 60 feet of your target. Move towards the target and hit it with your multiattack, using your talons to grapple it first, then your beak to finish it off. Then escape back to the sky with your target in your claws.

ROPER

 CR 5

A vast eye opens in this conical creature's front, just above a toothy mouth. Long strands of fibrous material whip from its sides.

Ropers hide in caverns posing as massive natural rock formations, waiting patiently for foes to come within their reach—which is 50 feet!

Fighting Style: Lurker. Although you are painfully slow, you have an exceptional reach of 50 feet and the Spider Climb feature, which allows you to escape into vertical areas that most foes can't reach.

Set-up: Caverns with High Ceilings. You have the Spider Climb feature and a 50-foot reach. Lurk in natural caverns with relatively high ceilings—30 to 50 feet—waiting for foes to pass. As a bonus, targets that escape your grasp will plummet to the ground and take additional damage.

Weaknesses: Slow. You have walking and climb speeds of 10 feet. When you emerge from hiding, you won't be able to escape quickly, so make sure that you set yourself up in areas where other creatures can't get to you.

Pair With Brutes, Controllers, and Minions. Use melee attackers to distract your foes while you grab them from above and controllers to blind, restrain, subdue, etc., the enemy, making it easier for you to hit with your attack rolls.

Tactics: Lurk, Grab, Wobble Away. Start combat attached to a high ceiling in a natural cavern disguised as a stalactite. When one or more targets come within your reach, use your Multiattack to grab and Reel them. Then start moving to a safe area, dragging them with you. On your next turn, reel more targets and bite those close to your maw. If necessary, grab more targets. Continue to move if necessary.

RUST MONSTER

 CR 1/2

This insectile monster has four legs, a strange propeller-shaped protrusion at the end of its tail, and two long, feathery antennae.

The bane of low-level warriors everywhere, rust monsters lurk in dark places looking for yummy ferrous objects—such as valuable weapons and expensive armor—to gobble up.

Fighting Style: Controller. You are a controller, albeit a passive one, thanks to the wide berth many metal-wielding and wearing creatures give you.

Set-up: Dark, Underground Areas. You wander around the subterranean realms sniffing for metal objects to eat, which often leads you to underground junk yards, armories, or battlefields where you can score meals. Such locations might also attract travelers carrying fresh items, a delicacy.

Weaknesses: One Track Mind. You aren't smart enough to recognize dangers before you encounter them and will especially ignore obvious threats if they're equipped with metal arms and armor. However, you are wise enough to recognize "pain is bad," forcing you to flee if something hits you. Fortunately, you move pretty fast.

Pair With Artillerists. You aren't smart enough to coordinate tactics with other monsters, but creatures armed with non-metallic ranged weapons may work alongside you, using you to "sheepdog" metal-clad fighters. As a bonus, they can use your large shell as cover.

Tactics: Dash and Gobble. Start combat within 30 feet of your targets, the range of your iron scene. On your turn, dash towards the source of the metal and start touching your antennae to it. Use your bite against targets that try to get in the way of your meal. If you have to flee, your fast movement speed should keep you relatively safe; however, you're not intelligent enough to know how to Disengage.

SAHUAGIN

 CR 1/2

This scaly humanoid has a long, fish-like tail. Its arms and legs end in webbed claws, and its piscine head features a toothy maw.

Sometimes called "devils of the deep," sahuagin are highly-disciplined, Intelligent self-appointed rulers of the ocean. They can control sharks with their minds, using them as fodder for their foes.

Fighting Style: Lurker. Although your offensive and defensive capabilities are nothing to write home about, your exceptional swim speed and darkvision range allow you to skirt just outside of most enemies' darkvision ranges, keeping you safe from attacks. Plus, you come in with built-in minions thanks to your Shark Telepathy feature.

Set-up: Dark, Underwater Areas. You want to fight in a deep, dark underwater area, where you will benefit from your swim speed and exceptional darkvision range. Make sure there are plenty of sharks around, too, since they work for you.

Weaknesses: Poor Offensive Capabilities. Although you have decent AC and hit points for a CR 1/2 creature, your offensive capabilities aren't exceptional. Furthermore, the long range on your spear isn't far enough to allow you to stay outside traditional darkvision ranges, meaning you won't benefit from the unseen attacker rule.

Pair With Brutes and Minions. Use melee attackers to distract your foes while you skirt along the edges of their darkvision and make ranged attacks with your spear. For brutes, use giant sharks or hunter sharks, and for minions, use reef sharks.

Tactics: Lurk and Toss. Start combat more than 60 feet away from your targets, outside their darkvision range. If you know your foe doesn't have a swim speed, always keep a minimum of 20 feet between you and them. Ready your spear to throw at any target that comes within 20 feet of you. Then, on your turn, swim back into hiding, using the Dash action if necessary. Reposition yourself elsewhere and repeat these tactics, using your sharks to cover your escape. Remember that you and your sharks have advantage on melee attacks against injured targets thanks to Blood Frenzy.

Sahuagin Baron. Barons are large sahuagin with four arms and even greater swim speeds than normal sahuagin. They are elite, capable of filling the brute, skirmisher, or tank roles. Like normal sahuagin, they can mentally control sharks, too.

Sahuagin Priestess. Priestesses are mid-tier clerics who function best as artillerists. They have darkvision out to 120 feet and *guiding bolt*, so they should try to stay outside of the enemy's darkvision range, rolling advantage on attack rolls with the guiding bolt.

SALAMANDER

CR 5

This snake-bodied humanoid hisses with anger. Spines of crackling flame dance along the creature's blackened, fiery-red scales.

The dreadful fire snakes hail from the Elemental Plane of Fire, where they frequently serve tyrannical efreet overlords. They are clever and efficient and recognize that most creatures that they fight don't have the same immunities as they do.

Fighting Style: Brute. Just being near you causes creatures to burn. Get close and wrap them up with your tail, ensuring they can't escape.

Set-up: Hot, Claustrophobic Environments. Fight in areas where constant fire hazards and obstacles prevent your targets from escaping quickly.

Weaknesses: Cold. You have decent defensive capabilities and even come with resistance to nonmagical attacks, but cold damage cuts right through all those immunities. Don't take any chances with spellcasters.

Pair With Artillerists and Controllers. Artillerists can keep a safe distance, thanks to your distracting nature. Meanwhile, controllers might help you gain advantage on attack rolls.

Tactics: Grapple and Smash. Start combat within 30 feet of your targets. On our turn, move close and hit the target with your tail, hopefully grappling them. Then attack with your spear while they're restrained. Continue to attack the same restrained target, potentially dragging it through hazards like lava pools or burning wreckage while you do.

SATYR

CR 1/2

This handsome, grinning man has the furry legs of a goat and a set of curling ram horns extending from his temples.

Known as fauns in some regions, satyrs are tricky, oft-chaotic fey who love to explore the depths of hedonism, which often gets them in trouble with other creatures.

Fighting Style: Artillerist. Assuming that you aren't using your panpipes, your best weapons are your quick movement speed and shortbow, which allow you to keep your distance.

Set-up: Wide, Open Spaces with Lots of Cover. You want to keep your distance and have places where you can hunker down between shots. Forests work well, but so do crowded streets with clear lines of sight.

Weaknesses: Chaotic. You're well-balanced for a CR 1/2 creature and even have Magic Resistance to boot. If anything will cause you trouble, it's your own unpredictable nature. Plus, 9 times out of 10, you're drunk (poisoned condition), which always leads to problems.

Pair With Brutes and Controllers. Use brutes to keep the enemy distracted and controllers to help you gain advantage on your attack rolls.

Tactics: Shoot From Cover. Start combat 60 to 80 feet away from your target behind cover. On your turn, emerge from cover and fire your shortbow at a target within the normal range of your bow. Then, duck behind cover or move if the enemy's melee attackers get too close.

SCARECROW

CR 1

It suddenly becomes clear that this is no ordinary pumpkin-headed scarecrow when its eyes glow and it comes to jerky life.

Scarecrows are horrible constructs powered by the bound spirit of an evil creature. Hags and witches frequently bind these creatures to their service.

Fighting Style: Controller. Although you only have attacks that require you to get up close to your targets, your claw attacks and glare frighten your targets, potentially paralyzing them. This fearsome effect helps other creatures working alongside you.

Set-up: Rural Environments. You resemble an ordinary scarecrow so long as you remain motionless. However, it will seem apparent to onlookers that you are not so ordinary if you try to hide in any environment other than rural farmland.

Weaknesses: Fire. "How about a little fire, scarecrow?" You better not since you're vulnerable to it. Stay away from fire and remove spellcasters as soon as you detect them.

Pair With Artillerists and Brutes. Work alongside other damage dealers who will benefit from your ability to frighten the heck out of your foes.

Tactics: Surprise and Claw. Start combat motionless to appear as an ordinary scarecrow. When a target comes within 30 feet of you, reveal your nature and charge it, then attack it with your claws. Alternatively, use your glare to target a creature within 30 feet of you; since you can use this feature while remaining motionless, it may not trigger creatures to your true nature. Of course, it may cause your enemies to burn you at the stake, so be careful.

SCOUT

CR 1/2

Scouts are easily one of the most dangerous low-CR creatures in the game thanks to their Stealth, multiattack, and longbow, which grants you a normal range of 150 feet.

Fighting Style: Artillerist. You are armed with a longbow with which you can make two attacks per turn from a distance of 150 feet.

Set-up: Wide Open Spaces with Lots of Cover. Use humongous areas with clear lines of sight to the enemy and plenty of cover to duck behind after you shoot at them.

Weaknesses: Enemy Artillerists. It's unlikely that evenly-matched melee attackers will ever get close to you. However, enemy artillerists possessing weapons or spells with similar ranges can fire back. Make sure you always take cover and be wary of enemies that Ready their attacks.

Pair With Brutes, Minions, and Tanks. Use melee attackers to keep your enemies distracted while you fire from the safety of cover.

Tactics: Shoot, Move, Take Cover. Start combat 120 to 150 feet away from your targets, just outside the range of most spells but still within the normal range of your longbow, preferably hidden. Fire at a target within your normal range, then move up to 30 feet to a new position and take cover, putting further distance between you and spellcasters (as well as enemies with longbows).

SHADOW

 CR 1/2

This shadowy figure sways and moves with an erratic grace as if lit by an unseen fire.

One could be forgiven for thinking these creatures are similar to specters, wraiths, and other incorporeal undead. However, they share more in common with oozes, slinking in and out of dark hiding places.

Fighting Style: Lurker. Your quick speed, defensive capabilities, exceptional Stealth, and amorphous nature allow you to make quick attacks and escape before enemies can counterattack.

Set-up: Dark Areas with Escape Routes. Pick places utterly devoid of bright light and far from the sun. You can escape through spaces as small as 1 inch wide without squeezing, so having plenty of places like this—city streets, dark castles, tombs, etc.—are the perfect environment.

Weaknesses: Bright Light. Bright light, especially sunlight, strips you of some of your most significant advantages. Never attack creatures carrying bright lights with them, and never attack creatures during the day.

Pair With Brutes and Minions. Use melee attackers to keep your foes distracted while you use ambush tactics against them.

Tactics: Lurk, Attack, Escape. Start combat hidden in dim light or darkness. When a target comes near you, attack it with your Strength Drain. Then slip away into an area they can't reach you using your Amorphous trait. Use back routes to slip away while the enemies try to find you and reposition yourself. Then, surprise the target with another ambush.

SHAMBLING MOUND

CR 5

A mass of tangled vines and dripping slime rises on two trunk-like legs, reeking of rot and freshly turned earth.

These lumbering devourers lurk in swamps, forests, and other places where vegetation is typical. Sadly, they don't come with the False Appearance trait, which would make them nearly perfect as lurkers.

Fighting Style: Brute. You come stacked with defensive and offensive capabilities, which allows you to give an evenly matched group of foes a run for their money.

Set-up: Wet, Green Areas. You have a swim speed of 20 feet, which isn't great, but it's probably better than your targets'. And since you're a creature made of vegetation, it probably makes sense that you lurk in such places as swamps and forests. However, it won't seem too out of place if you live in a sewer. Places heavily obscured by effects like *fog cloud* and magical darkness are also valuable hunting grounds since you have blindsight out to 60 feet.

Weaknesses: Slow. Although you have great defensive and offensive capabilities, you are relatively slow. Ensure you fight near water sources to hide and drag foes away after you capture them.

Pair With Artillerists and Elites. Although you are relatively intelligent, you are too consumed by hunger t cooperate. Still, artillerists can use you as a distraction, firing at targets from the safety of cover. Lightning damage heals you, so blue dragons and spellcasters capable of casting lightning might join forces with you, and you might even let them escape your hungry maw.

Tactics: Lurk, Slam, Engulf. Start combat either hidden or heavily obscured. When a target comes within 5 feet of you, emerge and attack with your Multiattack. If both Slam attacks hit, you automatically grapple the target, and you can use your Engulf on it. Once you Engulf a creature, there's no reason to stick around until you finish digesting it. Swim away.

SHIELD GUARDIAN

 **CR 7**

A tall, imposing humanoid figure made of wood and iron plates steps between you and your target, acting as a bodyguard.

Tanks, almost by definition, shield guardians are designed to take punishment and keep their masters safe. That's not to say they can't deal damage—with the right spells; they quickly become lingering menaces.

Fighting Style: Tank. You have AC 17 and 142 hit points, plus you regenerate. Your job is to interpose yourself between the attackers and your master, keeping them safe from attacks.

Set-up: Protector. No matter where you fight, make sure that there is a place for your master to hide or escape while you stand and take punishment.

Weaknesses: Your Creator. It's your job to defend your creator. And often, your creator is not nearly as durable as you are. Keep them safe because if someone kills them and steals their control amulet, you'll suddenly find yourself with a new boss.

Pair With Elites. Work alongside an elite (probably your creator), having them fill in with support, artillerist, or controller spells and features while you take punishment from your foes.

Tactics: Defend Your Creator. Before combat begins, ensure that your creator stores a useful, passive damage spell in you, such as *spirit guardians*. Alternatively, use *darkness* or *fog cloud* to blind your foes while you continue to function normally, thanks to your blindsight. Start combat within 30 feet of your enemies and your creator safely behind cover (such as you) or completely absent. Cast the spell stored in you and continue to hold your ground. Then, while your spell runs its course, take the Dodge action to improve your defenses. Don't forget that you regenerate every round, and you can use your reaction to shield your master.

SKELETON

 CR 1/4

The pile of bones suddenly stirs, rising to take on a human shape. Its long, bony fingers reach out to claw at the living.

Skeletons function as simple automatons working for necromancers, liches, and other evil or evil-leaning bad guys.

Fighting Style: Minion. You have a handful of hit points, a relatively low AC, and only average damage-dealing capabilities. Your job is to distract and slow down targets on behalf of your superiors.

Set-up: Spread Out. You come with both melee and ranged attack capabilities; therefore, you can fight anywhere you please. Wherever you go, make sure that you put at least 10 feet of space between you and your allies to reduce the risk of area-of-effect magic and to threaten as much area as possible.

Weaknesses: Individually Weak. As a single creature, you aren't much of a challenge. Your strength lies in working with throngs of other undead minions, protecting your unholy masters from their enemies.

Pair With Elites. Work alongside elites, such as spellcasters, who can control, support, or even provide extra artillery on the battlefield while you distract foes with your fellow minions.

Tactics: Attack! You are a relatively simple creature with enough intelligence to remember how to use your weapons. Start wherever your handler needs you. If you're within 30 feet of your foes, charge, and attack instead. Otherwise, rely on your shortbow. Your Intelligence score is 6, so you probably have enough sense to take cover and drop prone as needed.

SKELETON, MINOTAUR

 **CR 2**

This enormous humanoid skeleton has the skull of a bull and wields an enormous great axe in its bony claws.

While minotaur skeletons don't possess the defensive capabilities or the Reckless feature of their living cousins, they still deal a lot of damage with their Gore and Greataxe attacks. For all intents and purposes, they're "greater skeletons."

Fighting Style: Brute. Although you have the same Intelligence score as a living minotaur, you lack its common sense. As such, you throw yourself into combat without regard for your own well-being, aiming to hurt the enemy as much as possible.

Set-up: Charging Range. You have a 40-foot movement speed, like living minotaurs, which gives you a little buffer between enemy melee attackers with slower speeds. Your charge requires you to move at least 10 feet straight toward an enemy, so much sure you have clear lanes available.

Weaknesses: Bludgeoning. Although you aren't nearly as squishy (crumbly?) as a humanoid skeleton, you're still vulnerable to bludgeoning damage, effectively cutting your hit points in half. Unfortunately, your low Wisdom score isn't enough to alert you to this danger. Hopefully, controllers working alongside you will help you avoid this conundrum.

Pair With Controllers or Minions. Controllers will help keep you safe from enemy attacks while also setting you up to make attacks with advantage. Meanwhile, minions will benefit from the distraction you cause, attacking enemies too focused on removing you from the battlefield. Plus, your Charge knocks enemies prone, letting minions attack with advantage.

Tactics: Charge! Start combat 40 feet away from the enemy. On your turn, Charge toward the nearest enemy and hit it with your Gore attack, forcing a Strength saving throw. So long as the target remains within reach, hit it with your greataxe. If the target moves more than 10 feet away from you—or if you destroy it—charge again.

SKELETON, WARHORSE

 CR 1/2

This animated skeletal horse still wears scraps of barding it wore in life.

Skeletal warhorses are best used as mounts for other types of skeletons or other undead bad guys, giving their riders an improved movement speed.

Fighting Style: Support. You have a movement speed of 60 feet and will do pretty much whatever your rider tells you to do. While you can fight alone, it's better when you have a rider.

Set-up: Lots of Room to Move. Your 60 feet of movement makes you an excellent mount for monsters hoping to use artillerist or skirmisher fighting styles.

Weaknesses: Bludgeoning. Like the other types of skeletons, you are vulnerable to bludgeoning damage. Hopefully, your rider is smart enough to recognize this danger because you are not.

Pair With Artillerists or Brutes. Work with creatures who can benefit from your incredible movement speed. Because you're not an intelligent creature, the rider can have you move and take the Dash, Disengage, or Dodge action on your turn while still taking their own actions— that means that you can move a total of 120 feet while your attacker gets their whole action economy. Artillerists will benefit from the distance you can put between their targets and themselves. Brutes can use your ability to Disengage to make melee attacks and escape without suffering an attack of opportunity.

Tactics: Follow Orders. If you have an artillerist rider, start combat more than 60 feet away from your targets but still within the normal range of the rider's weapon. Otherwise, start within 30 feet of your targets. Use your movement to keep your rider safe by either putting space between you and the rider's targets or using your Disengage action to allow your brute master to make hit-and-run attacks without provoking attacks of opportunity.

SPECTER

 CR 1

This translucent, ghostly figure fades into view from the damp mist, its face distorted by wrath into a hideous mask.

Specters are vile, undead creatures filled with hate. They pose an immense threat against low-level adversaries, capable of wiping out entire groups.

Fighting Style: Lurker. You have a flying speed of 50 feet and can phase through difficult terrain. However, you're wise enough to recognize that hanging around too long allows your targets to gang up on you or, worse, use radiant magic. Fight through a series of ambushes.

Set-up: Dark, Claustrophobic Spaces. You want to fight in places with narrow corridors and side chambers so you can make attacks and then phase through the wall, ceiling, or floor for safety. Haunted houses and dungeons are your best bet.

Weaknesses: Magic. Your incorporeal nature gives you plenty of defenses against most mundane forms of damage. However, enemies armed with magic weapons and spellcasters capable of dealing force or radiant damage pose a considerable threat.

Pair With Controllers. Use controllers to slow down or subdue your targets, keeping you safe from reprisal while setting you up for advantage on your attacks.

Tactics: Lurk, Life Drain, Disappear. Start combat behind full cover. When you hear targets come near, phase into their area and make a Life Drain attack against the first target you see. Then, escape through the way you came or another solid surface. Don't worry about attacks of opportunity since one attack of opportunity is better than getting hit by multiple attacks when it isn't your turn. Reposition yourself and wait for the enemy to come by again, attacking the same target if possible.

Specter (Poltergeist). The poltergeist variant of specters makes you invisible and replaces your Life Drain attack with a slam attack that deals with force damage and a telekinetic attack. Despite these new features, your tactics remain the same, except you can use your Invisibility to remain hidden rather than escape through a solid surface.

SPHINX, ANDROSPHINX

 CR 17

This regal, bird-winged lion has a human's head, clad in the golden raiment of a mighty pharaoh.

Androsphinxes are the more powerful of the two sphinx types the Fifth Edition monster manual has to offer. The most significant difference between the two is that the androsphinx has a system of roars it can use to frighten, deafen, and destroy foes.

Fighting Style: Controller. You are a guardian who only fights creatures brave or foolish enough to circumvent your tests of courage and valor. You prefer to remove foes, relying on your exceptionally powerful (and weird) Lair Actions first. Failing that, you use your devastating roars and ability to cast spells as Legendary Actions.

Set-up: Your Lair. You have four Lair Actions, all of which are extraordinarily powerful. There is rarely a reason you should ever be encountered outside your lair since it is the source of your power and likely the place you were tasked to protect.

Weaknesses: Magic Weapons. You are immune to damage caused by nonmagical weapons, but magic weapons will get through your defenses.

Pair With Minions. While you're almost capable of taking on a well-armed group all by yourself, having a few minions to burn the enemies' action economy never hurts. Make sure your minions are immune to the effects of fear and being deafened, or they will not survive your first two roars. Animated objects are your best bet. Of course, they are highly vulnerable to thunder damage, so they won't likely make it past your third roar.

Tactics: See You Later. Before combat, make sure you have *freedom of movement* and *heroes' feast* affecting you and your allies. Start combat 100 to 120 feet away from your targets, so they're slightly in your truesight range but not close enough to reach you in a single turn without using magic. If the enemies fail to heed your advice, use your *plane shift* Lair Action to remove the troublemakers, then use your Lair Action to return home. You're a nigh immortal creature—you don't have time for such nonsense. Once you return, finish a short rest to recover this used legendary action. If the enemies somehow make it back to your lair before you finish your short rest, go into fighting mode. Stay in the skies above your enemies, far out of the reach of melee attackers. Use your roars in the listed order. Use your Cast a Spell legendary action in between your roars to further affect the targets. You have two slots to cast *flame strike*, your most potent damage-dealing spell. Once you use up your *flame strikes*, use your legendary actions to Teleport and claw just before the start of your turn, then use your turn to claw two more times and escape to a safe distance.

SPHINX, GYNOSPHINX

 **CR 11**

This creature has the body of a lion, the wings of a falcon, and the head and torso of a beautiful human woman.

Gynosphinxes are perhaps the best-known types of sphinxes, as they're the ones that challenge those who trespass in their lairs with riddles and puzzles. As lawful neutral creatures, they prefer to remove targets from their lair rather than fight them.

Fighting Style: Lurker. Although you prefer to remove targets with your *plane shift* Lair Action, if you must fight, you can do so wholly invisible or protected by darkness.

Set-up: See Them Coming. You are a guardian who only fights creatures brave or foolish enough to circumvent your riddles and puzzles. You prefer to remove foes, relying on your exceptionally powerful (and weird) Lair Actions first. Failing that, you can use powerful claw attacks and spells cast as Legendary Actions to destroy the insolent.

Weaknesses: Magic Weapons. You're fast and have decent AC for your CR, but you have relatively few hit points with only damage resistances to protect you. Make sure to stay out of range of melee attackers. Also, don't get grappled, as you don't have the same magical defenses against grapple attacks as the androsphinx.

Pair With Minions. While you're almost capable of taking on a well-armed group all by yourself, having a few minions to burn the enemies' action economy never hurts.

Tactics: See You Later. Start combat 100 to 120 feet away from your targets, so they're slightly in your truesight range but not close enough to reach you in a single turn without using magic. If the enemies fail to heed your advice, use your *plane shift* Lair Action to remove the troublemakers, then use your Lair Action to return home. You're a nigh immortal creature—you don't have time for such nonsense. Once you return, finish a short rest to recover this used legendary action. If the enemies somehow make it back to your lair before you finish your short rest, go into fighting mode. Use a Legendary Action as soon as possible to cast *greater invisibility* on yourself. When your turn starts, make invisible hit-and-run attacks against targets that can't see you. When it isn't your turn, use Legendary Actions to teleport near targets and claw them again. Do this right before your turn, so you can combo the claw attack with two more attacks. Then return to the skies. If your more significant *invisibility* drops, cast it again. You have up to four slots that you can do this with. If a target reveals that it can see you and will hit you, use *shield* to protect yourself. Then switch to *darkness* as your obscuring spell of choice. Cast it on an object you can carry with you, so you don't have to limit yourself to a particular area.

SPRITE

This lithe, diminutive creature looks like a humanoid with wispy, moth-like wings and long, thin ears.

Sprites are forest protectors who, while good-natured, take a more aggressive stance than creatures like pixies, who prefer non-violence. Still, they prefer to knock foes unconscious and drag them to the edge of their territory instead of killing them.

Fighting Style: Lurker. You can turn invisible at will and have a Stealth modifier of +8. Plus, you have a flying speed of 40 feet. Make your attacks, then get out of sight before the enemy can reciprocate.

Set-up: Lots of Hiding Places. Make sure to fight in areas where you can stage ambushes, then retreat after you make your attacks.

Weaknesses: 2 Hit Points. You only have 2 hit points. Don't get hit.

Pair With Controllers. You want to make sure every shot counts, so you can quickly subdue your enemies and eliminate them. Work alongside allies who can grant you advantage on your attack rolls by blinding, restraining, or stunning your foes.

Tactics: Lurk, Attack, Flee. Start combat invisible in full cover. When the enemies come within 40 feet of you, emerge and fire your shortbow. After you take your shot, fly to the nearest place of full cover. When it's your next turn, find a new spot to stage an ambush.

SPY

Spies are low-level rogues with Cunning Action and Sneak Attack. They also have exceptional social skills, making it easy for them to blend into any environment.

Fighting Style: Artillerist. The combination of your Sneak Attack, Cunning Action, and Hand Crossbow demands that you keep at least a little distance from foes, scoring heavy damage with successful Sneak Attacks.

Set-up: Lots of Room to Move and Take Cover. Fight in places where you can easily take cover between shots. Don't make it too large, however, since you must stay within the normal range of your hand crossbow. Having some difficult terrain or obstacles between you and your opponents is extremely useful since it'll allow you to stay within 30 feet of them without fear of them charging you.

Weaknesses: Relatively Squishy. You only have 12 AC and 27 hit points, which means it only takes a few good hits to eliminate you. Always keep your distance; if things get bad, beg or bribe your way out of the situation.

Pair With Anyone. Thanks to your Cunning Action and Sneak Attack, you can work with virtually any other creature so long as they either stay within 5 feet of your targets or set you up for advantage on your attack rolls, allowing you to score a Sneak Attack.

Tactics: Move, Shoot, Hide, Repeat. Start combat within 30 feet of your targets. On your turn, fire your hand crossbow at any target you have advantage against. Alternatively, look for a target that's within 5 feet of an ally that you won't have disadvantage on your attack roll. After you fire, move back at least 15 feet and use your Cunning Action to take the Hide action.

STIRGE

 CR 1/8

This insectoid creature has two pairs of bat wings, a tangle of thin legs, and a needle-sharp proboscis.

Often swarming in obnoxious numbers, these tiny bloodsuckers are the bane of many heroes.

Fighting Style: Minion. One stirge isn't scary. But a dozen? That's terrifying. Always work with plenty of your closest friends and family members.

Set-up: Tight Spaces. Although you have an excellent Dexterity score, you aren't necessarily stealthy—lair in places that offer few escape routes for creatures who happen upon you and your ilk. As a bat-like creature, you might even sleep hanging from the ceiling.

Weaknesses: 2 Hit Points. It only takes one hit to make you go "pop."

Pair With Controllers. While you aren't intelligent enough to work alongside other creatures, some creatures will see the advantage in working with you and using you as a living hazard for their enemies. Controllers can use spells and other features to blind, restrain, stun, or knock your targets prone, giving you advantage on your attack rolls.

Tactics: Swarm and Drink. Start combat within 40 feet of your targets. Immediately attack the nearest target with the intent to drain it of its blood. Once you drain 10 hit points from the target (or the target dies), find a nice, cozy place to nap.

SUCCUBUS/INCUBUS

CR 4

Tiny horns, bat-like wings, and a sinuous tail betray the demonic nature of this alluring humanoid.

Succubi and their male counterparts, Incubi, are attractive corruptors who use their charm, wiles, and—ahem—you know the—to attract and deceive simple-mind targets.

Fighting Style: Elite. You come with a bevy of features that let you fight any style necessary. Your Charm/Kiss combo does tremendous damage, making you a brute. You have enough defensive capabilities to play as a tank for weaker allies. You have a flying speed and can dip into the Ethereal Plane at will. And, of course, you're a controller, thanks to your Charm. The only thing you lack is a ranged attack.

Set-up: Up Close and Personal. Although you can fight in any terrain and style, your best attack combination—Charm and Kiss—requires you to get close to your enemy.

Weaknesses: Magic. Despite your strong offensive and defensive capabilities, you lack protection from most enchantments and illusions, as well as acid, force, necrotic, psychic, and radiant damage. Watch out for spellcasters and creatures wielding magic weapons.

Pair With Minions. Keep your targets busy with plenty of minions so you can perform your Charm and Kiss combination without interruption.

Tactics: Charm and Kiss. Even before combat starts, target one creature with your Charm ability while disguised or hidden. The target does not have to see you for the Charm to work. If you succeed, telepathically command the target to act normally. Eventually, get the charmed target to separate from the rest of its group, where you will meet it. Use your Draining Kiss to reduce the target's hit points, potentially killing it. If the kiss fails to kill it, slip away to the Ethereal Plane to avoid reprisal. Change shape and pick a new target, repeating these tactics, weakening as many foes as possible in 24 hours.

TARRASQUE

 **CR 30**

The beast towers over you, its massive form resembling that of a giant reptile with a heavily armored shell. Its jaws are gaping wide, revealing row upon row of razor-sharp teeth, and its horns, stretching a full six feet in length, gleam menacingly in the light. It's clear that facing this monstrosity will be no easy task.

The tarrasque is a classic "big bad" of Fifth Edition. But don't let its big Challenge Rating intimidate you; it's a pretty straightforward foe.

Fighting Style: Brute. You just want to smash everything that's in your path.

Set-up: Up Close and Personal. The longer you go without destroying buildings or eating things, the angrier you get. Get as close as possible to the target of your ire.

Weaknesses: No Ranged Attacks. All the strength in the world means diddly squat if your enemies can attack you from a distance and you can't attack them back.

Pair With Artillerists and Minions. One of the biggest glaring weaknesses of the tarrasque is its lack of ranged attacks. Work alongside artillerists and minions that can take out enemies who understand this weakness, especially rogues whose sneak attack will deal significant damage.

Tactics: Dash and Bash. Start combat within 40 feet of whatever you hope to smash. Then, go and smash it until it's no longer smashable. Move on to the next object. Repeat.

THUG

Thugs are mid-tier fighters who prefer to intimidate and crush their foes rather than chat.

Fighting Style: Brute. Although you carry a heavy crossbow, you prefer to fight up close, where you benefit from your Multiattack and Pack Tactics.

Set-up: Up Close and Personal. You don't want a lot of obstacles between you and your enemies. And although you might try to intimidate them into submission first, you inevitably go for your mace.

Weaknesses: Poor AC. Although you have decent hit points for a CR 1/2 creature, your AC is only 11.

Pair With Artillerists and Minions. Your brutal nature will keep your foes distracted. Meanwhile, artillerist allies can fire from the safety of cover. Plus, you have Pack Tactics, so if you can't work alongside other brutes, use minions to help you gain advantage on attacks.

Tactics: Dash and Bash. Start combat within 30 feet of the enemy already engaged with one of your allies in melee combat. On your turn, move within reach of your mace and attack the target. Once you defeat that enemy, move to another target that's getting ganged up on.

TREANT

 CR 9

This animated tree's bark is knotted into vaguely humanoid features, with branches for arms and roots for legs.

Ancient and powerful, treants are the legendary guardians and protectors of the wild. Traditionally chaotic good, they only fight if they feel great evil threatens their territory.

Fighting Style: Brute. Individually, you aren't that strong, as your defensive and offensive capabilities are dismal compared to other CR 9 creatures. However, you can animate trees to serve as additional damage dealers and tanks, making you extraordinarily dangerous.

Set-up: Near Trees. You're nothing with your animate trees action; make sure there are plenty of trees nearby for you to animate.

Weaknesses: You. Your animate trees action is extraordinarily powerful. However, your extra tree pals vanish if you die or move more than 120 feet away from them. After creating extra trees, ensure you stay within 120 feet of them and take defensive actions while your tree minions do all the work.

Pair With Controllers. You're strong and have exceptional attack rolls, but having advantage on those attacks is always lovely. Work alongside controllers like druids who can offer this to you.

Tactics: Tree Force Go! Start combat 60 to 120 feet away from your targets. If possible, animate trees before combat and place them within 30 feet of the enemies. On your first turn, throw rocks from your location while your animated trees enter melee combat. If the enemy demonstrates that they have dangerous magic, especially fire, take the Dodge action to improve your defensive capabilities.

TRIBAL WARRIOR

 **CR 1/8**

Tribal warriors represent low-level fighters who live outside of civilization. While they aren't necessarily individually challenging, they work better in small groups.

Fighting Style: Minion. Your defensive and offensive capabilities aren't quite good enough to qualify as a brute. However, your Pack Tactics feature says you enjoy fighting with other creatures.

Set-up: Spread Out. Although you aren't necessarily intelligent, you and your fellow tribal warriors have enough sense to spread out and surround the enemy; this reduces your risk for area-of-effect attacks while increasing your effective threat area.

Weaknesses: Squishy. You only have AC 12 and 11 hit points, which means it only takes a hit or two to drop you.

Pair With Artillerists, Brutes, and Tanks. Use brutes and tanks to distract your foes while you score attacks with advantage, thanks to Pack Tactics. Meanwhile, artillerists can fire from the safety of cover.

Tactics: Surround and Attack. Start combat within 30 feet of the enemy but spread out 10 feet from your allies. If you plan to fight with ranged attacks, take cover and Ready your action for when one of your allies gets within 5 feet of the enemy. Likewise, if you're a melee fighter, get close and Ready your action for when another ally comes within 5 feet. If you take damage and survive, Disengage and trade places with one of your spear-throwing allies.

TROGLODYTE

This humanoid's scaly hide is dull gray. Its frame resembles that of a cave lizard, with a long tail and crests on its head and back.

Typically described as "simple-minded brutes," troglodytes are the lizardfolk of the underground realms. Many worship evil, demonic deities and sometimes capture trespassers to offer as sacrifices.

Fighting Style: Brute. Your defensive capabilities aren't terrific (excluding your Stench feature), but you have excellent action economy for a CR 1/4 creature.

Set-up: Up Close and Personal. You fight with your bite and claws, and your Stench only works against creatures within 5 feet of you. Make sure there aren't a lot of obstacles between you and your enemies.

Weaknesses: Relatively Squishy. You only have AC 11 and 13 hit points. Fortunately, your Stench provides a natural layer of protection against melee attacks, but you're still vulnerable to artillerists. Make sure you wallop the enemy and fast.

Pair With Artillerists and Controllers. Artillerists will benefit from the distraction you cause. Use controllers to help you gain advantage on your attacks or prevent the enemy from making counterattacks.

Tactics: Dash and Thrash. Start combat within 30 feet of your enemies, ideally hidden. On your turn, get within reach of as many enemies as possible, so they have to make saving throws against your Stench. Focus all your attacks on the target that seems easiest to hurt (i.e., the one not wearing armor).

TROLL

 CR 5

This tall creature has a rough, green hide. Its hands end in claws, and its bestial face has a hideous, tusked underbite.

Trolls are famous for their disgusting appetites and ability to regenerate. They frequently serve other creatures as brute enforcers and bodyguards.

Fighting Style: Brute. Your Regeneration keeps you safe while you wail away with your bite and claws.

Set-up: Up Close and Personal. You're hungry. So make sure there aren't a lot of obstacles in the way of you and your meals—er, targets.

Weaknesses: Fire. Regeneration is your strongest trait. However, almost everyone in the world knows that fire (and acid) cancels your Regeneration. If you can't quickly kill the source of fire, escape.

Pair With Artillerists and Controllers. Use artillerists and controllers to deal with fire wielders while you attack with your teeth and claws. As a bonus, controllers may grant you an advantage on your attack rolls.

Tactics: Dash and Gnash. Start combat within 30 feet of your enemies. On your turn, get as close to a target as possible and attack with your multiattack. Look out for fire wielders—get rid of them before anyone else.

UNICORN

 CR 5

This magnificent beast looks like a white horse but with a goat's beard and a single long ivory horn on its brow.

Unicorns are divine guardians and forest lords best known for their sacred horns. They serve best as blessed mounts, amplifying their rider's capabilities.

Fighting Style: Support. You perform best as a mount for another good-aligned creature, effectively awarding the rider an increased movement speed, a shimmering shield, healing, and the ability to teleport.

Set-up: Your Magical Forest. You and your allies gain many benefits while hiding in your forest, detailed under your Regional Effects. The forest also provides excellent cover and places for you to hide.

Weaknesses: Poor Defensive Capabilities. Although you are a CR 5 creature, you have the defensive capabilities of a CR 1 creature. Fortunately, you can heal yourself and provide additional protection with your Legendary Actions. Just keep your distance between attack runs and take cover whenever possible.

Pair With Artillerists and Brutes. Use a damage dealer like artillerists and brutes to take offensive action while you provide defense and control. If you use a brute, ensure they have a 10-foot reach to avoid attacks of opportunity made against you and them.

Tactics: Skirmish, Control, Support. Start combat 60 to 90 feet away from your enemy, behind cover if possible. Cast *entangle* first while your rider either uses their own controller spells or makes an attack with a ranged weapon; otherwise, Dodge. Next, utilize skirmisher tactics while your rider makes attacks. If your rider is an artillerist, move and hide between their shots. If the rider is a brute, prepare the Dash action to retreat after your rider attacks a target. Always find cover, regardless of the rider's fighting style, since it'll help you both. Reserve your Legendary Actions to Heal Self. If your rider needs healing, spend the turn lurking in cover while you provide Healing Touch. Remember: while in your lair, both Heal Self and Healing Touch return the maximum number of hit points to the target. If it doesn't look like you'll win the fight, Teleport away.

VAMPIRE

 **CR 13**

This alluring, raven-haired beauty casually wipes a trickle of blood from a pale cheek, then smiles to reveal needle-sharp fangs.

Vampires are eternally cursed humanoids whose dark desires raise them from death as undead monstrosities. Chained to the grave, they endlessly strive to consume whatever drives them.

Fighting Style: Lurker. While you're tough enough to fill any fighting style, you have far too many vulnerabilities and too few hit points to risk engaging well-prepared enemies in protracted combat. Shapechanger, Misty Escape, and Spider Climb are all designed to help you ambush your foes and escape.

Set-up: Your Lair. As an ancient undead creature, you rarely have a reason or desire to leave your lair, as it is the seat of your power. Make sure this lair has plenty of escape routes and places to hide. Use hazards, traps, and obstacles to slow down creatures who lack your means of travel. Nobody enters your lair without you knowing about it. In fact, you welcome it. Once they're in your home, they're yours.

Weaknesses: Getting Caught. You have four weaknesses listed in your stat block. However, the common denominator between all of these is "getting caught." Never place yourself in a situation where the enemy can prevent you from escaping. Always have backup plans. And never let them know where you keep your resting place.

Pair With Brutes and Minions. As a lurker, you want creatures who can distract your foes while you strike from hiding or make your escape. Brutes and minions both do this well.

Tactics: The Long Game. You don't necessarily fight actual combats. Instead, you are a horror villain, content to pick off foes one by one. Use your extended darkvision range or Stealth to observe your enemies without them knowing about it. Use misdirection, traps, and obstacles to separate them. Determine ahead of time which is the most dangerous target to you. Then do what you can to get them alone. If it's too dangerous to go near them, use a charmed thrall (see below) to attack them, or summon your

Children of the Night to attack that foe specifically.

When you have weak-willed targets alone, use your Charm to make them your thrall, then send them back to their allies, acting as if nothing happened. The effect lasts for 24 hours and doesn't go away unless you or your companions do anything harmful to the target or you end it, thus making it one of the most potent charm effects in the game.

Look for weaknesses in the group, especially those injured while exploring your lair. Use your bat form to attack the target with your bite, then escape immediately. Don't worry about attacks of opportunity since your Regeneration will repair you while you hide.

Spellcaster Vampire. Spellcaster vampires are far more dangerous than their non-spellcaster counterparts. They can cast *dominate person*, which allows them to control two thralls at once (one from the spell and one from their Charm). They can also use *greater invisibility*, making it easier for them to attack and escape without getting caught.

Warrior Vampire. This version of the vampire provides better AC and gives the vampire a greatsword. Arguably, these do nothing to help the vampire except put it in greater danger of getting caught and subjected to its weaknesses. These vampires should use their main action to take the Dodge action while using their Legendary Actions to move and strike.

VAMPIRE SPAWN

CR 5

This alluring, raven-haired beauty casually wipes a trickle of blood from a pale cheek, then smiles to reveal needle-sharp fangs.

Vampire spawn are effectively "lesser" vampires, often serving an ancient vampire as its thralls.

Fighting Style: Lurker. Like the CR 13 vampires, you perform best when you don't hang around long enough for your enemies to trap you and exploit your weaknesses.

Set-up: Escape Routes and Places to Hide. You have Stealth +6, Spider Climb, and the ability to regenerate. Make sure your chosen battlefield has plenty of dark or hard-to-reach areas from which you can stage ambushes. Never fight in an area where the enemy may corner you.

Weaknesses: Getting Caught. You have four weaknesses listed in your stat block. However, the common denominator between all of these is "getting caught." Never place yourself in a situation where the enemy can prevent you from escaping. Always have backup plans.

Pair With Brutes and Minions. As a lurker, you want creatures who can distract your foes while you strike from hiding or make your escape. Brutes and minions both do this well.

Tactics: Ambush and Escape. Start combat hidden. Remember that you can climb walls and ceilings, so you can hide in high-up places, too, if necessary. When a target comes within your reach, attack it with your claws to grapple it, then bite to drain its blood. Then, escape. Don't worry about getting hit with attacks of opportunity since you regenerate. Repeat these tactics as often as possible. Don't get caught.

VETERAN

CR 3

Veterans are mid-tier fighters with plenty of action economy, perfect for tying up multiple enemies at once.

Fighting Style: Brute. Although you come armed with a heavy crossbow, you perform best at close range, where you get to make three attacks per turn with your swords.

Set-up: Up Close and Personal. You don't want a lot of obstacles in the way of your and your enemies. Make sure you get as close as possible to your foes on your first turn. Otherwise, Dodge until someone gets close enough for you to hit them.

Weaknesses: Relatively Low Hit Points. You have 58 hit points which are relatively low for a CR 3 creature. Fortunately, your AC and dazzling attack array make up for it. Just be careful not to get hit.

Pair With Artillerists and Controllers. Use controllers to help you score advantage on attack rolls and limit the action economy of your enemies. Meanwhile, artillerist allies can fire from the safety of cover while you distract the enemy.

Tactics: Dash and Slash. Start combat within 30 feet of your enemies. On your turn, move close and use your Multiattack against the most dangerous target on the field, likely a spellcaster or enemy artillerist.

WIGHT

 **CR 3**

The flesh of this walking corpse is rotting and putrid, its body skeletal in places, and its eye sockets glowing with red light.

Wights are undead life eaters whose touch can drain life from foes. In previous editions, this meant a reduction in levels—these days, it's just hit point maximum. Consider yourselves lucky, 5e players.

Fighting Style: Artillerist. Wights have decent defensive capabilities, but their real strength lies in the inclusion of their longbow, with which they can make two attacks per turn. Although it wants to drain the life from its foes, it's got enough sense to recognize it should soften up its foes from a distance before it closes in for the coup de grace.

Set-up: Distance and Darkness. As an artillerist, you want clear lines of sight and plenty of cover to duck behind between shots. Pick places of darkness where you can pick off foes carrying lanterns, torches, or other light sources.

Weaknesses: Magic. Spells and magic weapons avoid your resistances (excluding necrotic), which makes your relatively few 45 hit points seem even worse.

Pair With Brutes and Controllers. Use brutes to keep the enemy busy while you fire from cover and darkness. If the brute has light sources of its own, it can help you illuminate targets. Controllers can blind, restrain, stun, etc., targets to grant you advantage on your attacks.

Tactics: Fire From Hiding. Start combat hidden 120 to 150 feet away from your foes, just outside of the range of most spells. If the group doesn't have its own light source, wait until they come near one you set up in advance. Fire at the most dangerous target (likely a spellcaster) from the safety of your hiding space, then move to another area and take cover. Continue to move, shoot, and take cover, picking off foes one by one.

WILL-O'-WISP

 CR 2

This faintly glowing ball of light bobs gently in the air, the nebulous image of what might be a skull visible somewhere in its depths.

Will o' wisps are the souls of evil creatures who perished in agony or despair. Their appearance seems to bring hope to lost travelers, believing they are lanterns in the distance, only to discover the lights are cruel, life-eating horrors.

Fighting Style: Lurker. You can turn invisible at will and have a flying speed of 50 feet. This combination allows you to sneak up on targets, make attacks, and escape without fear of retribution.

Set-up: Dark Places with Lots of Cover. You have darkvision up to 120 feet, meaning you can see foes long before they see you (assuming you're invisible). You want to duck behind cover between your attacks, so make sure there's plenty around. Forests, swamps, tombs, and other dismal places are your top spots for hunting.

Weaknesses: Few Hit Points. You only have 22 hit points. Fortunately, your AC is 19, and you have plenty of methods to escape and hide between attacks. Just don't get hit.

Pair With Brutes and Controllers. Work alongside creatures that can distract or control your targets, allowing you to ambush without being noticed. Creatures capable of reducing your targets to 0 hit points are favorable since they do all the work for you. Sea hags and banshees both have this ability, as do devourers.

Tactics: Sneak and Zap. Start combat invisible; if you used your illumination feature to draw creatures to you, turn it off before they arrive. When a target comes within reach, appear and attack it with your shock attack. Then fly out of reach. On your next turn, turn invisible again. Wait until the targets have nearly forgotten about you to repeat this trick. Continue until you reduce a target to 0 hit points so that you can consume its life.

WINTER WOLF

CR 3

This bear-sized wolf has white fur and a rime of frost around its muzzle. Its eyes are pale blue, almost white.

These evil, dire-wolf-sized arctic creatures are far more Intelligent than most wolves and even capable of communicating in Common and Giant (and they have their own language, too). They often work alongside frost giants.

Fighting Style: Brute. Your strength lies in your offensive capabilities, particularly your devastating Cold Breath attack and Pack Tactics features. Plus, you have enough defensive features to last a few rounds in combat, devastating the enemy as you do.

Set-up: Arctic Environments. You are immune to cold damage and have the Snow Camouflage feature, which allows you to disguise yourself in snowy terrain. Make sure that the place you stage your attacks doesn't have many avenues of escape available to your targets.

Weaknesses: Relatively Poor Defensive Capabilities. You have only 75 hit points and AC 13; this is relatively low for a CR 3 creature, especially one that isn't immune or resistant to nonmagical weapon attacks. Make sure you get rid of your enemy before they get rid of you.

Pair With Artillerists and Minions. You have Pack Tactics, so you want to make sure that there are plenty of creatures within 5 feet of your targets so you can make your attacks with advantage. Plus, your bite attack knocks targets prone, so you can benefit those who don't have the Pack Tactics feature. These creatures should have immunity to cold, so they don't take damage from your Cold Breath. Meanwhile, artillerists can use the distractions you cause to take shots from the safety of cover.

Tactics: Ambush and Ravage. Start combat hidden in snowy terrain. When targets come within the range of your breath weapon, appear and attack, trying to hit at least two of them. Next turn, use your breath weapon again if it recharges. Otherwise, make a bite attack against whichever target is within 5 feet of one of your allies.

WORG

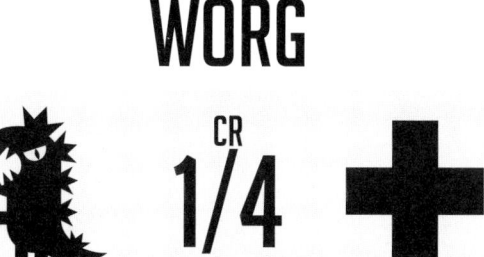

This enormous wolf has an evil, almost brilliant light shining in its deep red eyes.

Worgs are despicable predators who often serve goblins and hobgoblins as mounts. They can speak broken Goblin and have their own language, Worg.

Fighting Style: Support. Assuming you allow someone to ride you, you grant your target 50 feet of movement and can assist them in combat by knocking targets prone with your bite attack.

Set-up: Room to Move. Although you prefer to use brute tactics, you still want plenty of room to move around. Plus, your 50 feet of movement allows you and your rider to start outside most enemies' charging range.

Weaknesses: Temperamental. More of a roleplaying weakness than anything, worgs are intelligent creatures with a foul temper. If they feel that their rider is weaker or mistreating them, they'll eat the rider and leave.

Pair With Brutes or Minions. You offer your rider 50 feet of movement. In exchange, they help you double team targets. Choose targets with limited action economy but high damage output, such as bugbears or hobgoblins, the latter of which will benefit from its Martial Advantage feature while riding you.

Tactics: Charge, Trip, Ravage. Start combat 40 to 50 feet away from the enemy. If your rider's initiative order is before yours, the rider should Ready an attack action for when you get within reach of a target. Charge the nearest target and make a bite attack against it. Your rider then attacks, releasing a readied action or using their normal action economy. Continue these tactics until you defeat the foe, or the enemy gives you a reason to flee.

WRAITH

CR 5

This ghostly creature is little more than a dark shape with two flickering pinpoints of light where its eyes should be.

Crawled up from vile oblivion, these incorporeal creatures often serve as undead commanders, ruling legions of the dead.

Fighting Style: Lurker. You have a flying speed of 60 feet and the Incorporeal Movement feature, which allows you to phase through solid objects. Use this combination of features to ambush and retreat.

Set-up: Claustrophobic Areas with Lots of Cover. You don't want to linger too long after you attack a target. Fight in places where you can take full cover by fading through nearby walls, ceilings, or floors.

Weaknesses: Magic. Spells and magic effects, especially divine magic, cut through your resistances. Destroy spellcasters as fast as possible, or avoid them altogether. Also, don't get caught in direct sunlight—it weakens you.

Pair With Brutes and Minions. Use brutes and minions to distract your foes between attacks, allowing you to reposition without fear of the enemies seeking you for retribution.

Tactics: Ambush and Escape. Start combat hidden behind a wall, floor, ceiling, or another solid surface. When a target comes to the other side of that surface, phase through it and make a Life Drain attack. Then, escape back the way you came or into another area where you'll be safe from follow-up attacks. Don't worry about attacks of opportunity, as it's always better to take one attack than to stand around and wait for the enemy and all of their friends to attack you. After slipping away, reposition and find a new place to stage an ambush. Try to go for the same target, weakening it to the point where you can transform it into a specter minion.

WYVERN

 CR 6

A rust-colored dragon, its wings immense and its tail tipped with a hooked stinger, lands on two taloned feet and roars a challenge.

Wyverns are aggressive and reckless aerial hunters. While they aren't as intelligent as their "true" dragon cousins, they can still be tamed for use as a mount.

Fighting Style: Skirmisher. Whether you're fighting alone or with a rider, you prefer to use hit-and-run attacks, and you rarely, if ever, take to the ground to fight.

Set-up: Lots of Open Sky. As a flier, you want plenty of space overhead to perform your hit-and-run attacks. Without a Dexterity modifier or proficiency in Stealth, you like to let your targets know you're coming before you attack.

Weaknesses: Relatively Poor Dexterity. With a Dexterity score of 10 and no proficiency in Dexterity saving throws, you're a sitting duck for spells and effects that impose Dexterity saving throws. Although you can't spot a spellcaster in advance, you're clever enough to change tactics to target those once they hurt you.

Pair With Brutes or Controllers. Use brutes to keep your targets distracted while you make hit-and-run attacks. Or, if you're serving as a mount, the brute can toss in additional attacks when you're in range. Controllers are helpful, too, since they help set you up for advantage on attacks and prevent enemies from harming you.

Tactics: Hit-and-Run. Start combat flying 40 feet away in the air. On your turn, move within 10 feet of a target and attack it with your bite and stinger. Then, fly back 40 feet. So long as the target doesn't have a weapon with a reach greater than 5 feet, you can escape without fear of provoking an attack of opportunity, which outweighs the benefit of the extra damage your claws provide.

XORN

 **CR 5**

This squat beast is as wide as it is tall. Strangely symmetrical, it has three arms, three legs, three eyes, and one huge mouth.

Xorn are elemental travelers who can move through rock and stone as a fish moves through the water. They exist on gems and precious metals and frequently accost wealthy wanderers in the underworld for their precious "nom noms."

Fighting Style: Lurker. You can swim through earth thanks to Earth Glide and have tremorsense out to 60 feet. These features allow you to wait in full cover for a target carrying precious metals to come by so you can get the jump on them.

Set-up: Earthy Areas. You want to fight in areas with plenty of earth and stone for you to move through with ease.

Weaknesses: Being Grappled or Restrained. You're durable enough to absorb a few readied attacks and attacks of opportunity, but foes who grab you and stop you from moving will quickly end your tactical advantage.

Pair With Brutes and Minions. Work alongside other melee attackers who can distract your foes while you swim around the earth, ambushing them.

Tactics: Swim and Strike. Start combat 5 feet embedded in rock. Alternatively, use your Stone Camouflage feature to hide in a rocky area. When a target carrying treasure comes by, pop out and try to disarm them of the bag, pouch, etc., used to carry the goods; it's an attack roll contested by the enemy's Strength (Athletics) or Dexterity (Acrobatics) check. On a success, toss it in your mouth, and phase back through the rock. If you want to fight the enemies instead, ambush them like normal, but instead, use your Multiattack. After attacking, duck back into the earth and glide to a new area. Reappear and attack again. Don't worry about attacks of opportunity, as you're tough enough to withstand most punishment.

YETI

This creature stands like a man yet is half again the height of most men and covered with a coat of thick white fur.

Yetis are keen hunters that stalk the arctic wastes, their terrifying howl heard for miles around. As brutal rampagers, they use their hazardous environment for hunting, trapping, and ravaging their foes.

Fighting Style: Lurker. While you are undoubtedly fierce enough to fight as a brute, your ability to track with your sense of smell and hide in snowy environments means you're better equipped to ambush prey. If you can't kill your target with a single attack, your gaze can paralyze it, so you can drag it away to finish it off. Even if foes shake off the effects of your gaze, they're only immune for one hour.

Set-up: Snowy Conditions. You're immune to cold and have natural snow camouflage. Your sense of smell is strong enough to track enemies through blizzard conditions, which you can use to your advantage.

Weaknesses: Fire. You hate fire. Fire bad. When you take damage from fire, you have disadvantage on attack rolls and ability checks until the end of your next turn. As soon as an enemy shows up with fire, use your 40-foot movement and climbing speed to escape.

Pair With Brutes and Minions. Work alongside other cold-immune creatures who can act as a distraction while you lurk and strike from hiding. Plus, your ability to paralyze targets grants advantage to your allies' attacks.

Tactics: Ambush, Paralyze, Escape. Start combat hidden in a snowy environment. First, use your gaze to paralyze them. Then, claw them while they're paralyzed. If the target remains paralyzed, grab it and drag it away into difficult terrain or via a vertical passage its allies can't follow. If the target isn't paralyzed, escape without it. Find a new place to hide and stage ambushes.

Yeti, Abominable. Although abominable yetis are bigger and deadlier than normal yetis, they more or less use the same tactics. They also have a breath weapon attack which helps shake off creatures foolish enough to follow them.

ZOMBIE

 CR 1/4

This walking corpse wears only a few soiled rags, its flesh rotting off its bones as it stumbles forward, arms outstretched.

Zombies are mindless soldiers, often serving at the behest of sinister necromancers or other powerful undead. While they look similar to how they did in life, they often have disgusting injuries or rotting flesh, evoking terror in their victims.

Fighting Style: Minion. Although your attack isn't great, your Strength is in your tenacity and habit of swarming with others of your kind. Plus, your Undead Fortitude feature ensures that you stay up for countless rounds, much to the chagrin of those unlucky enough to fight you.

Set-up: Zombie Horde. You have no preference for the environment; you just do as you are told and smash things to bits. Your masters may know to separate you and your allies a bit to reduce the risk of area-of-effect attacks, but you're not intelligent or aware enough to know or care one way or the other.

Weaknesses: Radiant Damage. Two things cancel your Undead Fortitude: critical hits and radiant damage. You aren't clever enough to recognize a divine spellcaster before they cast a spell. But once they do, you know it's a good idea to crush them.

Pair With Brutes and Controllers. Use brutes to draw attention away from you and your fellow minions. Controllers are helpful, too, either working as your master and directing you or using their magic or features to grant you advantage on your attack rolls.

Tactics: Shamble and Slam. Start combat within 20 feet of your enemy and spread out 10 feet apart from other minions. On your turn, move towards the nearest enemy and attack it. If you can't reach the target, use Dash to at least get within reach. Once near an enemy, Slam it until it's dead, or it destroys you.

ZOMBIE, OGRE

 **CR 2**

This giant, walking corpse wears only a few soiled rags, its flesh rotting off its bones as it stumbles forward. It wields a rusting morningstar in his clawed hands.

Zombie ogres are mindless brutes raised by necromancers and other powerful undead. Like humanoid zombies, they look similar to how they did in life, albeit much more gruesome.

Fighting Style: Brute. Despite sharing the same CR as living ogres, you are far deadlier in nearly every aspect. Although you lose 10 feet of movement, you still move just as fast as most humanoids. Your AC is lower, but you have more hit points and the Undead Fortitude feature, which gives you a better chance at surviving.

Set-up: Up Close and Personal. Your job is to bash things, so you want to ensure there are no obstacles or difficult terrain in the way of that goal.

Weaknesses: Radiant Damage. Two things cancel your Undead Fortitude: critical hits and radiant damage. You aren't clever enough to recognize a divine spellcaster before they cast a spell. But once they do, you know it's a good idea to crush them.

Pair With Artillerists and Controllers. You'll keep foes distracted, allowing artillerists to take shots from the safety of cover. Meanwhile, controllers can direct your actions and use their spells and features to give you advantage on your attack rolls.

Tactics: Dash and Smash. Start combat within 30 feet of your foes. On your turn, move toward the nearest enemy and attack it with your morningstar. Continue to smash until the enemy stops moving, or you do.

BEASTS

Beasts are non-humanoid creatures that are a natural part of the fantasy ecology. Some beasts have magical powers, but most are unintelligent and lack any sophistication or language. Beasts include all varieties of ordinary animals, dinosaurs, and giant versions of animals.

For the sake of simplicity, I avoided writing out individual tactics for every beast in the Fifth Edition book for monsters. Instead, I've lumped them into categories based on their basic tactics, essentially the ones detailed on page 34.

4 THINGS TO KNOW ABOUT BEASTS

Here are a few things to know about beasts.

BEASTS USUALLY DON'T WANT TO FIGHT.

Except for a few predators, most beasts are terrified of humans and will flee as soon as they see one. Of course, this is a fantasy world, and cliches like "deadly wolf packs" or "bloodthirsty sharks" are commonplace. Furthermore, intelligent creatures like dryads, druids, vampires, and so forth may use beasts as low-level minions.

BEASTS USUALLY FLEE WHEN THEY ARE INJURED.

While beasts aren't very intelligent, they tend to have decent Wisdom scores, often 11 or higher; this means they have a well-developed sense of self-preservation. As soon as a beast takes damage, it will likely flee. The same goes for a pack of animals whose numbers are reduced by half or fewer.

BEASTS USE THEIR INSTINCTS TO FIGHT.

Although most beasts aren't smart enough to employ tactics, they are living creatures that have evolved to survive in a tough environment. They focus on attacks and features that benefit them the most.

BEASTS ARE USUALLY BRUTES, LURKERS, MINIONS, OR SKIRMISHERS (AND SOMETIMES SUPPORT).

The beasts included in the Fifth Edition manual for monsters are relatively unintelligent creatures. As such, they cannot devise complicated tactics. No beasts in this book are artillerists, controllers, elites, solo, or tanks, fighting styles that often require logistics and critical thinking. Instead, all the beasts fall into one of the other four categories: brutes, lurkers, minions, or skirmishers. Creatures that often serve as pack animals and mounts are considered support creatures, as they lend their speed and extra action economy to their rider.

BEASTS BY FIGHTING STYLE

The remainder of this chapter organizes the beasts from the Fifth Edition manual of monsters by their fighting styles. The notes in each category are somewhat generalized, but should work for a given monster, especially if you recall the four things to know about beasts above. Read about the 10 common fighting styles on page 34 for more information.

BRUTE BEASTS

Brute creatures start combat as close to their targets as possible. On their turn, they attack the nearest target and usually won't let up until the target is either dead or the target deals enough damage back to them to warrant a retreat.

Brute beasts include:

Ankylosaurus	Giant Badger	Rhinoceros
Ape	Giant Boar	Swarm of Bats
Black Bear	Giant Goat	Swarm of Insects
Boar	Giant Hyena	Swarm of Poisonous Snakes
Brown Bear	Giant Scorpion	Swarm of Quippers
Cave Bear	Goat	Swarm of Ravens
Elephant	Mammoth	Triceratops
Elk	Polar Bear	Tyrannosaurus Rex
Giant Ape		

LURKER BEASTS

Lurkers are beasts that prefer to wait in hiding or a heavily obscured area until their prey comes within reach. The creature then ambushes its prey,

Beasts

hoping to kill it with one strike. Some creatures, such as crocodiles and octopuses, have attacks that automatically grapple a target on a hit, allowing them to drag the target away. A lurker is less likely to stay in combat for more than one round—they want an easy dinner.

Lurker beasts include:

Badger	Giant Octopus	Octopus
Bat	Giant Poisonous Snake	Owl
Cat	Giant Shark	Panther
Constrictor Snake	Giant Spider	Plesiosaurus
Crocodile	Giant Toad	Poisonous Snake
Giant Centipede	Giant Weasel	Saber-toothed Tiger
Giant Constrictor Snake	Giant Wolf Spider	Scorpion
Giant Crab	Hunter Shark	Spider
Giant Crocodile	Killer Whale	Tiger
Giant Frog	Lion	Weasel

MINION BEASTS

Beasts that qualify as minions are those that usually have poor offensive and defensive skills and no way to lurk or skirmish. Many creatures with the Pack Tactics feature also qualify as minions since they tend to perform better when accompanied by others of their kind. Minions usually won't willingly enter combat unless they have strength in numbers.

Minion monsters include:

Baboon	Giant Fire Beetle	Quipper
Blood Hawk	Giant Rat	Rat
Crab	Hyena	Reef Shark
Deer	Jackal	Sea Horse
Dire Wolf	Lizard	Wolf
Frog	Mastiff	

SKIRMISHER BEASTS

Skirmishers are usually fliers or creatures with higher-than-average movement speeds that can make an attack and escape before a target can retaliate. These creatures sometimes have features like Flyby, which allows them to avoid attacks of opportunity when they fly out of the creature's reach.

Skirmisher beasts include:

Allosaurus	Giant Owl	Pteranadon
Eagle	Giant Wasp	Raven
Flying Snake	Hawk	Vulture
Giant Bat		

SUPPORT BEASTS

These beasts typically serve as mounts for other creatures, lending their movement speed, special features, and action economy to the rider. Without a rider, these creatures usually qualify as minions or skirmishers.

Support beasts include:

Axe Beak	Giant Lizard	Pony
Camel	Giant Sea Horse	Riding Horse
Draft Horse	Mule	Warhorse

APPENDIX A: HOW TO CREATE FIFTH EDITION MONSTERS

This appendix helps you understand how to create monsters. It includes multiple ways for you to do it: from tweaking existing monsters to applying simple templates to updating monsters from previous editions. I've omitted rules for building monsters from scratch since so much of what I would write would just be a retelling of the rules in the Fifth Edition guide for gamemasters, which I highly recommend you review, especially if you want to make new monsters.

BASIC DESIGN CONCEPTS

Before introducing templates, simple conversions, and edition updates, it's worth reiterating some basic monster design concepts.

DEFENSE AND OFFENSE CAPABILITIES AFFECT CR

The only two things that affect a monster's Challenge Rating are its offensive and defensive capabilities.

Its **offensive capabilities** are represented by the average damage it deals in a round of combat and the probability of hitting a character on its turn. Any special feature that would increase or decrease its damage output or the probability of it hitting a target—such as the ability to Hide as a bonus action every turn or extra damage dealt with a successful Charge attack—also affects these values.

A monster's **defensive capabilities** are represented by the total number of hit points it has and the probability of it avoiding attacks when it is targeted by characters. Any special feature that would increase or decrease its hit points or the probability of it avoiding attacks—such as the ability to Hide as a bonus action every turn or the ability to fly—also affects these values.

DAMAGE OUTPUT SCALING

The damage output of creatures scales at roughly the same rate within certain blocks of tiers.

Average Damage Increase by CR

CR	Average Damage Increase
0 to 1/2	Varies
1 to 19	6
20 to 30	18

When you increase a monster's average damage output by an amount equal to or greater than one of these values, you will likely increase the monster's CR.

HIT POINT SCALING

A monster's hit points also scale at fixed levels per tier as its CR increases, as shown in the table below.

Average Hit Point Increase by CR

CR	Average Hit Point Increase
0 to 1/2	Varies
1 to 19	15
20 to 30	45

Therefore if you increase a monster's hit points by an amount equal to or greater than one of these values, you will likely increase the monster's CR.

ARMOR CLASS SCALING

Fifth Edition monster ACs scale at approximately the same rate as the characters' probability to hit increases. The two major factors that increase the probability of a character's ability to hit a creature are its proficiency bonus and the relevant ability score modifier. Character proficiency bonuses increase at levels 5, 9, 13, and 17. And characters usually max out their ability scores by the 8th level, using the first two Ability Score Improvements to do so. Consequently, monster ACs increase at roughly the same rate, inevitably topping out at AC 19 once characters reach Tier IV play (levels 17 to 20). Monsters cannot normally have natural ACs above 22.

Typically, you can adjust a monster's AC by 1 either up or down without drastically affecting its CR. Once you increase or decrease it by 2 points or more, however, its CR changes, as the probability of characters hitting it (or not hitting it) becomes more varied.

TO-HIT SCALING

The probability that a monster will hit a character also increases at roughly the same rate the characters' own AC and defensive capabilities improve, beginning with the levels where characters reach new tiers of play (levels 5, 11, and 17), as well other important milestones, such as level 3 (where many classes pick up their first subclass), and levels 4, 8, and 16, where characters pick up Ability Score Improvements.

Typically, you can adjust a monster's to-hit modifier by 1 by 1 either up or down without drastically affecting its CR. Once you increase or decrease it by 2 points or more, however, its CR changes, as the probability of it hitting a character (or not hitting them) becomes more varied.

USING SIMPLE TEMPLATES

Simple templates can be applied during the game with minimal effort. This makes it easy, for example, to create new fiendish or celestial creatures conjured via a spell.

All simple templates have two categories of changes. The "quick rules" present a fast way to modify die rolls made in play to simulate the template's effects without actually rebuilding the stat block—this method works great for summoned creatures. The "rebuild rules" list the exact changes you make to the base stat block if you have the time to rebuild it completely. This method works best when you have time during game preparation to build full stat blocks. The two methods result in creators of similar, if not identical, abilities.

ADVANCED CREATURE (CR +1)

Creatures with the advanced template are fiercer and more powerful than their ordinary cousins.

Quick Rules: +2 on all rolls (including damage rolls) and special ability DCs; +4 to AC, and +2 hit points per hit die.

Rebuild Rules:

- **Armor Class (AC).** Increase natural armor by +2.
- **Ability Scores.** Increase all ability scores by +4 (except for Intelligence scores of 2 or less). Make sure to adjust the creature's AC, hit points, saving throws, skill proficiencies, save DCs, attack bonuses, and damage bonuses based on these changes.

ARTILLERIST CREATURE (CR +0 OR +1)

An artillerist is a creature that relies on long-ranged attacks to harm its foes. An artillerist creature's CR increases by +1 only if its AC remains unchanged.

Quick Rules: +2 to all Dexterity-based rolls; -2 to AC; give the creature a ranged weapon attack that deals the same amount of damage each turn as one of its melee weapon attacks with a normal range of at least 30 feet.

Rebuild Rules:

- Armor Class. If the creature has natural armor or wears manufactured armor, decrease its AC by -2.
- Ability Scores. Increase the creature's Dexterity score by 4.
- Multiattack. If the creature has the Multiattack action and it allows it to attack more than once with a melee weapon attack, replace that attack with its new ranged attack.
- Attacks. Give the creature a ranged spell or weapon attack that deals damage equal to one of its melee weapon attacks and has a normal range of at least 30 feet.

BRUTE CREATURE (CR +1)

A brute is a creature with powerful melee weapon attacks but relatively poor defensive capabilities.

Quick Rules: +2 to all Strength-based rolls; -2 to all Dexterity-based rolls; -2 to AC; give the creature the Brute trait (a melee weapon deals one extra die of its damage when the creature hits with it)

Rebuild Rules:

- **Armor Class.** Decrease the creature's AC by -2 (to a minimum of 10 plus its AC).
- **Ability Scores.** Increase the creature's Strength score by +4 and decrease its Dexterity score by -4.
- **New Trait: Brute.** A melee weapon deals one extra die of its damage when the creature hits with it.

CELESTIAL CREATURE (CR +0 OR +1)

Celestial creatures dwell in the higher planes but can be summoned using spells. A celestial creature's CR increases by +1 only if the base creature has a CR of 4 or less. Otherwise, it remains the same. A celestial creature's quick and rebuild rules are the same.

Rebuild Rules:

- **Senses.** The creature gains darkvision out to 60 ft.
- **Damage Resistance and Immunities.** If the creature's CR is 10 or less, the creature gains resistance to radiant damage and bludgeoning, piercing, and slashing damage from nonmagical attacks. If the creature's CR is 11 or greater, the creature gains resistance to radiant damage and immunity to bludgeoning, piercing, and slashing damage from nonmagical attacks
- **New Trait: Divine Smite (1/Day).** As a bonus action, the creature can cause its melee weapon attacks to magically deal an extra 10 (3d6) radiant damage to a target on a hit. This benefit lasts until the end of the turn.

CONTROLLER CREATURE (CR +0)

A controller is a creature that, whether through spells or innate magical abilities, is able to impose negative effects on its targets. A controller creature's quick and rebuild rules are the same.

Rebuild Rules:

- **Ability Scores.** Change the creature's Charisma score to 14 unless it is already higher.
- **New Action: Spellcasting.** The creature can cast the following spells, requiring no spell components, using Charisma as its spellcasting ability. The spell save DC for its spells equals 8 plus its proficiency bonus plus its Charisma modifier. At will—*command*; 1/day each—*bane, charm person, confusion, darkness, entangle, web*

FIENDISH CREATURE (CR +0 OR +1)

Creatures with the fiendish template live in the Lower Planes, such as the Abyss and Hell, but can be summoned using conjuration magic. A fiendish creature's CR increases by +1 only if the base creature has a CR of 4 or less. Otherwise, it remains the same. A fiendish creature's quick and rebuild rules are the same.

Rebuild Rules:

- **Senses.** The creature gains darkvision out to 60 ft.
- **Damage Resistance.** If the creature's CR is 10 or less, the creature gains resistance to cold, fire, and lighting damage and bludgeoning, piercing, and slashing damage from nonmagical attacks. If the creature's CR is 11 or greater, the creature gains resistance to cold, fire, and lightning damage and immunity to bludgeoning, piercing, and slashing damage from nonmagical attacks
- **New Trait: Fiendish Smite (1/Day).** As a bonus action, the creature can cause its melee weapon attacks to magically deal an extra

10 (3d6) necrotic damage to a target on a hit. This benefit lasts until the end of the turn.

GIANT CREATURE (CR +1)

Creatures with the giant template are larger and stronger than their normal-sized kin. This template cannot be applied to creatures that are Gargantuan.

Quick Rules: +2 to all rolls based on Strength or Constitution; +2 hit points per Hit Die.

Rebuild Rules:

- **Size.** The creature's size increases by one category. Make sure to change the creature's hit dice based on its new size using the rules outlined in the Fifth Edition guide for gamemasters.
- **Armor Class.** Increase the creature's AC by +2; it gains natural armor if it doesn't already have it.
- **Ability Scores.** Increase the creature's Strength and Constitution scores by +4.
- **Attacks.** Increase the damage dealt by the monster's weapon attacks by one die. For example, a creature that normally deals damage equal to 2d8 + its Strength modifier on a hit now deals damage equal to 3d8 + its Strength modifier on a hit as a giant creature.

LURKER CREATURE (CR +0)

Lurkers are creatures that use ambush tactics. Often, they wait in hiding for a creature to come within their reach. They then spring their trap, attacking fast and hard, then retreating with the prey captured in its jaws or claws.

Quick Build: +10 ft. to their primary movement speed; +2 to Dexterity-based rolls; advantage on Dexterity (Stealth) checks; when it hits a target with a melee weapon attack, the target is grappled (DC 10 + Str modifier)

Rebuild Rules:

- **Movement.** Increase the creature's primary movement speed by 10 feet. Alternatively, give the creature a new form of movement, such as a burrow, climb, fly, or swim speed equal to its walking speed.
- **Ability Scores.** Increase the creature's Dexterity score by 4.
- **New Trait: Camouflage.** Choose a type of natural terrain: the creature has advantage on Dexterity (Stealth) checks while it is in that terrain.
- **New Trait: Grappler.** When the lurker hits a creature of the same size category as the lurker or smaller with a melee weapon attack, the target is grappled. The escape DC is equal to 10 plus the lurker's Athletics proficiency or its Strength modifier (whichever is higher).

SKIRMISHER CREATURE (CR +0)

Skirmishers are creatures that use speed and reach to make hit-and-run attacks without fear of reprisal. A skirmisher's quick rules and rebuild rules are the same.

Rebuild Rules:

- **Armor Class.** If the creature has natural armor or wears manufactured armor, decrease its AC by -2.
- **Movement.** Double the creature's main form of movement, or give it a flying speed equal to its walking speed.
- **New Trait: Long Reach.** Increase the reach of the creature's melee weapon attacks by 5 ft.

SUPPORT CREATURE (CR +0)

Support creatures are creatures that have spells or innate magical abilities that allow them to create effects that help boost their allies. A support creature's quick rules and rebuild rules are the same.

Rebuild Rules:

- **Ability Scores.** Change the creature's Wisdom score to 14 unless it is already higher.
- **New Action: Spellcasting.** The creature can cast the following spells, requiring no spell components, using Wisdom as its spellcasting ability. The spell save DC for its spells equals 8 plus its proficiency bonus plus its Charisma modifier. At will—*prestidigitation*; 3/day—*cure wounds*; 1/day each—*bless, lesser restoration, sanctuary*.

YOUNG CREATURE (CR -1)

Creatures with the young template are immature specimens of the base creature. You can also use this simple template to create a smaller variant of a monster easily. This template cannot be applied to creatures that increase in power through aging or feeding (such as dragons) or Tiny-sized creatures.

Quick Rules: +2 to all Dexterity-based rolls; -2 to all other rolls; -2 hit points per Hit Die.

Rebuild Rules:

- **Size.** The creature's size decreases by one category. Make sure to adjust the creature's hit dice accordingly.
- **Ability Scores.** Decrease the creature's Strength and Constitution scores by -4 and increase the creature's Dexterity score by 4.
- **Attacks.** Decrease the damage dealt by the monster's attacks by one

die. For example, a creature that normally deals damage equal to 2d8 + its Strength modifier on a hit now deals damage equal to 1d8 + its Strength modifier on a hit as a young creature. If the creature only has a single die for its attacks and its CR becomes 0 from this adjustment, it only deals 1 damage on a hit, regardless of its modifiers.

TANK CREATURE (CR +1)

A tank creature is a creature with higher AC or improved defensive capabilities that spends combat distracting targets and threatening attacks of opportunity. A tank creature's quick rules and rebuild rules are the same.

Rebuild Rules:

- **Armor Class.** Increase the creature's Armor Class by +4, either increasing the natural armor it has or giving it a new type of manufactured armor to a maximum of 22.
- **New Trait: Intimidator.** The creature has advantage on Charisma (Intimidation) checks so long as it has more than half of its hit points remaining.
- **New Reaction: Parry.** The tank creature adds a bonus to its AC equal to its proficiency bonus against one melee attack that would hit it. To do so, the knight must see the attacker and be wielding a melee weapon.

TWEAKING EXISTING STAT BLOCKS

The next easiest way to create a monster in Fifth Edition is to take an existing monster stat block and adjust it. This works especially well if you don't change the two key dynamics in the monster's stat block that lend themselves to the Challenge Rating calculation, its defensive and its offensive capabilities.

STEP 1 - MATCH YOUR MONSTER CONCEPT TO AN EXISTING FIFTH EDITION MONSTER.

Say you have a concept for a monster that you want to make but don't want to go through the trouble of creating an entire stat block from the ground up. Consider the most important elements involving your monster concept:

- What CR do you want it to be?
- What size is the monster?
- What interesting traits does the monster have?

Once you can answer those three questions, it's just a matter of finding a creature in the Fifth Edition manual of monsters (or any other official monster book you like) that closely resembles your concept.

For example:

I want to make a two-headed undead child, and I want its CR to be 1/2. Checking out the 5e monster book, I decided that my concept is pretty close in size and CR to the deep gnome, which is also a Small creature at CR 1/2. So I will use the deep gnome as the basis of my new creature.

STEP 2 – EDIT ITS FEATURES WITHOUT ADJUSTING ITS DEFENSIVE AND OFFENSIVE CAPABILITIES.

Back in the section "Understanding the Monster Stat Block" (page 15), I mentioned that the only two features that affect a monster's challenge rating are its offensive and defensive capabilities. So long as you don't alter any features that would affect these two elements, the creature's CR will stay the same. Avoid altering Armor Class, hit points, to-hit modifiers, and average damage output, as well as any ability scores that would affect these ratings. Additionally, do not remove or add any of the following features:

- **Strength, Dexterity,** and **Constitution** usually have the biggest impact on the creature's offensive and defensive capabilities, as they may increase its hit points, Armor Class, to-hit modifiers, and damage output. If the creature has special features with DCs tied to its Intelligence, Wisdom, or Charisma modifiers, adjusting these may also significantly affect its offensive capabilities.

- **Damage Resistances and Immunities** significantly improve a creature's defensive capabilities, especially immunity to bludgeoning, piercing, and slashing damage. However, you are free to swap one immunity for another, such as cold for fire. Additionally, immunity to poison damage rarely comes into play since, in my experience, not many characters use features that deal poison damage.

- Giving a creature **more than two saving throw proficiencies** affects its defensive capabilities, as does each one added beyond three. As a good rule of thumb, avoid adding or subtracting saving throw proficiencies altogether.

- **Adding additional spells or spell-like abilities** that deal damage may affect the monster's damage output, especially area-of-effect spells.

- Giving a CR 10 or lower creature a **flying speed** affects its defensive capabilities, as they are harder for low-level characters to hit.

The CR-Affecting Monster Features list below includes a list of additional features that, when added, change a creature's special features. Avoid using these if you don't wish to recalculate the creature's AC.

Aggressive	Elemental Body	Pounce
Ambusher	Enlarge	Psychic Defense
Angelic Weapons	Fiendish Blessing	Rampage
Avoidance	Frightful Presence	Regeneration
Blood Frenzy	Horrifying Visage	Relentless
Breath Weapon	Legendary Resistance	Stench
Brute	Magic Resistance	Superior Invisibility
Charge	Martial Advantage	Surprise Attack
Constrict	Nimble Escape	Swallow
Damage Transfer	Pack Tactics	Undead Fortitude
Death Burst	Parry	Web
Dive Attack	Possession	Wounded Fury

Going back to my two-headed undead child example, using the deep gnome as my basis, I know that I want to change the following things.

Monster Type. I want to change its monster type from humanoid (gnome) to undead. Changing a monster's type won't affect its challenge rating.

Alignment. The undead child will be chaotic evil instead of neutral good.

Armor Class. The deep gnome has an AC 15 and wears a chain shirt. I don't foresee my undead two-headed child wearing a chain shirt, but I also don't want to adjust its AC, as that will affect its CR. Instead, I will retheme the AC 15 as natural armor. My kid has thick skin!

Damage and Condition Immunities. Nearly all undead are immune to poison damage and the poisoned condition. The deep gnome doesn't have any damage vulnerabilities, resistances, or immunities, nor does it have any condition immunities. Normally, I recommend that you don't add any of these features to a tweaked stat block, as it may affect the creature's defensive capabilities. However, characters so rarely deal poison damage, I find it doesn't hurt to add these into the block. So my undead two-headed child will have immunity to poison damage and the poisoned condition. Condition immunities don't normally affect a creature's defensive capabilities, so I could probably add more if I wanted, but I think I will leave it there for simplicity's sake.

Skills. I don't see my new monster being good at Investigation, so I remove that, too. However, I want it to still have proficiency in Perception and Stealth. And since it has two heads, I may actually double its proficiency modifier, taking it from +2 to +4.

Senses. If I change its proficiency modifier, I'll need to adjust its passive Perception score from 12 to 14.

Languages. I will replace Gnomish, Terran, and Undercommon with just Common.

Special Features. I want to eliminate its gnomish innate features, so I'll remove Stone Camouflage, Gnome Cunning, and Innate Spellcasting. I plan to add some new ones in the next step.

Actions. My two-headed undead child will have different attacks, so I'll need to eliminate the gnome's War Pick and Poison Dart attack. However, I need to make sure whatever attacks I give it have the same to-hit modifiers (+4) and the same average damage output (6 or 4 per round).

STEP 3 – "BORROW" FEATURES FROM OTHER STAT BLOCKS.

After you remove and edit the little details, so it better matches your creature, consider the special features that your concept has that the adjusted stat block doesn't. Then, find a creature that already has features similar to the ones you want to add and place those into the adjusted stat block. As before, ensure that the features you add won't affect its offensive or defensive capabilities.

For my two-headed undead child, I need to give it a feature that represents its two-headedness. Fortunately, there are a few monsters in the 5e manual for monsters that have appropriate features, such as the ettin and devil dog. I will copy over the Two Heads feature from the ettin verbatim.

Since it's undead, it also needs a feature that notes that it doesn't require the types of things other living creatures need, such as food, air, water, and sleep. Earlier editions of Fifth Edition called this Undead Nature and listed it outside of the stat block in the creature's description. The newest edition places this information in the stat block and calls it Unusual Nature. Regardless, the syntax is the same: "The undead child does not require air, food, water, or sleep."

STEP 4 - REPLACE THE CREATURE'S ATTACKS.

If you wish to change the creature's modes of attack, ensure that the new attacks have the same to-hit modifiers (or spell save DCs, if it relies mostly on spells or special attacks) and deal the same damage. You can change the damage type it deals, its reach, and even give it special secondary features that don't affect its damage output without altering its CR.

My deep gnome has a to-hit modifier of +2 and deals an average of 6 damage on its turn. I want to give my two-headed kid claw attacks, which it can use twice per turn thanks to Multiattack. So that means each attack must deal an average of 3 damage. With a +2 Strength modifier, that means if it uses a 1d4 for its damage roll; overall, it will deal an average of 4 damage per hit. Although this isn't exactly 6, increasing damage output by a couple of points shouldn't hurt anything, especially since we're getting rid of its ranged attack. If I wanted to keep it exactly the same, I would instead list its claws as a single attack (it rakes with both of its claws at the same time, like a bird), and just give it a 1d8 to deal damage.

STEP 5 - OPTIONAL: CHECK THE MATH

So long as you don't adjust the creature's offensive and defensive capabilities, its CR should stay relatively the same.

CONVERTING MONSTERS FROM PREVIOUS EDITIONS

Fifth Edition has plenty of monsters for gamemasters to use thanks to plenty of official and third-party books. But previous editions of the game, particularly the 2nd and 3rd editions, have even more interesting, zany, and fun creatures at your disposal. This section explains how to quickly convert these creatures so that they conform to Fifth Edition standards. The rules presented here are a "quick and dirty" way to convert without having to rebuild the stat block from the ground up.

Fourth Edition? Unfortunately, the creatures in Fourth Edition were so different in their balance and design, there is no quick way to change their stat blocks. You must build those creatures from the ground up.

CONVERTING FIRST AND SECOND EDITION CREATURES

Monsters in the first two editions were often weaker than those in current editions but often fought in large groups.

Armor Class. The creature's AC equals 19 minus the previous edition creature's AC, up to 22. For example, a First Edition monster with an AC of -1 would have an AC of 20 in Fifth Edition.

Attack Roll Modifiers. Determine the creature's attack roll modifier by dividing 2 into its original Hit Dice and adding +2 to a maximum of +12. For example, a creature with 10 Hit Dice in First Edition would have a +7 to-hit modifier in Fifth Edition.

Skill and Saving Throw Modifiers. If the creature has to make an ability check or saving throw and should be good at the roll, divide the creature's Hit Dice by 2 and add +2 to determine the bonus on the roll. Otherwise, use no modifier, or use a penalty to reflect something at which the creature is bad. For example, a First Edition creature with 12 Hit Dice that should be good at Dexterity saving throws does so with a +8 bonus to the roll.

CONVERTING THIRD (AND 3.5) EDITION CREATURES

Most lower CR creatures in Third Edition were balanced relatively the same way as creatures in Fifth Edition, with the same distribution of monsters per encounter.

Armor Class. The Fifth Edition version of the creature's Armor Class is either an average of the creature's touch AC and actual AC, or 20 percent lower than what it was in third edition, to a maximum of 22. For example, a Third Edition creature with a touch AC of 14 and actual AC of 22 would have an AC of 18 in Fifth Edition.

Attack Roll Modifiers. Determine the Third Edition creature's attack roll modifier by adding +3 to the appropriate ability score modifier. For example, a Third Edition creature with a Strength score of 17 would have an attack roll modifier of +6.

Saving Throw DCs. Determine the Third Edition creature's saving throw DCs by adding the appropriate ability score modifier to 10. For example, a Third Edition creature with a breath weapon attack and a Constitution score of 24 would have a saving throw DC of 17.

Skill Checks and Saving Throws. If the creature has to make an ability check or saving throw, use its ability score modifiers as normal and grant it a +3 bonus to the check if it should be good at the roll. For example, a Third Edition monster that should be good at Stealth checks that has a Dexterity score of 20 has a +8 bonus to its Dexterity (Stealth) checks.

APPENDIX B: ALTERNATIVE SPELL LISTS FOR SPELLCASTING NPCS

There are six "true spellcasters" in the Fifth Edition manual for monster's NPC section: acolyte, archmage, cult fanatic, druid, mage, and priest. This section offers new spell lists for those NPCs so that you can change the overall dynamic of the caster. Make a note that changing some of the spell lists may have an effect on the creature's CR, as noted in the description. I've also listed the creature's original spell list for your convenience.

ACOLYTE

The stock 5e version of the acolyte is a support caster, using the following spell list:

Cantrips (at will): *light, sacred flame, thaumaturgy*
1st level (3 slots): *bless, cure wounds, sanctuary*

These alternate spell lists change its dynamic, allowing it to perform different fighting styles.

ARTILLERIST ACOLYTE (CR 1)

Cantrips (at will): *light, sacred flame, thaumaturgy*
1st level (3 slots): *guiding bolt, healing word, shield of faith*

BRUTE ACOLYTE (CR 1)

Cantrips (at will): *light, sacred flame, thaumaturgy*
1st level (3 slots): *bless, healing word, inflict wounds*

CONTROLLER ACOLYTE (CR 1/4)

Cantrips (at will): *light, sacred flame, thaumaturgy*
1st level (3 slots): *bane, command, sanctuary*

LURKER ACOLYTE (CR 1)

Cantrips (at will): *light, sacred flame, thaumaturgy*
1st level (3 slots): *inflict wounds, sanctuary, shield of faith*

TANK ACOLYTE (CR 1/4)

Cantrips (at will): *light, sacred flame, thaumaturgy*
1st level (3 slots): *cure wounds, protection from evil and good, shield of faith*

ARCHMAGE

The stock 5e version of the archmage is an elite creature, using the following spell list:

Cantrips (at will): *fire bolt, light, mage hand, prestidigitation, shocking grasp*
1st level (4 slots): *detect magic, identify, mage armor, magic missile*
2nd level (3 slots): *detect thoughts, mirror image, misty step*
3rd level (3 slots): *counterspell, fly, lightning bolt*
4th level (3 slots): *banishment, fire shield, stoneskin*
5th level (3 slots): *cone of cold, scrying, wall of force*
6th level (1 slot): *globe of invulnerability*
7th level (1 slot): *teleport*
8th level (1 slot): *mind blank*
9th level (1 slot): *time stop*

It can also cast *disguise self* and *invisibility* at will.

These alternate spell lists change its dynamic, allowing it to perform different fighting styles.

ARTILLERIST ARCHMAGE (CR 14)

Cantrips (at will): *chill touch, fire bolt, light, mage hand, ray of frost*
1st level (4 slots): *expeditious retreat, fog cloud, mage armor, magic missile*
2nd level (3 slots): *acid arrow, mirror image, scorching ray*
3rd level (3 slots): *counterspell, fireball, slow*
4th level (3 slots): *dimension door, greater invisibility, stoneskin*
5th level (3 slots): *cloudkill, cone of cold, wall of force*
6th level (1 slot): *chain lightning*
7th level (1 slot): *delayed blast fireball*
8th level (1 slot): *sunburst*
9th level (1 slot): *meteor swarm*

BRUTE ARCHMAGE (CR 12)

Cantrips (at will): *light, mage hand, poison spray, prestidigitation, shocking grasp*
1st level (4 slots): *burning hands, mage armor, thunderwave*
2nd level (3 slots): *alter self, enlarge/reduce, mirror image*
3rd level (3 slots): *dispel magic, haste, vampiric touch*
4th level (3 slots): *faithful hound, polymorph, stone skin*
5th level (3 slots): *animate objects, cloudkill, wall of force*
6th level (1 slot): *sunbeam*
7th level (1 slot): *arcane sword*
8th level (1 slot): *mindblank*
9th level (1 slot): *shapechange*

CONTROLLER ARCHMAGE (CR 12)

Cantrips (at will): *dancing lights, light, mage hand, minor illusion, prestidigitation*
1st level (4 slots): *charm person, grease, mage armor*
2nd level (3 slots): *darkness, gust of wind, suggestion*
3rd level (3 slots): *counterspell, fear, slow*
4th level (3 slots): *confusion, ice storm, stoneskin*
5th level (3 slots): *dominate person, telekinesis, wall of force*
6th level (1 slot): *irresistible dance*
7th level (1 slot): *teleport*
8th level (1 slot): *reverse gravity*
9th level (1 slot): *prismatic wall*

LURKER ARCHMAGE (CR 12)

Cantrips (at will): *fire bolt, light, mage hand, prestidigitation, shocking grasp*
1st level (4 slots): *expeditious retreat, fog cloud, mage armor*
2nd level (3 slots): *detect thoughts, misty step, spider climb*
3rd level (3 slots): *blink, fireball, nondetection*
4th level (3 slots): *dimension door, greater invisibility, stoneskin*
5th level (3 slots): *cone of cold, mislead, scrying*
6th level (1 slot): *globe of invulnerability*
7th level (1 slot): *teleport*
8th level (1 slot): *mind blank*
9th level (1 slot): *power word kill*

SKIRMISHER ARCHMAGE (CR 12)

Cantrips (at will): *fire bolt, light, mage hand, prestidigitation, shocking grasp*
1st level (4 slots): *expeditious retreat, longstrider, mage armor*
2nd level (3 slots): *alter self, misty step, spider climb*
3rd level (3 slots): *fly, haste, phantom steed*
4th level (3 slots): *dimension door, polymorph, stoneskin*
5th level (3 slots): *cone of cold, scrying, wall of force*
6th level (1 slot): *globe of invulnerability*
7th level (1 slot): *teleport*
8th level (1 slot): *mind blank*
9th level (1 slot): *time stop*

SUPPORT ARCHMAGE (CR 12)

Cantrips (at will): *light, message, mage hand, mending, prestidigitation*
1st level (4 slots): *jump, longstrider, mage armor*
2nd level (3 slots): *darkvision, enlarge/reduce, gentle repose*
3rd level (3 slots): *fly, haste, nondetection*
4th level (3 slots): *greater invisibility, polymorph, stoneskin*
5th level (3 slots): *cone of cold, seeming, telepathic bond*
6th level (1 slot): *true seeing*
7th level (1 slot): *teleport*
8th level (1 slot): *mind blank*
9th level (1 slot): *foresight*

TANK ARCHMAGE (CR 12)

Cantrips (at will): *dancing lights, light, poison spray, ray of frost, shocking grasp*
1st level (4 slots): *false life, shield, mage armor*
2nd level (3 slots): *blur, mirror image, flaming sphere*
3rd level (3 slots): *counterspell, dispel magic, magic circle*
4th level (3 slots): *faithful hound, polymorph, stoneskin*
5th level (3 slots): *animate objects, conjure elemental, mislead*
6th level (1 slot): *globe of invulnerability*
7th level (1 slot): *teleport*
8th level (1 slot): *mind blank*
9th level (1 slot): *foresight*

CULT FANATIC

The stock 5e version of the cult fanatic is a controller creature, using the following spell list:

Cantrips (at will): *light, sacred flame, thaumaturgy*
1st level (4 slots): *command, inflict wounds, shield of faith*
2nd level (3 slots): *hold person, spiritual weapon*

These alternate spell lists change its dynamic, allowing it to perform different fighting styles.

ARTILLERIST CULT FANATIC (CR 2)

Cantrips (at will): *light, sacred flame, thaumaturgy*
1st level (4 slots): *bless, guiding bolt, healing word*
2nd level (3 slots): *hold person, spiritual weapon*

BRUTE CULT FANATIC (CR 2)

Cantrips (at will): *light, sacred flame, thaumaturgy*
1st level (4 slots): *bless, inflict wounds, shield of faith*
2nd level (3 slots): *enhance ability, spiritual weapon*

LURKER CULT FANATIC (CR 2)

Cantrips (at will): *light, sacred flame, thaumaturgy*
1st level (4 slots): *inflict wounds, sanctuary, shield of faith*
2nd level (3 slots): *enhance ability, hold person*

SUPPORT CULT FANATIC (CR 1)

Cantrips (at will): *light, resistance, sacred flame*
1st level (4 slots): *bless, sanctuary, shield of faith*
2nd level (3 slots): *aid, enhance ability*

TANK CULT FANATIC (CR 1)

Cantrips (at will): *light, sacred flame, thaumaturgy*
1st level (4 slots): *bless, sanctuary, shield of faith*
2nd level (3 slots): *enhance ability, spiritual weapon*

DRUID

The stock 5e version of the druid is a controller creature, using the following spell list:

Cantrips (at will): *druidcraft, produce flame, shillelagh*
1st level (4 slots: *entangle, longstrider, speak with animals, thunderwave*
2nd level (2 slots): *animal messenger, barkskin*

These alternate spell lists change its dynamic, allowing it to perform different fighting styles.

BRUTE DRUID (CR 2)

Cantrips (at will): *poison spray, produce flame, shillelagh*
1st level (4 slots): *entangle, healing word, thunderwave*
2nd level (2 slots): *barkskin, enhance ability, moonbeam*

LURKER DRUID (CR 2)

Cantrips (at will): *poison spray, produce flame, shillelagh*
1st level (4 slots): *entangle, fog cloud, jump, longstrider*
2nd level (2 slots): *pass without trace, spike growth*

SKIRMISHER DRUID (CR 2)

Cantrips (at will): *poison spray, produce flame, shillelagh*
1st level (4 slots): *entangle, jump, longstrider, thunderwave*
2nd level (2 slots): *hold person, spike growth*

SUPPORT DRUID (CR 1)

Cantrips (at will): *produce flame, resistance, shillelagh*
1st level (4 slots): *cure wounds, healing word, longstrider*
2nd level (2 slots): *darkvision, enhance ability, lesser restoration*

TANK DRUID (CR 2)

Cantrips (at will): *poison spray, produce flame, shillelagh*
1st level (4 slots): *entangle, healing word, thunderwave*
2nd level (2 slots): *barkskin, flame sphere, moonbeam*

MAGE

The stock 5e version of the mage is a lurker creature, using the following spell list:

Cantrips (at will): *fire bolt, light, mage hand, prestidigitation*
1st level (4 slots): *detect magic, mage armor, magic missile, shield*
2nd level (3 slots): *misty step, suggestion*
3rd level (3 slots): *counterspell, fireball, fly*
4th level (3 slots): *greater invisibility, ice storm*
5th level (1 slot): *cone of cold*

These alternate spell lists change its dynamic, allowing it to perform different fighting styles.

ARTILLERIST MAGE (CR 6)

Cantrips (at will): *fire bolt, light, mage hand, ray of frost*
1st level (4 slots): *expeditious retreat, fog cloud, mage armor, magic missile*
2nd level (3 slots): *mirror image, scorching ray*
3rd level (3 slots): *counterspell, fireball, slow*
4th level (3 slots): *dimension door, stoneskin*
5th level (3 slots): *cone of cold*

BRUTE MAGE (CR 6)

Cantrips (at will): *light, mage hand, poison spray, shocking grasp*
1st level (4 slots): *burning hands, mage armor, shield, thunderwave*
2nd level (3 slots): *alter self, mirror image*
3rd level (3 slots): *dispel magic, haste, vampiric touch*
4th level (3 slots): *polymorph, stoneskin*
5th level (3 slots): *animate objects*

CONTROLLER MAGE (CR 5)

Cantrips (at will): *light, mage hand, minor illusion, prestidigitation*
1st level (4 slots): *charm person, grease, mage armor*
2nd level (3 slots): *darkness, suggestion*
3rd level (3 slots): *counterspell, fear, slow*
4th level (3 slots): *confusion, stoneskin*
5th level (3 slots): *telekinesis, wall of force*

LURKER MAGE (CR 6)

Cantrips (at will): *fire bolt, mage hand, prestidigitation, shocking grasp*
1st level (4 slots): *expeditious retreat, fog cloud, mage armor*
2nd level (3 slots): *detect thoughts, misty step, spider climb*
3rd level (3 slots): *blink, fireball, nondetection*
4th level (3 slots): *greater invisibility, stoneskin*
5th level (3 slots): *mislead*

SKIRMISHER MAGE (CR 6)

Cantrips (at will): *fire bolt, mage hand, prestidigitation, shocking grasp*
1st level (4 slots): *expeditious retreat, longstrider, mage armor*
2nd level (3 slots): *misty step, spider climb*
3rd level (3 slots): *fly, haste, phantom steed*
4th level (3 slots): *dimension door, stoneskin*
5th level (3 slots): *cone of cold, wall of force*

SUPPORT MAGE (CR 5)

Cantrips (at will): *light, message, mage hand, mending*
1st level (4 slots): *jump, longstrider, mage armor*
2nd level (3 slots): *darkvision, enlarge/reduce, gentle repose*
3rd level (3 slots): *fly, haste, nondetection*
4th level (3 slots): *polymorph, stoneskin*
5th level (3 slots): *telepathic bond*

TANK MAGE (CR 6)

Cantrips (at will): *light, poison spray, ray of frost, shocking grasp*
1st level (4 slots): *false life, shield, mage armor*
2nd level (3 slots): *blur, mirror image, flaming sphere*
3rd level (3 slots): *counterspell, dispel magic*
4th level (3 slots): *faithful hound, polymorph, stoneskin*
5th level (3 slots): *animate objects*

PRIEST

The stock 5e version of the mage is an elite creature, using the following spell list:

Cantrips (at will): *light sacred flame, thaumaturgy*
1st level (4 slots): *cure wounds, guiding bolt, sanctuary*
2nd level (3 slots): *lesser restoration, spiritual weapon*
3rd level (2 slots): *dispel magic, spirit guardians*

These alternate spell lists change its dynamic, allowing it to perform different fighting styles.

ARTILLERIST PRIEST (CR 2)

Cantrips (at will): *light, sacred flame, thaumaturgy*
1st level (4 slots): *guiding bolt, healing word, shield of faith*
2nd level (3 slots): *hold person, spiritual weapon*
3rd level (2 slots): *dispel magic, spirit guardians*

BRUTE PRIEST (CR 2)

Cantrips (at will): *light, sacred flame, thaumaturgy*
1st level (4 slots): *bless, healing word, inflict wounds*
2nd level (3 slots): *enhance ability, spiritual weapon*
3rd level (2 slots): *dispel magic, spirit guardians*

CONTROLLER PRIEST (CR 2)

Cantrips (at will): *light, sacred flame, thaumaturgy*
1st level (4 slots): *bane, command, sanctuary*
2nd level (3 slots): *hold person, silence*
3rd level (2 slots): *dispel magic, spirit guardians*

LURKER PRIEST (CR 2)

Cantrips (at will): *light, sacred flame, thaumaturgy*
1st level (4 slots): *inflict wounds, sanctuary, shield of faith*
2nd level (3 slots): *aid, enhance ability*
3rd level (2 slots): *meld into stone, water walk*

SUPPORT PRIEST (CR 2)

Appendix B: Alternative Spell Lists for Spellcasting NPCs

Cantrips (at will): *light, sacred flame, thaumaturgy*

1st level (4 slots): *bless, cure wounds, healing word, sanctuary*

2nd level (3 slots): *aid, enhance ability*

3rd level (2 slots): *beacon of hope, revivify*

TANK PRIEST (CR 2)

Cantrips (at will): *light, sacred flame, thaumaturgy*

1st level (4 slots): *cure wounds, protection from evil and good, sanctuary, shield of faith*

2nd level (3 slots): *enhance ability, spiritual weapon*

3rd level (2 slots): *spirit guardians*

APPENDIX C: TACTICS VS SPECIFIC PLAYER CLASSES

This appendix covers tactics dealing with the twelve core player classes that appear in the Fifth Edition handbook for players. Any classes that don't appear in that guide are not included here, as we must stay within the confines of what the Fifth Edition Systems Reference Document allows.

BARBARIANS

In Fifth Edition, barbarians are rugged, primal characters who draw on their rage and physical prowess to overpower their enemies in combat.

Barbarians are almost always close combat fighters and frequently play the role of the tank or brute for their parties.

BARBARIAN STRENGTHS

The typical barbarian character has the following strengths.

High Defensive Capabilities. Barbarians have extremely high hit points and relatively good Armor Class provided by their Unarmored Defense feature. While raging, they have resistance to bludgeoning, piercing, and slashing damage, too. They are proficient in Strength and Constitution saving throws and have advantage on most Dexterity saving throws thanks to their Danger Sense feature.

Quick to Action. At second tier, barbarians gain the Fast Movement and Feral Instinct features, which allow them to often go first in combat and move quickly.

High Damage Output. While barbarians don't have the same action economy as fighters or monks, they do have Rage which significantly boosts their damage output. It is common for barbarians to wield two-handed weapons like greatswords and greataxes, too, giving them a higher damage output. When they reach the second tier, they gain an extra attack, and their critical damage improves, too.

Strong. Barbarians usually focus on boosting their Strength and Constitution. Many are proficient in the Athletics skill, too. And thanks to Rage, they get advantage on Strength checks while raging. This means they make for deadly grapplers.

BARBARIAN WEAKNESSES

While a barbarian's subclass features might account for some of its weaknesses, these are the barbarian's most common weaknesses.

Poor Mental Abilities. Barbarians are multi-ability, score-dependent characters, meaning they have to focus primarily on boosting their Strength, Dexterity, and Constitution scores. This often leaves them with relatively poor mental statistics. Combine this with the fact that they don't have proficiency in Wisdom, Intelligence, or Charisma saving throws—not without taking a feat—this leaves them vulnerable to most magical attacks, particularly enchantments.

Few Ranged Attacks. As tanks with high defensive capabilities, barbarians perform best in close combat. This isn't to say that they don't have ranged attacks—many carry javelins and other thrown items in case they can't reach their foe. But the typical barbarian would rather use its fast movement speed and bonus to melee weapon attacks in close combat.

FIGHTING BARBARIANS

Here are some basic tactics for dealing with most barbarian characters.

Keep Your Distance. Barbarians want to engage you in close combat. Make sure to keep plenty of distance from them. Rely on artillerists that deal damage other than bludgeoning, piercing, or slashing, such as barbed devils or mages. Don't forget that barbarians of 5th-level and higher can cover 40 feet with their movement, so place obstacles or difficult terrain in the way. Fliers work well against them, too.

Ignore or Separate Them. The barbarian's job is to tank and draw attacks. Therefore, if your monsters ignore them, they won't get a chance to do what they're good at. Alternatively, use lurkers or skirmishers to draw them away from the rest of the group. Wall spells are great for splitting them from the rest of the party, too.

Control Them. Most barbarians are weak against enchantment magic. Charm, dominate, or confuse them, so they turn against the rest of the party.

BARDS

Most bards are charismatic, artistic characters who use their skills in music, poetry, and performance to inspire and motivate allies, charm and deceive enemies, and uncover secrets and lore.

Although bards are highly versatile, most serve as support casters and elites for the party, helping out with whatever role is needed. Many are controllers, too.

BARD STRENGTHS

The typical bard character has the following strengths.

Enchantment Magic. Many of the bard's best spells are enchantment spells, forcing Wisdom saving throws on your monsters. These spells make them capable controllers who can easily take control of even your most deadly bad guys.

Dexterous. Bards have proficiency in Dexterity saving throws and often boost their Dexterity early on in their build. They gain the Expertise feature at 3rd level, so they may even have excellent Stealth proficiencies, allowing them to hide and lurk during combat.

Support Healers. Bards have many of the same healing spells as clerics, but are not as proficient with the spells as a Life cleric or similar specialist. These spells, particularly *healing word*, allow them to support their allies from safety.

BARD WEAKNESSES

While a bard's subclass features might account for some of its weaknesses, these are the bard's most common weaknesses.

Poor Defenses. Although there are some bards who come with better armor proficiencies, most bards rely on light armor and their Dexterity modifier to avoid attacks. They don't often come with the same extra defensive features as rogues and monks, such as Evasion and Uncanny Dodge, and their hit die is only a d8. Because they are a multi-ability, score-dependent class, they usually focus most of their effort on Dexterity, Intelligence, and Charisma, which sometimes leaves them with average Constitution scores. A brute focusing its attacks on a bard will make short work of such characters.

Jack of All Trades (Master of None). With the exception of bard builds that double-down on their controller features, most bard characters are versatile elite builds which make them decent at a lot of things but rarely as good at other fighting styles as other, more specialized classes.

FIGHTING BARDS

Here are some basic tactics for dealing with most bard characters.

Send Brutes After Them. The bard's relatively poor defensive capabilities make it easy to drop them with a few powerful hits from your strongest brutes or artillerists. Because bards tend to have subpar Strength and Constitution scores and usually aren't proficient in either saving throw, use brutes that force these saving throws on a hit, knocking them prone, poisoning them, etc.

Silence Them. The majority of the bard's spells require verbal components. Use the *silence* spell to quiet them. Alternatively, use creatures that can't hear the bard since many bard subclass features require the target to hear the bard for an effect to work. The deafened condition rarely limits what a creature can do and, if anything, serves to protect them from enchantment magic. This is especially useful against the bard's favorite cantrip, *vicious mockery*.

Roleplay. Bard characters are often played for laughs or by players that enjoy roleplaying. Use their character flaws against them—even if that means introducing some cringey situations.

CLERICS

In Fifth Edition, clerics are divine spellcasters who draw on the power of a deity or a pantheon of deities to cast spells and channel divine energy to smite and defeat their enemies and heal, protect, and bolster their allies.

Clerics have some of the most versatile subclasses out there, allowing them to take up nearly any role the party needs. They are usually played as elites or support.

CLERIC STRENGTHS

While few clerics are the same, many have the following strengths.

Undead Bane. Clerics are so powerful against undead that it's quite difficult for a party to fight a group of undead without a cleric in their party.

Healers. Although not all clerics specialize in healing, the vast majority of cleric characters have healing features. This keeps the party fresh even at early levels, and later, makes the party very difficult to defeat once the cleric gains the ability to *revivify* fallen characters.

Stackable Spells. The cleric spell list is full of spells that allow them to stack spells on spells on spells without having to concentrate. They also come with a load of bonus action spells, granting them incredible action economy even at early levels.

CLERIC WEAKNESSES

While a cleric's subclass features might account for some of its weaknesses, these are the cleric's most common weaknesses.

Distracted. While the cleric might try to assist in combat, they're often busy treating their allies' wounds and conditions. Therefore, dropping weak characters early in combat not only removes the weak character from the board, but also keeps the cleric busy—a two-for-one special.

Poor Dexterity. Most cleric builds focus on Strength, Constitution, and

Wisdom, foregoing Dexterity for medium or heavy armor. As such, they are relatively weak against effects and attacks that require Dexterity saving throws. Just be aware of any natural or magical elemental defenses they may have.

All Verbal Components. With the exception of some of their domain spells, there is not a single spell in the game that the cleric can cast that doesn't require verbal components. Silencing them keeps them from casting spells and turns them into relatively weak melee combatants.

FIGHTING CLERICS

Here are some basic tactics for dealing with most cleric characters.

Keep Them Busy. Focusing your attacks on the cleric is folly, as they tend to have relatively decent defensive capabilities and don't often put themselves on the front line. Instead, focus your attacks on the characters that are easy to drop to 0, as those will tie up the cleric's action economy and burn their best spell slots, especially at lower levels.

Force Dexterity Saves. If you do have to target the cleric, attack them with spells and effects that force Dexterity saving throws, as they usually have poor Dexterity saving throw modifiers.

Blind or Silence Them. Earlier, I mentioned that clerics need to be able to speak to use all their spells. But if you can't silence them, blind them instead, since nearly all spells need the caster to see their target to cast the spell. Clerics rarely have the ability to see through magical darkness. And if you don't have magical darkness on hand, use *fog cloud* or *cloudkill* instead.

Drown Them in Undead. Although undead are weak against clerics, they'll also keep the cleric busy, especially if it's clear that if the cleric doesn't deal with the undead, the party might be in trouble. This is especially useful for burning Channel Divinities of which clerics have a dreadfully low supply.

DRUIDS

In Fifth Edition, druids are divine spellcasters who draw on the power of nature and the spirit world to cast spells, transform into animals, and wield other magical abilities related to the natural world, such as control over the elements and the ability to shapeshift into various forms. Druids have diverse spell lists and features, letting them play the role of elite. Many druids, particularly those with stronger Wild Shape capabilities, often play the role of tank.

DRUID STRENGTHS

While few druids are the same, many have the following strengths in common.

Defensive Capabilities. Many druid players focus their efforts on the druid's ability to Wild Shape. While Wild Shaped, the druid gains bonus hit points, making it a formidable tank in combat.

Battlefield Controllers. Druid players who focus more on spellcasting often come loaded with battlefield control spells like *entangle*, *fog cloud*, and *spike growth*. These spells will make quick work of your minions and brutes.

Wisdom Saving Throws. Druids are usually highly proficient in Wisdom saving throws; not only does their class give them proficiency, but druid players tend to stack their Wisdom score to improve their spell save DCs. When it comes to tanking, this gives druids an edge over barbarians who are easily removed from combat with enchantment spells.

DRUID WEAKNESSES

While a druid's subclass features might account for some of its weaknesses, these are the druid's most common weaknesses.

Poor Damage Output. While the druid's Wisdom score might make it a better tank than barbarians, they aren't nearly as good at dealing damage, especially when they are wild-shaped, relying on the creature's natural attacks.

Poor Dexterity Saves. Druids don't have proficiency with Dexterity saving throws and most of their preferred wild shape forms won't have good Dexterity bonuses either. Focus on using spells and effects that require Dexterity saving throws, but don't necessarily focus only on dealing damage, such as *grease*, *web*, and *sleet storm*.

FIGHTING DRUIDS

Here are some basic tactics for dealing with most druid characters.

Tank the Tank. Druids that play the tank role are great at tying up your brutes and minions. Keep them busy with tanks of your own, especially since druids in wild shape form don't often have strong modes of attack.

Control the Controller. Use spells and effects on the druid that force Dexterity saving throws (or Strength, if possible), that keep them pinned in combat. This is especially useful against druids that prefer to tank over casting spells. If the druid prefers spellcasting, instead blind them with *darkness* or *fog cloud* so they can't see their targets.

Distract Them. If the druid comes with an array of healing spells, focus attacks on weak foes, forcing the druid to burn their action economy and spell slots to heal their allies.

FIGHTERS

The Fighter is a versatile and formidable warrior in the world of Fifth Edition, skilled in both hand-to-hand combat and the use of weapons such as swords, axes, and bows. They are known for their physical prowess and exceptional defense abilities, able to withstand even the toughest of blows.

FIGHTER STRENGTHS

The fighter class is extremely versatile. However, they usually have the following strengths in common.

Action Economy. Fighters have some of the best action economies in the game, especially once they get past the 5th level and they pick up their first Extra Attack.

High Armor Class. Most fighters have impressive AC, bolstered by expensive armor and shields, or high Dexterity and other defensive abilities.

Elite Combatants. Nearly all fighters can fill multiple roles, casually switching from tank to artillerist to brute without breaking a sweat.

FIGHTER WEAKNESSES

While it might seem like fighters are good at everything, they do have some glaring weaknesses.

Poor Mental Saving Throws. Fighters have proficiency in Strength and Constitution saving throws. And since they tend to be multiple attribute dependent, they rarely boost their Intelligence, Wisdom, and Charisma scores, favoring the physical ones. This leaves them vulnerable to many spells and magical effects, particularly enchantments.

Equipment Dependent. A fighter is nothing without their arms and armor. Unless they're equipped head-to-toe with magical gear, creatures like rust monsters, oozes, and other things capable of destroying armor and weapons are especially effective against them. The *heat metal* spell is another fun trick.

Lack of Mobility. While fighters, barbarians, and monks usually comprise the front line of many parties, fighters lack the speed of barbarians and monks. Furthermore, they rarely have the ability to fly or swim effectively. This makes it hard for them to reach enemies, forcing them to rely on ranged weapons which they might not be as good with.

FIGHTING FIGHTERS

Here are some basic tactics for dealing with most fighter characters.

Enchant and Bewilder. Use spells and effects that force the fighter to make Wisdom, Intelligence, or Charisma saving throws. This is especially useful at higher levels when the Fighter's low bonuses will render them useless against such effects.

Keep Away. Fighters deal a lot of damage. Keep your distance from the fighter or use minions to keep them tied up in combat.

Destroy Their Toys. Use rust monsters, oozes, or the *heat metal* spell to cause damage to the fighter's expensive armor and weapons. At the very least, it'll force them to avoid the monster.

MONKS

In Fifth Edition, Monks are martial artists who have honed their bodies and minds to a state of near perfection. They use their mastery of the body and mind to perform incredible physical feats and can strike with deadly accuracy. Monks can also harness their inner energy, known as ki, to perform powerful and unique abilities, making them formidable foes in combat.

MONK STRENGTHS

Monks are a relatively diverse class, giving them various strengths.

Action Economy. Monks are one of the few classes in the game that starts with a bonus action attack, thanks to their Martial Arts feature. As they increase levels, they get even more attacks.

High Defensive Capabilities. The monk's Unarmored Defense gives them an impressive AC. As they increase in levels, they gain Evasion, Stillness of Mind, Purity of Body, Diamond Soul, Timeless Body, and Empty Body, all incredibly powerful defensive features which make them extraordinarily difficult to harm.

Dextrous. Most monks rely on Dexterity as their highest ability score since it fuels almost all of their attacks and defenses. Once they gain Evasion, it's almost impossible to harm them with Dexterity-based attacks.

MONK WEAKNESSES

Monks don't have a ton of weaknesses, making them tricky foes. Still, here are a few that stand out.

Relatively Low Damage Output. Although monks have a lot of action economy, the damage they deal with their hands and weapons is relatively low compared to the heavy weapons of fighters and barbarians.

Poor Constitution, Intelligence, and Charisma Saving Throws. Monks are multiple attribute dependent, focusing much of their effort on Dexterity and Wisdom. Granted, Diamond Soul gives them a proficiency in all saving throws at 14th-level and beyond. But before then, they're wide open to attacks and spells that target saving throws other than Strength and Dexterity.

Ki Limitations. Monk features, particularly those used for dealing damage, are limited by their ki. At early levels, it drains quickly, leaving them with only their basic features.

FIGHTING MONKS

Here are some basic tactics for dealing with most monk characters.

Draw Them Away. Monks are fast and capable of subduing foes during the first round of combat thanks to their Stunning Strike. Use your faster monster to draw them away from the rest of the party, keeping them distracted.

Burn Their Ki Early. Create low-stress combats with lots of minions that will force the monk to burn a lot of their ki using flurry of blows and other action economy boosting effects.

Tank the Tank. A lot of monks rely on their defensive capabilities to tie up combatants. Turn the tables and do the same to them, keeping them occupied.

PALADINS

Paladins in Fifth Edition are holy warriors who draw their strength from their faith and devotion to a higher power. They are known for their ability to perform miracles, smite evil, and heal the wounded, making them valuable allies in any adventuring party.

PALADIN STRENGTHS

Everything, really. But here are the ones that rise above the others.

Damage Output. The paladin's smite is one of the most devastating attacks in the game, capable of dealing damage on par with a high-level rogue's sneak attack. And since it's radiant damage, there aren't many creatures capable of resisting it.

Protective Auras. When the paladin hits 6th level, they get to add their Charisma modifier to the saving throws of everyone within 10 feet of them. This is perhaps their greatest strength (and their most annoying feature).

Elites. Paladins are extraordinarily diverse. Even before factoring in their subclass features, a stock paladin can heal, deal damage, tank, and support allies. The only area where they lack is in skirmishing and artillery, but it only takes a few quick fixes and useful magic items to fix that.

PALADIN WEAKNESSES

Paladins, especially high-level ones, don't have a whole lot of weaknesses. Still, there are a few things to recognize.

Poor Mobility. Like fighters, paladins aren't the fastest melee combatants in the game. Unless they use a mount, they are severely limited in their speed.

Hero Mentality. Perhaps this is a bit stereotypical, but many paladin players tend to play the hero role. As such, it's easy to taunt them into combat through roleplaying. Granted, this is an overgeneralization, but it tends to work quite well.

Poor Ranged Attacks. Many paladin players focus on boosting their character's Strength, Constitution, and Charisma, ignoring Dexterity. Plus, they can't smite using a ranged weapon.

FIGHTING PALADINS

Here are some basic tactics for dealing with most paladin characters.

Draw Them Away. The paladin's auras are arguably their single greatest power, making the entire party that much better for having them around. Try to keep them away from the rest of the party however you can, using grapplers, pit traps, etc., to keep their auras off their allies.

User Fliers or Swimmers. Not a lot of paladins have the ability to fly (unless they conjure a celestial horse, of course) or swim. Force them to rely on ranged attacks against flying creatures. They're even weaker when they have to fight in water.

Cut Them Off. If you can't draw them away or keep your distance, use magic and effects that divide them from the rest of the party. Magical walls, *forcecage*, *spike growth*, etc., are all great tools for dividing them.

RANGERS

Rangers in Fifth Edition are skilled hunters and trackers who are at home in the wild. They use their knowledge of nature and their expertise in archery to survive and defeat their enemies, making them formidable opponents even in the harshest of environments. Rangers are also known for their stealth and cunning, allowing them to move unseen and strike from the shadows, making them valuable assets in any situation.

Editor's Note: keep in mind that many of the notes here do not take into account non-SRD ranger subclasses and variants.

RANGER STRENGTHS

Arguably, most of a ranger's strengths lie in their non-combat abilities. However, they do have some cool features to consider in combat, too.

Hunter's Mark. Possibly one of the best 1st-level spells in the game, *hunter's mark* lets the ranger deal extra damage to a target and track it indefinitely all for the cost of a bonus action. Then, after it kills the target, it can shift the target away to another creature. The only drawback is that it burns the ranger's concentration.

Elites. While rangers aren't as good at playing the elite role as the paladin or other spellcasters, their naturally high Dexterity and a wide array of spells, many of which are usable through bonus actions even at early levels, allow them to fill multiple roles in the party.

Ranged Attacks. Most rangers are built with high Dexterity scores. Plus, they're one of the few classes that starts with a longbow, easily the best ranged weapon in the game. They make fantastic artillerists.

RANGER WEAKNESSES

Here are a few glaring weaknesses that the ranger class possesses.

Jack of All Trades, Master of None. Rangers have a lot of interesting features, but they rarely gel well together. Even as a ranged combatant, they're nowhere near as competent at being an artillerist as a rogue, fighter, or even a warlock. Their spellcasting list is all over the place. And their defensive capabilities are only so-so, achieving the ability to Hide as a bonus action only when they reach the 14th level.

Funky Action Economy. The biggest issue with the ranger is that many of their cool features burn too much of their action economy to be useful. They're stealthy, certainly, but until they reach the 14th level, they have to burn an action to hide. They have some decent bonus action spells (see *hunter's mark* above), but they're nowhere near as useful as the paladin's smite spells. Finally, they only get one Extra Attack.

Not Built for Combat. Ultimately, the problem in ranger lies in the fact that it just isn't a class built for combat. Rangers were designed to be good at exploration. And when they are in a campaign that sees a lot of hex crawl and travel, they're great. Otherwise, they tend to lag behind other classes regarding combat usefulness.

Stay Out of Sight. A lot of rangers are built for artillery. Keep your monsters distant and out of sight, taking full or at least three-quarters cover. Don't forget that you can have your monsters drop prone to impose disadvantage on ranged attacks made against you.

FIGHTING RANGERS

Here are some basic tactics for dealing with most ranger characters.

Non-Dexterity and Strength Saving Throws. Although some players may focus on boosting their ranger's Wisdom score, the majority of the ranger player's focus will probably be Dexterity, especially since they don't get the same number of Ability Score Improvements as rogues or fighters. Target them with spells and effects that force Constitution, Intelligence, Wisdom, and Charisma saving throws.

Run Away. This one is a bit cheesy, but once a target gets the *hunter's mark* on it, have that target run away. This forces the ranger to either track the target or forego the use of *hunter's mark*, making them burn another slot to recast it.

Ignore Them. Not to sound mean, but most ranger builds (at least the SRD ones, those gloom stalkers can be nasty!) aren't big enough of a concern to focus your efforts. Instead, make them one of the last enemies you target, focusing your efforts on

ROGUES

Rogues in Fifth Edition are cunning and stealthy individuals who rely on their wit and charm to get what they want. They use their quick reflexes and agility to avoid danger and slip into the shadows, allowing them to take what they want without being detected. They also have one of the best features in the game, Sneak Attack, allowing them to deal significant damage.

ROGUE STRENGTHS

Rogues are blessed with a variety of strengths.

Damage Output. No matter the build, most rogues are incredible damage dealers thanks to their Sneak Attack. And since most of their Sneak Attacks rely on having advantage, they usually hit their target, despite their limited number of attacks per round.

Single Ability Dependent. Rogues really only need to be good with one ability score to be effective: Dexterity. From their attack and defense, skills, and saving throws, everything is tied to Dexterity.

Cunning Action. As if the other two strengths weren't enough, rogues from 2nd-level and up can Dash, Disengage, or Hide as a bonus action, a remarkably powerful feature that all but ensures that they'll rarely get targeted by your monster's attacks and will almost have advantage on their own attacks.

ROGUE WEAKNESSES

Fortunately, rogues do have a few weaknesses which you can exploit.

Poor Non-Dexterity Saving Throws. With maybe the exception of Intelligence, most rogues have pretty lousy saving throws that aren't Dexterity. This leaves them wide open to most spells. They get slippery mind at the 15th level, but by then, the party is completely trashing all of your encounters anyways.

One Attack Per Turn. Most rogues only have one attack per turn. And while it's likely they'll have advantage on that attack, or at the very minimum Sneak Attack, if it misses, they have to wait until the next round—or best case scenario, someone triggers an attack of opportunity—to try again.

Sneak Attack Dependency. A rogue in combat is nothing without its Sneak Attack. If it has disadvantage on its attack or if there is no ally within 5 feet of the target, it can't use it, reducing it to making an attack with a weapon that usually does no more than 1d8 + Dex damage.

FIGHTING ROGUES

Here are some basic tactics for dealing with most rogue characters.

Target with Enchantments. Until a rogue reaches the 15th level, it is usually incredibly susceptible to enchantment spells. And with a poor Wisdom saving throw, it likely won't recover fast from it, either. If that doesn't work, use Constitution-based spells instead.

Remove Sneak Attack Opportunities. Be aware of your rogue's potential targets. Unless you're using a minion or a tank, don't get within 5 feet of the rogue's allies. Stay completely hidden between your turns, forcing the rogue to Ready attacks. Or fight in settings that naturally impose disadvantage. Don't forget to drop prone and Dodge, too.

Ready Attacks. Although the rogue has excellent saving throws, their actual defenses are usually limited by light armor and their Dexterity modifier. Ready your monster's ranged attacks and spells so that they hit the rogue just as they pop out of hiding to make their attack.

SORCERERS

Sorcerers in Fifth Edition possess innate magical abilities, using their powers to control the elements and shape reality to their will. Their spells are often more instinctive and less studied compared to those of wizards, but they can still unleash devastating effects with a flick of their wrist.

SORCERER STRENGTHS

Sorcerers are unique in that they are usually very good at a few things but pretty bad at many other things.

Durable. Although sorcerers are multiple ability dependent, sorcerer players tend to focus on boosting their character's Constitution and Charisma. And since they're naturally proficient in Constitution saving throws, they're often resistant to most forms of poison and other attacks that force such saves.

Focused. The best way to build a sorcerer is to pick one specific type of magic or spell and focus on it, making it the best thing they do. This is especially true when they get metamagic, which allows them to further amplify and alter their spells.

Mobile. Many sorcerer subclasses grant them additional means of movement when they reach higher levels, such as dragon wings or the ability to fly in a storm. This not only helps them engage foes faster but also helps them escape from foes.

SORCERER WEAKNESSES

While sorcerers are fun and come with some unique features, they also tend to be one of the weaker classes in the game.

Poor Saving Throws. The sorcerer's best saving throw is its Constitution. It also has proficiency in Charisma saving throws, but so few effects target Charisma it might as well not be there. As such, they suffer quite a bit when targeted by effects that force saves.

Limited Magical Capabilities. The sorcerer's greatest strength, their ability to focus, is also one of their weaknesses. Sorcerers have a limited array of spells that they can cast. As such, they must rely heavily on their cantrips and whatever casting niche they've put their faith in.

Poor Armor Class. With a limited knowledge of spells, sorcerers don't have the luxury of learning spells like *shield* and *mage armor* to keep them safe. Plus, unlike warlocks, they don't start with proficiency in any type of armor or shields. And if that wasn't bad enough, since they're mostly dependent on Constitution and Charisma, they might not even have great Dexterity. As such, they tend to come equipped with relatively poor AC, too.

FIGHTING SORCERERS

Here are some basic tactics for dealing with most sorcerer characters.

Target Them First. Sorcerers are often the weakest link in the party and easiest to drop using either spells, ranged attacks, or other harmful effects. Take them out as fast as you can. Not only will this remove their spellcasting ability, but it will force the healers to scramble and protect them.

Burn Their Slots Early. Like most spellcasters, the best way to handle a sorcerer is to use up their spell slots as fast as you can. Toss groups of minions or other forms of distraction at them and the party early in the session or combat to force them to blow their biggest spells early.

Turn Them Against the Party. Many sorcerers don't come with high Wisdom saving throws, making them a vulnerable target for enchantment magic. Charm them early and use their spells against their allies.

WARLOCKS

Warlocks in Fifth Edition have made a pact with a powerful entity, granting them access to dark magic. They use their powers to manipulate and control others. They also come packed with one of the best cantrips in the game, *eldritch blast*.

WARLOCK STRENGTHS

While warlocks may have limited casting capabilities, they do have a few interesting strengths which more than makeup for it.

Eldritch Blast. Not only is *eldritch blast* an awesome spell, but the warlock's invocations allow them to modify the spell the same way a sorcerer's metamagic boosts their spells. But unlike the sorcerer, the *eldritch blast* invocations aren't hampered by sorcery points.

Decent Defenses. Although this isn't a strength compared to the martial classes, it's at least better than most of the other full casters, as the warlock not only has proficiency with light armor but also gets a better hit die. And even if that isn't enough, they can take Armor of Shadows as an invocation, giving them permanent *mage armor*.

Elite. Warlocks, like bards, can fulfill many different roles in the party. They come with decent weapons and armor proficiencies, have a deadly cantrip capable of dealing high damage, and they've even got a pretty snazzy spell list that, while limited, does let them carry some "nukes" in case things get bad.

WARLOCK WEAKNESSES

Of course, warlocks aren't without their weaknesses.

Few Spell Slots. Often the subject of memes and jokes, warlocks never get more than 4 spell slots throughout the entire game—and they don't even get the fourth one until they reach the 17th level.

Poor Physical Saving Throws. Warlocks do not have good physical saving throws. As such, they are usually sitting ducks when it comes to spells and effects that force Strength, Dexterity, or Constitution saving throws.

One-Trick Pony. The warlock's primary mode of dealing damage is almost always its *eldritch blast*. If it goes up against a creature immune to force—which is relatively rare, mind you—or the creature knows enough to hide or drop prone, the warlock is at a disadvantage.

FIGHTING WARLOCKS

Here are some basic tactics for dealing with most warlock characters.

Force Saving Throws. Warlocks are proficient in Wisdom and Charisma saving throws but lack everywhere else. Most of the time, they'll have poor Strength or Constitution saving throws. Use this to your advantage.

Burn Their Spell Slots. Toss out early encounters or waves of minions that force the warlock to burn any area-of-effect magic or strong spells they have.

Impose Disadvantage on Ranged Attacks. The warlock's *eldritch blast* relies on ranged spell attacks. Dodge or drop prone to avoid the spell and jump behind full cover whenever possible.

WIZARDS

Wizards are scholarly individuals who have devoted their lives to studying magic. Whether they're blasting their enemies with powerful spells, creating illusions to confuse their foes, or using their knowledge of the arcane to uncover hidden secrets, wizards are known for their mastery of magic and their ability to bend the rules of reality to their will.

WIZARD STRENGTHS

A classic class, wizards are still one of the best options in the game.

Powerful Magic. Wizards are arcane casters, giving them access to some of the most powerful spells in the game. And although they don't immediately have access to every spell permitted to them like clerics, they can easily learn new spells with a little downtime.

Mental Saving Throws. Wizards have strong Wisdom and Intelligence saving throws. As such, enchantments, illusions, and psychic attacks don't work as well against them.

Damage Dealers. Wizards, especially evokers, are known for their big damage-dealing spells. And since they have more spell slots than warlocks and a greater variety than sorcerers, they are arguably the best at it.

WIZARD WEAKNESSES

Although wizards are strong offensively, most of their weaknesses lie in defense.

Glass Cannons. Wizards deal a lot of damage but have relatively low hit points and typically have AC values, too. They can boost their AC with *shield*, but that usually burns a valuable spell slot.

Limited Spell Slots. While wizards may have access to more spells than some other casting classes, they are still limited in what they can cast, especially at low levels.

Poor Physical Saving Throws. Wizards are strong against mental attacks but severely lack defense against attacks that force physical saving throws.

FIGHTING WIZARDS

Here are some basic tactics for dealing with most wizard characters.

Drop the Wizard First. Like sorcerers, wizards are physically weak, with lower hit points and AC than the other classes. Plus, the damage they deal causes a huge problem, especially once they get access to 3rd level and higher spells. Always target them first. Not only does this remove their damage-dealing capabilities, but it also forces the rest of the party to scramble to defend them.

Burn Their Spell Slots. Because wizards have a limited number of spell slots, throw out minions in pre-encounters or during the first wave of an encounter to force them to use up their higher-level spell slots.

Blind Them. Nearly every spell the wizard casts requires them to see. Take that sense away, and they lose their effectiveness. Furthermore, most spells and effects that blind targets force Constitution saving throws, one of the wizard's weaker saving throws.

Appendix C: Tactics vs Specific Player Classes

APPENDIX D: POWERFUL SPELLS AND HOW TO AVOID THEM

As a gamemaster, it's important to understand the impact that spells can have on combat and to be prepared for any situation. It only takes one spell to completely "ruin" a combat, ending it way earlier than you anticipated.

BASIC TIPS

Here are some basic pointers for avoiding all spells.

1. KNOW THE SPELLS

- Read the handbook for players to familiarize yourself with the spells available in the game.
- Pay attention to what spells your opponents have access to and what they can do.
- Study the spell descriptions, including their range, damage, and any special effects they may have.
- Keep a list of the spells you're likely to encounter and their effects, so you can quickly reference it in combat.

2. KEEP YOUR DISTANCE

- Most spells have a range, so if you can stay outside of that range, you'll be safe.
- Use terrain and obstacles to your advantage to block line of sight and prevent spells from hitting you.
- Keep moving and stay unpredictable to make it harder for spellcasters to hit you.
- If a spellcaster is closing in, consider retreat or using a distraction to create space between you.
- Use cover.

3. BURN SPELL SLOTS EARLY

- Use minions or other distractions to force spellcasters to use their best spells early in the session or combat.
- Encourage spellcasters to waste their spell slots on non-threatening targets, so they have fewer options later in the battle.
- Try to force spellcasters to choose between using their spells on your minions or their allies, forcing them to make difficult decisions.
- If a spellcaster is low on spell slots, they are less of a threat, so focus your attention elsewhere.

4. REMOVE SPELLCASTERS FIRST:

- Focus on removing spellcasters, especially glass cannons like wizards and sorcerers, as fast as you can.
- Spellcasters can be dangerous, so take them out quickly before they have a chance to unleash their full potential.
- If a spellcaster is down, they can't cast spells, so take advantage of the opportunity to neutralize them.
- Remember, the best defense is offense, so don't be afraid to take the fight to the spellcasters.

INDIVIDUAL SPELL TACTICS

Here are some of the most "infamous" spells for disrupting combat during the game and ways to avoid them.

BANISHMENT

With one bad saving throw, a tough creature gets sent to another dimension. And it only costs a single 4th-level spell slot to do it.

Fortunately, *banishment* is a concentration spell, meaning that the spellcaster needs to maintain concentration lest the foe return. Use auto-hit attacks such as save-for-half area-of-effect spells or *magic missiles* to force the spellcaster to make Constitution saving throws. Also, spells like *private sanctum* prevents dimensional travel, so it could, in theory, protect creatures from this spell, too.

COUNTERSPELL

The bane of many players and GM's existence for numerous editions, *counterspell* stops a spellcaster from casting a spell, disrupting their action economy and invalidating the entire round.

Overcome *counterspell* by forcing the target to burn higher-level spell slots during the early game. Also, most spellcasters are allowed only one reaction per turn. Use minions to provoke attacks of opportunity from the spellcaster before you cast your big spell. Alternatively, use a cantrip to draw the spellcaster's *counterspell* usage, then follow up with a bonus action spell (or vice versa).

Don't forget that you can *counterspell counterspell*, too.

ELDRITCH BLAST

Possibly the strongest cantrip in the game, *eldritch blast* grants warlocks incredible damage dealing and control capabilities.

Eldritch blast requires a ranged spell attack roll. The easiest way to avoid ranged attacks is to make it harder to hit your target. Place your target into cover (full, whenever possible), and don't forget to drop prone between attacks. Because *eldritch blast* can target multiple targets, use minions to burn the individual bolts, letting your bigger targets move about the battlefield unimpeded.

GOODBERRY

A quirky druid and ranger spell, *goodberry* grants spellcasters a cheap way to bring unconscious allies back to life.

The thing to remember with *goodberry* is that they only heal one hit point, and they take an action to use. This already is a big action economy burner for the characters. And since it takes an action to eat one, it similarly should take at least one action to feed it to a downed opponent.

If players rely too heavily on *goodberry*, letting their characters always hover around 1 hit point, target them heavy damage dealing effects that would exceed their hit points maximum. This is a cruel tactic, but it'll quickly get them to stop doing *goodberry* cheese.

FOG CLOUD

As a 1st-level spell, *fog cloud* is a cheap and effective way to allow characters to escape unseen. Fortunately, there are some ways to get around this.

First, the spell requires concentration. Damage the caster (using an area of effect attack if you can't see them) and force them to roll Constitution saving throws to maintain concentration.

Additionally, *fog cloud* blinds most creatures, except those with blindsense or tremorsense. Even truesight fails to see through fog clouds. Use this against the party, since they likely won't have a way to see through the cloud themselves.

HEAT METAL

Another spell known for its cheesiness, *heat metal* deals 2d8 damage per turn to a creature wearing heavy armor or holding a metallic item. Plus, it imposes disadvantage on attack rolls and ability checks while they continue to hold or wear it.

Heat metal is a concentration spell, so use effects to disrupt the caster's concentration. If the target is wearing armor that's getting heated, consider making the target grapple with the spellcaster or one of its allies. While it doesn't say it directly in the rules, common sense would dictate that any damage the target takes, the grappled person should also take.

MAGIC MISSILE

One of the oldest and cheesiest spells in the game, *magic missile* allows a caster to launch a volley of force bolts, each one dealing 1d4 + 1 damage with no save or attack roll required.

If you're worried about *magic missile*, use minions to distract the caster. Jumping behind full cover also hampers the caster, since they need to see the target in order to use the *magic missile*.

Keep in mind, too, that the caster using *magic missile* causes them to burn through their 1st-level spell slots, which in turn, forces them to use up higher-level spell slots to cast valuable low-level spells such as *shield* or *mage armor*.

MAGNIFICENT MANSION

This high-level spell is basically a "safe zone" for the party to rest and regroup while in the middle of a dungeon.

Of course, it requires the 13th level to gain access to it. At that point, the players are fighting much more dangerous enemies. And although they're in an extradimensional space, the spell is not immune to *dispel magic*. All it takes is a *detect magic* spell or truesight to locate the invisible entrance and a high-level *dispel magic* spell, and poof, all of the characters are spit out into unoccupied spaces within 5 feet of the entrance. Is this mean? Yes. But do they deserve it? Probably.

REVIVIFY

Most parties gain the ability to bring their dead comrades back to life when they reach 5th-level, as they gain access to *revivify*. Once death is off the table, parties tend to get a little more reckless with their actions.

When *revivify* starts making the rounds (and spells like it), you need to decide if you want to be a nice GM or a mean one. A nice GM lets the party *revivify* their party members without any trouble. A mean GM destroys the corpse, keeps it away from the healer who has to touch the target to use the magic, or—most diabolically—remind the players that they can't use the spell unless they have a diamond worth 300 gp or more on hand.

SILENCE

This obnoxious little spell allows casters to create an area of complete *silence*, essentially taking away most caster's ability to cast spells. And since it has a 120-foot range, it's hard to *counterspell*, too.

Avoiding *silence* requires smart placement of your caster at the start of combat. Make sure they always have a way to step out of the aura, either by moving, leaping off a cliff and *feather falling* or *dimension doorings*, or some other nifty escape method.

Silence requires concentration, so use minions and those not caught in the field of *silence* to damage the spellcaster, forcing them to make Constitution saving throws to maintain concentration.

TINY HUT

At 3rd-level, some spellcasters gain the ability to create a little "tent" made of force magic that allows them to rest and save in the middle of a dangerous place.

There are a lot of ways to get around *tiny hut*. First, it can be dispelled, no upcasting necessary. It's also an object of force magic, so *disintegrate* will blow a hole right through it. If your monsters don't have access to spells, you can also have the monsters place rocks on top of the hut, fill the area with water, set it on fire, and so on.

WALL OF FORCE/FORCECAGE

These two spells allow a spellcaster to create a permanent barrier of force through which your monsters won't be able to get through. *Forcecage* doesn't even require concentration!

Still, there are some clever ways to get around these. First, *forcecage* has a cost component, so you can simply ask the player if they have ruby dust worth 1,500 gold pieces (not likely). Note that creatures too large to fit in the area—arguably most Gargantuan creatures, despite the cage form's 20-foot dimensions—are immediately pushed out of it, too.

Spells will always be the best way to get out of *forcecage*, especially if the caster has Legendary Resistances, allowing them to succeed on a failed saving throw automatically.

When it comes to walls of force, remember that they are either a flat surface or a dome. This means that there's always an open side. Your target can move or fly around it or even burrow below it to escape.

APPENDIX E: MONSTERS BY FIGHTING STYLE

This section organizes the monsters by their fighting style.

ARTILLERISTS

Bandit	77
Centaur	87
Devil, Barbed	111
Elf, Drow	136
Genie, Efreeti	145
Goblin	164
Hag, Night	175
Lycanthrope, Wererat	197
Manticore	202
Satyr	245
Scout	247
Spy	260
Wight	274

BRUTES

Animated Object, Armor	67
Animated Object, Flying Sword	68
Animated Object, Rug of Smothering	69
Awakened Tree	75
Basilisk	80
Berserker	82
Bulette	84

Monster	Page
Chuul	89
Cyclops	97
Demon, Balor	102
Demon, Hezrou	105
Devil, Bearded	112
Elemental, Fire	134
Ettin	139
Ghast	147
Giant, Fire	155
Giant, Frost	156
Giant, Hill	157
Golem, Clay	165
Golem, Iron	167
Gorgon	169
Half-Red Dragon Veteran	177
Hell Hound	179
Hydra	184
Lycanthrope, Wereboar	196
Minotaur	211
Ogre	219
Ogre, Half-	220
Ooze, Black Pudding	222
Ooze, Ochre Jelly	225
Orc	226
Otyugh	227
Owlbear	228
Revenant	238
Salamander	244
Shambling Mound	249
Skeleton, Minotaur	252

Tarrasque	263
Thug	264
Treant	265
Troglodyte	267
Troll	268
Veteran	273
Winter Wolf	276
Zombie, Ogre	283

CONTROLLERS

Cult Fanatic	95
Devil, Chain	114
Druid	129
Dryad	130
Elemental, Water	135
Faerie Dragon	140
Flumph	141
Genie, Djinni	144
Genie, Marid	146
Giant, Cloud	154
Gibbering Mouther	160
Hag, Sea	176
Harpy	178
Jackalwere	187
Lamia	191
Mephit, Dust	204
Merrow	209
Mummy	212
Mummy Lord	213

Naga, Guardian	215
Naga, Spirit	216
Pixie	232
Rakshasa	236
Rust Monster	241
Scarecrow	246
Sphinx, Androsphinx	255

ELITES

Archmage	71
Bandit Captain	78
Cambion	86
Death Knight	100
Demon, Glabrezu	104
Demon, Marilith	106
Demon, Nalfeshnee	107
Devil, Erinyes	115
Devil, Horned	116
Devil, Ice	117
Devil, Pit Fiend	120
Dragon Turtle	127
Drider	128
Duergar	131
Gladiator	161
Hobgoblin	181
Knight	188
Lich	192
Lycanthrope, Weretiger	198
Lycanthrope, Werewolf	199

Medusa 203

Priest 233

Succubus/Incubus 262

LURKERS

Ankheg 70

Assassin 75

Behir 81

Bugbear 84

Cloaker 90

Darkmantle 98

Demon, Quasit 108

Demon, Shadow 109

Devil, Imp 118

Doppelganger 121

Elemental, Earth 135

Ettercap 138

Ghost 148

Giant Spider 152

Giant, Stone 158

Gnome, Deep 163

Grick 170

Hag, Green 174

Intellect Devourer 185

Lizardfolk 194

Mage 200

Mephit, Ice 205

Mephit, Magma 206

Mimic 210

Oni 221

Ooze, Gelatinous Cube	223
Ooze, Gray	224
Phase Spider	231
Pseudodragon	234
Purple Worm	235
Remorhaz	237
Roper	240
Sahuagin	242
Shadow	248
Specter	254
Sphinx, Gynosphinx	257
Sprite	259
Vampire	270
Vampire Spawn	272
Will-o'-Wisp	275
Wraith	278
Xorn	280
Yeti	281

MINIONS

Awakened Shrub	74
Commoner	92
Crawling Hand	94
Cultist	96
Demon, Dretch	103
Devil, Lemure	119
Fungus, Violet	142
Ghoul	149
Gnoll	162
Grimlock	172

Guard	173
Homunculus	183
Kobold	189
Magmin	201
Merfolk	208
Skeleton	251
Stirge	261
Tribal Warrior	266
Zombie	282

SKIRMISHERS

Angel, Deva	64
Banshee	79
Blink Dog	83
Chimera	88
Cockatrice	91
Demon, Vrock	110
Devil, Bone	113
Dragon, Wyrmlings	123
Dragons, Young	124
Elemental, Air	132
Gargoyle	143
Giant Eagle	150
Giant Elk	151
Giant Vulture	153
Griffon	171
Hippogriff	180
Invisible Stalker	186
Knight	188
Mephit, Steam	207

Peryton	230
Roc	239
Wyvern	279

SOLO

Aboleth	61
Angel, Planetar	65
Angel, Solar	66
Demilich	101
Dragon, Adult	125
Dragon, Ancient	126
Giant, Storm	159
Kraken	190

SUPPORT

Acolyte	63
Couatl	93
Nightmare	217
Pegasus	229
Skeleton, Warhorse	253
Unicorn	269
Worg	277

TANKS

Azer	76
Golem, Flesh	166
Golem, Stone	168
Lycanthrope, Werebear	195
Noble	218
Shield Guardian	250

OPEN GAME LICENSE Version 1.0a

The following text is the property of Wizards of the Coast, Inc. and is Copyright 2000 Wizards of the Coast, Inc ("Wizards"). All Rights Reserved.

1. Definitions: (a)"Contributors" means the copyright and/or trademark owners who have contributed Open Game Content; (b)"Derivative Material" means copyrighted material including derivative works and translations (including into other computer languages), potation, modification, correction, addition, extension, upgrade, improvement, compilation, abridgment or other form in which an existing work may be recast, transformed or adapted; (c) "Distribute" means to reproduce, license, rent, lease, sell, broadcast, publicly display, transmit or otherwise distribute; (d)"Open Game Content" means the game mechanic and includes the methods, procedures, processes and routines to the extent such content does not embody the Product Identity and is an enhancement over the prior art and any additional content clearly identified as Open Game Content by the Contributor, and means any work covered by this License, including translations and derivative works under copyright law, but specifically excludes Product Identity. (e) "Product Identity" means product and product line names, logos and identifying marks including trade dress; artifacts; creatures characters; stories, storylines, plots, thematic elements, dialogue, incidents, language, artwork, symbols, designs, depictions, likenesses, formats, poses, concepts, themes and graphic, photographic and other visual or audio representations; names and descriptions of characters, spells, enchantments, personalities, teams, personas, likenesses and special abilities; places, locations, environments, creatures, equipment, magical or supernatural abilities or effects, logos, symbols, or graphic designs; and any other trademark or registered trademark clearly identified as Product identity by the owner of the Product Identity, and which specifically excludes the Open Game Content; (f) "Trademark" means the logos, names, mark, sign, motto, designs that are used by a Contributor to identify itself or its products or the associated products contributed to the Open Game License by the Contributor (g) "Use", "Used" or "Using" means to use, Distribute, copy, edit, format, modify, translate and otherwise create Derivative Material of Open Game Content. (h) "You" or "Your" means the licensee in terms of this agreement.

2. The License: This License applies to any Open Game Content that contains a notice indicating that the Open Game Content may only be Used under and in terms of this License. You must affix such a notice to any Open Game Content that you Use. No terms may be added to or subtracted from this License except as described by the License itself. No other terms or conditions may be applied to any Open Game Content distributed using this License.

3. Offer and Acceptance: By Using the Open Game Content You indicate Your acceptance of the terms of this License.

4. Grant and Consideration: In consideration for agreeing to use this License, the Contributors grant You a perpetual, worldwide, royalty-free, non-exclusive license with the exact terms of this License to Use, the Open Game Content.

5. Representation of Authority to Contribute: If You are contributing original material as Open Game Content, You represent that Your Contributions are Your original creation and/or You have sufficient rights to grant the rights conveyed by this License.

6. Notice of License Copyright: You must update the COPYRIGHT NOTICE portion of this License to include the exact text of the COPYRIGHT

NOTICE of any Open Game Content You are copying, modifying or distributing, and You must add the title, the copyright date, and the copyright holder's name to the COPYRIGHT NOTICE of any original Open Game Content you Distribute.

7. Use of Product Identity: You agree not to Use any Product Identity, including as an indication as to compatibility, except as expressly licensed in another, independent Agreement with the owner of each element of that Product Identity. You agree not to indicate compatibility or co-adaptability with any Trademark or Registered Trademark in conjunction with a work containing Open Game Content except as expressly licensed in another, independent Agreement with the owner of such Trademark or Registered Trademark. The use of any Product Identity in Open Game Content does not constitute a challenge to the ownership of that Product Identity. The owner of any Product Identity used in Open Game Content shall retain all rights, title and interest in and to that Product Identity.

8. Identification: If you distribute Open Game Content You must clearly indicate which portions of the work that you are distributing are Open Game Content.

9. Updating the License: Wizards or its designated Agents may publish updated versions of this License. You may use any authorized version of this License to copy, modify and distribute any Open Game Content originally distributed under any version of this License.

10. Copy of this License: You MUST include a copy of this License with every copy of the Open Game Content You Distribute.

11. Use of Contributor Credits: You may not market or advertise the Open Game Content using the name of any Contributor unless You have written permission from the Contributor to do so.

12. Inability to Comply: If it is impossible for You to comply with any of the terms of this License with respect to some or all of the Open Game Content due to statute, judicial order, or governmental regulation then You may not Use any Open Game Material so affected.

13. Termination: This License will terminate automatically if You fail to comply with all terms herein and fail to cure such breach within 30 days of becoming aware of the breach. All sublicenses shall survive the termination of this License.

14. Reformation: If any provision of this License is held to be unenforceable, such provision shall be reformed only to the extent necessary to make it enforceable.

15. COPYRIGHT NOTICE Open Game License v 1.0a Copyright 2000, Wizards of the Coast, Inc.

System Reference Document Copyright 2000-2003, Wizards of the Coast, Inc.; Authors Jonathan Tweet, Monte Cook, Skip Williams, Rich Baker, Andy Collins, David Noonan, Rich Redman, Bruce R. Cordell, John D. Rateliff, Thomas Reid, James Wyatt, based on original material by E. Gary Gygax and Dave Arneson.

The Fifth Edition Gamemaster's Survival Guide Copyright 2023, Hamrick Brands, LLC; Author Dave Hamrick.

END OF LICENSE

MORE FIFTH EDITION TITLES FROM DMDAVE

THE FIFTH EDITION GAMEMASTER'S SURVIVAL GUIDE

Quick Tactics Deck #1: CR 0 - ¼
Quick Tactics Deck #2: CR ½ - 2
Quick Tactics Deck #3: CR 3 - 6
Quick Tactics Deck #4: CR 7 - 30
The Gamemaster's Playbook The Ultimate Encounter Cheat Sheet
The Fifth Edition Gamemaster's Survival Guide GM Screen
Battlefield Modification Deck

DUNGEONS & LAIRS 5E ADVENTURES

Forest of Peril
Shores of Silver
Cursed Locations
Desert of Dread
Frostlands

JUST PASSING THROUGH

20 Small Villages for Any Fantasy RPG
12 Mid-Sized Towns for Any Fantasy RPG

MORE MONSTERS

Arctic Adversaries

ADVENTURER'S ARSENAL

The Complete Arctic Survival Handbook

WWW.SHOPDMDAVE.COM